The Nylon Pirates

by the same author

THE SHIP THAT DIED OF SHAME
THE TRIBE THAT LOST ITS HEAD

The Nylon Pirates

by Nicholas Monsarrat

William Sloane Associates New York 1960

Library of Congress Catalog Card Number 60–14542
Printed in the United States of America
by H. Wolff
designed by Robin Fox

Third Printing

part one 1

"Meticulously planned with just YOU in mind."

part two 33

"Your travelling companions are like you—gracious, fun-loving, eternally young at heart."

part three 111

"You will thrill to the colorful, pirate-haunted Caribbean, surrender to the fiesta mood at Carnival Time."

part four 199

"Enjoy long, thrill-packed days at sea on the way to your rendezvous at the Tavern of the Seas—Cape Town."

part five 279

"Listen to the heart-beat of savage, untamed, mysterious Africa."

part six 369

"The ULTIMATE in cruise adventure."

part one

"Meticulously planned with just YOU in mind."

chapter 1

THE girl, who was very beautiful, turned away from the window. The view, of Central Park and the Fifth Avenue skyline on a crisp winter morning, was exciting, but the height made her dizzy. Hotel suites, even suites as elegant as this one, should never be higher than the third storey; the twentieth was almost at cloud-level, the thirty-fourth was crazy. . . . She drew her silk robe about her, feeling it embrace her warm, still faintly excited, still languorous body; then she crossed the sittingroom, her bare feet brushing against the luxury of the carpet, and picked up the telephone.

"Room service," she said, to the alert voice which presently answered her. Then she put her hand over the mouthpiece, and called out: "Carl!"

A man's voice, deep-chested, throaty with the remembrance of love, came through the open door leading to the bedroom.

"Yes? What is it?"

"I'm ordering something to eat. You should have something. And the others are sure to be hungry. What would you like?"

After a pause, the man's voice said: "I'll leave it to you."

"You always do that," she grumbled. But she was smiling gently; the confluence of love still bound them.

"That's because you always give me what I want. . . . Did I say thank you, Kathy?"

"You said thank you. And what did I say?"

"You said, 'It was a pleasure.' Was it, my darling?"

"Yes."

She became aware of a voice over the telephone repeating "Room service, room service!" on an increasing note of impatience, and she uncovered the mouthpiece.

"Sorry," she said. Her voice changed, to a more incisive tone. "This is thirty-four twenty one. Send up some sandwiches, please. Enough for five people. Beef. Chicken. Ham on rye. Cheese-and-tomato. And coffee." Her glance travelled to the side table where the bottles and the glasses were ranged. "And a bottle of Johnny Walker, six sodas, some ice."

When the order was acknowledged she replaced the telephone, and turned towards the room again. There was a huge mirror on the opposite wall, and she looked at it with the fleeting satisfaction of a beautiful young woman who need make no special effort, either now or later, to continue in loveliness. Her hair was blonde and smooth, still gracefully shaped to her head in spite of its gentle disorder. Her grey eyes were wide; underneath them, the faint shadows, the fatigue of love, showed like tiny brush-strokes—but discreetly, as if complimenting her in an undertone on a task well done.

The man's voice came again from the inner room.

"You are very efficient."

Slightly startled, she turned her head. "How do you mean?"

"The ordering."

"Oh, that. . . . The cheese-and-tomato is for you."

"To give me strength?"

She smiled at her reflection. "You don't need strength."

After a moment the man's voice said: "You're looking at yourself in the mirror."

She was never surprised, now, at anything he knew or at anything he said. It was enough for her that they had been lovers since she was sixteen years old; that she knew a good deal about him, and that he knew every conceivable thing about her. If he had the edge, in knowledge or in power, it did not matter; it was a part of love—the natural shadow cast by a man. It was the reason why a girl lay *so,* and a man lay *so.* . . . Her daydreaming was interrupted again.

"What do you see in the mirror?" his deep voice asked.

"You know what I see."

"Tell me."

"A girl."

"*That* I know."

"Tall."

"Medium."

"Medium to you. . . ." She looked at herself with an increased attention, as though it were really important to give him an accurate picture. "Smooth blonde hair. An oval face. Pale at the moment. Mouth rather big. Long neck." She paused, looking down at herself.

"Continue," came his voice.

She shook her head. "You're making me shy again."

"Again?" He sounded surprised.

"You often make me shy. . . . Are *you* looking in the mirror?"

"Yes. I'm tying my tie."

"What do you see?"

"An old man."

She frowned at her reflection. "Carl, you are not old."

"I don't feel old, at these moments." There was a smile in his voice. "You were kind enough to demonstrate that I am not. But the mirror's against us." Suddenly his voice changed, as if disposing of the subject. "A happy new year, Kathy."

She turned from the mirror, and looked towards the bedroom door. "You've been saying that to me for the last four days."

"That's the way I feel." His voice was coming nearer. "Tell me once again, how old will you be this year?"

She smiled. "Twenty-two."

"I shall be fifty," he said, and came briskly through the doorway.

If Carl Wenstrom was fifty, she thought, then fifty was the exact age for a man to be. . . . He was very tall, so that she, at five-feet-seven, scarcely came up to his chin; his broad tough body was of the kind to excite second glances from women or policemen, and to keep bar-strangers in order. Norwegian ancestors had given him his blond coloring; an American father his air of decision and command, an English education his accent and phrasing. When she was sixteen, his ruthless good looks had totally overwhelmed her, just as her innocent loveliness had induced in him a shaking abdication of self-control; six years later, the ruthlessness still softened only for her. She was the sole taming agent of a man who for some reason—for many reasons—regarded the world simply as a target.

Of course, he was not young any more. . . . At fifty, the sinews set, the chin thickened, the waistline lost its flattened trimness; Carl was hard and tough still, but the twenty-eight years that divided them were now (she knew) a challenge to him, instead of an adorable piece of flattery. He was dressed, as always, in dark grey: "Bright colors are for children," he had once said, long ago, when they were watching the whirling skaters on the Rockefeller Plaza rink: but when he had first said it, it had sounded confident and benign, with no trace of wistfulness.

He had been a magic lover in those old days; the magic was still there, undeniably, but there were moments—and this had been one of them—when his potency took on a faint, forgivable air of contrivance, when the physical price for him was, by a few hard-breathing seconds, too high. She knew the strength of his love, in this special realm of achievement; but she felt that between them there ought now to be other measurements of strength, other private tide-marks.

Indeed (and now her sad thoughts multiplied, in the savage headlong capitulation of youth) this particular tide might already have turned; the inevitable ebb could already be in being. They both knew this, but they had not yet confessed it to each other; and in this, manhood's most touchy area, she could not be the first to say: *You need not do that. Do this instead.*

If she had dared to tell the truth, she did not expect the transports of love any longer, nor welcome them with the same fervour. She would have been just as satisfied (in a whisper to herself) with the role of loving daughter.

Or was this, she wondered, simply *post coitum triste*—the let-down after the build-up? If she had given voice to such thoughts, he would only have answered ironically: "Of course you feel that, *now*." Carl always had all the answers, whether the topic were tender or tough. Of such a man, presently, one hesitated to ask questions; and in the end one stopped altogether.

Now, face to face with her, he said, incredibly accurate: "You are thinking sad thoughts, Kathy," and as soon as he spoke, on the instant, she knew that her doubts were gossamer, and that she would love him according to any fashion he chose. It did not need his touch on her shoulder to confirm this.

"Just for about twenty seconds," she answered. She looked up at his face, where the heavy lines at brow and nostrils showed deep in the strong light. "Are you tired, darling?"

He smiled. "I am as tired as I have a right to be, at this moment."

"Perhaps we shouldn't have done that, just before the meeting."

With his arm round her shoulder: "When the day comes," he said, "that I can't make love to you, and preside at a meeting of three or four people, within the space of an hour, then I'll abdicate—from the meetings."

That wasn't true, she knew; it was simply his accolade, his spoken tribute to her loveliness—the words he thought she wanted to hear. Carl would never abdicate from power; and his true power was outside their love, it concerned other people, other plans, other achievements altogether.

She slipped from his arms, and crossed to the big record-player which dominated one corner of the room.

"Music?" she asked, over her shoulder.

He glanced at his watch. "Something short—the others will be here in ten minutes."

"Chopin," she said.

There was a knock at the door, and the floor-waiter came in, pushing a loaded trolley. He was old and rather slow; Kathy delayed starting the record until the trolley had been laboriously unloaded onto another table, the bill signed, the two-dollar tip transferred from hand to hand. As the waiter went out of the door, profuse with thanks:

"You're too generous," she said. "No wonder we have to become pirates."

"I want to be a pirate anyway."

The heavenly music filled the room, smoothing all cares, solving all problems. Above the liquid notes he asked:

"What were those sad thoughts, Kathy?"

She shook her head. "Really nothing, Carl. All gone now, anyway. Are you happy about the plans?"

"I will be, in about an hour's time."

"The cruise should be wonderful, in any case."

He was sitting down now, in a deep armchair, with his back to the window; drawing on a cigar, he nursed in his free hand the drink he had abandoned, twenty minutes earlier. When he was fully at ease, and the caressing *nocturne* had made its gentle statement of intention, he began to speak. It was a special, measured voice which she knew well, and perversely enjoyed; however irrelevant, it was a part of their next love-making, even though that might be three days away.

"One of the delights of a life of crime, at our level, is that we can choose our surroundings, and make them add pleasure and elegance to the occasion." Listening to his voice, she felt herself surrendering to it once again; it was as true now as it had been when she was a sixteen-year-old, head-in-the-clouds, senses-in-a-whirl virgin no longer—this fantastic man was for her like an outlawed god. For him, robbery was an intellectual exercise; but it was still robbery, often dangerous, brutal, and without pity, and it was with this consistent wickedness in his head that he lived, made love, was kind to children and old people, paid his taxes, gave improvidently to beggars.

"To steal in sordid circumstances?" he went on. "What a horrible thought! *Not* to stay in hotels like this?—inconceivable! Of course the cruise will be wonderful. Long romantic nights under the tropical stars—wasn't that what that ridiculous brochure promised us? We will have them, Kathy. But we shall have everything else as well. We'll live like kings and queens—far better, indeed—and we will spoil the Egyptians at the same time. I wonder—" he mused "—if there *will* be any Egyptians. Many of them are inordinately rich. And cunning also, which makes it more enjoyable. . . .

"In any case," he continued, "we will spend three months in circumstances of the utmost luxury, and make them highly profitable at the same time. That is crime, according to my personal dictionary. Plush plunder—nylon piracy—I am sure Madison Avenue can find us the right title. I can't tell you how much I am looking forward to it."

"You *have* to do it, don't you, Carl?"

"Certainly."

"Why?—after all these years?"

"My private compulsion." He leant back, flicking the ash off his cigar with a light tap of his forefinger. She thought suddenly what a wonderful actor he would have made. The deep voice, the formidable presence, the slightly studied English delivery were all tailor-made for stardom—and his next words were ridiculously appropriate to this. "Do you remember the opening dialogue of 'The Seagull'? It tells the entire story of the play. '*Why do you always wear black, Masha?*' '*I am in mourning for my life.*' In the same way, if you ask me, 'Why do you steal?' I would answer: 'I am at war with the world.' That is the story of *my* play."

"But doesn't it ever end?"

He smiled. "It's the only play ever written with an unlimited number of acts. . . . You know that I have planned this particular piece of my war for many months. It has aspects of the most delicious irony. A millionaire's cruise—forgive the vulgarity, but I fancy that is an accurate description. More than three hundred very rich men and women, enjoying luxury and leisure in the sunshine. But all the time, they know they are in danger! They have been warned! There are pirates, sharks, thieves, at every port of call. Indeed, we will warn them ourselves that everywhere they go, confidence-men and tricksters are waiting to plunder the simple tourists. And the real danger?

Us! The true pirates are on board already, standing right behind them, travelling first-class."

She felt herself warming, as so often before, to the infectious pleasure in his voice. It was hard to resist a connoisseur's enthusiasm, even in this dubious field.

"That's what I call an inside job. I hope we can make the most of it, Carl."

"Oh, I am sure we will. To begin with, there are you and I." He waited while a phrase of the Chopin *nocturne* came to its delicate closing. "There was never a better team, Kathy." He chuckled. "We have only to remember the customs inspector at El Paso."

Kathy nodded. "Or that inquisitive policeman at Saint Raphael."

"Or the currency switch in Zurich."

"Or Lord Merriwether and the blonde in the bathroom."

He lifted an eyebrow at the memory. "You looked charming, my darling. For a moment I was genuinely jealous."

"It was so *cold*. . . ."

"I don't doubt it. . . . Well, there are you and I. Then there is Scapelli, who, though an objectionable young man in many ways, has done two jobs with us without putting a foot wrong. Then there is Diane." He paused.

"I wish I knew more about her," said Kathy.

"You might not like what you found." He shook his head. "Oh, Diane will do well enough. She is tough and—shall we say—accomplished. Of course, you and she make a most curious contrast. She debases love, you adorn it. It is strange how identical bodily movements can be so widely different in quality. . . . While I remember, you had better be cousins, not sisters. Otherwise we may have passport trouble. But I'll explain all that in detail, later."

"I would rather be cousins."

"Agreed. Then finally we have our old friend the Professor."

"Is he really coming with us, Carl?"

"Yes. I promised him."

It was enough; she would never have argued the point. But at that moment they were cut short, in any case, by the telephone. It was the inquiries desk in the lobby downstairs.

"Are you expecting visitors, Mr. Wenstrom?" asked a guarded voice.

"Yes, I am," answered Carl.

"Miss Loring and Mr. Scapelli have just inquired for you."

"Have them come up, please."

"Very well, sir."

Carl found himself smiling at the slight edge of disbelief which lingered in the man's voice. It was probable that, in this hotel, Diane and Louis Scapelli might give a certain amount of pause to the management. It was possibly their bearing, probably their clothes, and he made a mental note of the fact. If they looked out of place in the François Hotel, then they would look out of place on board the *Alcestis.* It would be a point to watch, perhaps a point to mention.

He turned back to Kathy. "They're coming up now. Louis and Diane."

"Good," she said.

As she did not move from her chair, he added: "Darling, aren't you going to dress?"

Kathy looked down at her robe, and the tiny brocade mules on her feet.

"This is all right, surely?"

"Don't be so lazy." There was a chiding good-humour in his voice, but something else as well. "Put some clothes on."

She stared up at him. "Carl, what *does* it matter if I'm like this?"

"It's not—businesslike."

Standing up, smiling faintly, she said: "Carl, you're wonderful."

"What do you mean?"

"Never mind. . . ." As she moved towards the bedroom she said, over her shoulder: "Stockings as well—sir?" But she did not wait for an answer.

Left to himself, Carl Wenstrom was momentarily thoughtful, the furrows deep on his forehead. Kathy, of course, was allowed to make such remarks; indeed, this gentle mockery was part of their shared love, for he ruefully acknowledged, to her as well as to himself, that his total direction of her life sometimes took absurd forms. (He had once forbidden her to read a book of scandalous memoirs by one of Hollywood's more scabrous harlots. "It is simply not suitable for you," he had said, with finality. At that time, Kathy had just turned seventeen; by conservative estimate, she and Carl must have made love at least four hundred times during the preceding year.) But perhaps, on this occasion, she had been a little too direct, a little too appropriate? He did not want to be called "Sir" at any time, and particularly not this afternoon, when he was reminded by a slight headache that lovemaking and consecutive thought were not, at the age of fifty, perfect bedfellows.

Was she, perhaps, hinting at such a thing? If so, she had chosen an uneasy moment, one that a man who was unsure of himself would have resented. On board the *Alcestis,* she was to be his step-daughter; but they were not on board yet.

He allowed the Chopin record to come to a finish, and turned off the record-player. Then there was a knock at the door, and when he called "Come in—it's open," Diane and Louis Scapelli entered the room.

Carl saw immediately what it was that had checked the clerk at the inquiries desk downstairs. Diane Loring could pass muster, in a brassy sort of way; she did not look like a lady, but she did not miss it by too wide a margin. Louis Scapelli was something else again. He was a dark young man, very small, very pale, with the kind of thin pruned moustache affected by gangsters of several decades ago; he had the available air, the jaunty self-consciousness, of a man prepared to be whatever suited his company—a great or small lover, a homosexual, a gambler, a pickpocket, a dancing instructor. On a good day, in a good light—the sort of day on which Carl had hired him—Louis often seemed handsome, in a cut-rate animal way which won applause from appropriate female hands; but today was not his day, nor had it been so for many a raffish moon. Today, especially, his clothes were terrible—and

Carl, who had not seen him face to face for some months, knew that he would have to make that point very succinctly.

He wore a dark tussore suit, extravagantly draped; a white tie anchored by a jewelled clip; a drooping gold watch-chain; two signet rings; and patent-leather shoes with three-inch elevator heels. Carl stared at him as they shook hands. This young man, who was due to masquerade as his nephew—his favorite sister's child from upper-crust New England—looked at the moment like a caricature of one of the boys in the back room.

He also talked like one. "Hi, chief!" he said to Carl, hitching his shoulders as he glanced round the room. "Big deal . . . How much does this joint set you back?"

"Plenty," answered Carl coolly. "That's why we're in business." He turned to the girl. "Well, Diane. Nice to see you again."

It was not nice to see her, but it was nicer than Louis Scapelli. . . . Diane Loring was small and dark, with beautiful legs and a pointed bosom fiercely, arrestingly upthrust. She had the most unvirginal face Carl had ever seen on any woman—pretty, bold, and corrupt. He was reminded of an English phrase he had heard during the war—"She's covered a lot of carpet in her time." Diane must have done just that. She looked as though she would be wonderful in bed, agile, athletic, highly efficient; but speedy and totally disengaged also—looking at her wrist-watch at intervals, counting the hours remaining out of the working day or night. She was English, but someone had wangled for her an American working-permit as a "model."

She had been a gruesomely successful call-girl when Carl had first met her. He had been looking for a girl to use as a come-on for a race-track swindle down in Florida, and Diane had certainly filled that assignment. Himself, he could never imagine making love to that rubbery, machine-made, fully-packed body; but in America, he knew, he was in a minority. Among other things, she was a coarsely sensual dancer; she had once boasted that five minutes on a dance-floor with her was as good as—well, even the thought was now unphraseable, but he believed her. ("Ever danced with a Latino?" she had once asked him. "No, of course you haven't, but believe me it's an education. They all use the Spanish grip—they must learn it in school, the dirty bastards—that's the knuckles pressing hard on the middle of your spine, so that you can't back away and you finish up practically *underneath* the delegate from Nicaragua. But believe me, they get a surprise when they give it to little Diane!")

Now she said: "Hallo, Carl! My, you look tired. What have you and Kathy been doing?"

"We've had some late nights." He spoke as briefly and as coolly as he had done to Louis Scapelli; he did not intend to receive either commiseration or conjecture from this dependent tramp.

"Where is Kathy, anyway?"

"Dressing."

Diane opened her mouth to comment, caught his eye, and changed her mind. Louis Scapelli crossed to the side-table where the food and drinks were set out.

"I'm bushed," he announced. "Mind if I help myself, chief?"

"Go ahead," said Carl.

Snatching a sandwich: "Where's the Prof?" Scapelli asked, between bites.

"He'll be here in a minute."

"Half corned, if I know anything about him."

"Oh, the Prof's O.K.," said Diane. "He just likes his little drop of comfort."

"Who doesn't?" said Scapelli. "Trouble is, he can't take it."

"Look who's talking!"

"Oh, lay off me!" said Scapelli irritably. "Yak, yak, yak! Don't you ever get tired?"

"Of you, yes."

"All right," said Carl coldly. "Let's not start arguing. Diane, help yourself to a drink. The Professor will be here when he gets through. He's been collecting the tickets and the travellers' checks. He had to pick up his passport, too."

"*His* passport?" Scapelli's tone showed his astonishment. "Is he coming on the trip?"

"Yes."

"Gee, chief, why?"

"He'll be useful."

"That I wish to see."

Carl frowned, and his voice grew rough. "He's done a lot of work on this project already. And if I say he'll be useful, then he'll be useful, and that's all there is to it."

Kathy, entering at that moment, heard the words and the tone. It was astonishing how Carl's voice and even his accent could change, according to the people he was talking to. With herself, he used his "actor's" voice—measured, benevolent, rather English—while with Scapelli and the others the tone of command was almost obtrusive, and his accent took on an American briskness. It was not an affectation, she knew; he spoke to her as he felt, while he spoke to the rest of the world as he thought—and his thoughts in that direction were always brusque and masterful. The way he was talking to Louis Scapelli now meant that Louis had annoyed him—which was not the best start to their meeting.

She came forward with a certain determination, intent on smoothing things down.

"Hallo, Diane. . . . Hallo, Louis."

Diane Loring greeted her with guarded enthusiasm; Louis, who was ready to turn sulky, scarcely acknowledged her arrival before saying to Carl:

"But what's the Prof going to *do*?"

Kathy took the initiative before Carl could answer. "He's going to work on his book."

"You're kidding," said Scapelli scornfully.

"It's true—he's writing a book about pirates," said Kathy. "Didn't you know that? He's been working on it for years. Doesn't that fit in?"

"O.K., it fits in. But where's the percentage for us?"

Now it was Diane's turn. "All right, so he won't make us a million dollars and he won't lay all the rich old dames till they're dizzy. That's your job, Romeo. Can't you handle it?"

"I can handle it," said Louis sulkily.

"Don't knock yourself out trying."

"What's that mean?"

"You won't be the only *man* on board." Diane managed to put the word "man" into quotes, so that it seemed to pose a whole series of crude question-marks. "There might be some *real* competition."

"On a cruise ship? You're nuts! There won't be a guy under sixty. Man, they come on board in wheel-chairs! On these trips, men are as scarce as hen's teeth. Isn't that so, chief?"

Carl had not been listening. He had been watching Kathy. She had "put on some clothes," as he had directed, but the clothes were somehow rebellious—a clinging white sweater, and a pair of lizard-green slacks that showed off her slim build with startling candour. She looked about sixteen, a sensual, provocative, free-moving child. She had done it on purpose, of course; but what was the purpose—and what, indeed, was "it"? A demonstration of independence? A challenge to authority? A statement that she would still decide how much of her body was to be on public view? Or were the trousers somehow symbolic—he caught himself up at that, and smiled in spite of his uneasy thoughts. He knew her quite well enough to ask the answer to the riddle, later. In the meantime, there was work to do.

"Children, do not quarrel, do not argue." His tone was more relaxed, more friendly, but the note of command was still there. "I am promoting this enterprise, and the people I take with me are my choice, no-one else's. I want the Professor on board. Indeed, I need him. We will call him my confidential secretary. On the surface, he will be there because I am a man of affairs, and I require the services of such a companion. In actual fact, he will do the leg-work." He caught Louis Scapelli's sneering smile. "My dear Louis, there is slow leg-work as well as quick. . . . He will run messages, arrange meetings and introductions, serve as part of our background; he will be a link between the family—my family—and those people on board who want to meet it. Above all, he will be the one man whom no-one could possibly suspect. For that reason, he will collect the loot from you all, whatever form it takes, and he will go ashore with it at the end of the voyage."

In the silence that followed, Scapelli said: "Hell, chief, you're taking a chance on that."

"I am not," answered Carl curtly.

"But what's to stop him—"

"He won't need stopping. We will make an appointment to meet on shore, and the Professor will keep it."

As if to point the remark, the door now opened quietly, and the old man came in.

Unless one kept him under close-range scrutiny for quite a long time, the Professor was a figure of undoubted dignity. He was tall, and thin, and old; above the wizened face the mane of white hair rose like some ancient crest. He had a courteous, venerable charm which delighted almost all women, causing them to look discontentedly at their more free-and-easy escorts; *this,* their glances said, was the proper way to treat a lady. . . . His clothes were those of the old school, the black coat greenish with age, the collar high and stiff, the thin knitted tie held in place by a gold ring belonging to a vanished age of elegance; as he stood in the doorway, he held in his hand a grey bowler hat with a curly brim, and a gold-headed malacca cane which must, it seemed, have been won from its Malayan palm-grove when Queen Victoria was young.

Of course, close-to, he was a little seedy, a little shaky in the hand, a trifle rheumy of eye; but so were many fine old gentlemen for whom the modern world had proved somewhat too exhausting. It was no shame (he seemed to say) to show the weight of three-score-years-and-ten, no disgrace to have abdicated from the cut-throat marathon which was the twentieth century's measurement of achievement. There was indeed a disarming humility in the Professor's bearing which had proved, to innumerable people for more than half a century, the most costly calling-card of all.

It was only when one came to know him very well indeed, or was exposed to that frail and fallacious charm for a long period of time, that the façade betrayed, beneath the patina of age, the fissures of corruption. But even at first appearance, small hints of imperfection sometimes obtruded. There was such a moment now; for, as he stood framed in the doorway, it was clear to the roomful of people who knew him that the Professor was more than a little drunk.

He carried it well, as he had done for thirty years, but the slightly swaying stance and the pinkish flush under the eyes were unmistakable signs. So was his voice, as he raised his cane in solemn salute and enunciated:

"A happy new year to one and all!"

Carl smiled in spite of himself; their joint past had contained much that allowed the old man such latitudes as this, and after all they were not yet in action. The others greeted the Professor according to their several habits of mind; Diane exclaimed, half admiringly: "Why, you old devil!" and Kathy said: "You'd better sit down, Professor," and led him towards a chair. Only Louis Scapelli, lounging in the background, glass in hand, had a sour note in his voice as he said:

"What did I tell you? Prof, you're stinking!"

The Professor, struggling with his overcoat, paused to glare at him.

"I can carry my drink, sir! Which is more than can be said for your generation."

"You're sure carrying it now, daddy-oh. Didn't they tell you, New Year's was over four days ago?"

Carl interposed. "Professor, have you just left the shipping company? Did you come here directly?"

The Professor, who had lowered himself gingerly into an armchair, blinked at him.

"Not *directly* here, Carl," he answered. His voice was grave, almost senatorial, as if he were pronouncing a verdict upon the Far East. "I completed our business—let me see—some little time ago."

Carl nodded, satisfied. "I'm glad to hear it. Otherwise they might have got the wrong impression."

"Impression? What impression?"

"He means," said Louis, "the shipping clerks might think you were stinking *all* the time. They might not like it. They might even cancel your ticket. You know how these things get about."

The Professor, with much effort, turned in his chair to face his tormentor. "Young man—" he began.

Kathy, crossing between them, broke in. "All right—let's cut out the comedy. Professor, do you want a drink?"

"Two guesses," said Louis spitefully. "For sixty-four thousand dollars."

The Professor ignored him. "Thank you, my dear. You're very kind. If I may—a small scotch and water?"

Kathy busied herself at the side-table, while silence and calm returned to the room, broken only by the hum of traffic far below on Fifth Avenue. Carl found that he did not mind these small evidences of discord. The five of them had to work together as a team, but they did not have to love each other; their voyage of piracy could well profit from an injection of competitive ill-humour. There might come to be smaller cliques within their circle, but it would be as well if these did not flourish unduly. The only natural partners were himself and Kathy; the rest were mere allies—useful, indeed essential, but never to gain strength enough to challenge his leadership.

"Well, let's settle down," he said presently, when the Professor had his drink and a sandwich comfortably close at hand, and Kathy had returned to her chair. "We've got a lot of things to talk about, and this is the first time we've all met together in one room, though of course we've talked or telephoned individually. . . . First, the tickets. Are we all set there, Professor?"

The Professor nodded slowly and wisely, as if anything else were out of the question. Then he patted his breast pocket.

"I have everything here. The tickets, the passports, the passenger-list, the itinerary, and the cabin-plan."

"Did we get the accommodation we applied for?"

The Professor nodded again. "Yes, exactly. Five single cabins and a stateroom. Four of the cabins are on "A" deck, and the fifth—presumably mine—is one deck below."

"What was the total bill?"

"Twenty-six thousand dollars and forty-two cents," answered the Professor precisely. "At par in the city of New York."

Diane Loring was the first to react, with a low whistle of surprise.

"Twenty-six—gee!" she exclaimed. "It's like the national debt!"

"We're in the wrong business," said Louis sarcastically.

Carl shook his head. "On the contrary, we're in exactly the right business," he answered, with firmness. "I told you this was going to be a big operation, and that initial bill for twenty-six thousand dollars is a good illustration of it. Of course it's a huge outlay, but think of the stakes! They call this a millionaire's cruise, as you know; whether that's true or not, the label has stuck and the label means plenty. It means that there will be about one hundred and fifty men on board whose annual income must total at least fifteen million dollars. It means there'll be women—rich widows with nothing to do but stare out of the window, divorcees who have so much money that even their psycho-analysts can't think up ways of spending it fast enough. There'll be jewellery by the sack-load! There'll be wives looking for off-beat romance, and husbands looking for anything—anything but their wives. And we're going to live with these people, mix with them, relax with them when they're in a spending mood, for three months at a stretch. Personally, I shall be very disappointed if I haven't made the cost of my round-trip ticket by the time we reach Martinique, and I hope the rest of you have the same kind of luck."

"What's your angle, chief?" asked Scapelli, in a subdued, almost impressed voice.

"Poker."

Hearing him utter the single, loaded word, Kathy nearly laughed aloud. But it would have been a loving laugh, a shared joke. Carl had spoken the word "poker" just as he felt about the game itself—as something special and significant, as a habit of life rather than a game of chance. For him, it contained everything because it demanded everything; skill, nerve, knowledge of human strengths and human weaknesses, mental endurance, and above all luck. . . . She had once watched him play for fourteen straight hours, for stakes which he could not afford to lose, with men as tough, cunning, and fundamentally ruthless as himself. The game had started at eight in the evening, in a San Francisco hotel room; by midnight he had lost eighteen thousand dollars, at dawn he had been level, at ten o'clock of a crisp September morning he had pushed his winnings above the thirty thousand mark. What had impressed her especially was the fact that, on the last hand, after all the nervous ordeal of the night, he had given as much attention to squeezing out two other players for a pot worth twenty-seven dollars, as he had done six hours earlier when a monumental bluff had earned him a hundred times that amount, on cards which, seen from any angle, were still utterly worthless.

For him it was the great game. She could even feel jealous of it; there had been very few times during their life together, and those only at the beginning, when it was beyond doubt that he would rather make love to her than cut the pack for a fresh round of seven-card stud. But now, at this moment, she did not feel jealous. She even felt relieved. If Carl were going to concentrate on poker during their cruise, at least he was not going to operate in another well-qualified area which, taking him from her bed, would land him squarely and permanently in someone else's.

She let him know this by saying, almost in a whisper:

"That's a very good choice, Carl."

He turned to smile at her, completely understanding, before he said:

"I hope it will prove so. . . . Mind you, I'm under no illusions as to the competition. To make it worth-while, I shall have to be playing with men who treat the game as I treat it—seriously. Of course, there will be suckers on board, but they won't all be suckers. And that's something I want all of you to remember, all the time. Basically, rich men are not fools. They are rich only because they have outsmarted other men, at whatever game they've chosen. And they have a life-long preference for hanging on to what they have won. If we are going to separate anyone, man or woman, from their bankroll, we can't afford to underrate them, even though they may seem half-asleep or stupid. Stupid men have moments of perception; stupid women have intuition. They also have lawyers and policemen. Don't ever forget that."

There was another silence, reflective, rather foreboding, as if they were now moving nearer to some testing area, and then Diane Loring broke in again.

"How's it going to work, Carl?"

"Well, now. . . ." Carl, leaning back in his chair, looked round the room. He had the attention of all of them except the Professor who, after his precise enunciation of the figures, seemed to have succumbed to the effort and nodded off into a doze. It did not matter; the old man's tasks were simpler than anyone else's; he did not need a detailed picture, he only needed encouragement. . . . "You all know why we are making this trip; to take our fellow-passengers for every cent that the traffic will bear." Carl's voice had changed now, Kathy noticed; it was no longer free and easy, it had overtones of that ingrained contempt which made him the man he was. "But everything we do is going to be *practically* legal. We will give people what they want—give them good measure, too—but we'll make them pay a great deal extra for it. Kathy and Diane are really the spearhead of the operation—" he smiled, not amusedly, "—our front-line nylon pirates. They will supply *romance*—" Carl put a grotesque inflection on the word, so that it sounded coarsely obscene, "—which can prove extremely expensive, particularly when there is, by coincidence, a very real chance of discovery. Few married men will argue with a girl who suddenly develops scruples, who might even call for help. . . . 'He said he wanted to show me his exposure-meter,'" he mimicked, with ferocious sarcasm, "'and now—look!' There are a number of variations on the same theme. I'll be glad to supply ideas, if you should ever run out of them."

Both girls were smiling as Carl paused; his mimicry of outraged virtue had been horribly accurate. But Scapelli, seemingly deprived of a leading role, was less amused.

"That's O.K. for them," he said shortly. "What about me?"

Carl turned to face him. "You will be operating in the same area, Louis, among the female lonely-hearts. You will make it clear that, though love has blossomed like an orchid in the sun, you are, like all young men, perennially short of money. Apart from money, I dare say you will be given trinkets—jewellery, cuff-links, cigarette cases—for your trouble. Middle-aged women can be *very* grateful. You might even *take* trinkets. What woman would confess that the only time her earrings could have disappeared off her dressing-table was when she was drowsy after saying goodnight to Mr. Scapelli? What woman would care to say that to her husband?"

Carl paused again, while Kathy found herself, for the hundredth time, marvelling at the pure hypnosis which he could inject into discussions like these. It was really extraordinary how he was able to make such propositions sound normal and acceptable. His sardonic recital had conjured up, not a picture of evil intent but only the farcical dilemma of some forlorn matron, stunned by domestic complication at breakfast-time. Even Louis Scapelli, whose role had been spelled out as some kind of bedside sneak-thief, with overtones of sexual blackmail, was not surprised thereby; he was now smiling, as the girls had smiled, at the inverted theme of Carl Wenstrom's prize sculpture—Self-Indulgence Caught In The Toils Of Social Pressure.

After a moment, seeing that they had no comments, Carl went on:

"The Professor's job I have already outlined—he is part of my business set-up, and of our family background." He looked across at the old man, dozing in his armchair, and raised his voice slightly. "Professor!"

The Professor opened his eyes instantly. "Yes, Carl?"

"You are not to get drunk on board in public."

"No, sir!" The ancient head inclined gravely, as if assenting to some broad proposition in moral philosophy. "I will not. Rely upon me."

"And no—" Carl's hand rose and fell delicately, milking the air, "—no light-finger stuff. That's Louis' job, and then only in special circumstances."

"Agreed, sir, agreed."

"Very well. . . . For myself, I shall be playing poker, as I told you. That, again, will be practically legal: if I am good enough to win, I shall win: if I am outclassed, I will take precautions. And—" he smiled, "—if the game turns out to be crooked anyway, I will join in, with added enthusiasm. Apart from that, I am there to apply pressure

—family pressure—if it ever becomes necessary. The outraged father, the jealous uncle—there are various ways in which I can give you all necessary support. Which reminds me. . . ."

He took a slow sip of his drink, while they continued to watch him. He was going through the drill of giving them confidence, Kathy realised; this was the coach, telling them to get in there and hit the bastards hard, assuring them, before the vital play-off, that he would be up there pitching with them, every second of the game. Presently, as he still kept silent, Louis asked:

"You mean, like we're all related?"

Carl nodded. "I think that's the best way to do it. We've got to produce passports, and passports have names on them. Of course—" he looked at Louis Scapelli, "—you could tag along as a fiancé or a friend, but that might put the customers off—the girls have got to be absolutely free to operate, with no strings attached. The same is true for you. So we'd better be one family, more or less; all cousins, let's say. Kathy is my step-daughter, my dear wife's child by her first marriage." Carl's tone and look as he said this were steeped in an almost terrifying cynicism. "We have always been very close, particularly since my wife passed away so tragically. . . . Diane is a niece—my sister's child. And Louis is my nephew, the son of another sister."

"Jesus!" said Diane inelegantly. "How did she go wrong?"

Louis scowled at her. "Cut out the cracks! If you can be a niece, I can be a nephew."

"You can be a niece if you like."

Carl broke in, stemming the incipient clash. "You should all refer to me as Uncle Carl, except for Kathy, who will call me Carl."

After a pause, Louis said: "But how are you and Kathy going to fix —I mean—" he gestured round the suite, "you know, like this?"

Carl surveyed him bleakly. "You can leave that to us."

Louis shrugged. "O.K."

"We'll have a stateroom—a day-cabin—for all of us to use. My own cabin leads out of it, Kathy's is on the opposite side." His tone was factual and without special emphasis. "Yours and Diane's are just across the corridor, next door to each other. We could have saved money by sharing, but we shall undoubtedly make a great deal more if we're all in single quarters. The whole idea, of course, is that though we constitute one family, each member can lead his own life in isolation. I fancy the customers will come to appreciate that."

Diane said: "Carl, have you actually picked out the customers?"

"I have done some home-work, certainly." There was such confidence in his tone, such controlled certainty, that it was like a loving father saying: *Santa Claus is reading your letters at this very moment.* "I've seen the preliminary passenger-list, and it's extremely promising. There will be at least a dozen people on board who are exceptionally vulnerable, for one reason or another; people who have made these mistakes before and can afford not to learn from them, couples who have agreed to loathe one another, women who have always had to buy it, men who have never experienced any other sort of transaction." His voice now was in the full flower of contempt, scorning these weaknesses, loving the chances they offered, hating the delay which kept him a full week away from punitive action. "But I don't want to finalize any of our plans, at this stage. These people should only be names, until we actually meet them; when we *do* meet them, we can then look up the file and see what the basic form is. The Professor already has a note-book full of such helpful information . . . Remember that we don't need to hurry anything. We have three months, twelve weeks, eighty-four days. Ideas will flow, opportunities will happen, quickly enough; a man who is just a dull face on Tuesday morning can become a pair of drunken, mauling hands by night-fall. He can also be a terrified check-signer by Wednesday midday. None of us need choose without forethought. None of us should do so. And the fewer checks we take, the better."

"How do we get round that?" asked Diane.

"Ships' pursers cash checks," answered Carl, "for the people who sign them. Especially travellers' checks. You should always be ready to point that out."

He was communicating more than enthusiasm, Kathy realized; he was communicating his own sense of power. Now they all saw themselves as small and large dictators, able to say to any man or any woman: "The terms are cash, by six o'clock this evening." Carl *was* a wonderful coach, there was no doubt about that; she knew it because she was totally subject to his mind and body, the others knew it because he could hammer home his quality of ruthlessness with a few key words, a few special inflexions. When they were on board ship, he would be conducting this small specialized orchestra; and they would be glad of his all-embracing control because they might be lost without it.

The Professor awoke to their silence, opening his eyes with practised wariness, raising his glass unhurriedly as if the time between sips had been a matter of a few moments. His eyes fell first on Louis Scapelli, whom he did not like, and then on Carl, his last and longest ally in a world lately grown hostile and scornful. He asked:

"Do we all meet again, Carl? Before going on board?"

"One more meeting," answered Carl readily. "A week from today—that is, the day before we sail. Of course, you can call me up at any time, if there are questions or problems. I don't see why there should be; we won't be starting anything until we have scouted the market, until our fellow-passengers have fallen into place." He sat up suddenly, tall in his chair, and looked round him with steady, almost baleful concentration. "I'm paying for this trip," he said, with crude emphasis. "My stake is twenty-six thousand dollars, and you are all working for me. Don't forget that. There will be no independent operating of any kind. And nothing—*nothing*—is going to be done that I don't know about beforehand. Clear?"

They nodded. It was a moment when an answer of any kind would have seemed presumptuous and dangerous. After a pause, Carl turned a direct glance on Louis Scapelli.

"Clothes," he said. "We are medium rich—by *Alcestis* standards—and so we will dress medium quiet. The girls should always be as simple as possible; very little jewellery, and the minimum of make-up. There will be plenty of time for orange lipstick and sequined bikinis when we get down to the Caribbean." Kathy smiled with private pleasure: in a single phrase Carl had managed to conjure up a grisly picture of what Diane Loring might have been tempted to wear, and to steer her away from it. "Louis—" his glance narrowed further, "keep it down, keep it quiet. You're a simple, unassuming young man, probably studying for an accountancy job in New York or Philadelphia. You're going to coax them into bed, not scare them half way up the cabin wall."

"I don't dig it, chief," said Louis, disgruntled. "What's wrong with this suit? It's real sharp."

"Extremely sharp," agreed Carl. "A riot at Birdland. But this is a cruise with some of the world's nicest people. Slacks for you, Louis—dark grey or green; *conservative* sports shirts; ties like the one I've got on now. You could lose that moustache, too."

"So what's wrong with the moustache?"

"It makes you look—" Carl decided to compromise, "—too old."

"O.K."

"And put in a few hours under a sun-lamp . . . Professor," Carl turned, "you'll do as you are. But get yourself some white flannels and a Panama hat."

"I have them," said the Professor.

"Good for you. . . . Anyone got any questions?"

"Yeah," said Scapelli, who was not wholly appeased. "That jewellery bit—you know?"

"You mean the jewellery they *don't* give you?"

"Yeah. It's dangerous, lifting stuff that way. How do I know they won't start screaming?"

"You must choose people who daren't scream." Carl, always economical of gesture, suddenly slammed his fist down on the arm of his chair, so that their attention was instantly held. "*That's rule number one for all of you!* There isn't going to be an epidemic of thefts—*reported* thefts—and there isn't going to be an epidemic of complaints of rape, either. The last thing we want is a show-down or a scandal. In fact, we can't afford a single one. You, Louis, will never take anything from anyone who would dare to say: 'This man was in my cabin. He must have stolen it.' And the girls are going to cultivate the art of *not* being found in the wrong bed"

"I don't exactly get that. Carl," said Diane.

"I'll give you an example. . . . You, Diane, will be dancing one night with one of the five or six men who have got to know you during the preceding week. He will almost certainly be a married man. He will indicate his admiration—his urgent need. You will indicate that he has put your head in the most fantastic whirl, and you just can't resist him a moment longer. You will take him to your cabin, or you will go to his. At some undetermined time, he will probably offer you a hundred dollars."

"I would hope," said Diane.

"It turns out that he has the right idea," said Carl, "but he's got the amount wrong. For you now realise that you have never been so insulted in all your life. This man has broken into your cabin—or he has lured you to his. Scandalous. Disgusting. Unheard-of. In fact it's so unheard-of that your asking price is a minumum one thousand dollars, cash, in small bills. Otherwise Uncle Carl—just across the corridor—will either call the duty-officer, or go straight to the man's wife and make a complaint."

Once again Carl had done it very well; they could all see the darkened cabin, the suggestive disarray, the flustered or frightened man, the scandalized and avenging uncle. . . . But Diane, whom life had turned into a literal, one-track creature, was still not entirely satisfied, and she did not pause long for her crucial question.

"O.K., so he folds, and pays up. But does he get his hundred bucks' worth, to start with? Or his thousand?"

Carl smiled at the form of words which, for Diane, was distinctly refined. "That's for you to decide. I think it would be more persuasive if he did get his money's worth. Guilt is a wonderful purgative."

Diane nodded carelessly. "O.K. with me. But—Kathy too?"

After a deep silence, Carl answered: "If necessary—Kathy too."

Kathy felt her face suddenly burning, as if she had been declared diseased or defective before a huge audience. Carl would explain it differently afterwards, she knew; he would indicate that her approach and her appeal were so much more subtle than Diane's, that she could do with a word what Diane needed half her body to effect. He would make it clear also that the matter would be left to her own judgment, at all times. He would rationalize the whole thing. But just at that moment, the raw terms of her employment, so baldly stated before them all, shocked her unreasonably. Of course Carl had used her many times before, for occasions when a girl was the appropriate bait. But always he had maintained a fiction that she was innocent, that she did not really do these things, that she remained his, in spite of all evidence, all probability.

He used her as a weapon, but it was as if he used her with his eyes shut, aloofly, not acknowledging that the things which gave him such delight were often hazarded, as a matter of policy, in a very different field. And he had never yet admitted, either publicly or privately, until today, the fact—the actual proposition—that in order to collect, she might have to deliver.

It was something new, it had a sting and a bite and a troublesome pain, centred under the heart. . . . When next she came to the surface she discovered, to her surprise, that they were all saying goodbye. Diane and Louis left together; the Professor lingered to deliver his file of papers, and then stumbled off in search of the haven of his own room. Within two minutes, Carl and she were alone.

Aware of her moods, responsive to the thinnest of tensions between them, Carl was not the man to hold back, or let things lie when they should be restored to balance. He sat still in his armchair, in the darkening room now deserted by the afternoon sun, and said:

"You were very quiet, my darling."

She was looking out of the window, her back towards him; waiting to be reassured, she wanted to do nothing to delay it. After a moment she answered:

"You and I have talked more than the others, much more. I didn't have so many questions."

"Have you any questions now?"

"No, Carl."

He answered the only one he was sure about. "Of course you won't have to sleep with those men."

"Won't I, Carl?"

"You know you won't! When Diane asked me like that, I couldn't very well differentiate between you. I had to put you on the same level. But it's not true."

"Perhaps we *are* on the same level."

"Oh, nonsense!"

"It's only a matter of degree, isn't it?"

"You know that's not so. You are—" he gestured, "—totally different in quality. There are things Diane has to do which you don't have to do."

"But would it matter if I did them?"

"Of course it would matter! Do you think I would let you get involved in that way? I love you!"

She took the soothing draught, savoured it, allowed it to warm her. She turned from the window, slim against the pale light, and said:

"All right—I just wanted to know. . . . Why does Diane needle Louis like that, all the time?"

He took the obvious cue from her, content to follow her down this different, safer, better-buoyed channel. "I think she has doubts about his virility. And that's what he's been hired for, after all."

"Do *you* doubt it?"

"Well, he's not my first choice. . . . That's literally true, as you know; I wanted to get Brownell, but Brownell isn't available. However, Louis will be all right, with the correct kind of encouragement. He has basic good looks: he can be improved on; we will improve on him, with a kindly hint here and a brisk kick there. And women in search of youth—*his* designated targets—are not too particular, anyway. How can they be?" He mused, chin in hand. "Of course, Louis' basic trouble is signalized by his elevator shoes. He wants to be taller all over. . . . You know those small men who send you long-stemmed roses? The symbolism is positively degrading. But it supplies the clue."

"But suppose he—"

"Oh, he will be effective enough. And if not, the ladies will think it's their own fault. There is often fantastic humility in that area. I know something of it myself. . . . So they will simulate, they will pretend an antique lust—"

She looked down at him. "Carl, you really are awful, you know."

"I have to be. . . . Why did you put on slacks, Kathy?"

"My declaration of independence." She stretched her arms above her head, sensuous, luxuriating. She felt beautiful once more; she *was* beautiful; his glance upon her lifting breasts was an authentic signature to this. "But that was an hour ago. I don't want it now."

"What do you want now?"

"To be with you. To pick up the pieces."

He sighed, in grateful relaxation. "Let's do that, together. Put on some music, Kathy. Shall we go out to dinner?"

"No."

She shuffled through their stock of records, chose one, put it on the record-player. It was Chopin again, but of a different mood: a *polonaise*, slow at first, rising to martial triumph and ardor, the dancers leaping, the frogged uniforms catching the torch-light. . . . He sat back, at ease, content to close one account for the day, to open another if the mood favoured them.

"How did you guess?" he asked presently.

"Guess what?"

"The music."

"I know you. Are you tired, Carl?"

"A little." He wished it were not so, but in their shared confidence it did not matter. He grinned suddenly, boyishly, his face shedding on the instant twenty infamous years. "All I really need, my darling Kathy, is a long sea voyage."

part two

"Your travelling companions are like you—gracious, fun-loving, eternally young at heart."

chapter 1

CAPTAIN William George Harmer, master of the *Alcestis,* sat at his desk in the cabin high above the fore-deck, dealing with the thing he liked least in the whole world—his pre-sailing paper-work.

Ashore or afloat, in uniform or street clothes, he could not have been anything but a sailor. He was small, and broad, and tough; his skin was wind-roughened and sun-tanned from one end of the year to the other; he had walked with a roll since he was six years old. The habit of command sat easily in his face, and in the way he moved his head, chin up, when he had to face a man or a situation. He was fifty-five, not far from retiring-age; he had been facing men and situations, in war and in peace, for all his working life. To take charge, to deal with, to dispose of—all the hallowed names of action—were by now so much second nature that he could not have imagined any other alternative.

If his ship were in hazard, he pulled her out; if a pilot proved inefficient, he was tapped on the shoulder and told to get out of the way. If a man got drunk, he was punished; if one of his officers botched a job, he was shown how never to do it again. When passengers grew obstreperous, they were quietly reminded that they could, within the law, be locked up indefinitely at the Captain's sweet will. If a woman overstepped the permissible limits of misconduct, the fact was pointed out to her in crude terms which seldom proved ineffective.

Men liked him because they felt safe in his hands; women, because they did not. But the women could not have been more wrong. He was good-looking still, and, like most sailors, deeply sentimental; but William George Harmer was only sentimental about one person—his wife—and the rest of the sex existed only as fare-paying passengers who either did, or did not, behave themselves.

Before him on his desk was a mound of papers, some important, some nonsensical, fed to him in an unending series by the First Officer, the Chief Steward, the Purser, the booking agents, and the various officers in charge of stores, baggage, charts, catering, entertainment, security, and hygiene. Mostly they only needed his signature; sometimes they needed attention; occasionally they needed memorizing. None of them needed action; the only action required from him would be in two hours' time, when he would take his ship down river, past the Statue of Liberty, past Sandy Hook Light, and due southeast towards Bermuda.

The ship's noises, now loud, now subdued, were comforting; they meant efficiency, organization, smooth-running order. The shadow of a derrick moved across the carpet at regular intervals; that was the last of the stores coming aboard. The dull clattering, more distant, was the hand-baggage trolleys running up the after gangway. The whining rise-and-fall was a pump somewhere (what pump? a compression engine—something to do with the heating); the steady hum of a generator, one deck below, meant that the radio-office was open for business.

He signed his name four more times—"W. G. Harmer, Master" in firm large script—and then he threw down his pen and walked across to the shore-side port-hole.

The view was of the grey customs sheds of Pier 26, and above them the skyline of New York on a drab winter afternoon. It was a skyline he could never quite believe in; and he did not like it anyway. In truth, he did not really like anything except certain isolated parts of the South Atlantic, and the small house in distant Birkenhead which he knew as home. Anything else was either the sea, the element he earned his living on, or simply *land*—to be avoided, visited only when necessary, and left behind as soon as possible.

He turned, crossed to his desk, and rang his bell. In answer, his cabin steward appeared, with that promptness which, in stewards, could only seem suspicious.

"Sir!" said the steward, whose unlikely name was Brotherhood.

"Brotherhood!" barked Captain Harmer, and pointed.

He was pointing towards a side-table on which were ranged the various bottles necessary to a ship's captain who, working through his invitation list, must be ready to entertain anyone, from the president of Specific Motors to a Bolshoi Theatre ballerina. There was whisky (Scotch, Rye, and Bourbon), gin, sherry, vodka, rum, vermouth, Dubonnet, Kina Lillet, and Angostura bitters. There was not, however, any ice, and this was what had caught his eye.

As Brotherhood, trim and spotless in his white uniform, assumed the professionally injured air of a man certain that he could have forgotten nothing, the Captain said:

"Ice!"

"Sorry, sir," said Brotherhood promptly. "I thought you'd ring."

"God damn it!" said Harmer. "I always need ice. You know that."

"Yes, sir," said Brotherhood, and withdrew.

Left to himself, Captain Harmer frowned, but only at his own irritation. Of course, he always rang for ice when he needed it, and so far none of his visitors had rated a drink of any kind. Brotherhood would never make this, or any other kind of mistake; he was the best steward in the ship, otherwise he would not have held down his honourable and highly influential job, nor would he have been trusted, as he was, to garner for the Captain's benefit appropriate titbits from the ship's most efficient grapevine—the body of eighty stewards and stewardesses who, with access to every cabin, kept tally of everything from the number of drinks served before ten A.M. to the number of people in any one bed at any one time.

It was not Brotherhood who was at fault; it was the fact of being in harbour, where the Captain was always uncomfortable and irritable, and the other fact, more annoying, more disturbing still, that this time there would be no real relief even when they put to sea. For they were going on a cruise, which was something Captain Harmer loathed with all his heart and soul.

He should not have done so; to take the *Alcestis*, flagship of the line, on her annual Caribbean and South African cruise, was meant to be the plum assignment of the year, a reward for braving the bleak North Atlantic run for the other nine months. The crew, to a man and to a boy, certainly thought so; each year, they were on their best behaviour for fully four weeks beforehand. But the Captain could never see it that way. For him, it meant that he had to change from being a sailor to being a glorified *maître d'hôtel;* he had to drop the sextant and pick up the Martini shaker; he had to forget he was commanding a ship and learn the trick of running a three-months' non-stop party. And, above all, there was always a woman, sometimes several of them, who interpreted her current mission in life as the duty of bringing comfort and warmth to the lonely sex-starved hero on the bridge. That was the worst hazard of all.

Of course, the peak of sea-going, for him, had been the war, and the dedicated masculine world to which command of a destroyer had confined him. Twenty years earlier, as Commander Harmer, with an escort group to run in the wild and murderous North Atlantic, and a D.S.O. to prove that he did it well, he had been a fundamentally happy man—a seaman in a seaman's tough job. Now, as senior Captain of Myth Lines, his reward for good behaviour was to triple as Santa Claus, Charles Boyer, and John Paul Jones, for the benefit of three hundred super de luxe passengers, whose idea of fun was to bombard each other with paper streamers, to get intoxicated in paper hats, and to gamble on the ship's daily run at a minimum one hundred dollars a chance.

His jaundiced eye left the skyline of New York, the towering jungle which probably housed the majority of these characters, and travelled down the length of his ship. Her, at least, he loved. . . . He had been master of the *Alcestis* for eight years; she would be his last command, and she had certainly been the best. As he looked at her, he saw more than the newly-painted funnel with its golden Myth Lines crest; more than the long row of canopied life-boats, centred to an inch underneath their davits; more than the clean sweep of the decks and the controlled bustle of embarkation. He saw an idea, an idea which was his own creation; the idea that one could take 16,000 tons of steel, twenty miles of wiring, and a mass of complicated machinery, and turn the whole thing into a living, assessable personality.

After eight years, Harmer knew every rivet of *Alcestis;* but she was more than rivets, more than steel. She *worked.* . . . Built on the Clyde, manned predominantly from her home port of Liverpool, she was no longer in the first flush of youth; indeed, she was fourteen years old now, a little creaky here and there, a little old-fashioned in her ways. But those who sailed in her always grew fond of her, whether they were top-flight tourists or apprentice-engineers; she had that element more valuable than any speed-record or split-second schedule; she had a name that people warmed to. Everyone nodded or smiled when they heard the name *Alcestis;* it was shorthand for something good, something glamorous, something of quality. She had been built as a luxury "one-class" ship, and she had always kept that distinction; she lost money steadily for most of the year, unable to compete with the bigger tourist ships and even less with a 6½-hour jet service and an "economy" air-fare, between London and Montreal, of $247. But she made it up, with something to spare, on this once-yearly millionaire's cruise, when she carried half her usual complement at much more than triple her usual price. She was about to make it up now.

The phrase "millionaire's cruise" was of course never used in the advertisements, where a decent British reticence spoke only of traditional courtesy and the best service in the world. But the phrase reappeared time and again in the newspapers and in conversation, and it was implicit in an *Alcestis* booking. If you were on board, it was presumed firstly that you were having a wonderful time, and secondly that you were loaded. The shore prices of everything, from curry to coconut carvings, tripled accordingly. There was even a rumour, which

Captain Harmer had never been able to check, that the taxi drivers of Johannesburg, in South Africa, made an annual, 930-mile *trek* down to Cape Town, especially to gyp the *Alcestis* passengers when they came ashore. Whether true or false, it was part of the legend. But that "traditional British service," whether it concerned swinging out a life-boat or serving twelve different kinds of canapé between 6 P.M. and 7.30, was certainly true. The Captain saw to that.

There was a step in the passageway, and when he turned, it was Brotherhood again, bearing, by way of rebuke, not one but two buckets brimming with ice.

The Captain, smiling inwardly, offered an olive-branch for his earlier irritation by asking something which he knew Brotherhood would have attended to.

"Did you get those pipe-cleaners for me?"

"Yes, sir," answered Brotherhood.

"And the Gent's Relish?"

"Yes, sir."

Not only the passengers had their particular tastes and foibles; Captain Harmer had a weakness for a certain kind of English sandwich-spread with the odd name of "Gentlemen's Relish," and, being the Captain, he was entitled to have it taken care of. It could hardly be said that the passengers were stinted of such individual care, either. Earlier, he had been leafing through a list of stores which had had to be topped up in New York; it was a formidable reflection of the kind of cossetting which was *Alcestis*' pride. There were sides of beef from Calgary; salmon from the Gaspé, soft-shell crab from San Francisco; five hundred pheasants which a sister-ship had brought out from Scotland; thirty cases of Beluga caviar; champagne, rye whisky, and Coca-Cola; 20,000 Frankfurters, 500 lbs. of hamburger meat, ice-cream by the ton; an entire truck-load of South African lobster-tails; prunes, bottled snails, canned Vichyssoise, small complimentary tubes of striped toothpaste. . . . It would keep them happy for a while, Harmer reflected, and then they would grow restive, and start complaining about the food; and at that point, with luck, they could go ashore and break the monotony by gorging themselves on fly-specked West Indian village cooking. Passengers. . . .

Brotherhood, the watch-dog, hearing a movement outside, walked to the doorway and peered out. Then he turned back.

"That's Mr. Barrett now, sir."

"Ask him to come in."

Jack Barrett, the chief booking agent and usually the last man from "shore side" to call on the Captain, was an energetic, fast-talking man with an air of tremendous self-confidence. Everything about him was at the alert: the spotted bow-tie, the wiry crew-cut, the bouncing walk. Only the protuberant belly gave the lie to the picture of taut efficiency; and he contrived to carry even this as if he had won it at cards. The Captain sometimes wondered if Barrett actually woke up looking like this, or whether he achieved it gradually between breakfast-time and his office—firming up stage by stage, tightening the muscles with some Rotarian draw-string, steeling the jaw, glinting the eye. Harmer always found him annoying to deal with: his obvious conviction that he had done every single thing himself was sometimes hard to take; but there was no doubt that Barrett knew his job, as *Alcestis'* perennially full passenger-lists testified.

They shook hands. "Hi, Bill!" said Barrett, as if he were giving an order to fire. "All set to take off?"

The Captain nodded. Only in America was he called "Bill," and he could never quite get used to it; in England his friends called him "Willy," but that again was really quite unsuitable to the Captain of the *Alcestis*. He said, briefly: "Drink, Jack?" and motioned to Brotherhood.

"Just a thin Scotch on the rocks," answered Barrett. He sat down at the table, and opened his briefcase. Over his shoulder he said: "Thought I'd run through the list with you."

Jack Barrett always "ran through the list" before sailing, as though it were a brand-new alphabet he had invented, engraved, and illuminated. Once again, as usual, the Captain found it vaguely annoying; the implication, that he would be utterly lost without this fatherly briefing, was obvious and mortifying. He remembered feeling the same way during the war, when the shore-gang made it clear, before each convoy, that he and his escort-group were only the blunt instruments—the real skill, the true finesse, lay enshrined in their parting words, which he could disregard at his peril. Indeed, this whole present interview reminded him of those wartime pre-convoy sessions. Jack Barrett, implying that the voyage of 20,000 miles which lay ahead was only entrusted to him as a last resort, inevitably recalled Lieutenant-Commander Binghampton, back in the early forties, instructing him that if he were really serious about getting his convoy across to Halifax in the face of persistent U-boat attacks, this last-minute contact with brains might just see him through.

He awoke from his brief, bad-tempered daydream to hear Jack Barrett say:

"—got a nice group for you this time, Bill, a real top-notch group. Should be a fine trip, from that angle. Of course, there's bound to be the odd-ball here and there. F'rinstance, that van Dooren dame drinks like a fire-horse. The way I heard it, she *showers* in eight-to-one Martinis. You might have a snitch of trouble there."

"The weather," said Lieutenant-Commander Binghampton, portentously, his voice like treacle running over enormous boulders of self-importance. "You should have no difficulty—ah—Harmer. There's a low-pressure area south of Iceland. Of course, it might break up. I wouldn't waste any time if I were you."

"Three hundred-eight passengers," said Jack Barrett. "Couple dropped out from Tacoma, Washington. Illness or something. We kept their dough. There was a bit of a run-in about who should have the Princess suite. I gave it to the Tillotsons, finally. After all, he *is* the president of Steel & Tool."

"Eight escorts, sixty-seven ships," said Binghampton. "We put the Commodore in a Danish packet called the 'Elsevier.' She's not the biggest, but the accommodation's better, we think, from the communications point of view. Of course, he kicked up a row about it. Silly old sod."

"I'm told the Bancrofts don't get on well with the Gersons," said

Barrett. "So, what the hell! If they start feuding, you know what to do. At least, I would hope so. Anyway, it wouldn't be a cruise without some sort of brawl, would it?"

"You can expect trouble HERE and HERE," said Binghampton, stabbing the chart with his pencil. "There have been eight U-boat sighting-reports since noon yesterday. Frankly, we're not too happy about the position west of forty-two degrees. However, that's your worry. We can't do everything."

"Walham is a big shot from Chicago," said Barrett, running his finger down the passenger-list. "Something to do with farm-equipment. The Beddingtons—well, you know about them. They're taking that homely daughter along again. Mr. and Mrs. Kincaid; he ran for Governor in Florida, way back, but it came unstuck. She's a real bitch. Carl Wenstrom—that's a party of five, cousins or something. Nothing on them. Sir Hubert and Lady Beckwith. He's a long, snooty bastard. She's American, and tough as old boots. They say he was broke, and she bought him and the title. Don't know who won out on *that* package deal. . . . George M. Simms. Broker. He's an old guy, been sick for a long time. Got a nurse with him. Maybe—well, we'll see."

"The biggest ships are the 'Wensleydale,' the 'Empire Buttress,' and the 'Shroveport,' " said Binghampton. "The rest are just run-of-the-mill. There's one we're not sure of—the 'Arkwright Courier.' She's been reported in trouble twice before—making too much smoke, and bad station-keeping. If she can't keep up, send her in."

"Mrs. Consolini is making the cruise again," said Barrett, grinning knowingly at the Captain. "*And* Mrs. Stewart-Bates. They both particularly asked after you when they made the bookings. You should be all set there."

"We're sending an escort tanker with you," said Binghampton. "You can top up with fuel any time."

Jack Barrett turned in his chair, and began to tap his nose lightly with his pencil. It was a sign, the Captain knew, that Barrett was about to step into some area of delicacy, to broach a subject which even he, with all his brashness, recognized was really none of his business. It wasn't *much* of a sign, thought Harmer grimly, but at least it was something.

"Then there's your table," said Barrett, with smooth self-confidence, as though this were the next item on the agenda, which it patently was not. "Usual thing, nine places for ninety candidates. . . . But the competition's real rough this time."

"I'll arrange who sits at my table," said Harmer coldly. This was a recurrent tussle, now dormant, now in full swing. "With my purser and my chief steward. You know quite well that I always do that."

"Yes, I appreciate that, Bill, but I just thought I'd mention a few names." As the Captain said nothing, he continued: "You know how it is—the front-office gets first sight of these people. We can give you a useful steer sometimes. . . . First, there's the Tillotsons. Like I said, they've booked the Princess suite. They rate a seat with you."

The Captain still said nothing. Indeed, he was only half-listening, just enough to memorize Jack Barrett's candidates, who might or might not be his own. This was one area where, within limits, he pleased himself; the decision as to who, out of three-hundred-and-eight passengers, sat at the Captain's table, had never belonged ashore, and he was going to keep it that way, for as long as he had a sea-going command.

"Then there's the Beckwiths," Barrett went on. "Handle to their name. You can't very well pass them up. Then the Kincaids. He's still pretty big in politics, even if he didn't make Governor. That's six." He saw the Captain frown. "I mean, it's six if you see it my way."

"I don't see it any way, so far," said Captain Harmer. Somewhere inside, he was enjoying this minor collision; it marked the division between shore-side and ship-side, and very soon every single thing in sight, from people to places, from the bridge to the distant horizon, would be ship-side—his side.

"Then," said Barrett, with exceptional care, "I half-promised the Beddingtons."

The Captain awoke with a jerk at that.

"You had no business to do anything of the sort," he said hardly. "I've told you before, this is *my* table."

"I know that," said Barrett. "But hell, Bill, I've got to sell this cruise! It's public relations!" He said this as another man might say: *It's in the Bible!* "The Beddingtons have made two trips with the *Alcestis* already. I thought this would make a kind of dividend for them."

"If I have Mr. and Mrs. Beddington," said Harmer, with curt emphasis, "—who incidentally never utter a word—I would have to have the daughter as well." His jaw came up. "*I will not look at that girl twice a day for eighty-four days.*"

"What's wrong with the daughter?"

"You know damn' well what's wrong with the daughter! She is, without exception, not only the plainest human being I have ever set eyes on, but also the silliest. That laugh alone is enough to turn the cream. I won't do it, Jack, and that's all there is to it."

"Well, think it over," said Barrett gamely, as if the Captain had expressed interest instead of returning this flat negative. He gathered up his papers, stuffed them into his briefcase, and swallowed the remainder of his drink, all in one swift series of movements which looked as though they were part of a time-study run-through. Then he stood up.

"That's it, then, I guess," he said. "Unless you've anything for me."

"Nothing," said Captain Harmer.

"You're sure, now? You wouldn't like me to come along as cruise-director?"

This was a traditional joke: the *Alcestis* was one of the few ships of any line which never carried a cruise-director; it was Captain Harmer's boast that his men could, without shore-side aid, take care of any problem in any area.

"Quite sure," he said.

"O.K. I'll get back to the jailhouse." Barrett held out his hand. " 'Bye now, Bill. Have fun!"

Fun, thought Harmer angrily, looking at his retreating back; this cruise is *fun?* . . . Then he sat down at his desk again, prepared to continue with his paper-work. It was a mistake to let these things get under one's skin. Jack Barrett, by way of working a farewell point, might draw a distinction between the "jailhouse"—Myth Lines' glass-and-chromium palace on 57th Street—and the "fun" supposedly involved in piloting a big ship, with one thousand people on board, in and out of thirty-eight assorted harbours; but it was not important, it was childish stuff, suitable to landsmen. The comparative level of achievement must be clear to anyone with a grain of sense in their head. . . . And anyway (he smiled to himself as he took up his pen) he *had* made his own point, once again, about his table.

He was not left in peace for long; indeed, with less than two hours to sailing time, he did not expect to be. Within a few moments, as Brotherhood was tidying up the bar, there was a knock at the door, and a deep, rather fruity voice said:

"Captain, sir!"

Tiptree-Jones. . . . Captain Harmer frowned briefly, as much at the exaggerated Royal Navy style of the greeting as at the man who made it. First Officer Tiptree-Jones was everything that the illustrations to Myth Lines' advertisements promised: tall, dark, good-looking, wavy-haired—just the man to accompany the caption: "*Our officers are there to see that you have a perfectly wonderful time on board.*" Harmer did not like him—he could not like him, though he acknowledged his competence and was forced to agree that he was an undoubted asset on a trip such as this. But there was too much of a contrast between the two of them. Tiptree-Jones was smooth where the Captain was rough, at ease where he was awkward; he was *social*, in a way that Harmer could never attain to, and secretly envied.

He remembered one of the women passengers, a few trips back, saying, between Martinis: "That first officer of yours is a living *doll!*" For the Captain, this just about summed it up. He did not like dolls, living or otherwise. He only liked sailors, and not too many of them. One day Tiptree-Jones would have his own command, and then he could be whatever kind of a doll he chose. But in the meantime. . . .

"What is it, T.J.?" he growled. With Tiptree-Jones, he always exaggerated his own roughness; sometimes he went so far as to use the old-style Merchant Service title "Mister!" simply to see the look of pain cross those noble features.

"Sir," announced Tiptree-Jones, tremendously correct, "we're finished storing. I've secured number two hatch."

His voice had a reassuring, leave-it-all-to-me tone which the Captain did not appreciate. The fact that he himself could remember taking the same encouraging line, twenty years earlier, with his own superiors, made no difference at all. Points of view tended to change, and a damned good thing too.

He said grumpily: "What took so long?"

It was possibly the one sentence which Tiptree-Jones had not expected to hear; but he did not falter. Instead, standing erect in the doorway, cap under arm, heels together, he answered:

"I think the men did well, sir, considering. Some of the stuff was late in arriving."

The Captain, recognizing a soft answer, made a noise which sounded like "M'm," and Tiptree-Jones continued:

"There's one man still ashore, sir. Absent over leave."

"Who's that?"

"Barkway, sir. Steward."

The Captain glanced at his watch. "I'll log him when he turns up. *If* he turns up. . . . Are the passengers coming on board yet?"

"Some, sir. About twenty so far. They're just moving through immigration now."

"I want to know when the Tillotsons arrive. And Sir Hubert Beckwith."

"The purser's got that in hand, sir."

"All right." The Captain got up from his chair, and walked towards the doorway. Tiptree-Jones stood aside, gracefully, deferentially. The Captain stared aft. He had to find something. He was in that kind of mood. And he was the Captain, anyway. . . . His eye was caught by the ensign-staff, at least four hundred feet away. A cross-wind had whipped the flag several times round the staff, where it hung forlornly, limp and unrecognizable.

"Mister!" growled Captain Harmer, and pointed. "If you're not proud of that ensign, I am!"

Tiptree-Jones swallowed. "Sorry, sir. I'll have it seen to immediately."

"Ship looks like a Liberian tramp." In his maritime dictionary, the scale went no lower. "It's the quartermaster's job to watch out for that sort of thing."

"I'll see to it, sir," repeated Tiptree-Jones, and turned to leave.

By way of farewell, the Captain said: "I'm putting the Beddingtons at your table."

Tiptree-Jones, scarcely pausing to answer "Yes, sir," walked aft with the gait of a shaken man. Captain Harmer grinned to himself. That would take care of the living doll. . . . There were certain moods when he enjoyed the pleasures and vices of autocracy, and this was one of them.

Knowing that Brotherhood must have remained within earshot from force of habit, he called out: "Brotherhood! What's happened to Barkway?"

Brotherhood came to the doorway from his small pantry alongside. His face, normally thin and inquisitive, was now impassive, almost theatrically so.

"I couldn't say, sir."

The Captain recognized the gambit, the conventional loyal disclaimer. "Think," he commanded. "He's late reporting back. The only one of the stewards, the only one of the whole crew. Spoilt our record. And he may even miss the ship. Do you know what he does in New York?"

Brotherhood shrugged, wrinkling his pointed nose slightly. "I've seen him ashore, sir."

"And?"

"If you'll excuse the expression, sir, he's got this woman."

The Captain looked at him. "Tell me something new. What sort of woman?"

"She does this act, sir."

"Act? Is she an actress?"

"Sort of, sir. It's like a music-hall, 52nd Street. She plays the accordion, but she's got nothing on behind it, just beads. See what I mean, sir?"

"I think so," said Captain Harmer. "What else does she do?"

"She puts down the accordion and plays the flute."

"Is she any good?"

"Oh yes, sir! She's not *young*." He said this as if it would have made the whole thing highly irregular. "I saw the act once. It's really quite refined, sir."

"How does Barkway come into this?"

"He carries her accordion home, sir."

The Captain sighed. "All right. I think I've got the picture. Well, Barkway's in trouble. And if he misses the ship, he'll be in trouble with the British Consul as well as me."

"Sir," said Brotherhood formally.

"What is it?"

"Could I slip ashore and make a phone call?"

"Yes, but be quick."

"Yes, sir." As Brotherhood backed away, intent on whatever sort of rescue operation he had in mind, he said: "Here's Mr. Mansell, sir."

There were times when the Captain, looking at Tim Mansell, his fourth and junior officer, was seized with an almost violent wish to be twenty-four again, full of the vitality and the incomprehensible optimism of youth; and other times when he thanked his stars that he was quit of such nonsense for good. If the Captain had any favourites among his four deck officers, three apprentices, and sixteen engineers, it was Mansell; though the latter would scarcely have guessed it during nine-tenths of his working day, when he seemed to draw as much invective, scorn, and impatient correction from the Captain as from anyone else in authority, including First Officer Tiptree-Jones.

But though he was the dog's-body on board the *Alcestis* (for so he phrased it ruefully, and so it was phrased for him, when there was any question of overtime on watch or extra duty in harbour), yet he was a resilient young man, and seemed to thrive on it. His boyish good looks always made him a great favourite with passengers; above all, he had that unassailable good humour, that intense physical well-being, which could carry young men of his age past any danger, any despair short of death itself. It was obvious that he loved the life of a sailor, that he loved the sea; there was on his face now a glowing satisfaction that they were about to set out on another voyage, another adventure—and this time to the Caribbean, to Africa! The Captain did not find the feeling infectious, but he found it endearing. If he had had sons, he would have hoped to have such a one as this. Though that did not mean that he would have spared the rod, at any time.

Tim Mansell was smiling, entirely without reason, as he said:

"Sir, the purser's compliments, and Mr. and Mrs. Tillotson have just come on board."

"Are they being looked after properly?"

"Yes, sir. Purser's shown them to their suite."

The Captain nodded. "What are they like, Fourth?"

"Rather small, sir. But lots of luggage."

For some reason the Captain found that an entirely adequate picture of the Tillotsons.

"All right," he said. "I'll come down in a minute."

"Very good, sir." Mansell turned to go.

"And Fourth—"

"Yes, sir?"

"See that you sweat up on navigation, this voyage."

"Oh yes, sir!"

"Yours is terrible. Worst I've ever seen. You'll never get a mate's ticket at this rate."

"I'll work on it, sir."

"See that you do." He nodded in dismissal, and Tim Mansell strode off down the passageway as if making straight for his books.

Left alone once more, the Captain thought briefly of the Tillotsons. "Small, with lots of luggage"—the description fitted countless passengers who thronged the *Alcestis*, year in and year out. Small men made money—it was a law of nature, it failed only with ship's captains. . . . Pursers made money, too; pursers, chief stewards, and head-barmen. It was another law of nature, with the same mortifying exception. But if his own purser were looking after the Tillotsons, then the Tillotsons were getting the full treatment, the way he wanted it. A good purser, money-maker or not, was in many ways the mainspring of a ship, and *Alcestis* had one of the best.

There was a quick step in the passageway, reminding him that even short daydreams were out of place, so close to sailing time. It was Brotherhood returning again, breathing rather heavily with the effort of speed.

"Well?" asked Captain Harmer curtly.

"Barkway's on his way now, sir."

"I should bloody well think so!"

"His alarm didn't go off, sir."

"I'll make his alarm go off," said the Captain grimly. But secretly he was pleased at the outcome. A man left on shore, particularly at the beginning of a long voyage, was a damned nuisance, posing endless problems with reports, cables, and explanations; everyone from the Labour Exchange to the local Consulate-General had to hear about it in triplicate. At least he had been saved all that bother.

He was pleased in another way also, on a less official plane. Barkway had been rescued from really bad trouble by a shipmate on board the *Alcestis*. Harmer was always glad to know that his crew were ready to dig each other out of such holes as these. It marked the difference between a crew, and a collection of six-hundred-and-forty-two men. Essential during the war, it often proved a blessing in peace-time also.

Brotherhood, seeing the Captain relaxed, less grim of brow, added:

"Sir, the first officer told me to tell you, the other passengers you were waiting for just came aboard."

"The Beckwiths?"

"That's them, sir."

Captain Harmer picked up his cap.

"All right. I'm going aft. Let me know when the pilot comes on board."

"Very good, sir."

"And give him a drink if I'm not here. One."

"Yes, sir."

"I'll be in the Princess suite. Or next door in A 6."

It was time to start wooing the customers.

chapter 2

IN a broadening, talkative stream, the passengers moved along the quay, up the gangway, and into the warm embrace of the *Alcestis*. For them, preparing to escape New York's raw winter air, she was more than a handsome ship; she was the whole promise of the future, she was spring and summer rolled into one. Once aboard her, and in a few hours—days at the most—they would be installed in a glamorous tropical haven where nothing could harm them. No ship ever sailed without excitement and expectancy, but this was something special. For when the *Alcestis* sailed, she sailed straight into paradise, and everyone knew it.

Among the passengers and their friends, some were frolicsome—it was only three o'clock, farewell lunches had a tendency to prolong themselves, and precautions had to be taken against bars which could not legally be open for business until the ship sailed. Some, again, were sad—almost incomprehensibly, until one remembered that, like weddings and christenings, all sailings were vaguely sad. Some were efficient and determined, others dropped their tickets and mislaid their hand luggage. Some were blasé, some were impressed. But they all had one thing in common. There was a prosperous air about this invasion which stuck out like a church spire on Wall Street. These were solid citizens on the move, and everything about them—the complicated cameras, the pig-skin luggage, the voices, the massive purple orchid-corsages—proclaimed it at full strength.

Above the gangway, discreetly masked by a boat-awning, a handful of young officers, Tim Mansell among them, watched with care as the passengers trooped aboard. They were gauging the ordeal of their future.

It was in many ways a crucial moment. From this time onwards, they were assigned to full-time duty; company rules dictated that for the next eighty days they had to exert themselves at every conceivable aspect of shipboard sociality, from playing bingo to escorting shore-trips, from shuffleboard to fancy dress, from deck-tennis in the sun to cha-cha in the twilight. They had in fact, to knock themselves out amusing the customers, and they wanted to see which, if any, of the customers might possibly repay the trouble. It was a time-honored embarkation drill known as "inspecting the talent." Though *other* company rules, less explicit but formidably clear, forbade them to compete with the male paying passengers in the realm of love, yet there was always a chance that the male paying passengers—so ancient, so decrepit, so indisputably over thirty years of age—might not recognize a good thing when they saw one. The phrase for this particular slice of good luck—"broaching the cargo"—did not need elaboration in any ship over 500 tons.

So far, however, the exercise as observed from the boat-deck had not been rewarding. Indeed, within the frame-work of "talent inspection," the assorted female passengers had stirred no single ripple of any kind.

"All these old trouts look exactly alike," said Fleming, a young engineer-officer who should by rights have been at least four decks below, checking pressure-gauges. "Have you noticed?"

"We've noticed," said Tim Mansell.

"It's their hair, really," said Beresford, an apprentice, who was included among his seniors because he was over six feet tall and a terror on the dance-floor. "It's *blue*. And those curls. . . . Looks like steel wool."

"They must all buy it at the same shop."

An old man, propelled along the dock in a wheel-chair, now came into view. His knees were covered by a rug, and the nurse pushing the chair bent over him with professional solicitude as they traversed a rough patch of concrete. Under an old-fashioned travelling cap, his face was yellowish-grey, skull-like in its bony emaciation.

"Typical," observed Fleming unfeelingly.

"Burial service," said Beresford, an equally hard-hearted young man. "Somewhere near Cape Town. Rig-of-the-day, dress whites with black armbands."

"Stop engines!" intoned Fleming. "For as much as it has pleased Almighty God—"

"But the nurse is pretty," said Tim Mansell suddenly.

At that moment the nurse looked up and caught their eye. She *was* pretty, slim and demurely attractive in her blue uniform; the slight smile which crossed her face as she observed their interest seemed to promise something short of an absolute, twenty-four-hour dedication to her job.

"We'll count her," said Fleming. "Name?"

Tim Mansell consulted his copy of the passenger list. "The old boy must be Simms," he announced. "I remember the office putting in a slip about him. All meals in his cabin. . . . Yes, here he is. 'George M. Simms'," he read out. "Bracketted with Miss F. Bartlett, Registered Nurse."

"Nurses know everything," said Fleming, with authority.

"I wonder what F. stands for," said Beresford.

"Didn't your mother tell you?"

The nurse and the wheel-chair and the old man disappeared from view below them. Next up the gangway were a man and a woman, engaged in brisk argument with a horrible-looking youth of about fifteen. He wore a white cowboy hat and ornamental spurred boots, and he carried a leather switch with which he lashed rhythmically at the gangway-stanchions.

The voices came up to them clearly.

"Quit horsing around with that thing!" commanded the man. "You'll hurt somebody."

"Wish I could," said the youth. He looked up at the tall, towering side of the *Alcestis*. "Gee, what a crummy outfit! Why we sailing in a British ship, for Chris-sakes?"

"Because we are, that's all," said the woman.

"Bunch of nose-bleeds," said the youth. "Pip, pip, old fruit. . . . Hah d'yew dew? . . . Oh, veddy well indeed!"

The woman, who was small and muscular, gave him a powerful shove from behind. "Move on, can't you? You're blocking the doorway."

"Aw, shit, Ma!" muttered the youth.

The woman gave him a second, more vindictive push. "How many times have I told you?" she shrilled, with violent emphasis. "*Don't call me Ma!*"

Tim Mansell consulted his passenger list again. "Master Barry Greenfield," he reported after a moment. "The only child on board."

"That's a child?" asked Fleming.

"There'll be trouble with that one," said Beresford.

"It'll be a pleasure."

"All right for engineers," said Tim Mansell. "*We* have to keep the little stinker happy."

"Get him a horse."

"One that bites."

Now there was a disturbance at the bottom of the gangway; a tall blonde woman, forty-ish, brilliantly dressed in cream and red, had embarked upon a scene of classic proportions. It seemed to concern a ticket or a pass; whatever piece of paper the dock-policeman wished to see was not available or had been lost. As the woman waved her arms, heavy gold bracelets caught the wan sunlight; as she argued, rocking slightly on her heels, snatches of invective reached them, ripping through the air like poisoned darts. When the phrase, "I'll tell you one thing—this God-damned hooker won't sail without me!" reached their ears, the bustling figure of First Officer Tiptree-Jones appeared, hastening down the gangway to the rescue.

"Don't look now," said Blantyre, the Third Officer, who had so far been watching in silence, "but this one's drunk."

"I know her," said Tim Mansell suddenly. "That's Mrs. van Dooren. I've seen her photo in the papers."

"Doing what?"

"Drinking, mostly."

Presently the scene resolved itself. Tiptree-Jones remained behind to appease the policeman, who was sulkily fingering his revolver;

Mrs. van Dooren, with an air of triumph, negotiated the modest slope of the gangway as if she were conquering Everest, and stumbled out of their line of sight. To the very last moment, she continued to argue with thin air, and her load of jewellery, storm-tossed, sent out recurrent call-signs.

"Tight as a tick," said Blantyre appreciatively. "Sort of starved-looking, too. She'll be selling tickets for it, by the time we get to Bermuda."

"Not a bad looker, all the same," put in Tim Mansell. "We count her?"

"Too old," said Beresford.

"Too rich," said Fleming.

"Too tight," said Blantyre.

"We count her," said Tim Mansell, and pencilled a note on his passenger list. "You've made her sound ideal."

There was a pause now, while Mrs. van Dooren's voice faded out, and peace was restored. First Officer Tiptree-Jones made his way up the gangway again, forcing his watching juniors to withdraw from view behind the nearest boat; when next they were able to look down, a small dark woman in a magnificent mink coat was half-way up the slope.

"Ah!" said Blantyre. "Mrs. Consolini. The merriest widow of them all. . . . Stand by to repel boarders!"

"Always nice to see an old friend," said Fleming.

"She's not *our* old friend," said Tim Mansell. "She's the skipper's old friend."

"Do you really think so?"

"He was fighting her off with a fire-axe, all last trip."

"Why fight?" asked Beresford, world-weary. "Sit back and enjoy it."

"He's a funny old sod," said Mansell. "He *wouldn't* enjoy it."

"Talking of old friends," interrupted Fleming, who was long-sighted, "here comes Bernice."

"Oh, God!"

They all watched, with no great enthusiasm to be nearest the rail, as the Beddington family made their way along the dock and approached the gangway. The parents were small, quietly dressed, unobtrusive; the daughter, a full head taller, plodded in their wake like a laden scow. She was a big girl, but that was about all one could say for her; for the rest, the pasty moonlike face, the beefy legs, the gleaming spectacles, needed only a single caption: "Miss X., BEFORE attending our Charm School."

"Well, thank God it's not *my* turn," said Fleming, with satisfaction. "I had it last time."

"You *had* it?" asked Beresford, astounded.

"Be your age," said Fleming austerely. "I was stuck with the privilege of leaving no stone unturned to see that Bernice Beddington enjoyed the voyage. Never again. Someone else can get that medal."

The family drew nearer; while the parents attracted no special attention, Bernice Beddington seemed to loom into view like a mournful lighthouse, warning them all never to go to sea. With one accord they edged back from the rail, as if fearful of coming within the beam of that foreboding gaze; so that the girl, mounting the gangway at a heavy shambling walk, was met by the odd sight of four disembodied naval caps poised above the edge of a lifeboat. It could have been something which, with variations, she had seen many times before, for she gave no sign as she passed into the entrance-foyer below.

"What a huge girl!" said Beresford. It was his first cruise in the *Alcestis*, and he had not yet encountered the Beddingtons. "I'd hate to go ten rounds with her."

"I'd hate to go one of anything with her," said Fleming. "I tell you, that girl dances like a ton of steak-and-kidney pudding."

"But lots of money," said Blantyre. "Old man Beddington makes hearing aids."

"The news falls on deaf ears."

"You'd think that *someone* would marry her."

"There are times when you can't give it away."

Tim Mansell fingered his passenger list, and then looked along the quay towards the customs sheds.

"I hope that isn't all," he said anxiously. "We really *must* do better than this."

Captain Harmer paused before knocking at the door of the Princess suite, and listened to the sounds of his ship. They were not sea-going sounds, the best sounds in the world, but they were at least the noises of departure, and these—even if it was only departure on a cruise—were still heartening to a sailor who loathed the land. There was the usual internal hum of any ship—the dynamos, the forced-draught ventilation. There was the scurry of baggage-porters with trolleys of luggage, stewardesses with flowers, stewards with telegrams; there were people wandering up and down the corridors, greeting their friends, comparing their cabins with others. There were early good-byes being said, and the sound of an orchestra, two decks above, playing selections from *H.M.S. Pinafore.* There was above all the *smell* of a ship—salty, painty, exciting; the warm smell of boilers, the warm whiff of oil.

No matter how many times it happened, thought the Captain as he raised his hand to knock on the cabin door, sailing time was the best moment in all the world.

The voice which called "Come in!" was forceful, and the man who turned towards him as he entered was forceful also. At a swift glance, Tillotson was almost a caricature of American power and prosperity. He was small and compact; the wiry grey hair was crew-cut, the jaw prominent, the blue eyes direct and level. Any whisky advertiser would have been glad to feature him (head and shoulders) as a Man of Distinction. At the moment he was holding a tiny microphone in his hand, and dictating into a small portable tape-recorder. He finished a sentence—"I do not agree, and therefore do not choose to proceed with it" were the final words—before he stood up and gave attention to his visitor. But then, as he glanced down at the four rings on the Captain's sleeve, his expression altered on the instant, from one of preoccupied arrogance to a hearty good-fellowship, and he held out his hand with a smile.

"Afternoon, Captain."

"Good afternoon, Mr. Tillotson," said Harmer, shaking hands. "I just looked in to see if you were comfortable."

"Very good of you. I appreciate that." Tillotson turned, and raised his voice slightly. "Honey! Here's the Captain come to see us."

"Well, isn't that nice?" came an answering voice from the adjoining cabin, and within a few seconds Mrs. Tillotson appeared. She was as the Captain had imagined her; the wife of a very rich man who had not been rich, thirty years earlier. She might have been pretty in those early days; now, in middle-age, Mrs. Tillotson was simply a work of art—the conformist art of the cosmetician, the hair-dresser, the masseur, the makers of perfume and foundation-garments and shoes and jewellery. She was small, plain, undeniably plump; she gave the impression of being held together—by her clothes, by her tight blue-grey curls, by dollar bills. But she was simple and pleasant at the same time, and the Captain warmed to her as she came forward, with a rather shy smile, and said:

"Well, isn't this the nicest thing. . . ."

"Just looked in to see if you were comfortable," said the Captain again, on a more gallant note. He waved his hand round the panelled magnificence of the Princess suite. "I hope you like your quarters."

Mrs. Tillotson nodded vigorously. "It's the most elegant thing I've seen in years! Those chair-covers are just a dream! And the bathroom!" She giggled, eying the Captain uncertainly. "You can tell I'm just a home-maker. . . . We always heard the *Alcestis* was wonderful. But my goodness!"

"She's a fine ship, Captain," said Tillotson, plainly impressed.

There was an agreeable deference in both their voices which Harmer, though he had heard it countless times before, always reacted to. Ashore, Tillotson could probably buy the *Alcestis* five times over, just by initialling a contract, while he himself was a poor man who would never have got past the chairs in the outer office of Steel &

Tool, Incorporated. But once on board, the roles were reversed; passengers were only people, but the Captain was the Captain, and Tillotson was a big enough man, and a simple enough man, to recognize the fact.

Harmer, on an impulse, said: "I've arranged for you to sit at my table, if you'd like that."

"We'd be honoured, Captain," said Mrs. Tillotson, and her husband nodded.

"Excellent," said Harmer, and turned towards the door again. "Well, I can see you're busy," he said to Tillotson. "And even I have one or two things to see to." It was a mild joke he had used innumerable times before, and it was answered according to the usual pattern.

"Well, I should just think so," said Mrs. Tillotson, with a laugh.

"You go right ahead," said Tillotson heartily. "You must have a whole raft of things to do. . . . Thanks again for visiting with us."

"We'll meet later, then," said the Captain. It was a good moment to trot out another hallowed joke. "But if I'm not down to dinner, don't worry. Someone's got to point the ship in the right direction. And to begin with, it has to be me."

Their appreciative laughter followed him as he closed the cabin door. So far, so good. . . . He had liked the Tillotsons on sight, and he was glad that they had been given the best suite in the ship.

He was even more glad a few moments later, when he made himself known to Sir Hubert and Lady Beckwith in suite A 6 next door. This time it was a woman's voice, harsh and irritable, which answered his knock; and the fact told him half the story, just as the first few moments with this infinitely sordid couple told him the rest. Part of his sudden liking for the Tillotsons had sprung, he realised, from the fact that, though inordinately rich, they had been impressed by their surroundings, and deferential to him as the Captain; now he had the feeling that if both the Beckwiths had fallen on their knees as he entered, he would still have found them intolerable.

Lady Beckwith was a grim-looking woman with the kind of ravaged face sometimes to be glimpsed over other people's shoulders at nightclubs. If she had been beautiful when young, no trace of it now remained; her expression alone—supercilious, selfish, almost vindictive in its air of settled boredom—must long ago have destroyed all elements of grace. She was clearly very rich; everything about her—the wonderful chinchilla stole, the open jewel-cases spread on the table, the masses of flowers that filled one entire wall of the cabin—proclaimed an almost frantic opulence. But her manner proclaimed, with equal clarity, something else: that the opulence was all hers, and hers alone. A single glance at her husband confirmed the fact abundantly.

Sir Hubert was a type, an English type; the Captain recognized it, and him, with an immediate sinking dislike. He was tall, grey-haired, beautifully tailored; he had an ex-Army air, a touch of polo, a whiff of India before the coolies took over. At a first glance, he seemed to have everything: monogrammed shirt (he was for the moment coatless), boned shoes, heavy gold cuff-links, a platinum watch-chain, an elegant topaz signet ring. But then suddenly, at a closer look, he had nothing, nothing at all. A few seconds' inspection made it blindingly clear that he was a dependent, a creature of another's whim; as clear as if everything he wore had been shamefully labelled "HERS." He had been rented, hired at the price of the things he wore, the money he jingled.

The facts were implicit in his manner; the suave grooming was synthetic, the coolness was plainly faked. All he had left was an expression of public disdain. It was as if, having ceased to fool other people, he was now concentrating, with forlorn desperation, upon himself.

Captain Harmer recalled Jack Barrett's words—"He was broke; she bought him, and the title"—but he would have known the truth anyway. Sir Hubert proclaimed his status in a dozen ways; his wife proclaimed hers in one—the look she now gave the Captain as he stood in the doorway, and she snapped out, with consuming impatience:

"What is it?"

He was not going to take that, the Captain decided instantly; not from this haggard bitch, not from anyone. He came forward a couple of steps, so that they could see his uniform beyond a doubt, and said simply:

"Good afternoon."

Sir Hubert Beckwith muttered: "Afternoon," in an off-hand way, jerking his shoulders irritably as he said it. If his wife were annoyed at the interruption, then he had to be annoyed too . . . Lady Beckwith continued to stare at her visitor as if he were a steward who had come in not only without knocking, but with a lot of his buttons undone as well. Then something in his manner, unimpressed, entirely unmoving, broke through to her; and with a flicker of a glacial smile, a second's fractional unbending, she said:

"I guess you must be the Captain."

Harmer nodded, somewhat bleakly. "Yes."

"I'm Lady Beckwith."

Her accent was curious; a basic American, overlaid with the kind of phoney gentility affected by the more refined type of English street-walker. For a moment Captain Harmer had a wild idea that she might be a tremendously bad American actress impersonating one of the English upper classes. Then he took a second look at the chinchilla stole, and he knew that, for good or ill, Lady Beckwith was real. He said:

"I know."

Lady Beckwith frowned. Clearly he had failed her; he had not fainted dead away, he had not even bowed deeply from the waist. As at many other moments of frustration, Harmer guessed, she spoke brusquely over her shoulder to her husband:

"Cigarette, Hubert!"

Sir Hubert's hand went swiftly to his trouser pocket, following, for the millionth time, his private drill manual. Click! went the gold cigarette-case as it was opened: snap! went the gold lighter as he leant over to proffer the flame: pouf! went the elegant expulsion of breath as he extinguished it. With a curt nod, and through a cloud of blown smoke, Lady Beckwith said:

"Is it about the suite?"

"What suite is that, Lady Beckwith?" Harmer felt he could relax now; the only point of status which he wished to make had been made. "As a matter of fact, I just looked in to see if you were comfortable."

"I told them at the head office, I wanted the something suite—" she snapped her fingers at her husband, "—what's that damn-fool name?"

"Princess," said Sir Hubert readily.

"The Princess suite. Isn't that supposed to be the best one in the ship?"

"It's certainly very comfortable indeed," answered the Captain reasonably. He gestured round the plush splendour of suite A 6, which was panelled in rosewood and carpeted in a soft shade of pink. "But don't you like this one?"

"That's not quite the point, is it, old boy?" said Sir Hubert, with extreme hauteur.

"Hubert!" said his wife sharply. And then: "I asked for the Princess suite. What happened to it?"

"It was allocated to someone else."

"Who?"

"Mr. and Mrs. Tillotson."

"Never heard of them. Who are they?"

Captain Harmer looked at her. It was not his job to snap at the customers—the reverse, in fact—but sometimes the temptation was overwhelming.

"The Tillotsons are an American couple," he answered coldly. "They also asked for the Princess suite. Probably their application went in earlier, so they got it. First come, first served, you know." He decided, with regret, that he was doing less than justice to Myth Lines and the *Alcestis*. "I'm sure you'll be comfortable here," he went on. "We chose it specially for you. The Princess suite and this one are almost identical."

"What does 'almost' mean?" asked Lady Beckwith, tartly.

"You can hardly tell them apart."

"But is the other one *any* better?"

"It is six feet wider," answered the Captain, with sarcastic, painstaking accuracy. "It has an extra armchair. It has a fixed bar instead of a side-table. It costs four hundred dollars more. And it has a name instead of a number."

"Ah!" said Sir Hubert, as if the Captain had at last confessed his crime. "That's rather the point, what?"

"I don't quite understand," said Harmer politely.

"Hubert!" said Lady Beckwith. "Go fetch my manicure set. It's in the alligator case, someplace. And for the love of God put your coat on!"

"Yes, my sweet," said Sir Hubert, and disappeared into the cabin next door.

Lady Beckwith expelled another cloud of smoke, and looked levelly at the Captain. The light caught the jewels at her throat, and, less flatteringly, the etched lines from nostrils to mouth, the collapse of pleasure into discontent.

"Not such a hell of a good start," she observed, disagreeably.

"How do you mean?"

"I'm paying top prices," said Lady Beckwith. "I expect to be looked after properly. Your ads certainly talk enough about it. . . . Now I find that the best suite, the only one I wanted, has been given to God-knows-who from Kokomo. What sort of a deal is that?"

"Lady Beckwith," said the Captain firmly, "you really cannot expect me to turn people out of the accommodation assigned to them, just because you want it yourself."

Lady Beckwith looked at him as if this were just what she did expect. But the firmness of his tone forbade her to make the point; she knew she would have lost, and that would have been intolerable.

"Well, I hope they appreciate it," she said unpleasantly. "Though it doesn't exactly sound—"

Her husband appeared at the communicating door. "Sweetheart," he began hesitantly.

"What is it?"

"I can't find it."

"Look again. Get the stewardess. And I want my fur coat too. This place is like a morgue."

"Yes, my darling."

"Well," said Captain Harmer, "I must get back to work." It would have been bliss to add: *And thank God I'm not working for you, like that poor chewed-up piece of string.* But there were certain luxuries which a ship's captain could not afford, and this was one of them.

Lady Beckwith suddenly came to the alert.

"Thanks for calling, Captain," she said unexpectedly.

"Not at all," said Harmer.

"We'll be seeing you at dinner," said Lady Beckwith, with unblinking confidence.

It would have been further bliss, a whole mountain of it, to have answered: *Yes—I'll wave to you across the dining-saloon.* But once again, it had to be foregone. Jack Barrett was right: Sir Hubert and Lady Beckwith, by virtue of their rank, had to be seated at his table, even if they appeared in rags and ate with their feet. It was unfair, it was disgusting; but it was a fixed item in that adroit social blandishment which (it must be faced) kept the *Alcestis* afloat. Rich people had to be flattered; people with titles had to be appeased. The end-result was a full passenger-list at the highest prices in the world: dollars for Britain, dividends for stock-holders, material joy at an official level. If it meant excruciating headaches for captains at the same time, that was what they were paid for.

He said: "I'll look forward to that," and turned towards the door. As he opened it he heard Sir Hubert's voice, plaintive yet appeasing, saying: "Are you *sure* you packed it, old girl?" and as it closed behind him he caught the beginnings of an answering snarl. The Beckwiths were *en famille* once more.

Alone in the corridor, Captain Harmer drew a long breath, conscious of relief and of a vague discomfort at the same time. There were not many passengers like the Beckwiths, thank goodness; but they could too easily make their destructive mark, they could poison a whole cruise if they were not closely watched. There was a choice of two things to be done with people like that; they could be disciplined, or they could be flattered and appeased. The latter was preferred company policy; he, and every man under him, had to lean over backwards to avoid a clash—even the negative clash of criticism—and to satisfy any whim which did not inconvenience other passengers. It was like the company policy on love, he reflected. It had to be accepted that people slept with other people; sometimes they came on board with nothing else in mind; it was a fact of life, and therefore a fact which had to be catered for. In so far as he set any rules, they could be summed up as no open scandals, and no screams in the night. Apart from that, the passengers were free to tear each other to ecstatic ribbons. At sea, love did no damage, and it was generally held to be good for the bar trade.

He began to walk forward slowly along the corridor, making for his cabin again. Stewards stood aside formally as he progressed; stewardesses smiled at him; passengers stared in his direction and sometimes whispered. At the corner of the main foyer, a mink-coated figure detached herself from a group of other people, and waylaid him with a firm determination. It was Mrs. Consolini.

She was a good-looking woman; she seemed to admire him tremendously; it was her third cruise. The three facts knitted together into a pattern which the Captain had found distinctly trying in the past. He did not want Mrs. Consolini; he did not want anybody except his wife. But it had proved difficult to make the fact plain, and still retain feminine good-will during a close-quarters voyage of eighty-four days.

She was looking at him now with those magnificent brown eyes, her face mysteriously alight. His heart sank as he saw it. It was clear that Mrs. Consolini was already coming up for the third round, fighting fit and as fresh as ever, her footwork unimpaired.

But he had a job to do, and this was part of it.

"Why, Mrs. Consolini!" he exclaimed. "How very nice to see you again!"

She smiled at him as if they shared a secret, standing almost touching him.

"How could I possibly miss the *Alcestis?*" She had a pretty voice, an Italian lilt to her speech; not for nothing did his officers (as he knew) call her the Merry Widow. "I've been looking forward to nothing else, the whole of this awful winter."

"That's very flattering indeed." He saw that other passengers, and some of his crew, were looking at them, and he fell back a pace, seeking to disengage. Out of the corner of his eye he noticed Tiptree-Jones standing at the head of the gangway, and he lifted his hand. The First Officer hurried over.

"Please excuse me," said the Captain to Mrs. Consolini, and half-turned aside. Foolishly, he could think of nothing of any consequence to say to Tiptree-Jones, and he was reduced to asking:

"Everything all right?"

"Yes, sir," answered Tiptree-Jones, faintly puzzled.

"You remember Mrs. Consolini?"

"Oh yes!" Tiptree-Jones smiled his best smile directly at her. "We've said hallo already."

"Well. . . ." Captain Harmer shifted from one foot to the other. This was the only sort of situation which ever embarrassed him. *Women*, he thought irritably; they ought to be locked up, every last one of them, and the key thrown over the side. . . .

Annoyingly, it was Mrs. Consolini herself who rescued him.

"I'm sure you're busy, Captain," she said, with an understanding air which was somehow a public demonstration of their intimacy. "Don't let me keep you now. We'll be seeing *lots* of each other, won't we?"

"I certainly hope so," answered the Captain, and smiled before he turned away. As he moved off, he thought: Now why in God's name did I have to say that? But at least he was temporarily freed.

He began to climb the companionway leading to the promenade deck. Then, at the head of the stairs, he paused, attracted by loud voices—or rather, by one loud voice and one soft one. When he came level with the next deck, he saw that the loud voice belonged to Mrs. van Dooren, whom he had recognized earlier. The soft answers, as usual, were being supplied by Edgar, the head barman of the *Alcestis*.

Edgar, like all head barmen, was a character; and, by unspoken protocol, he was allowed to be. It was Edgar whom people chiefly remembered, after a voyage in the *Alcestis*: "Give my best to Edgar" was the standard message, from any former passenger to any prospective one. He was fat, he was cheerful, he was a wonderful listener; and he had that fantastic, flattering memory which persuaded each customer that he was Edgar's personal favourite. If a man ordered a pink gin with eight drops—no more, no less—of Angostura, then he was given eight drops the next time; if he liked a touch of Pernod in his Martini, the same touch of Pernod greeted him the following lunch-time. It was a professional trick, of course; but it paid off every time. The amount that Edgar made in tips each voyage was more than four times his basic salary.

He was other things besides a highly talented head barman; some of them were legitimate, from the Captain's point of view, others were marginal. Edgar ran things. He ran the daily sweepstake on the ship's run during the preceding twenty-four hours. He held large, undercover raffles for cases of whisky and bolts of Chinese silk. He introduced people who wanted to play cards, people who wanted to dance with the pretty girl entrenched behind her family at Table 8. He fixed things. He took messages. He sold Irish Sweep tickets. At every port of call, from Liverpool to Montreal, from New York to Barbados, from Cape Town to Teneriffe, he could be ready with fool-proof introductions: to shops that sold suspect jewellery, to gambling clubs, to chiefs of police, to people's sisters.

He presided, like a jovial fat spider, over the core of the *Alcestis*—the Tapestry Bar. He had six men working under him, smart as paint, willing as ponies; but none of them stirred a finger without a nod from Edgar. Of course, he had too much power, too much influence, too much squeeze. But he was a prodigious asset to the ship; and the Captain, recognizing him for what he was—a rare man in a rare job—gave him free play to an extent allowed to no-one else on board.

Just now, the Captain observed, Edgar was standing at the doorway of the Tapestry Bar, engaged in a standard routine—refusing a passenger a drink. In his best social manner, he was dealing with Mrs. van Dooren, a formidable if handicapped opponent. Mrs. van Dooren wanted a rye-and-water: not outside the three-mile limit, which was legal; not as soon as they sailed, which was practically legal; but then and there—illegal.

"What's the matter with this hooker, anyway?" demanded Mrs. van Dooren discontentedly. "You mean I can't get a *drink?*"

"It's regulations, madam," said Edgar, with smooth insistence. "If it was just myself, I'd start pouring for you now. But it's the customs."

"The customs!" Mrs. van Dooren's voice was suddenly strident with indignation. "You know what?—they tried to stop me coming on board!"

"I can hardly believe that, madam."

"They said I hadn't paid my income tax."

"I'm sure you have, madam."

"Well, I haven't. It's deducted at source by my ex-husband." She swayed slightly, and Edgar put out a practised hand to steady her. "That's what threw them, the sons-of-bitches! Deducted at source."

"It must be very convenient, madam."

"What's your name, George?"

"Edgar, madam."

"How about that rye-and-water, Ed? Just a little one. Who's to know the difference?"

Across the twenty yards of space between them, Edgar caught the Captain's eye. But even if he had not done so, the Captain knew that Edgar would not have transgressed this particular rule. There were rules that could be broken, rules that could be bent, rules that were rules. Customs regulations about liquor in bond were the latter.

"You don't want me to lose my job, madam, do you?" he asked persuasively.

"I just want a rye-and-water, that's all," said Mrs. van Dooren, and collapsed into the chair nearest the doorway.

Edgar arranged the cushions round her shoulders, and then stood back, a benign, understanding presence.

"It won't be long now, madam," he assured her. "It really won't be long."

Indeed, it would not be long. Blue Peter, the sailing flag, had gone to the yard-arm; the first gongs for "All ashore" were now sounding faintly along the lower reaches of B deck; a few premature paper streamers already stretched from ship to shore. But a fair number of passengers were still arriving—life at the *Alcestis* level did not breed habits of punctuality; and among the slow-moving voyagers, a single weaving figure, a small furtive man in a hurry, could be momentarily glimpsed. Sighted by a deck-hand in the stern, pointed out to other shipmates, greeted by cat-calls from cheerful men in chef's hats poking their heads out of portholes—Barkway the missing steward made his embarrassed way on board. The Master-at-Arms touched him briefly on the shoulder as he disappeared from sight.

Up on the boat-deck, the group of young officers were still maintaining their watch for "talent," though with increasing despondency. A single solitary girl had been added to Tim Mansell's quota; they had not been able to identify her from the passenger-list, but she was at least slim, moderately good-looking, and under thirty years of age. Now, with the flow of newcomers easing off, depression had set in; it seemed likely to be one of those voyages which made Jack a dull boy. Beresford, the young apprentice, voiced it for all of them when he observed dejectedly:

"I don't know about you, but I feel like missing this trip altogether."

"Romance!" intoned Blantyre, sardonically. "Glamour. Sun-drenched days. Never-to-be-forgotten nights. Once-in-a-lifetime thrills. Baloney!"

"I wonder who writes those ads," said Tim Mansell.

"Some bloody liar!"

"He should try dancing with Bernice Beddington."

The long-sighted Fleming, scanning the length of the quay, suddenly exclaimed: "Wow!"

"What is it?" asked Blantyre.

"Dawn is breaking," said Fleming. "Just look at those two girls!"

They watched with interest, and then with goggle-eyed concentration, as Carl Wenstrom's party of five approached the foot of the gangway. The three men they scarcely saw, though the Professor, his white hair topping a magnificent old-fashioned travelling ulster, was an arresting figure. But it was the girls who claimed the attention, and held it irresistibly. Diane Loring, quietly dressed in grey, still failed to disguise her air of sensual readiness; the pretty pale face was composed, but the walk was a mobile invitation, the figure a challenge to every male within range. Beside her, Kathy looked remarkably lovely; her blonde hair shone brilliantly against the drab dockside, her face was a grave oval, delighting the eye, promising infinite pleasures. Work seemed to stop, enraptured silence seemed to fall, as she first smiled at the dock policeman, and then set foot on the gangway, leading them all on board.

When she was half way up, and Diane a few paces behind her, she chanced to raise her eyes to the level of the boat-deck. The four young men gazing down at her were almost ludicrous in their combined air of admiration, their hungry unanimity. Kathy was used to such glances, from almost every man she encountered; but the quartet above her, united in their longing, suspended in space like love in aspic, were suddenly disconcerting. Carl had coached them all towards making a delayed, eye-catching entrance; but this was almost too successful. . . . Her chin rose a fraction; she caught Tim Mansell's glance, and held it coolly for a moment, before passing out of sight.

"Gee!" said Tim Mansell, almost whispering. "What a girl!"

"Both of them."

"Probably come to see their father off, or something," said Fleming, pessimistically.

"I couldn't bear that," said Tim Mansell. "Gee!"

A formidable voice behind them said: "Well, gentlemen?"

They turned as one body, though they did not need to do so in order to recognize the voice. It was the Captain, surveying them from a distance of a few feet, his expression bleak.

"If you have nothing to do," he said after a moment's awkward silence, "you ought to have more sense than to advertise the fact in public."

Blantyre, the senior of the four, summoned his courage. "We were just checking up, sir."

"I know damned well you were just checking up!" said the Captain, on a note of the sternest discipline. Then his face relaxed suddenly, and he smiled, the sort of smile which, on its rare appearance, could made a simple hero-worshipper out of any man on board. He looked directly at Tim Mansell, still holding the passenger-list. "How many, Fourth?"

"Sir?" said Tim, abashed.

"You heard me. How many?"

"Four, sir."

"Five, if we stretched it a bit," said Fleming, who sometimes took chances with the Captain's humour.

"We must be slipping," said the Captain. "*Alcestis* ought to do better than that."

Tim Mansell grinned, still rapt in his private joy. "But, sir—one's an absolute knock-out!"

The tugs nosed up and took their lines, and then waited, while the last gong sounded, the last visitors walked ashore, the last gangway was hoisted and swung out-board. The orchestra played "Old Lang Syne," and then "A Life on the Ocean Wave"; the coloured paper streamers, doled out by busy stewards, bound the ship tenuously to the land in a last brief contact. Up on the bridge, the pilot cocked an eye at the wind-indicator, and put his whistle to his lips; a plume of steam came from the huge siren, and then a shattering, deep-toned roar as the *Alcestis* made her farewell salute to New York. At the pilot's side, the Captain hunched his shoulders deeper into his greatcoat, conscious of satisfaction, conscious of the weight of command, and of the nervousness which not a thousand sailings could ever cure.

Up on the fo'csle-head, in the very eyes of the ship, First Officer Tiptree-Jones stood staring at the bridge, waiting for the signal to cast off; far aft, out of sight, Tim Mansell pressed the telephone closer to his ear, awaiting the same order. The pilot, a small non-committal man in a shabby peaked cap, glanced sideways at the captain.

"O.K.?"

Captain Harmer nodded. "Go ahead." And then, to the quartermasters at the telegraphs: "Stand by engines!"

Outside the Tapestry Bar, two decks below, Mrs. van Dooren stirred in her chair, looked out of the nearest big porthole, and sat up with a start.

"We're afloat!" she said.

"I certainly hope so, madam," said Edgar.

"I mean, we've started."

Edgar glanced down at the receding dock wall. "That is so, madam."

Mrs. van Dooren levered herself upright. "How about it, then?"

"Rye and water, madam," said Edgar promptly, and advanced a loaded tray. As she took the glass, he continued: "Can I interest you in the first sweepstake ticket on the day's run?"

"Sure," said Mrs. van Dooren readily, between gulps. "How much?"

"One hundred dollars, madam. We divide it up into pools of ten people each. The prize is nine hundred dollars."

"*Nine* hundred?"

"We always deduct ten per cent, madam," answered Edgar, with practised smoothness. "Ship's charities."

chapter 3

PASSING the Statue of Liberty, the passengers flocked to the rail, cameras clicking and whirring like castanets, like crazy clocks. They even left the haven of the Tapestry Bar, where Edgar was now doing a roaring trade in late lunch-time liqueurs, early cocktails, and the first harvest of his endless series of sweepstakes. To Mrs. van Dooren, who did *not* leave her station at the brass rail, Edgar remarked:

"They say it's built on top of a prison."

"What's that, George?" asked Mrs. van Dooren.

"The Statue of Liberty. There used to be a prison underneath it, in the old days."

"So?" said Mrs. van Dooren, rather belligerently.

"Nothing really, madam. It's just an interesting fact. Sort of symbolic."

"Are you a radical?" asked Mrs. van Dooren.

"Far from it, madam."

An inwardly brooding man, sitting a few feet away down the bar, said: "There's an elevator going up inside the arm, too. Sensational!"

"Facts, facts," said Mrs. van Dooren.

Above their heads, the siren suddenly sounded, in a series of ear-splitting blasts which rattled every glass in the bar.

"Who in God's name is sounding off *now?*" asked Mrs. van Dooren peevishly.

"Boat drill, madam," answered Edgar. "You may have seen a notice about it in your cabin. Passengers are asked to assemble on the boat-deck."

"Baloney."

"Do you know your station, madam?"

"White Plains," said Mrs. van Dooren.

The brooding man got down from his stool. "Well, I guess we ought to obey orders," he remarked uncertainly. "Like they say, *noblesse oblige*."

"The Captain doesn't actually insist on it," said Edgar, in a confidential undertone. "He knows he can rely on all of you in an emergency."

"I buy that," said the man. "Integrity." He walked unsteadily towards the door.

"Integrity?" queried Mrs. van Dooren, astonished.

"That's Mr. Zucco," Edgar informed her. "He's in the film business. Hollywood."

"Gee whiz!" Mrs. van Dooren looked at Edgar with sudden, owlish concentration. "Has this ship ever been sunk?"

"No, madam."

"Just keep that up! And give me a rye-and-water."

Boat drill was indeed a somewhat sketchy affair, a sort of marine get-together with very slight overtones of crisis and actuality. It was true that Captain Harmer never insisted on a hundred-per-cent turn-out; he had long ago realized that many of his passengers resented it, that they considered themselves either too comfortable to be disturbed or too rich to drown. His officers went through the motions of mustering their crews and checking their allotted passengers; at least one of them—Tim Mansell—was delighted to find that he had drawn a winner, the beautiful blonde girl, together with her step-father (a lightning check at the purser's office had established this relationship, and their names as well). He did not speak to Kathy; she seemed aloof, unapproachable, staring about her at the unfamiliar scene as if it were something she did not choose to be involved in.

The truth was that she was cold, and also somewhat nervous. Everything so far—the size and luxury of the ship, the number of passengers, their air of sureness and consequence—had conspired to make her feel that they had taken on something too big, too complicated, too dangerous. They would hardly be able to make a dent in this quality of armour. . . . But when she mentioned this to Carl, after the drill was over and they were back in their day-cabin, he scoffed at the idea.

"Nonsense, my darling!" He was sitting back in a comfortable armchair, leafing through the wine-list which was part of the ship's 'directory.' "In a week we'll be running this ship—or as much of it as we want to. You're going to be a tremendous success, Kathy—I can see it already."

"What makes you think that?"

"The way people look at you." He put out his hand to touch her shoulder. "You really are extremely decorative, you know."

She shrugged slightly, unconvinced, irritated. "But that's nothing, Carl, that's just the beginning of it. This is all so—" she frowned,

"—*so organized.* As if they could deal with anything, including us."

"They've never had people like us," answered Carl decisively. "That I can guarantee."

"I wonder. I still get the impression that nothing is new around here. They've seen it all before. They've got answers to everything."

"Not to us," he said again.

The cabin floor lifted suddenly, a slight rocking movement, and a patter of spray sounded against the plating outside. There was a knock at the door, and their steward, a small, rather harassed man, entered.

"Barkway, sir," he said to Carl. "Just checking the portholes."

"Please go ahead," said Carl.

Barkway crossed the cabin and started to put a few extra turns on the fastenings of the main porthole, which was already closed.

"Is it going to be rough?" Carl asked.

Barkway, turning, shook his head, summoning a weak grin. "Oh no, sir. We wouldn't do that to you. It's just a little lift. We're outside now."

"Does she roll much?"

"No, sir. The Captain takes care of that."

Kathy laughed. "Now how can he do that?"

"Captain Harmer takes care of everything, miss," answered Barkway, a trifle dispiritedly, and withdrew.

He spoke with feeling: the Captain had already found time to have him brought up, logged, scathingly rebuked, officially reprimanded, and fined to the limit that the regulations allowed. Barkway, who would have had a hangover anyway, was already sick of the sea.

Mr. Cutler, the purser, sat in his small cubbyhole of an office, just off the 'entrance foyer' of the *Alcestis,* and waited for the first complaint. He knew exactly what the complaint would be about; he knew the extent to which it was justified; he knew what his answer would be. It was the duty of the best pursers never to be surprised, and Mr. Cutler, senior purser of Myth Lines, was one of the very best. He was a very small, very sharp, very grey man of fifty; he was known to anyone who had anything to do with big liners, the world over, as "Foxy" Cutler, but the nickname was admiring and affectionate, never derogatory. For Foxy Cutler knew it all—that was a matter of common agreement; the pointed, questing look had, over the years, ferreted out all conceivable answers.

He knew, down to the last packet of pins, how to run the inside of a ship; how to see that people—any number of people between one and one thousand—were bedded down, woken up, fed, amused, financed, mollified, kept happy, and unobtrusively disciplined.

He could tell a bouncing cheque before it hit his desk for the first time. He knew the kind of cossetting which made honeymoon couples happier still in their entrancement. He knew about stewards—all about all of them, from the good eager youngsters to the snivelling old drunks. Looking at any pair of passengers, he could smell out benefit of clergy, or the lack of it, and tell whether it really mattered or not. He knew the exact extent of Edgar the head barman's various rackets, and at what point they stopped being good for the *Alcestis*, and were simply good for Edgar. He had his own rackets, naturally: they were monumental in some cases, modest in others; they were reflected in his No. 2 bank-account ashore, which was a remarkable monument in itself. He had always remained a bachelor—"the purser is married to the ship" was his explanatory comment upon this, but the truth was far different. The simple fact was that he knew how to do too many things too perfectly. Mr. Cutler, the all-competent housekeeper, organizer, banker, and disciplinarian, would have driven any woman round the bend in six weeks.

In ships of the size and complexity of the *Alcestis*, there were sometimes feuds between the purser's side of the ship—the organizational, administrative side—and the seamen up top who worked her. In Foxy Cutler's mind, there was no such feud, and no occasion for it; and he took good care to communicate this to everyone around him. He knew that he could not have done the Captain's job; and the Captain could not have done his. Similarly, a good deck-hand would make a terrible steward, or no steward at all; and the oldish men who ran the elevators with ceremonial courtesy could never change jobs with the oldish men who watched the pressure gauges, four decks below. But they were all, every last one of them, essential to the *Alcestis.* That was his personal creed; and an endlessly repeated *You do your job. I'll do mine* was the phrase which enshrined it. While Mr. Cutler was around, no-one traded inter-departmental insults, no-one swore that stewards were free-wheeling loafers, or deck-hands the dregs of the Liverpool water front; and, on board the *Alcestis,* they said it very seldom when he was out of hearing, either.

Now, while he waited for that first, foreseeable complaint, he tuned his ear to his part of the ship, and was satisfied. He could hear cabin doors being opened and closed—that was the stewards obeying the bridge-order "Secure ports and deadlights." He could hear the restless creak of woodwork, as for the thousandth time the *Alcestis* faced the open sea. He felt the laboured motion as she shouldered her burden, and heard the wash and drip of spray, and the gentle working of her ribs and joints, and he was glad of all of them.

A slight sea to begin with always had a settling, salutary effect; it made people realize they were in a ship, part of her lading, and no longer sheltered by a run-of-the-mill roof ashore. It made them behave better, and stop whooping it up aimlessly, and drink for comfort instead of hilarity. It took the edge off bad behaviour; it would even do this for the child, young Master Barry Greenfield, whom an hour earlier a steward had observed in two separate misdemeanours—peeping through a keyhole into an adjoining cabin (which was traditionally fruitless, since there were protective flaps on either side), and poking his whip, or whatever it was, into one of the big electric fans in the corridor, which could be dangerous, or expensive, or both. Master Greenfield, with luck, would soon feel slightly queasy; he would be given two tablets of dramamine, and wake up a better boy. The whip itself might well disappear, sunk (literally) without trace.

Presently Mr. Cutler's phone rang; answering, he said: "Purser's office," and then: "Yes, Mr. Walham." He had known all along that it would be Walham, because Walham was in Cabin B.23, and B.23 had a kind of primal curse upon it—a steam-joint which, for some reason locked deep in the hearts of the builders, picked up and magnified a rhythmic thudding sound from a valve at least forty feet away. They had tried everything with that steam-joint, and with the valve too; they had repacked them, altered their arc of curve, turned them sideways and then upside down, adjusted the pressure, invented an entirely new type of spring-loaded valve as gentle as a butterfly's kiss; all to no avail. The steam-joint still thudded, steadily and metallically, from one end of a voyage to the other, and B.23 was its sounding-board.

Thus Mr. Cutler had known that his first complainant would be Walham; and he knew quite a lot about Walham, too. He was a Chicago industrialist with interests in steel and farm equipment; he was very rich; he would probably be seated at the captain's table; and though married, he was travelling alone. What Mr. Cutler could not have foreseen about Walham was his voice, a sort of nasal bark like a petulant sergeant-major; and his outlook on life, which came through with alarming clarity in the first few sentences. Mr. Walham was mean; not poor-mean, which was often forgiveable, but rich-mean, which was invariably odious.

"There's some damn' pipe or other making a racket, just outside my door," began Walham, as soon as he had announced himself. "I want it stopped."

Mr. Cutler, soothing, courteous, explained as well as he could, from a well-worn rubric, that unfortunately this particular pipe always made that noise, and there was nothing he could do about it.

"Like hell!" said Walham disagreeably. "I don't pay good money for that sort of thing. How do you expect me to get to sleep nights?"

"We have found," said Mr. Cutler patiently, "that people grow used to the noise."

"I don't care about *people*." Walham made his point very clearly. "I want you to take care of *me*. I didn't pay nearly five thousand bucks, just to listen to some damned steam hammer. I can get that sort of racket back home in the boiler factory."

"I'm very sorry—" began Mr. Cutler.

"You'll be sorrier still," barked Walham, "if you don't see this thing my way."

"But fortunately," continued Mr. Cutler, controlling himself with a practised hand, "I can offer you another cabin."

"I should damn well hope so."

"We happen to have one free. It's a double cabin. Slightly larger. B.14."

There was a silence, suspicious, loaded. Then:

"Same price, though," said Walham. It was a command rather than a query. "You're not going to rail-road me into paying—"

"Same price," said Mr. Cutler. Occupation of cabin B.14 did in fact involve an extra two hundred dollars, but there was (as Cutler sometimes phrased it to himself) a time to go fishing and a time to dry the nets. This particular net, if he was any judge at all, was worth two hundred dollars to Myth Lines; it was certainly worth it, in the general interests of harmony on board. "If you would like to make the move, I'll send a message to your cabin-steward."

"Sure I'd like to make the move." Walham did not sound in the least grateful; the grudging nasal twang was unaltered. *I'm getting what I paid for*, the tone said, unmistakably; *you're not doing me any favours. . . .* "Can't be too soon for me, with this damned racket going on all the time. And there's another thing. Afternoon tea."

"Afternoon tea?" queried Cutler, surprised.

"Yes, afternoon tea!" There was a rustle of papers over the telephone. "It says here, afternoon tea is served *daily* in the Olympic Lounge."

"That is so, Mr. Walham."

"I went there at half after four," said Walham deliberately, as if he were giving evidence in some massive crime. "I waited. No tea. I waited a full half-hour. No tea. Then I asked a steward. He had the gall to tell me they weren't serving it today."

"That is so," said Cutler again. "You see—"

"Now what sort of a deal is that?" demanded Walham, his sharp voice rising a full half-octave. "You put out this catalogue, or whatever it is, saying what you're going to give us. Then when the time comes to deliver, we're told it's not available. Like hell it's not available! You make a contract, you've got to stick with it. You can't chop and change, just the way it suits you. If I ran my business like that, would I be *in* business? No, I'd be in jail! Afternoon tea daily means—"

"Mr. Walham!" Cutler, faced with this rising tide, decided that he must stem it somehow, and his voice was loud and clear and crisp.

"What is it?" asked Walham, caught in mid-sentence.

"We didn't sail till four o'clock," said Cutler, going straight into his explanation while he had the chance. "By the time we were clear of harbour, it was nearer five, well past teatime. We don't serve tea on the first day. We never do. The times just don't fit in."

"The first day is a day like any other day," said Walham stubbornly, "and this trip started at four P.M. You can't get round that, whatever you say."

Cutler sighed. "Mr. Walham, I don't want to get round anything. That's not our policy at all." He made his decision. "Would you like to have some tea now?"

"I'd like the afternoon tea that's in the catalogue," said Walham, suspicion in his voice. "Not a special tea, or an extra tea. Just tea, like it says in the book."

"You mean, a free tea?"

"Just that."

"I'll have it sent along directly. And then we'll move your cabin."

"I'll be waiting," said Walham, with simple churlishness, and hung up.

Passengers, thought Mr. Cutler, as he lifted the receiver again to make these minor dispositions; *dear* passengers. . . . The *Alcestis* had six hundred crew members to look after three hundred of them. Somehow, every time she put to sea, they still discovered new things to bitch about.

chapter 4

THE first dinner on board the *Alcestis* at the start of a cruise was never an easy affair; it was the first "shake" of the shake-down process, and thus a period of trial, not the least for Chief Steward Vincent, who had a large number of things on his mind. Vincent, a fat man who was an excellent advertisement for the *Alcestis* menus, had first of all to produce a satisfactory meal; this would be, for nearly all the passengers, their first sample of their projected "way of life" for the next few months, and it was necessary to give them confidence and set an appropriate tone—in spite of supplies that might have failed to arrive, cooks who might have hangovers, and stewards who could take an immediate dislike to their customers. There was also the table plan, a fruitful source of argument and embarrassment.

The Captain had picked his own table; in thirty years afloat, Vincent had only known this to be changed once, when one of the elect was so invariably drunk at meal-times that he was relegated to his cabin half-way through the voyage. The First Officer had had his table picked for him; the Chief Engineer and the Purser took what was left of the cream; the rest of the passengers had to be settled in their allotted places, and persuaded that these were ideal. It was never easy. Some of them wanted to be alone; some objected to being behind pillars, or too near the door, or too far from it; some did not like the people they were with, and spent this first meal-time making the fact plain and scheming how to change their table. Some had fads, often extraordinary; special foods, special sauces, special brands of aerated water, boxes of pills, flowers which relieved their allergies, cushions at their backs, even footstools; they all had to be catered for.

Some, owing to the slight roll, had no appetite, but sweated out the meal notwithstanding, queasy and ominous; some ate too much, or got drunk, or were drunk already, and thus grew boisterous or troublesome. Some table-hopped, spilling wine or upsetting glasses in the process. Some thought they ought to be seated at one of the officers' tables, and sneered at the usurping incumbents. When a young steward dropped a heavy metal dish-cover with a reverberating clang, and a momentary silence fell, it reminded Vincent of the start of a new round, with the contestants glaring at each other and flexing their muscles. It was a daunting thought that he would have to preside at a minimum of two-hundred-and-fifty ensuing meals.

Nowhere was this air of unease more apparent than at the Captain's own table.

The Captain himself was not present. He never came down to dinner on this first evening; his excuse, that the *Alcestis* was still weaving her way across half a dozen busy shipping lanes and that he was required on the bridge, was valid enough, but the real reason was personal—he was somewhat shy, even after so long in the service, and he preferred to leave it to his guests to get acquainted, rather than to assume the burden himself. Sir Hubert and Lady Beckwith, Mr. and Mrs. Tillotson, and Mr. Walham were the first to arrive at table; characteristically, when Vincent announced that the Captain would not be coming down, only Walham commented on the fact.

"Fine thing!" he said disagreeably. He was surveying—perhaps he was even counting—the supply of olives, salted almonds, and sticks of celery which lay on a dish in the middle of the table. Then he looked up at the chief steward. "You mean, the Captain's missing dinner?"

"He will have his up on the bridge, sir," answered Vincent.

Walham's face, which was thin and pursed, as if he had just bitten on a lemon, tightened even further. "Why not here? Isn't this the Captain's table?"

"I'm sure he has plenty to do," said Mr. Tillotson, "at the beginning of the voyage."

"He's got to eat," said Walham.

"He always stays on the bridge," explained Vincent, in faint reproof, "when we're anywhere near land, or near other ships."

"The Captain's table," repeated Walham. "At least, that's the way I heard it."

Sir Hubert Beckwith, tall, aloof, supercilious, leant across the table. "The Captain never comes down, the first evening," he said coldly. "Most people know that."

Walham looked at him. The Beckwiths were the only ones who

had changed for dinner, which was traditionally optional on this occasion; it gave them a dividing superiority which nothing in their manner diminished. He set his thin jaw, and helped himself to celery. Then he said suddenly:

"What's your line?"

"Line?" repeated Sir Hubert.

"Yeah, line. I'm in farm equipment, biggest in the Middle West. Mr. Tillotson here is Steel & Tool—" he cocked an eye at Tillotson, "—in fact, we do business together, when there *is* any business. What's your business?"

"I have no business," answered Sir Hubert after a pause. "Not in the accepted sense."

"You're lucky," said Walham. His eyes swivelled round to Lady Beckwith, whose bracelets, earrings, and three-tier necklace, all of emeralds, were exceptionally prominent. His lips pursed again. "I'd say you were *very* lucky."

Round them, the clatter of dishes and the buzz of conversation was suddenly loud as silence fell on their table. Lady Beckwith, her face set in a furious scowl, concentrated on her soup. Sir Hubert was staring at a point six inches above everyone's head. Tillotson consulted a wine-list as if it were the most engrossing thing he had ever clapped eyes on. It was left to Mrs. Tillotson to step in.

"I wonder," she said, gesturing round the empty places, "who else is sitting with us."

"Whoever it is," said Walham, who was not sensitive to the atmosphere around him, "they'll miss the soup if they don't watch out."

"Oh, surely not," said Mrs. Tillotson. "It's right here on the menu."

"So was afternoon tea," said Walham, his mouth full.

"How's that again?" asked Tillotson, looking up.

"Did you have afternoon tea?"

"I guess not."

"You *could* have. It's on the menu."

"I didn't want it."

"Well, I did. And they tried to give me the run-around. Said it wasn't being served today. But I got it" He looked around him, in triumph. "I tell you, you have to watch out for these things! Otherwise they'll gyp you every time. That's why they're in business."

"Who?" asked Lady Beckwith, coming belligerently to the surface.

Walham waved his hand round the room. "The shipping line. They have to shave their costs all the time. And they don't care how they do it."

"I doubt if they'll go bankrupt over one afternoon tea," said Lady Beckwith, with disdain.

"It all adds up, percentage-wise," said Walham. "But I guess you wouldn't know about that."

"As it happens," said Sir Hubert austerely, "my wife has an acute business sense."

Walham grinned, as if in the bitten lemon he had hit suddenly on a brief, thin rind of saccharine. "That must come in handy," he said, "in the circumstances."

Now there was an interruption, welcome for many reasons, as Chief Steward Vincent led forward two more of their fellow guests. He stood over them as they sat down.

"I'd like to introduce Mr. and Mrs. Kincaid," he said, professionally hearty. "Sir Hubert and Lady Beckwith, Mr. and Mrs. Tillotson, Mr. Walham."

The newcomers were greeted with slightly overdone enthusiasm; in the circumstances, any dilution of the table could only come as a relief. Kincaid looked what he was: a tough professional politician who had failed to make the grade from medium to top rank, from the hatchet to the walking-stick. The shock of grey hair and the gaunt face might have suited a Governor or even a senator, if Kincaid had ever succeeded in becoming either; as he had failed, in circumstances of some notoriety, the hair looked, subtly, like a wig, and the gaunt face seemed merely hungry. His wife had that disappointed look peculiar to women who, goading their husbands by every means short of a spear between the shoulder-blades, see the goal receding, the world passing them by, the plums of office shrinking like raisins in the sun. But whatever the set-backs, the betrayals, the deals that came unstuck, the Kincaids were still in the ring, as their manner showed unmistakably; their reaction to "Sir Hubert and Lady Beckwith" was little short of a round of cheers, and their greeting of the others was on the same scale of buoyant good-fellowship. The habit of vote-snagging clearly died hard. On this occasion, they only lacked babies to kiss.

"Well, well, well," said Kincaid heartily, rubbing his hands. "Looks like we're all set for a wonderful trip."

This had not been the general impression a few seconds earlier; but such was the power of suggestion, the contagion of good-humour, that for several minutes all was love. Tillotson and Kincaid discovered some mutual acquaintances in New York; Mrs. Kincaid was so determinedly obsequious to Lady Beckwith that the latter actually gave her a faint sketch of a smile; and Walham, burrowing his way into a second helping of the fish course, was for the moment neutralized. Then two spanners, one of them obscure, alighted in the works with successive thuds.

The first came when Mrs. Kincaid made the error of assuming that the Beckwiths had the Princess suite.

"I hear it's lovely," she said enthusiastically. "How wonderful for you!"

"It certainly would be wonderful," said Lady Beckwith, with a return of her most acid manner, "if we had it. But we haven't. There was some stupid mix-up over the bookings."

"Oh," said Mrs. Kincaid, uncertainly. "I was sure—"

Mrs. Tillotson, who had overheard, leant forward, unwisely happy. "We have the Princess suite," she said, with ingenuous satisfaction. "And you're quite right—it's a dream!"

"There was some mix-up," repeated Lady Beckwith, busily murdering a soft roll.

"I hadn't heard that," said Mrs. Tillotson quietly.

"Well, obviously there must have been," said Lady Beckwith. She made a gesture which somehow managed to include her husband's dinner-jacket, her own extensive jewellery, and Mrs. Tillotson's modest cocktail dress. "I mean to say. . . ."

There was a glacial silence. It was broken by Walham, who leant across the table towards Kincaid, his mouth crammed, and asked:

"How are things in Dade County?"

Kincaid's expression changed, from public well-being to a kind of wary hostility. "You know Dade County?" he asked curtly.

"Only what I read in the newspapers." Walham's tone was offensively loaded. "But that's enough, for sure."

A hood seemed to come down over Kincaid's eyes. "You have to know all the circumstances—" he began.

His wife interrupted him. "The chief of police was a crook," she said, almost snarling. "That was proved!"

"I only asked," said Walham. "You've got to admit, Dade County was in the news."

Sir Hubert Beckwith, who had been dissecting his pheasant with the grace and skill common to all titled Englishmen eating off the cuff, looked up.

"Am I the only one," he asked superciliously, "who knows nothing at all about Dade County—not even where it is?"

"It's in Florida," said Walham. He grinned, unpleasantly. "Or it was, up till the time we sailed."

"Now just a minute—" began Kincaid angrily.

"The whole thing was a frame-up," said Mrs. Kincaid, near to shouting. Gone with the wind were public relations. "Those photostats were all fakes. What would my husband want with land-options? Just tell me that! Everyone knows this other gang had every hoodlum in Miami working for them! It was just smear, smear, smear, from beginning to end. Even the call-girls were fixed!"

In the interested silence that followed, Sir Hubert said coldly:

"I have never really understood American politics."

Unseen by him, a man and a woman had approached their table and now stood behind him, waiting uncertainly. The chief steward was busy with another table, and had not noticed their entrance. Finally the man, who was the sombre man from the Tapestry Bar, came forward a pace, bowed formally, and said:

"Zucco."

"No, thank you," said Sir Hubert, without turning his head.

"Zucco, Transaction Pictures," said the man again. He was now wearing a white tuxedo, a red bow tie, and a scarlet cummerbund edged with sequins, but his expression of gloom was unaltered. "We're proud to be sitting with you fine people," he went on, as if he were the heavy lead in some stark Biblical drama. "And now I'd like you all to meet my lovely wife."

The men stood up awkwardly as the introductions were made. Mr. Zucco's lovely wife was an exceptionally ugly woman of about fifty, the planes of whose face seemed long ago to have dissolved like melting gelatine. The wardrobe department of Transaction Pictures might well have had a hand in her jewellery, which was uniformly barbaric—enormous single-stone rings, bangles like slave-shackles, earrings like dwarf chandeliers. As she sat down she said: "I hope we haven't missed all the go-go-go-stuff."

Her husband remained standing, looking down at the table full of glum or angry people. Suddenly he stepped back, "sighting" them through his half-clenched hand against a background of cold ham and Stilton cheeses on a centre table. Then he shook his head, and said: "Meaningful."

"Hannibal never stops running," said his wife in explanation.

Mr. Zucco said: "I'd like to get a shot of this whole significant group. Gracious living goes to sea. Fabulous! I can see it visually."

Sir Hubert Beckwith, whose expression indicated unmistakably that he feared the Zuccos were Jews, inquired acidly:

"How else would you see it?"

Mr. Zucco turned the full force of his sombre gaze on Sir Hubert. "That's something you can never get on film," he said finally. "No matter how hard you try."

"Try what?" asked Sir Hubert. "I don't understand."

"The British sense of humour," said Mr. Zucco, sitting down at last. "It just doesn't translate. Controlled! Razor-sharp! And subtle as hell!"

"I can assure you—" began Sir Hubert.

"Hubert!" said his wife crisply.

"Yes, dear?"

"Break off this scintillating conversation," said Lady Beckwith, "long enough to order some wine."

"Of course, dear."

"And I'd like a cigarette."

"Sorry, darling."

"And I want my other stole from the cabin."

"I'll get the steward."

"And pass the salt," said Walham.

First Officer Tiptree-Jones, in spite of an impeccable social manner, was having a hard time, and he was beginning to show it. At his table there was (as he privately phrased it) a really ripe collection of dead-beats; the three Beddingtons, who were uniformly speechless, the Gersons and the Bancrofts, who loathed each other, Mrs. Consolini who thought she ought to be at the Captain's table, and Mrs. van Dooren, who by now had gone about as far as she could, alcoholically, without actually falling head first into the fruit basket. In the intervals of trying to entertain this truly remarkable mélange of misfits, Tiptree-Jones brooded on the fact that the Captain must have done it to him on purpose. But why? It was not reassuring that he had eighty-four days in which to find out the answer.

The Bancrofts and the Gersons came from the same smart suburb of Chicago; if they had been told that, as married couples, they were as unique and as distinguishable from each other as two pairs of hard-boiled eggs, they would have laughed the idea to scorn, but it was depressingly true. The men were both bald, fat, and talkative; the women were smart, grey-haired, blue-rinsed, community-minded. Back home, the Bancrofts and the Gersons lived a half-mile from each other in identical split-level, ranch-type homes, built on commodious estates of 1¼ acres each; the Gersons boasted a luminous sun-dial, the Bancrofts a barbecue-pit with terrazzo-style tiling; in both their two-car garages, a 1958 Cadillac nuzzled a 1960 Ford station-wagon. The Bancrofts went for hi-fi, the Gersons for home-movies. They all went for vodka Martinis, the higher reaches of country club life, and marathon sessions of bridge.

The men were much given to the kind of self-conscious 'joshing' which took the place of conversation over large tracts of America. Mr. Gerson was in oil—"though not very deep" was Mr. Bancroft's reiterated comment. Mr. Bancroft manufactured a well-known brand of bar supplies, including ornamental bone-handled cork-screws. ("Even the products are crooked," said Mr. Gerson, on every possible occasion.) Their invariable greeting to each other was: "Putting on a little weight, eh?" Then Mr. Bancroft would tell the story about Mr. Gerson and the oilmen's convention at Edmonton, Alberta, in 1951 ("They sold him the drilling rights, all right—he was in the wrong hall—they were *dentists,*") and Mr. Gerson countered with the one about Mr. Bancroft and the two male cabaret dancers in Paris in 1948 ("You know, there's something *queer* here"). Then, with luck, they got drunk, and quarrelled, and their wives hauled them off to bed, while they made wild backward threats to kick each other's teeth in. In the morning they would say, almost simultaneously: "Boy, you certainly tied one on, last night."

At the moment, to a listless audience of nine at Tiptree-Jones' table, Mr. Bancroft was trying to get Mr. Gerson to admit that he had been drunk at a certain party in New York about three years previously.

"Boy, you certainly tied one on, that night."

"I was cold sober," said Mr. Gerson. "I drove home."

"You drove home! That doorman had to pour you into the back seat. Millie drove home. Didn't you, Millie?"

"I don't remember," said Mrs. Gerson.

"I'll bet Jack doesn't remember, either."

"I remember every little thing," said Mr. Gerson, "including you and that hat-check girl."

"It wasn't a hat-check girl, it was a cigarette-girl," said Mr. Bancroft triumphantly. "*That's* how much you remember. I told you, Jack, you shouldn't have switched to Bourbon. You can't take it." He turned to Tiptree-Jones. "That was his trouble, see? He switched to Bourbon."

"Really?" said Tiptree-Jones, laughing heartily. "It sounds rather unwise."

"I can switch to Bourbon, any time," proclaimed Mr. Gerson.

"He *thinks*," said Mr. Bancroft, with heavy sarcasm. "But boy, you should have seen him that night!"

"Well, who picked up the check, anyway?"

"The waiter picked up the check. It was on the floor." Mr. Bancroft bellowed with sudden laughter. "You knocked it onto the floor, and the waiter had to pick it up. Boy, you certainly tied one on, that night."

"I was cold sober," said Mr. Gerson. "It was you that tied one on."

"In a pig's ear!" said Mr. Bancroft. "*You* tied one on, Jack, and you might as well admit it."

"I drove home," said Mr. Gerson. "All the way from that crummy joint to that crummy hotel on 56th Street."

"And all the way into the fire-hydrant," said Mr. Bancroft. "Boy, you certainly had a skinful, that night."

Silence fell all round the table; the topic, significant, absorbing, seemed to have been exhausted. The Bancrofts and the Gersons, smiling reminiscently on one side, scowling slightly on the other, went on with their meal; Bernice Beddington continued to stare straight ahead, rapt in some interior dream from which her spectacles kept the prying world; Mrs. van Dooren, weaving slightly, fished for her lost shoes under the table. Mrs. Consolini might have helped things out, but she had, in a relatively charming way, turned sulky. She had expected to be seated at the Captain's table; she did not like the one she was at; the fact that her long-term rival, Mrs. Stewart-Bates, was only at the *purser's* table, did little to assuage a feeling of time wasted, opportunity lost, indifference and cowardice in high places. She was prepared to smile if need be, but no words, no contribution. . . . Tiptree-Jones finally broke the silence, addressing himself bravely to the most forlorn quadrant of all, the Beddingtons.

"I expect," he said to Mr. Beddington, with exceptional brightness, "that you've been looking forward to this trip?"

Mr. Beddington, a stolid man who gave the impression that he was smoking a pipe even when this was not the case, considered the question at a comfortable length. Then he nodded ponderously, and said:

"I reckon that's a fair statement of the facts."

"What about you, Miss Beddington?" inquired Tiptree-Jones, when it was clear that Mr. Beddington was not going to add to this pronouncement.

Bernice Beddington, who was sitting directly opposite to him, continued to stare at a nearby pillar as if it had some compelling symbolism which a girl of her age ought to appreciate. She had eaten well of lobster cocktail, soup, fish, and saddle of lamb; she was waiting now for a choice of *Bombe Surprise, meringues à la glace,* or Cherries Jubilee, and after that for release, or Alka-Seltzer, or something—anything—whatever came next. In her huge myopic world, she was content, or at least reconciled. She was certainly not listening.

Her mother, who had for years worn the guilty, beaten look of a very small woman with a six-foot daughter, nudged her unobtrusively.

"Bernice."

Bernice Beddington broke surface slowly, like a suet dumpling coaxed towards the boil.

"Yes, mother?"

"Mr. Tiptree-Jones was speaking to you, dear."

Bernice Beddington looked at him, blinking. Then she turned to her mother. "What did he say?"

Mrs. Beddington searched her memory, which was unreliable. Finally she asked: "What was it you said, Mr. Jones?"

Tiptree-Jones smiled manfully, caught in a lunatic realm of reported speech. "I said, was she looking forward to the trip?"

Mrs. Beddington turned back to her daughter, waiting. The rest of the table waited also, staring at the girl as if willing her to formulate a reply. Finally it came, accompanied by a scarlet blush which might have been the onset of indigestion.

"I don't know," she said.

Tiptree-Jones tried again. "I hope you enjoyed it last time, anyway."

"Oh, she did!" said Mrs. Beddington, filling another lengthy pause.

"I'm so glad," said Tiptree-Jones. "It makes a lot of difference to us, you know."

Mr. Beddington took the spectral pipe out of his mouth. "What does?"

"If people enjoy it," said Tiptree-Jones. "It makes a difference."

A disturbance by his side resolved itself into Mrs. van Dooren who, having reclaimed her shoes, was finding difficulty in putting them on again. But presently, having won this private wrestling match, she straightened up, and asked:

"What makes a difference to what?"

Tiptree-Jones felt he could not go through it all again. "Are you all right, Mrs. van Dooren?" he asked, by way of a change of pace.

"Why wouldn't I be all right?"

"I thought you were looking for something."

"You're damn' right I was looking for something! My shoes. Some jerk kicked them away to hell and gone."

Tiptree-Jones, conscious of a certain lack of decorum at his table, decided to apply a minor measure of discipline. He looked at Mrs. van Dooren with as much hauteur as the regulations would stand for, and asked coldly:

"You have them on now?"

"Wouldn't you like to know. . . . What's this thing that makes such a difference?"

"I was saying to Miss Beddington," answered Tiptree-Jones heavily, "that it makes a lot of difference to us—the ship's personnel—if people enjoy these cruises."

"It would make a damn' sight more difference if we *didn't* enjoy them." Mrs. van Dooren snapped her fingers suddenly, and then, as no steward appeared, rapped smartly on the table.

"Is there anything you want?" asked Tiptree-Jones.

"Rye and water," said Mrs. van Dooren.

"Do you find," asked Tiptree-Jones guardedly, "that rye whisky really *goes* with a meal like this?"

"It goes with me," said Mrs. van Dooren. "East, west, old friends are best."

Mr. Bancroft looked at his old friend Mr. Gerson. "Maybe if you'd stuck to rye," he said, "you wouldn't have started all that uproar, that night."

"I started no uproar," said Mr. Gerson.

"Boy, it was certainly a good imitation. You even fooled the management."

"Now look here—" began Mr. Gerson angrily.

"Boys, boys," said Mrs. van Dooren. "If you *both* got loaded to the eyeballs, what's the difference? Look at me! I've been loaded since November nineteen-forty-eight."

"What happened then?" asked Tiptree-Jones, as no-one else seemed inclined to lift this dubious stone.

"Truman was re-elected."

At Carl Wenstrom's table, by contrast, a happy relaxation ruled. It was a good table, under the central skylight of the dining-room; collectively, they could see and be seen from every angle, and Carl was conscious, as when they had boarded the ship earlier, that they were making a good start. The two girls were indisputably the best-looking in the room; Louis—a much-improved Louis—was attracting the speculative glances which indicated that he looked 'eligible,' in the shipboard sense; even the old Professor managed to shed an air of romantic, old time gallantry. His eyes were bright as he sipped his wine and talked about his hobby, the history of piracy. His audience was not at all attentive, but it did not seem to matter. Everything was benign, this evening; even the manifest rocking motion of the *Alcestis* was rhythmical and kindly.

"Then there was Ned Teach," said the Professor, to no-one in particular. "An unusual character—I am giving him a whole chapter in my book. He went by the name of Blackbeard, and he operated in these very waters. A most blood-thirsty villain. . . . He marooned his own crew, every last man of them, in order to steal their share of the general plunder. He used to have the hair on his chest made up into small pigtails, and tied with coloured ribbon."

"What was that?" asked Diane, her attention caught at last.

"Ned Teach, the pirate," said the Professor. "They say he was covered with thick black hair from head to foot. And he went into battle with flaming sulphur matches stuck into his beard. People thought he was the devil himself."

"That figures," said Louis.

"What was that about the hair on his chest?" asked Diane again.

"He had it curled and tied into pigtails."

"Why? Was he queer or something?"

"That I would doubt," answered the Professor, in a mellow mood of reminiscence. "His aim, I think, was to present a bizarre appearance to his enemies."

Louis turned from a roving-eye survey of the neighbouring tables. He had been doing well, even at this early stage; there was a woman nearby—elderly, beautifully made up—whose glance seemed especially ready to meet his. This was going to be a breeze. . . .

"Are you really writing a book, Prof?" he asked, more attentively.

"Certainly," answered the Professor. "I have been working on it for more than twenty-five years."

"With all these nutty characters?"

"Many of the old-time pirates were distinctly eccentric."

"So who's interested?"

The Professor stared at him over the rim of his wine-glass. He was too contented to take offence, and he was not going to have his evening spoiled by argument.

"It is a field which has always intrigued me," he said finally. "I hope that will prove true for other people."

"And you make a million dollars? This I wish to see!"

Kathy interrupted. "Lots of people will be interested," she said encouragingly. "How far have you got, Professor?"

"Page two-hundred-and-twenty-five," answered the Professor, from an exact, painstaking memory. He gestured, spilling a few drops of wine down his ancient cream flannel suit. "It goes slowly, of course. The scope of research is tremendous. But it is worth it. It is well worth it."

"Excuse me, sir," said a voice at his elbow. It was Vincent, the chief steward, whose eagle eye had caught the small mishap. He advanced with a napkin, and gently mopped up the spilled wine.

"Thank you, thank you," said the Professor, courteously. "Entirely my fault."

"Accidents will happen, sir," Vincent reassured him. It was a phrase he had to use at least fifty times on each voyage. He smiled and straightened up, looking at Carl, the natural head of the table. "Everything all right, Mr. Wenstrom?"

"Oh yes," said Carl. "We have had an excellent dinner. That saddle of lamb was delicious." He glanced round his table benevolently, very much the senior member of the family. "At this rate, we shall have to consider going on a diet."

"Plenty of time to think about that, sir," said Vincent heartily. He also looked round the table, professionally inquisitive. "Excuse me, sir—I was just wondering—are you all one family?"

Carl smiled, with considerable charm. "Not exactly, but we are related." With a careless finger he indicated each of them in turn. "My step-daughter—my nephew—my niece. . . ." Coming to the Professor, he added: "And my business associate."

Vincent beamed on them all impartially. "How lucky for you to be able to take a holiday together."

"It just worked out right," said Carl.

The voice of young Master Barry Greenfield rose from a nearby table, changing every subject within earshot.

"I don't want any old ice-cream," he proclaimed disagreeably. "It stinks. I want a piece of pie."

"There isn't any pie," said his mother. "Eat up your ice-cream."

"No pie?" The voice was now an incredulous whine. "What sort of a crummy outfit—"

"Excuse me, sir," said Vincent, and turned swiftly away towards the centre of crisis.

Louis glanced sideways after him. "Nosy bastard," he said.

Carl shook his head. "That sort of thing doesn't do any harm. It saves us a lot of explaining. He's the talkative kind. The word will get around."

"You can say that again."

Kathy, chin on hand, dreamily beautiful in pale green, stirred and sat up straight. This was the first mention that evening, even indirectly, of their plans for the voyage, and she was not yet in the mood for it. The ship had captured her now; sitting at ease in the huge dining saloon with its banks of flowers and multiple mirrors and superb service, she wanted the enchanted moment to last for ever, she wanted never to wake up. The idea of using a talkative chief steward to broadcast details of their family set-up was somehow intrusive and gross. She looked round the table.

"Let's go up," she said. "It must be beautiful outside."

"You want to get to work?" inquired Louis, eying her.

"What else?" Refusing to surrender her mood, she could only give a flippant answer. "Remember, only eighty-three shopping days till Christmas."

chapter 5

AFTER dinner, an unmistakable air of lethargy pervaded the *Alcestis;* the nine hours of intermittent drinking since lunch-time meant that afternoon hangovers had now reached their peak, and the ship's steady rolling induced sleep, prudent inactivity, a comfortable sense of well-being—everything but energy. Wexford, the assistant purser, who was running the first bingo game of the voyage (there would be at least fifty others) was having a hard time injecting life into the time-honoured pattern of jollity.

All the traditional jokes fell flat; and the new ones, which might develop during the voyage, were not yet born. Wexford,Tim Mansell who was helping him, and the steward who was producing the numbers from the wire cage, all beamed universally upon the customers; but the customers were not yet ready to be wooed. "Legs—eleven!" called out Wexford, with an air of epigram; and "Doctor's orders—

number nine!" and "Any way up—sixty-nine!" and "Life begins at —forty!" But there was no reaction, no confederate giggling. When, on the third game, the prize of thirty-eight dollars was carried off by Master Barry Greenfield, who called out "Bingo!" with a piping malevolence which won him very few friends, it was obvious that a change of pace was needed.

"Better pack this up," said Wexford, out of the side of his mouth. "We're never going to get it off the ground."

"Orchestra?"

"Orchestra."

Presently the orchestra filed in—six players in dinner-jackets which had a seedy, somewhat rented air. Their first few bars of "*On the Street Where You Live*" were enough to produce an inescapable suspicion that their instruments might be rented also. They sounded terrible.

"Oh God!" said Tim Mansell, back at the officers' table. "Have we had union trouble again?"

"They need practice," said Fleming, the engineer officer, who was in a generous mood.

"They need shooting," said Wexford. He looked round the half-filled room, and the space which had been cleared for dancing in the middle. "Is this going to take, do you think?"

"Like yellow fever."

Mr. Cutler, the purser, passing their table on his way to the bar, looked down at them with mock sternness.

"Gentlemen, do your duty," he commanded.

"Do we have to?" asked Beresford, the young apprentice. "This band is worse than the last lot."

"Nonsense," said Cutler, who had hired them. "Three of them are straight from the Palladium."

"The police must have moved them on."

Tim Mansell also looked round the room. He saw that the only girl he wanted to dance with, Kathy, was not at the moment in view, and might have gone to bed already. The other girl, the dark one with the sit-up-and-beg figure, was circling the floor with her uncle, or whatever he was. Mansell sighed, conscious of bereavement, and of duty not yet fulfilled. The band, launching out into "*Time On My Hands,*" hit a clinker which made even the bass-player wince. Wexford stood up.

"All right, boys," he said bravely. "We dance. . . . You take the one with the squint, Tim, and I'll have a crack at the six-footer."

Later, after talking idly with Carl, Diane Loring danced with three of the young officers. At this stage, she performed sedately, holding her partners at arm's length, setting her figure in well-defined profile, exhibiting her wares within a cool, self-evident vacuum. For her, it was a practice run, using these uniformed children as pace-makers. But presently it paid off; a man whose name she did not catch—a middle-aged, middle-weight, middle-definition man—came up and asked if he might dance with her. On the second turn around the floor, to the music of "*Begin the Beguine,*" the man, who up till then had been rather drunk, gave her waist a small, speculative squeeze. Diane responded with a movement which, as she phrased it later, nearly made him jump out of his underwear. Within a few moments, looking thoughtful, they disappeared in the direction of the boat-deck, while Carl, noting that Kathy was not in view and that Louis, busy on the dance-floor, was not disgracing himself, made for the Tapestry Bar. It was possible that Diane was moving too fast, but he was prepared to take that chance. Their first night on board was not an appropriate occasion for cracking the whip.

Kathy was not moving too fast; on this first evening, she was scarcely moving at all. The mood of enchantment had persisted, inducing a sense of deep contentment; tomorrow would bring its problems and its manoeuvres, but tomorrow was still over the horizon, tomorrow could keep its place. Tonight she would, and could, be solitary. She had watched the bingo-game briefly, but it had seemed a forced and silly enterprise; then she had set out on a slow, wandering tour of the ship, down the long alleyways lined with cabins, through the near-empty public rooms, up to the deserted sun-lounge under the stars.

She met a few people, wanderers like herself, she smiled at stewardesses, she watched, from outside an uncurtained window, four people playing cards with slow, ridiculous absorption. Deep down in one of the B-deck corridors, an old steward asked: "Are you lost, miss?" and she answered: "Yes," and they had both laughed with the same delight. Then she had climbed up to the sun-lounge again, and sat in a deep chair, her head back, and watched the mast and funnels rocking through their slow majestic arc against a canopy of a million cold stars. For a brief moment she wanted to cry, and then she wanted to sit there for ever, lapped in this private heaven.

Much later, a movement nearby disturbed her, an intrusion; two people—and one of them was Diane—out on the boat-deck, closely entwined, writhing in preliminary skirmish. So soon, so early? She could not watch them; this was the task of tomorrow, and was not yet due. She walked slowly back to her cabin, and presently lay in her bed in the half-darkness, still private, still uncommitted, still dreamily happy. She was waiting for Carl, and she loved him; but if he did not come to her tonight, it would not matter.

Louis Scapelli said: "Would you like to dance?" and the oldish woman who had caught his eye in the dining-room looked up, unsurprised but slightly flustered, and answered: "That would be very nice." She put aside her *petit point* evening bag, and stood up. She was small and, in spite of tremendous aid from science, almost shapeless.

Within the first few moments they agreed that the band was awful, but might improve; they agreed further that there were difficulties about dancing on a floor which shifted its position rhythmically at every third step. Then it was time for the introductory confidences, and nearly all of them came from her, in a free-flowing stream. She was Mrs. Stewart-Bates, she told him; it was her third voyage in the *Alcestis*; she knew the Captain *very* well, but this time she was sitting at the purser's table, really (with a laugh) so as to give somebody else a chance. She lived in Connecticut, near Georgetown; she had lost her husband, a banker, three years earlier; she was absolutely crazy about travelling. She always had been. It really did broaden the mind —didn't he agree? Of course, there were difficulties now. A woman travelling alone. . . . When her husband was alive it had all been different. He had taken care of everything. They had been ideally matched, too, in every way. He had been interested in physical culture. Now it was often so lonely.

Louis listened carefully, taking in the facts, estimating the right speed of advance, pacing himself to match it. The old bag was obviously nuts; a woman of fifty pretending she was thirty-five, acting up like an old movie, stretching out and asking for it; she probably hadn't been laid for ten years, and then it was just for Christmas. But the rocks were really something—diamond rings, diamond bracelets, drop-earrings, the lot. It would be worth closing his eyes for. . . . He came out of his daydream to hear her asking:

"Is that your family you're sitting with?"

He looked away, conscious of delicate ground. The band wound up their rendering of "*Arrivaderci Roma*" with a Latin flourish and an entirely inappropriate shout of "Olé!"; the dance floor shifted gently but decisively under their feet; then they stood together with the half-dozen other couples, waiting to see if the band would continue. He said:

"We're a family party, sure. Mr. Wenstrom is my uncle. The girls are cousins."

"They're both very pretty," said Mrs. Stewart-Bates, watching him with close attention.

Louis gestured carelessly. "Oh, they're just kids. . . . Not my type."

The band put down their instruments, to mark the end of the current session. Louis and Mrs. Stewart-Bates remained where they were, smiling at each other. His hand was still loosely on her arm.

"Just what is your type, Mr. Scapelli?" she inquired archly.

Louis looked at her, making a conscious effort to keep out of his eyes the derisive contempt which now flooded in. Imagine making a pass like that, at her age. . . . Under the enamelled make-up and the elaborate pyramid of hair, a disgusting oldness peeped through; "falling to bits" was how Louis phrased it to himself; she must be nuts to think that any man of any age would make a bid for it. And yet that was just what he was going to do. In cards and spades.

He said: "You ought to know," and gently, very gently, squeezed her arm.

They were still sitting on the sofa an hour later, sipping their drinks, talking companionably. "You just don't know how careful I have to be," Mrs. Stewart-Bates was saying, her eyes swimming. "A woman travelling alone . . . ."

There were not more than a dozen people left in the Tapestry Bar, and Carl Wenstrom was the only one sitting up at the counter. It was eleven o'clock; according to invariable custom he was drinking brandy-and-soda, and smoking his last cigar before going to bed. He felt tired, but pleasantly so; the first day seemed to have gone very well, and he was sure that Diane, off to a romping start with a man he had identified as Mr. Bancroft from Chicago, would not become too heavily involved before getting the signal to go ahead. That was the understanding, and the understanding was law. . . . Now, in this leisurely hour, he would have liked to talk to Kathy; but Kathy, when he had glanced into her cabin, had been asleep already. Instead, Carl talked, or rather listened, to Edgar the head barman.

He had said: "A very quiet evening." It was enough to precipitate one of Edgar's celebrated monologues.

"Usual thing, sir—first night out. There's four classes of customer tonight, if you care to work it out." Edgar was polishing an ashtray, slowly and deliberately; the glass of whisky which he felt entitled to accept at this time of night was discreetly masked by an ice-bucket. "People who don't like any kind of motion—they've turned in already. People who don't mind the sea, but who've been at it since lunch-time, if you'll excuse the expression. They're mostly asleep, by now. People who don't like to drink anyway—you'd be amazed how many that is, even on a cruise like this. Even—" he coughed, having decided to size Carl up as a man of the world, "—even among Americans. That leaves people like yourself, who always have a drink at this time of the evening; you haven't got anything better to do, since there's no entertainment, and you don't have to worry about a bit of seaway. But that's not so many." He glanced round the room, figuring with an expert eye. "In fact it's eleven people exactly, which is a fair average. Of course, later on—"

The gossipy, rather self-satisfied voice continued, bridging all gaps, bruising no egos, breaking no bones. Carl recognized Edgar for what he was—a competent operator, smooth, expert, accustomed to his own way. It was a type, a useful type, a type to be enlisted, if possible, on one's own side. He dicided that it would be wise to over-tip Edgar (twenty dollars? even fifty?) rather early in the voyage. People like Edgar were inquisitive, and often privately vindictive, but they had a blind spot. They could be bought; by flattery, or by money, or by both. Money was quicker and, in this particular case, more certain. It would be a worth-while expense, a small shading of the odds, to be in Edgar's good books.

During a pause, he said: "I see you've made quite a philosophical study of us. How long have you been in the *Alcestis?*"

"Since she was first commissioned, sir." Edgar put down the polished ashtray, picked up his glass, sipped it without seeming to move either his hands or his lips, put it back behind the ice-bucket. The series of movements was at once apologetic and determined, like a conjuror before royalty, like a hangman. This won't hurt, he seemed to be saying. And if it does, it goes with my job, doesn't it? *Standing behind a bar for twelve hours on end. Of course I can have a drink. . . .* "I remember it like yesterday, that maiden voyage. Liverpool to Montreal, sixteenth of July, nineteen-forty-seven. If you think back to those days, sir, just after the war—"

It was a long story, posing no problems either for the listener or the non-listener; it had a beginning, a middle, and a neat ending (something to do with immigrants to Canada sleeping four in a cabin, women on one deck, men on another); it lasted over ten minutes. When it was done, and Carl had laughed appropriately, Edgar returned to duty with a graceful air of transition. Motioning towards Carl's empty glass, he asked:

"Something similar, sir?"

"Thank you," answered Carl. "Just one more. Then I must really go to bed. And have one yourself, if you care to." He turned on his stool, surveying the room negligently. "I wonder," he threw over his shoulder, "if we have any card-players on board."

"Sure to, sir," answered Edgar. He poured the drinks with the minimum of movement, swabbed down the section of the counter in front of Carl, pushed forward a fresh bowl of salted almonds and olives. "In fact, sometimes you'd think that cards is all people want to know about, even on a cruise. I've had people come aboard who played bridge for three months on end, rain or shine, and never even looked out of the window, from one end of the trip to the other. Balmy, I call it. At least—" he hedged promptly and expertly, "—it seems a funny way of passing the time, with all that expensive scenery going by. But there's no accounting for tastes. Is bridge your game, sir? There'll be a notice posted about it tomorrow. You sign your name on a list on the notice-board."

"Not bridge," answered Carl. "I'm not really good enough. I prefer poker, actually."

Edgar nodded, reacting to the sophisticated word. "Wonderful game, they say, sir. I don't play myself. But I'm sure you could find some people who'd be interested."

"It's really a question," said Carl, with great deliberation, "of finding the *right* people." He looked straight at Edgar, man to man, frankness to frankness. "I'm sure you know what I mean. I just want a nice easy game. No—" he waved his hand, emphasizing the important point, "—no professionals."

Edgar nodded again. "Know what you mean, sir."

"If you get a chance, you might mention it."

"I'll do that, sir."

"Good." Carl looked towards the swing doors, attracted by a movement. "Ah," he said, on a new and cheerful note. "Here's some of my family."

Diane made her way towards him between the tables. She was alone and (he noted with relief) entirely well-groomed and undishevelled. He said as she approached: "It's long past your bed-time, my dear girl," and motioned towards the stool beside him. When she had ordered a drink, and Edgar had supplied it, Carl went on: "Where have you been all evening? If an uncle may ask?"

Diane looked at him, cynically self-possessed. Then she glanced at Edgar who, with thirty years of training behind him, had already withdrawn out of earshot to the other end of the bar. Then she said, in a voice discreetly low:

"I've been working."

Carl, aware that they could not be overheard, took up the subject without hesitation. "Working?"

Diane shook her head. "Nothing to report." Her face was young and mature at the same time, infinitely knowing, corrupt in its competence. "But it was a near thing. It still is."

Now it was Carl's turn to glance sideways at Edgar, but Edgar was still busy. He drew on his cigar, watching the smoke curl upwards towards the ceiling. "What happened?" he asked. "I saw you leave the dance-floor. His name is Bancroft, by the way."

Diane nodded. "Yeah. But call me Jerry, won't you, please? He's in hardware." She smiled, mirthless and amused in the same squalid moment of recollection. "That was some of the hardest ware I've ever met."

"And?" prompted Carl.

She tossed her head carelessly. "Oh, we wrestled. I thought it was too early. He didn't. We've got a date later on, but I can always junk it."

"Later tonight?"

"Sure. Midnight, in my cabin. Knock three times, then once, then wait. How corny can you get?"

"What does he expect?"

Diane grimaced, inelegantly. "Are you kidding? He's *hot*. . . . Does he get it?"

Carl considered the question carefully. Of course it was really too soon for them to start "operating," in any serious sense; they ought to find out a great deal more about Bancroft—how tough he was, how vulnerable, how rich. But in one area, enough was known already; the omens were good; the bait was tempting. Bancroft was travelling with his wife; he was with another couple, the Gersons, who were friends from the same suburb. There were indications of social pressure there; an inexorable need to stay in line. . . . Presently Carl answered:

"Yes. He gets it. The way we planned."

"How much do I roll him for?"

"This time, whatever he's got in his wallet. We'll take a chance on that. He's just come on board. He might be loaded."

"O.K." Diane was astonishingly matter-of-fact; Carl hoped that her nerve would always be as good. "I'll suspend credit for the duration."

A sudden voice behind Carl said: "Zucco. Good evening."

Carl turned swiftly, to find a mournful man in a white dinner-jacket climbing onto the next stool. Warily he answered: "Good evening to you."

"Saw you folks enjoying yourselves," said Mr. Zucco. "Thought I'd join in and spoil it. How about a drink on that?"

"Well—" began Carl.

"Oh, come on—it's going to be a long voyage." He beckoned to Edgar, and then looked towards Diane. "Perhaps the little lady will join us."

"The little lady is going straight to bed, like a good girl," said Diane, and promptly climbed down off her stool. "Good night, folks."

"Hope I didn't break anything up, there," said Mr. Zucco uncertainly, when she had gone.

"The little lady," said Carl, with a certain austere emphasis, "happens to be my niece."

"Togetherness!" exclaimed Mr. Zucco, unabashed. "Wouldn't you know it!" He raised his glass, and suddenly everything was involved, from Lincoln to motherhood. "Togetherness! If there's any toast in America I'd rather drink to than that, I've never heard it!"

"Togetherness," answered Carl, with modest irony, his thoughts already ranging far afield.

Mr. Zucco shook his head, regaining his status as a mourner. "If you could only get it on film. . . . Tell me, has the little lady ever taken a test?"

After midnight, a deep peace reigned on board the *Alcestis;* the bars were shut, the elevators stilled, the lights switched out in the public rooms. Though the noise of the fans continued, and the pulse of the engines, and the Master-at-Arms' rounds, yet the ship seemed deserted; silently making her passage southwards, she was a ship without people, self-propelled, supernaturally navigated. The occasional figures—in the corridors, on the stairways—were like ghosts inhabiting a vessel which wandered the seas of her own accord.

Yet some few were still wakeful. Up on the bridge under the enormous stars, the Second Officer, who had the middle watch, stared ceaselessly ahead; occasionally he glanced at the dimmed compass, or made a note in the deck-log, or raised his binoculars to examine a light on the horizon. Behind him, the apprentice who shared the watch stood sentinel over the radar-scan, searching it for the warning of distant ships, calling out the bearings of others nearby. In the green phosphorescence of the screen, his face was studious, and intent, and very young. Between the two officers, the stolid quartermaster at the wheel let the spokes slide off his fingers, and gripped them to check the yaw as the ship swung off, submitting to the sea, and stared unwinkingly at the compass-card, his only horizon, his only charge. High above their heads, the mast head look-out in the crow's-nest completed the pattern of vigilance.

Four decks below, at the end of a shadowy deserted corridor, a single figure also kept his vigil. Surrounded by forty-four pairs of shoes, male and female, the B-deck shoe-steward worked methodically, at a pace long ordained by custom and his own dejection, to spin the task out till four bells sounded—cocoa time. He was an old man; he had waited on captains and rich folk in his day, and then on tourist passengers; later, the failing years had seen him tend the deck-chairs, and then the lifts, and then the ashtrays; now he was cleaning shoes, in the twilight of all his worlds. The shaded light overhead fell on a bald pate, on sparse grey hairs, on a blue-veined tremulous hand which, polishing and polishing, often paused for a long space, as if the hand itself were dreaming. Without pride or hope he sat enthroned in his grudging corner of limbo, an old man attending, like some ancient acolyte, the last humble ritual of the night.

Tearful, terrified, beseeching, Mr. Bancroft—a ridiculous figure without his trousers—whimpered his prayers for release.

"My wife will kill me!" His voice was hoarse, thick with fright. "You must be fooling—you asked me to come in! You know you did!"

"Stay where you are!" commanded Diane threateningly. Twice as naked as he, she was still in full control. "You forced your way in here, you bastard, and you're going to pay for it."

"Just give me back my pants," he begged. "Then we'll talk."

"You try to take them, and I'll scream! . . . You want my uncle to hear?—you want him to come in and find you here, bare-assed? He'll beat the hell out of you—and then he'll ring the bell and call the Captain."

"Keep your voice down, for Christ's sake! What is it you want?"

Diane, superbly unconcerned in her nakedness, felt for the wallet she knew was there. "This," she said finally. "All of it."

"It's two thousand dollars," wailed Bancroft, his pudgy face desperate, and started forward. Diane opened her mouth. "All right, all right!" he called out, petrified, trembling. "Take it—take the whole lot. Just let me out of here! Jesus God, what a lousy shake-down!"

She peeled off the notes, and tossed the empty wallet, and then the trousers, at his feet. He drew them over his plump thighs with frantic speed, tripping over, nearly falling. His face was still glistening with fear.

In the heavy-breathing silence: "Don't you want your money's worth?" she asked crudely.

"Why, you—! I'll see you in hell before I touch you again!"

She shrugged; it was an arresting movement. "Well, don't complain I short-changed you. If I say I'll deliver, I deliver."

He paused then, and looked at her. Ten minutes before, his flabby body had been at the peak of desire; it still pricked him powerfully, even now, even after this vile treachery. "You'll scream again," he said uncertainly.

"Try and make me." She threw the money into a drawer, locked it, and then turned again. Her naked form, poised before him, began a practised undulation, like a fish swimming in warm sluggish water. "Just try and make me," she said, in sudden raw invitation, "for two thousand bucks."

part three

"You will thrill to the colourful, pirate-haunted Caribbean, surrender to the fiesta mood at Carnival Time."

chapter 1

AS usual with an old man, the Professor rose early; indeed, the pale light creeping through his porthole at six A.M. found him already wakeful, already primed for the new day. At his bedside was the spirit-stove, the miniature kettle, and the earthenware tea-pot which accompanied him everywhere: when he had made tea, with slow ceremonial, he sipped it delicately, savouring every moment of this private initiation, the start of another prized twenty-four hours. There was no flavour like Lapsang Soochong, no warmth like its scalding fall upon a tongue furred by alcohol, no comfort to match it, save in the forgotten areas of love and triumph. After the third cup, he lay back on the pillows and dozed peaceably for five minutes; then he rose, and wrapped his thin shanks in a threadbare dressing-gown, and walked through to the bathroom to shave off, for the twenty-thousandth time, the white stubble of seventy years, the last evidence of an ancient virility.

He dressed carefully, as always; he had bought no new clothes for more than a decade, but those that he had, ordered and paid for during some vanished era of prosperity (in England? in Paris? in San Francisco?—only the labels could confirm this aspect of the past, and he never looked at labels) were well-cut, still infinitely durable. As he dressed—the pace was slow, as all things now were slow, but pleasurable and reassuring all the same—he kept returning to the writing table, to read what he had added to his manuscript on the previous night. He had written half of a whole paragraph—sixty-one words! It was another solid pleasure, another pledge that the wiry thread of life persisted, that it was still good. He touched and stroked the very surface of the page as he read it over again.

"*We come now,*" he had written, in his spidery long-hand, "*to one of the most iniquitous characters ever to stain the pages of the long, blood-thirsty history of piracy. This was a Frenchman, of noble or at least honourable birth; he was called Simon de Montbars, but by reason of his wickedness he came to be known by the frightful pseudonym of 'The Exterminator,' Simon de Montbars—*"

There the writing petered out, as his energy and interest had failed, at midnight last night, when the whisky finally took its toll. But it was tangible progress none-the-less, it was part of The Book, it would be page two-hundred-and-thirty-two when it was formally transcribed. . . . Even in the midst of dressing, his hand returned again and again to the tattered manuscript book, and to the typescript that lay by its side; hope mounted afresh, as it had done on successive dawns stretching far back into the past. At this rate, another year or two—say five, to be on the safe side—would see his task completed, his great work acclaimed as the definitive one. Let them then laugh, when he mounted the rostrum to receive the Nobel Prize from the King of Sweden's own hands! Let them laugh—and then crowd round him to claim, if they could, a bare acquaintance!

He knotted his stringy tie with a firm hand, drew on his blue blazer, pinched the creases in the old, yellowing flannel trousers; then he tilted his be-ribboned Panama hat at a lively angle and stepped out—jaunty, ageless, and undefeated—to meet the promised day.

It was now half-past seven; when he reached it, the boat-deck of the *Alcestis* gleamed cheerfully in the early sunshine, freshly sluiced down by deck-hands who were now rolling the hoses towards the after-part. As far as the eye could see, the sun sparkled on a calm wide sea, translucent, green—the peerless colour which the Caribbean seemed to have at its command always. They had now advanced twelve days on their voyage, with three of them spent in harbour at Bermuda and

Puerto Rico; today they were nearing Antigua, threading their way through the magic island necklace of St. Croix and Anguilla, Barbuda and St. Kitts. The weather after the first day had been very kind, and the mellowing sun a blessed comfort for an old man's bones. Under its benign influence, the whole ship-load of people had blossomed anew. Clothes became casual and often bizarre; the traditional drinks of North America—Martinis, old-fashioneds, Scotch-on-the-rocks—had given place to rum in all its garish aspects—Bacardi cocktail, planter's punch, frozen daiquiri. It was as if the whole passenger-list were melting into a beach-combing informality. The process had advanced their own affairs considerably.

The Professor began his customary constitutional, a circle at easy speed past the port-side boats, across the back of the bridge, round the funnel, and down the other side towards the after-rail. There were a few people about already, and he gave them each a cheerful greeting; to those who rose early, he was by now a familiar figure. But on all these morning walks, he surrendered as far as he could to the pleasure of speculative thought. There was to be a meeting later that morning with all the 'gang' (really, no other word could be used), and at this meeting they would give an accounting of the progress they had made up to date. Later still, alone with Carl, the Professor would present his own report of what he had observed so far—a report not on the other passengers, but on their own personnel. That was his true job within the party, and if it put him in the category of company spy, he was still content. It was an essential job, and he was proud to have been assigned to it.

He had known Carl Wenstrom for many years; known him, admired him, and (the most important aspect of all) trusted him. Carl talked to him as he talked to no-one else—unless it were to Kathy, and that was bound to be love-talk, pillow-talk, traditionally inaccurate and vague. It was *himself* that Carl relied on, to keep track of what was happening, what might go wrong, what major or minor dishonesties might be coming into practise. The Professor had an idea, for instance, that Diane Loring had lied about the extent of her first killing. A thousand dollars was a lot of money, but this sum, as reported, was too pat, the figure too round. No-one carried *exactly* one thousand dollars in their wallet. Since it could not have been less, it was likely to have been more—twelve hundred? fourteen hundred? There was no accurate way of checking, but it was certainly worth a mention, in private.

Rounding the funnel for the fourth time, he came face to face with another early riser whom he felt he must greet personally—Mr. Walham. Mr. Walham was, from their point of view, an unattractive prospect; he was so monumentally mean, so eternally worrisome about money, that it was already a ship-board joke. But he was also monumentally rich, and there were still many days and nights in which to ensure that he went ashore with less money to worry about.

"Hallo, Mr. Walham!" said the Professor cheerily. "Trust you to be up and about early!" (*Getting your money's worth*, he added privately, but it was not a thought to be voiced save in an entirely complimentary sense.) "Are you looking forward to our visit to Antigua?"

Mr. Walham, as lean and disagreeable as ever, gave the matter some thought, as they stood together in the long shadow of one of the ventilator cowls. Finally he answered:

"God knows. I expect we'll all be gypped again."

"Gypped?" echoed the Professor.

"Yeah—short-changed. Like at San Juan, Puerto Rico."

"What happened there?" asked the Professor, puzzled.

Mr. Walham looked at him as if he were half-witted. "Gee, doesn't anyone around here read the *programme*? Remember what it said? 'Ten A.M.—Excursion to the casino.' Did we get there? Did we hell! We finished up at the airport, with a free pass to the public concourse! What kind of a deal is that?"

"But I understand," said the Professor equably, "that the casino was closed for redecoration. They really can't help that sort of thing, you know."

"Of course they can help it!" said Walham violently. "They say we go to the casino, why don't we go? I tell you, they're trying to shave this trip all the time. A bit off here, a bit off there. Next thing, we won't *get* to Cape Town, or something. We'll go straight home from Rio, and they'll say they ran out of fuel."

"I'm sure they wouldn't do that."

"You've got to watch it all the time," said Walham. He looked closely at the Professor. "Have you had your morning tea, for instance?"

"Of course," answered the Professor. "I make it myself."

"Make it yourself! Why, for God's sakes? Tea's available from seven A.M. It says so in clear print. I ought to know. That's the time that *I* have it, every morning. I put in a standing order. And if it doesn't turn up, on the dot, *with* a jug of hot water as well, I want to know why."

"But I *like* to make it myself," said the Professor. "It tastes better."

"Tastes?" repeated Walham. "What's that got to do with it? They say you can have tea. Then have tea. Whose side are you on, anyway?"

"No side," answered the Professor, with dignity. "I've usually found that it's perfectly easy to arrange these things without any unpleasantness."

Walham shook his head, irritated and unappeased. "It's people like you," he said, "who let them get away with murder. First thing you know, they'll put a ten-per-cent surcharge on all the stuff you order at the bar. They'll tell you the cost of living's gone up, or some damn thing."

"Oh, I hope not," said the Professor, with feeling.

"Don't say I didn't warn you," said Walham. He prepared to resume his walk. "Well, let's get our money's worth out of the deck, at least."

"Does that sort of thing really worry you?" asked the Professor innocently.

"It pleases me!" answered Walham, with sudden grisly relish. "Budgeting! I built up my business by watching the budget. Not just half the time, not just when I remembered to check, but *all* the time. Ten cents here, fifteen cents there—that's cost-accounting! And it's not just a hobby, it's a science. The greatest!"

After a pause: "If it is not impertinent," said the Professor, preparing to move on, "might I ask how that fits in with—" he waved his hand round the *Alcestis,* "—with all this? It's very much of a luxury, surely?"

"It's a vacation," Walham corrected him, with clipped determination. "I've earned it, I've paid the asking price, and I'm getting my money's worth. Just watch me!"

"But what about the budget? What about extras?"

"What extras?" asked Walham suspiciously.

"Well—" the Professor cast about for an innocuous phrase, "for pleasure, for entertainment, for—shall we say—the bright lights?"

"Sex," said Walham, reaching past the unessentials. He seemed within an ace of reaching for his note-book as well. "I'm not all that dumb, you know. And I'm not dead yet, either. You'll find an entry under sex in my budget. It's down there in black and white."

No man alive could have resisted the vital question. "How much?" asked the Professor.

"Two hundred dollars," said Walham promptly. "Maximum, twenty dollars a throw—I've been around, I know the prices, don't fool yourself! That's ten throws, spread over three months. It's plenty for a man of my age."

"Two hundred dollars," the Professor repeated, thoughtfully. "I wonder if you can stick to that."

"I'd just like to see the situation," answered Walham, "where I can be gouged for one red cent more."

He took his leave, fiercely confident, while the Professor, shaking with inward laughter, continued on an opposite course. He had a sudden vision, delicious yet terrifying, of the confronting of Diane and Walham—whether before or after the act did not matter—when the question of a twenty-dollar fee was brought squarely into the open. He saw it taking place at dawn; in the wan light Walham was counting out twenty one-dollar bills—no, the last dollar would be in quarters—while an enraged Diane stood with her hand open, repeating, " 'Ere, wot's this?" like a London taxi-driver. The Professor laughed aloud at that, and, laughing, was himself confronted with someone else he must talk to. It was Mrs. Kincaid, making an early foray into the world of public relations.

"Why, Professor!" She looked at him with a hard stare of speculation, as if the time might have come to re-assess his category. *This one could be nuts,* her glance seemed to say: *I'll have to go over the files.* . . . "I declare, someone must have told you one of those men's stories!"

The Professor raised his ancient hat, bowing with the irresistible courtliness which had made him very popular on board. "Dear lady!" he exclaimed. "How very nice . . . No, no story—just a passing thought which I won't inflict on you. And how is the senator, on this fine morning?"

"You know darn well my husband isn't a senator." But Mrs. Kincaid was smiling; she liked the Professor, in the sense that he was a nonentity who could neither help nor harm her, and therefore demanded no special handling.

The Professor smiled in turn. "I merely anticipate. As a humble voter, I know a prospective senator when I see one. . . . You are out very early, surely?"

"Just looking round," answered Mrs. Kincaid—and it was bound to be true. She had already established herself as the most inquisitive woman on board; if you wanted to know anything about anyone's antecedents, you came to Mrs. Kincaid. "I was woken up early this morning—a lot of cabin-doors were opening and shutting." She smiled—a crocodile smile which creased her mouth but left her eyes unblinkingly alert. "There's a lot going on in this ship that people don't know about."

"Dear me," said the Professor mildly. "I had no idea. *What* is going on?"

"I'd hate to tell you. . . . You know that couple that always sit by themselves—the big man, and the blonde girl with the terrible legs?"

The Professor nodded. "The Burrells?"

"The Burrells." Mrs. Kincaid sniffed, as if an air of corruption had invaded the boat-deck. "I don't think they're even married!"

"Dear me," said the Professor again. "What makes you say that?"

"Oh—just a hunch. She's French, you know, or she says she is. There's always something off-beat about continentals. They don't think the way we do. Sort of loose. You know what I mean?"

"Well—" said the Professor.

"And another thing." Well launched, Mrs. Kincaid held him with a hypnotic glance. "Those Zuccos, the ones that sit at the Captain's table with us. You know, I think they're actually Jewish!"

"I had no idea."

"Oh, you can always tell. Haven't you noticed how he talks with his hands? Gee, I hate that! Their cabin is near ours—too near, if you want to know the truth. They just never stop arguing. I didn't think we'd get that sort of thing on board a boat like this."

"It takes all sorts to make a world," said the Professor, finding refuge in sententiousness. Privately, he considered Mrs. Kincaid entirely odious, but she was a useful channel of communication none-the-less; long training in the unique arena of Florida politics had given her a matchless instinct for detection—the probing and ruin of the weak, the suspicion and undermining of the strong. If there were any short-cuts to hurtful knowledge, Mrs. Kincaid could supply them. Intent on this aspect, he took pains to produce a conspiratorial smile. "What was that you said about cabin-doors opening and shutting?"

"Now, Professor!" she said, catching his mood. "Sometimes it doesn't do to ask too many questions."

"But really," he insisted.

"Well, I'll tell you." She came close to him—a tough, sketchily-groomed woman in the hard morning sunlight. She looked awful—awful and useful. "You know there's a woman called Mrs. Stewart-Bates?"

"Certainly." Sudden wariness made him confine his answer to this single word.

"She's made one or two trips on this boat already. Claims she's like that with the Captain." Mrs. Kincaid laid one finger on top of the other, in a crude gesture. "I wouldn't know about that. But I *do* know that someone—maybe the Captain, maybe not—pays a hell of a lot of visits to her cabin. You can hear voices all the time. Don't ask me what the attraction is. Maybe they talk about world conditions. Maybe he's nuts—maybe he'd have to be." Her expression was indescribably vicious and unpleasant. "But the traffic to-and-fro—I can tell you, it's quite something!"

The Professor, now fully alerted, sought to pass the matter off. "Well, well. . . . Perhaps *Honi soit qui mal y pense* would be an appropriate motto in this case."

"How's that again?"

"I don't think we should jump to conclusions."

"The trouble with you, Professor," said Mrs. Kincaid, "is that you're too darned sweet. Personally, *I'm* jumping to conclusions, and it's not such a hell of a big jump either." She stretched, raising her thin pointed nose to the virgin air. "Well, I must see what that husband of mine is getting up to. 'Bye now!"

She left him, and the Professor, now deep in more urgent thought, continued his walk. He had been brought to the alert because the recurrent nocturnal visitor to Mrs. Stewart-Bates was almost certainly Louis Scapelli; if his visits were already public property, it could be dangerous. *Our boy,* thought the Professor, as near to a sneer as he had ever been, *getting his name into the Alcestis gossip columns. . . .* It was something else which he must raise at the meeting later; it might mean that Louis would have to change his tactics, whatever those tactics were. So far, he had not been given the go-ahead by Carl; if his movements were being watched, and if (say) Mrs. Stewart-Bates became suddenly distraught, or publicly embarrassed, then two-and-two could be put together with uncomfortable precision by those in authority. The whole strength of their operations, as Carl had long ago pointed out, lay in their *not* causing the smallest ripple of public interest. One woman—or one man, for that matter—who betrayed, even inadvertently, the fact that they had been under pressure, could put Carl Wenstrom out of business in a single hour.

He had reached this stage in uneasy thought, and reached also the after-rail of the boat-deck, when there was another interruption, this time the most intrusive of all. Above the noise of the hoses sluicing down the decks, there came the sound of an argument; the broad

Liverpool voice of one of the sailors suddenly called out: "Get out of the road, you little booger!" in a tone of final exasperation; then there was a sound of running feet, and Master Barry Greenfield, seemingly propelled from behind, shot into view and landed squarely in the Professor's midriff. He was dishevelled, and very wet; the Professor was glad of this, but it failed to soothe his anger at the onslaught.

"Look where you're going, boy!" he said crustily. "You nearly knocked me down!"

Barry Greenfield shook himself, then darted a furious glance behind him. "He kicked me!" he said angrily. "The lousy son of a bitch kicked me!"

"I am sure you deserved it," said the Professor tartly. Young Master Greenfield, during the past twelve days, had attained a position approximating to total loathing throughout the ship. "I have not the slightest doubt that you were making yourself insufferable, as usual."

"I'll have that guy fired," said Barry, with another dark glance. "Who the hell does he think he is? Just one of the stinking crew! I'll get him thrown off the boat."

The culprit, a broad middle-aged man with a hose in his hand, suddenly appeared from behind one of the boats. He pointed a stubby finger at Barry.

"You try that lark again," he called out, with refreshing lack of deference, "and I'll haul you up before Captain, and he'll kick your bloody arse off, same as me." He then withdrew.

"But what did you do?" asked the Professor, intrigued in spite of a natural distaste. The entire crew of the *Alcestis* normally behaved so angelically, putting up with every kind of passenger misbehaviour as an inescapable part of their duty, that the outburst could only have been provoked by an unmistakable act of barbarism.

"Nothing," said Barry sulkily.

"Don't lie to me, boy!"

Barry Greenfield, recovering his self-assurance, looked at the Professor.

"What's with you, old timer?" he asked derisively. "You got a candid camera or something?"

"You must have done something," answered the Professor, weakening already. This was the younger generation, he supposed; across such a yawning chasm, he could never compete, nor even enter a token appearance. It must be true, what one read from time to time in the newspapers. . . . "People don't get angry for no reason at all."

"That stupid jerk!" said Barry malevolently. "I'll fix his wagon for him. . . ." He looked again at the Professor, his surly eyes turning lewd in the space of a single instant. Under the warming sun, it came as a disgusting shock, like indecent exposure in surroundings of the utmost innocence. "How are those two broads of yours?"

"I beg your pardon?" said the Professor.

"You know—those girls. Especially the one with the—" his small claws sketched twin balloons of obscene size. "Boy, what an operator!"

"I don't know what you mean," said the Professor, and in truth he scarcely did know.

"O.K., Daddy-oh! Play it stupid if that's the way you like it. But you'd better watch out, or you'll be raided. I've seen a few things going on. We're not all dopey, don't you kid yourself!"

"You are talking nonsense," said the Professor firmly.

Barry Greenfield shrugged; it was difficult to tell, at that moment, if he were fifteen or fifty-five. "O.K., O.K. . . . You know what? There's an old guy on board, he's even older than you are."

"Indeed?"

"Yeah. But he's dying."

"I am going down to breakfast," said the Professor, dismissively.

Barry Greenfield spread his hands, in a terrible caricature of Jewish well-wishing. "Eat it in good health," he said, and walked away whistling.

chapter 2

IT was mid-morning, an hour of great variety. For some it meant *bouillon* and gossip on the promenade deck, for others the first cold beer of the day; there were already some bridge-players imprisoned in their private world, there was ping-pong, and shuffle-board, and deck-tennis, all played with plodding devotion. There were people bathing in the lime-green open-air pool in front of the bridge; there were people reading thrillers, and writing letters to be posted at Antigua, and speculating about their ticket on the ship's daily run, and trying to cure their hangovers. Some were thinking about money, some about politics, some about their children left at home, some about the homes themselves. There were a few—a very few—thinking about love. There were dining-room stewards eating before they went on duty, and stewardesses making up beds and collecting soiled towels. There was a trio of officers on the bridge taking expert care of their southward progress.

There was, in Carl Wenstrom's stateroom on A-deck, an incipient row.

It was probably the Professor's fault, thought Carl, sitting at the head of the table and surveying his quarrelsome brood. The old man was obviously dying for a drink; the way he passed his hand across his lower jaw every few moments was a dead give-away, to anyone who had watched the ten A.M. tortures of representative citizens outside a Sixth Avenue bar. But he was ashamed to ask for what he craved; instead, he had channelled his misery into comment which, though it fell short of nagging, had a fussy air of criticism. He was unsure of this, he could scarcely recommend that—the pinpricks were only occasional, but they were enough to inject a measurable poison.

Carl himself was irritable; he had been up till four o'clock that morning, in a poker game which, though profitable, had taken toll of his energy. Everyone else in the room seemed wonderfully fresh; even Diane, who, he knew, had stayed up at an advanced sort of party at least as late as he. Perhaps it was this which was the irritation—the knowledge that the time was past when he could keep the hours of the young without paying the price of the old. There was no aspect of age more mortifying than this.

Louis Scapelli spoke first. He was a much improved Louis, something like the kind of young man Carl had had in mind when he was planning their enterprise. The moustache was gone, the clothes were simple, and casually correct; the sun had done wonders for his complexion. If some of the pallor was still there, it could be the pallor of a man who spent too much time as a plush night-club customer, rather than as one of the boys wearing green eye-shades in the back room. He was even good-looking again; the snide urban skin, peeled off, revealed a small but sensual animal.

"I've got two things going for me," he reported, with novel and convincing authority. "Maybe more, but at least two you can count on. One is Mrs. Stewart-Bates—she's pretty near ripe." His expression as he said this was so utterly contemptuous that Kathy, who had been staring out of the porthole, turned her head and looked at him closely. Could he really be so full of contempt, and yet go through the motions of love convincingly when the time came? Apparently he thought he could do so. "We're taking a run ashore together when we get to Antigua," he went on. "I think that should fix it." He cocked an inquiring eyebrow at Carl. "O.K., chief?"

"What do you propose to do?" asked Carl.

"Come back on board early," answered Louis, "when there's not too many people about. Then go into action."

"Where?" inquired the Professor suddenly.

"In her cabin. It's—" his grin was unpleasant, "—more discreet, like they say."

"It has certainly not proved so," said the Professor flatly.

"What's that meant to mean?" snapped Louis.

"The fact that you have been to her cabin several times is already common gossip. One can hardly recommend—"

"Wait a minute," interrupted Carl. "How do you know that?"

"I heard of it this morning. From Mrs. Kincaid."

"That long-nosed bitch," said Louis. "Anyway, what the hell? I've been seen going to her cabin. So what? I'm going again—once more."

The Professor raised an admonishing finger. "That is precisely where the danger lies. If you suddenly stop going—"

"Just a moment, Professor," interrupted Carl again. He turned back to Louis. "What's this about her cabin?" he asked.

"I've just been there, that's all."

"Doing what?"

"Talking, mostly. Holding her hand. And practising dance-steps."

"Gee!" said Diane, ironically. "Big deal, Romeo. How's her cha-cha coming on? You get paid by the lesson?"

Louis surveyed her, with cold dislike. "Not yet. But I will be. And the price is going to be right, don't you worry. You saw that cigarette case she gave me. Eighteen carat, from the best jewellery store in San Juan."

"Yeah, we saw it. When are you going to turn it in to the Prof?"

"At the end of the deal," Louis snapped. "How can I turn it in now? She sees me using it every day. How do I explain if it's not there?"

"You can say you gave up cigarettes to improve your dancing."

"I still think that the amount of public attention—" began the Professor.

Louis, nettled, goaded on many fronts, turned on him with a snarl. "What the hell are you bitching about, Prof? I'm doing my job. You get on with yours, whatever it is. Of course I've been going to her cabin. It's part of the build-up. And when I stop going, she won't squawk. Not in public. She won't dare. And your gossiping pals can forget all about it—till I switch to someone else. Then maybe they'll start all over again. *And it doesn't matter!*"

The Professor opened his mouth again, but Kathy unexpectedly forestalled him. The point intrigued her, as a woman; she felt she could make a contribution; and indeed, it was high time that she did so, and earned some of her passage-money. "I think Louis is right," she said firmly. She was addressing the people round the table, but she was talking to and for Carl—Carl who, short of sleep, his nerves too taut, was not handling this thing at all well. "The fact that there's gossip about him and the old girl is useful. I bet she knows about it—women always do. It'll make her more nervous of public opinion. *Therefore*, when the pressure's put on, she 's more likely to crack."

Louis gave her a mock salute. "Thanks, kid. I'm glad somebody else around here knows what the score is." He looked at Carl. "Do I go ahead, chief?"

"Yes," said Carl, making up his mind a shade too quickly. "Play it your way. But just watch it. I'll come back to that a bit later." He turned again. "Diane?"

Diane, trim and tanned in a strapless sun-dress which did a great deal for her figure, smiled back at him. She was very confident, very sure of herself. There could be no complaints about what she had done so far. She was the big winner; indeed, the only one.

"No dancing lessons," she reported coolly. "This is the advanced course. . . . You know about Bancroft—he came across for a thousand dollars, the very first night. Since then I've been lining 'em up." She ticked off the names on her fingers. "There's a pal of his called Gerson—maybe Bancroft's been talking to him, but whatever he said, it must have been sweet talk. He can't wait for it. There's Zucco, next down the queue. He wants to give me a film test." She laughed, without humour. "What a line! He'll learn. . . . Then there's an old guy who's been nibbling at it—Walham. He—"

"Walham?" repeated the Professor, on a note of petulant disbelief. "I hope you are not placing any great hopes in that particular quarter."

Diane's chin came up. In the full tide of recital, she did not relish the interruption. "Why not?" she demanded.

"I have it on the very best authority," he said, "that his idea of a —suitable fee is twenty dollars."

"What the hell are you talking about?" asked Diane. "What *authority?*"

"His own. He told me so."

"*Told* you so? Twenty dollars? I don't get it. Have you been talking prices with him?"

"We were discussing matters in general terms. But he was quite explicit. He is extraordinarily mean, as we all know. Twenty dollars is his firm price."

At that, Diane exploded, into inevitable vulgarity. "Firm price? What do you know about it? What does *he* know? I'll tell him what the price is, and I'll tell him when it's firm too." She leant forward, raising her finger. "You better keep out of this, Prof, before you screw the whole thing up. I've done better than anyone so far—"

"You have indeed done very well." The Professor passed his hand, for the twentieth time, across his dry lower lip. "A thousand dollars, wasn't it?"

"Yeah."

"Exactly a thousand?"

Diane stared at him, frowning. "Exactly. What are you getting at?"

"It's such a round figure."

"That's what he was paying for, you old goat! Are you hinting that I've been holding out?"

Carl raised his hand. "For heaven's sake stop it! You're like a bunch of children."

"If he's insinuating—"

"He's insinuating nothing." Carl rapped sharply on the table. "Let's all do a little work, for a change. That's what you've got so far, is it, Diane? Gerson, Zucco, and possibly Walham."

"Yes," answered Diane sulkily. "There's a couple of the officers, but you can't count them." She looked sideways at Kathy. "Or can you?"

"Why ask me?" asked Kathy coldly.

"I thought you were interested."

"I am not."

Carl broke in again. "All right, all right. I think you can go ahead with Gerson, Diane, but leave it for a day or so. If he's a friend of Bancroft, it might be a bit dangerous. Try and get a line on what Bancroft told him, if he told him anything."

"I know just what he told him," answered Diane, not less sulkily. "You've got to understand this—they're friends, but they don't like each other. Not one little bit. Bancroft got hooked, so he wants the same thing to happen to Gerson. All he would say is—" she gestured, with exceptional crudity, "—go ahead, boy, it's wonderful, it's red-hot, and it's yours for the asking."

"You think so?" asked Carl.

"I know so."

"All right. But wait a little longer, like I said." He sat up straight, flexing his sore shoulder-muscles. "That leaves me," he said, "and you might as well know what's been happening in the wonderful world of poker. We've got a good school going—reasonably skilful, except for one man; we've played every night, and I've won about nine thousand dollars."

Louis whistled, admiringly. "Hell, chief—that's not peanuts!"

"It's a no-limit game," explained Carl, "and I've held good cards all the time."

"Straight?"

"Oh yes."

"Who's the one man?"

"Greenfield. The father of the brat." He smiled. "Maybe his home life drove him to poker. But he *is* bad."

Since no-one seemed to have anything else to say, Carl looked inquiringly round the room, prepared to finish off the meeting. Kathy, he knew, had nothing worth-while to report; he was not disappointed, certainly not surprised, but he did not want to draw attention to the fact among the others. She would go to work when the moment and the occasion suited her; if this seemed to place her in a favoured position, then that was where she belonged, and he was not inclined to discuss the point. They had been very happy during the last few days; lovingly happy, at ease with each other and with the whole world. Perhaps it could not stay like that, when Kathy started 'operating'; whatever she did would not come between them, in any emotional sense, but it would encroach on their peace. He was selfish enough, or loving enough, to want to postpone that.

"All right," he said, more briskly. "Professor—treasurer's report!"

The Professor smiled, and leant forward, a touch of pride in his bearing. "A simple balance-sheet so far, Carl. Yourself, nine thousand two hundred dollars. Diane, one thousand dollars. Louis, one gold cigarette case, worth—" he looked up, directing his query down the table.

"Seven hundred and fifty bucks," said Louis, with a smirk.

The Professor made a pencilled note on a pad. "That's fifty dollars short of eleven thousand. Nearly half-way to our original stake. I would call that very satisfactory."

Carl nodded. "So would I. Particularly as we've hardly got started yet."

"Some of us," said Diane, not quite under her breath.

"What's that?"

"I said, 'Some of us,' " repeated Diane, more loudly. "Some of us haven't got started at all yet."

Carl was about to dismiss the comment, when Kathy herself took it up. "That means me, I suppose."

"Yeah. We haven't heard any report from you."

"You haven't heard anything," said Kathy, "because so far there's nothing to tell."

"Just so long as we know."

The tone was unpleasant, but Kathy would not be provoked. "I've got three things in mind," she said slowly. "One of them is Beckwith—Sir Hubert himself." She gave the title an ironic emphasis. "He may be too scared of his wife. But I don't think so. Another is Zucco—your Mr. Zucco. He's offered me a film-test too."

"Those cameras of his are sure going to be whirring," said Diane. But she had a point to make, and she was not going to be deflected. "What about that tea-party?"

"What tea-party?"

"Those kids who call themselves officers."

Kathy shrugged. "I had tea with them in their saloon, or whatever it's called. They invited me along. What about it?"

"They invited *me*," said Diane. "But I turned it down."

"So?"

Diane was not getting anywhere, and the fact annoyed her further. "It's just a waste of time, that's all."

"Oh, I agree."

And indeed, it had been a waste of time, from all points of view. There had been eight of them at the tea-party; she was the only woman; they had laid on a tremendous meal—tea, bread-and-butter, crumpets, scones, jam, Devonshire cream, little cakes, big cakes—the lot. Their efforts to please, to entertain, to appear sophisticated men-of-the-world, had been unmistakable; in between times, in the silences, they all ate enormously. It had been pathetic, rather endearing, and dull. That song about sailors should really have been called "*Heads* of Oak." . . . Even Tim Mansell, whom she liked best of the assembled collection, had shown himself astonishingly innocent and unaware. He was a few years older than herself, yet he made her feel about fifty years of age. Compared with Carl—

Her daydream was broken into, roughly, by Diane. "Why go to the party, then? We're meant to be *working*. Remember?"

Kathy looked at her, frowning. She did not want to argue; it was futile; Diane was one kind of animal, herself another—they could not meet, they did not need to, they could go their separate ways and, if necessary, compare results at the end. She had gone to the party because she had been asked, and because she had nothing better to do. It was as simple as that. Perhaps it had better be kept simple.

"I don't think it matters at all," she said briefly. "This was an officers' tea-party. I went, you didn't. There's no crisis, no bones broken, no need to panic. The whole thing took an hour. . . . My third possibility," she went on, in a voice studiously devoid of emphasis, "is Tillotson."

The name produced the effect she had expected. Even Carl repeated it, surprised. Diane opened her mouth, and then shut it again; the Professor raised his bushy eyebrows. Louis voiced all their thoughts when he said:

"Tillotson? The big, *big* shot? Don't tell me he's got hot pants, same as everyone else!"

"It's only beginning," answered Kathy. "That's about all I can say. But if we're making out lists, he's certainly on mine."

"Baloney!" said Diane rudely. "I don't believe it. Tillotson is married with a capital M. He's married to his money, too. He wouldn't recognize a proposition if it climbed up and sat on his face."

Kathy shrugged, not caring to argue. "Have it your own way. I'm just telling you that Tillotson is due to make a play sooner or later. When it's going to happen is anybody's guess. But that's for me to worry about."

There was a knock on the cabin door, startling them all. Before Carl could answer, the door opened, and Barkway, the steward, appeared.

"Compliments of Mr. Tillotson, sir," he said. "Don't forget you're having a drink with him at noon."

Carl swung round, genuinely shaken, while an electric silence settled on the others. Barkway's face was absolutely expressionless; it was quite impossible to judge whether the sudden entrance were innocent or not. It was quite true, thought Carl swiftly, that he was due to have a drink at noon; Tillotson was one of their poker-school; there had been some talk, when they broke up, of a pre-lunch party. But the timing of the message was remarkable; and so, in Barkway's mind, must be the fact that they were all sitting round the table, clearly holding some kind of meeting. Had Barkway waited outside the door? Had he been listening? Had he chosen the exact moment, so as to achieve surprise, or—more likely—to enjoy the shock which was his to give? Carl looked at him again. The face was still blank, almost theatrically so. But then, stewards often *did* look like that; it was a badge of service, copied from God-knows-what ancient dynasty of film butlers. If they ever betrayed emotion, they were betraying Paul Lukas, Arthur Treacher, William Powell. . . . But it was time for him to answer, if the moment were to be passed off naturally.

"Thank you, Barkway," he said. "Please tell Mr. Tillotson that I'll be there."

"Very good, sir." Barkway withdrew, smooth, expressionless, without allusion or accent of any kind. They could hear vague voices in the lobby outside as he spoke, presumably, to another steward. Then there was silence again.

Louis expelled a long breath. "Jesus! How about that, chief? That guy could have been listening outside, all the time!"

"I'll bet he was, too," said Diane. "What in hell were we saying, anyway?"

"Just that you and Kathy aim to get laid by everything that breathes. That's all!"

Carl raised his hand. "Let's take it easy. If he was listening, even all the time, I doubt if he could have really understood what we were talking about. Most of it wouldn't mean a thing, unless he'd been listening to a lot of *other* talk as well. He probably overheard the name Tillotson, and decided it would be funny to deliver the message just then."

"It was funny, all right," said Louis.

"Or it may have been a coincidence." Now that the small crisis was past, Carl was inclined to take this comforting view. He also wanted to finish off the meeting, which had run its course and served its purpose. "But in any case, it's a good illustration of what I wanted to say, before—" he looked at his watch, "—before I go to have my drink with Mr. Tillotson. We want to be careful all the time. We want to attract as little attention as possible. It doesn't really matter if Louis is seen going to Mrs. So-and-so's cabin; this whole ship's a gossip factory, as you know—you can't have corned-beef-hash for breakfast without half the passengers congratulating you by lunchtime. There's bound to be talk, whatever he does, whatever the girls do. But there's talk and talk." He looked round the table slowly, intent on making his point. "It's a matter of degree. If it's just talk about who's dancing with who, or even who's sleeping with who, it doesn't really matter. We're on a cruise, these things go on, love is in the air. . . . But if there's *conflict*—if there's *drama*—if Mrs. Stewart-Bates goes into shock for the next ten days, if Gerson wanders out of Diane's cabin shouting and waving an empty wallet, even if my poker friends start complaining in public about their losses—then we're in for trouble. It's a matter of handling, and of course it comes down to the individual. I can't tell you how far you can go, in each case. That's up to you. But try and attract the minimum of attention, when the pressure's on." He pushed back his chair, formally ending the session. "I must break this up," he said, "because I've got to keep that date. But just remember, and take it easy."

Louis left first, then Diane; the Professor remained where he was at the table, and Kathy also, standing by the porthole. After a moment she came forward.

"Anything I can do, Carl?"

"No, my darling." He looked up at her. "I want to talk to the Professor for a moment."

She nodded. Then she came up behind him, and put her hands softly over his temples. "Do get some sleep, when you can. You were terribly late last night."

"I'll sleep this afternoon."

"Promise?"

"I promise."

After a moment she added: "Those officers were just babies."

He smiled, covering her hand with his own. "I haven't a doubt of that."

When she was gone, leaving behind her, where she had touched him, the faint perfume which he knew so well, Carl came briskly to attention. It was his most formidable capacity, to be able to isolate contrasting moods and to concentrate on one or other of them at the flick of a switch.

"Were they?" he asked almost harshly of the Professor.

"What's that, Carl?" The Professor's hand had wandered again to his mouth, and he was looking sideways at the wall-table laden with drinks.

Carl said: "Help yourself, Professor," and the old man crossed to the table with unashamed alacrity. There was a rattle of bottle against glass as he poured himself a drink. After two gulps of whisky, also audible, he turned and said:

"Were they what? Were *who* what?"

"The officers. She said they were babies. True?"

The Professor was not surprised. Between himself and Carl there was an absolute frankness; no question was too inquisitive, no answer too squalid, no topic unmentionable.

"Perfectly true," he answered readily. "There's nothing there. She likes one of them—Mansell, his name is—but it's nothing serious. They've danced together a few times. He asked her to go ashore with him when we were at Bermuda, but she wouldn't."

"What's he like?"

The Professor spread his hands. "A child, just as she said."

"O.K." Carl dismissed the topic. He looked at his watch again. "I've got ten minutes still. Anything for me?"

The Professor, enormously comforted and reassured by the mere feel of a glass in his hand, sat down again.

"One or two things," he answered. "First, there's Diane's one thousand dollars. The Bancroft affair."

Carl nodded. "Why did you raise that? You think she's holding out?"

"Frankly, I do. It's such a round figure, and—" he threw back his head in a dignified movement, "—I still use that phrase, in spite of any coarse comment she may make. It was probably a great deal more."

"Difficult to find out."

"Indeed, impossible. But there's no harm in indicating that we are keeping our eyes open."

Carl nodded again. "Agreed. I think we've got to accept the fact, Professor, that both she and Louis will get away with whatever they can. There can't be an effective check. It's like the income-tax assessment of a waiter's tips—educated guesswork. We must take a likely figure, and raise hell if they seem to be getting out of line."

"We'll do that. . . . Then there's Louis," the Professor went on. "I mentioned the matter of Mrs. Kincaid, and the amount of gossip there is already. You dealt with it yourself, perfectly adequately. But I think it's *probable*," he said carefully, "that Mrs. Stewart-Bates has already given him other presents, besides the cigarette case. They have been together—dancing and such-like—for nearly two weeks now. He has been uniformly attentive. Now she is not a stupid woman, though of course she is incontestably foolish. She surely regards him as a dancing-partner; with all the self-flattery in the world, she must realize that he is a full quarter of a century younger than herself, and that the relationship is that of gigolo to client. She *must* have been paying him—with jewellery, cuff-links, even money—on a more-or-less continuous basis."

"There's no check," said Carl again.

"No," agreed the Professor. "But I have compiled a list of the jewellery she has worn in public. If that is what he proposes to take from her, I will certainly make a note of what she no longer wears, during the rest of the voyage."

Carl smiled, with genuine amusement. "Professor, you're wonderful."

The Professor sipped his drink, well satisfied. "I dislike being fooled," he said, "particularly by my inferiors. One must take certain precautions. . . . I also had a confusing encounter with young Barry Greenfield."

"Bad luck."

"That young man," said the Professor, with feeling, "should have been exposed at birth. More and more do I come to believe in the old Spartan customs. However. . . . It was a curious conversation; I must admit that I did not fully understand all of it. He seemed to be hinting that the girls—and Diane especially—were engaged in some operation, of which he at least—at the age of fifteen—was fully aware."

"You're fooling."

The Professor passed his hand over his brow. It was a much more relaxed gesture than hitherto, but it demonstrated a degree of inadequacy none-the-less.

"I am not fooling," he answered, "though I may have been mistaken."

"But what did he say?"

"Just that he was keeping an eye on all of us."

Carl laughed aloud. "Barry Greenfield? But that's wonderful! Perhaps we should cut him in."

The Professor shuddered. "No, no! There is a capacity for evil there which I for one could never compete with. I can assure you, he would have acquired a controlling interest, inside of a week."

"If we can't lick him we must join him. . . ." Carl stood up, stretching. "I must go, I'm afraid. That's all?"

"Yes." The Professor, soothed in spirit, already regaining his normal hazy contentment, looked at Carl. "If you are satisfied, that is."

"How do you mean?"

"As regards Kathy."

"What about her?"

"I think she *is* being a little lazy, Carl."

Carl frowned, considering the remark. He would have taken it from no-one else; but the Professor was allowed infinite latitude in this area, as well as all the others. It was his contribution, the role of the small voice made audible.

"O.K.," he said, curtly. "I will deal."

chapter 3

AS if making a distant curtsey, the *Alcestis* altered course at the first glimpse of the ruffled crinoline of Montserrat Island, far to the south, and set her bows towards Antigua, thirty miles to the eastwards. The weather still held, peerless, magically clear; when, coasting down Nevis, they passed through shallower water—ten fathoms, eight fathoms—they left behind them a broad boiling wake of pink and brown, a hundred million coral atoms stirred up by the pressure of their passing hull. Flying fish gave them brief escort, whirring alongside in company until their wings dried and they dropped back into the placid water; dolphins, the clowns of the sea, tumbled across their bows like children clamouring for attention from a huge grown-up. When the new course was set, the wheeling sea-birds settled down again in a long stationary line on the edges of the boats; hitch-hiking from island to island, uncommunicative, surly, they seemed to have made up their minds to stay with this complaisant traveller for a few more miles. The *Alcestis,* closing yet another island in her long chain of landfalls, had much maritime attendance as she ploughed her lazy furrow eastwards.

In his day-cabin under the bridge, Captain Harmer was talking to Mr. Cutler the purser. It was a routine meeting; Cutler was the man who customarily brought him up-to-date; once in each twenty-four hours, they held this same colloquy. They were holding it now because the Captain, as so often at sea, was temporarily unemployed. He was awaiting the call from the bridge which would tell him that Antigua was within an hour's easy steaming, and that it was time for him to take over.

Within sight of land again, he was less than happy. For him, deep water was the only true element; nothing had made him more content than to be out of soundings, as they had been within the last few days, rolling nobly across the Puerto Rico Trench with thirty thousand feet under *Alcestis*' keel. It was the deepest part of the Atlantic, deeper than Mount Everest was high; to be afloat above this fathomless pit, this fantastic canyon in the ocean bed, was all the romance he needed. Let others fall in love with beckoning lights, with harbours, with the disciplined line of buoys marking the mainstreets of a hundred coastal approaches. For him, to see nothing on any horizon, to feel nothing for five miles beneath his ship, was a sailor's seventh heaven.

Now, as Brotherhood, his steward, poured drinks for Cutler and himself, he brought his mind to bear on the other mundane aspect of sea-going—the internal affairs of his ship. Between the two of them, the talk was always clipped and elliptical; they had sailed together for many years; there were no new ship-board problems, only variations on the same twin themes—complaints and scandals. But before they dealt with these, there was a small departure from the normal. It was not new, alas, but it was rare. It was death.

"How's the old man today?" the Captain asked. "Mr. Simms."

Cutler, accepting his drink from Brotherhood, shook his head.

"Not too good, I'm afraid. Doc says he's pretty well fading away."

"I ought to put him ashore, really."

"He's tremendously against it—Simms is. Doc asked him, and he said he'd sue us for a million dollars if we even tried it."

The Captain grinned. "I bet he would, too. He's a tough old bird. . . . But I don't like it, all the same. You know how unsettling those things are. Do people know about it?"

"Yes."

Harmer would have been surprised if this were not so. In a ship, the sounding-board for the faintest breath of gossip, a rumour of illness or death travelled fastest of all. It was as if, listening to a multitude of heart-beats, people could detect a single one that lagged, a pulse that even fluttered. Fearing their own mortality, they feared most of all any fore-runner of it.

"I'll think about it," said Harmer. "Any other troubles?"

Cutler sipped his pink gin. "The usual one about clothes. You know we always get it about now. Bikinis. . . . Mrs. Kincaid thinks they ought to be banned."

"So do I, by God! If those people could only see what they look like. . . . Who's been wearing one now?"

"Bernice Beddington, of all people."

"What a horrible thought."

"She looks like a minaret with string round it. But we can't do much about that. They always buy awful clothes when we get down here. Floppy sun-hats—Bermuda shorts—shirts with funny pictures on them—sometimes I wonder if they ever look in the mirror before they come on deck. Even Mrs. Consolini went and bought herself a set of horsehair slave-bangles. But you must have seen them yourself."

"No," said the Captain. "I have not."

Cutler smiled. "Not pressing you this time?"

"No, thank God."

"Just as well you didn't put her at your table again."

"We could use a bit of life there," said the Captain, "but not that much. . . . Of course," he went on, referring back to Bernice Beddington without need for explanation, "it's her parents' fault really."

Cutler pursed his lips caustically. "It's her parents' *idea.*"

"I wish she *would* get married. . . . What else?"

"Walham, as usual." Cutler expelled a long breath. "I swear to God, that man would complain if we gave him the whole ship for Christmas!"

"Anything special?"

"No, just bloody nagging the whole time. Where's my tea—why can't we have kedgeree for breakfast—" Cutler put on a very creditable mimicry of Walham's nasal whine. "—why did we only stay ten hours at St. Thomas when the programme says 'Half a day'—why is the deck so slippery after it's been washed down in the morning? One day he's going to come up and say he's actually enjoying himself. Then we'll all drop dead."

Harmer was smiling. "You know there's one in every ship."

"This one's getting me down."

"Cheer up, Foxy."

"Oh, I can take it. It's just that it annoys a lot of other people as well. There'll be an anti-Walham brigade before we get to Rio. Like Little Nuisance. Only there's an anti-*him* brigade already."

"How *is* Master Greenfield?"

"Awful. We really ought to have an age limit, skipper."

"Upper *and* lower. Though I must admit, this one's a winner. Tiptree-Jones had to chuck him off the bridge yesterday."

"What was he doing?"

"Stamping on the quartermaster's foot."

Cutler nodded. "That's just about the size of it. Ah well. . . . Then we have Sir Hubert Beckwith."

"What's his worry? Apart from—well, let's not be morbid."

"Bingo jokes. Apparently Wexford used the old one about 'The Kremlin—Number 10,' and Beckwith thought it was an insult to the entire British Empire."

"He would. But better tell Wexford to leave that one out in future." The Captain looked sideways, towards the small pantry out in the passageway. "Brotherhood! Same again."

Brotherhood entered, collected the empty glasses, and began to refill them at the sideboard.

"Any scandals?" asked the Captain, after a pause.

"Nothing much. Mrs. van Dooren's been falling about a bit. But we've had them worse."

"What does she do all day?"

"Just that."

"H'm." The Captain looked up at Brotherhood, standing by his elbow with the fresh drink. "Who is Mrs. van Dooren's steward?"

"Pennington, sir," answered Brotherhood, without hesitation.

"How's he holding out?"

"No complaints, sir."

"Very well." Harmer nodded, and Brotherhood withdrew again. "But you'd better watch it, Foxy. I don't want her breaking a leg or anything."

"I'll watch it."

The ship rocked gently over a long swell. Automatically the Captain glanced up at the repeater-compass which was fixed to the bulkhead behind him. He followed it as it swung off two or three degrees, then looked away again as it settled down on course once more. They weren't asleep up on the bridge. . . . He took a slow pull at his drink.

"How's our gigolo?"

"Still on the pay-roll, apparently."

"I suppose she knows what she's doing."

"Well, she's old enough."

"They're a funny family. . . . Tim's well smitten with the blonde girl."

"Oh, he's a case, all right. . . . I'm not sure about the other one."

"What about her?"

Cutler shrugged. "I've just got a feeling. She has all the men panting, and I'm not surprised. It's the uncle that puzzles me—Wenstrom. He doesn't seem to worry about it at all."

"Why should he?"

"*I* would."

"Oh, you know what kids are like, these days. The girls are practically born with make-up on. . . . He plays poker, doesn't he?"

"All the time. Very hot stuff, so Edgar says."

"Big winner?"

"Up in the thousands."

Harmer raised his eyebrows. "Is that so? Any complaints about it?"

"No, no, nothing like that. They all seem very happy. It's a daft way to spend your money, I say, but I suppose they've got plenty of it."

"They're a funny family," said the Captain again. "Who's looking after them?"

"Barkway has three of their cabins."

"He'll keep an eye on them. Is he still bloody-minded, by the way?"

"Very."

The buzzer sounded on Harmer's desk. He pressed the switch of the inter-com; Tiptree-Jones' voice came through, elegantly controlled.

"Captain, sir!"

"Yes." Harmer winked at Foxy Cutler. "What is it?"

"I have Antigua on the plot, sir. Bearing one hundred degrees, about fifteen miles."

"Very good. I'll be up."

He stood up, and reached for his cap. "That's it for me, Foxy. But don't hurry. Finish your drink."

"Thanks, skipper."

"I'll want to know about Simms. Any change."

"I'll tell the doctor."

"Apart from that," said the Captain, preparing to take his leave, "it looks like just another cruise."

chapter 4

A WHOLE fleet of buses and taxis had been chartered to take the *Alcestis* passengers from St. John's, their anchorage on the north coast of Antigua, to English Harbour on the other side of the island, and thence to the Millreef Club for a gala dinner. The passengers streamed ashore from the launches—the *Alcestis* being too big to come alongside—in a brightly-coloured, chattering throng. They were stared at, even giggled at, but they paid no attention to this. It was just something that happened, in this part of the world.

They knew already that natives hereabouts simply weren't used to tourists—not their kind of tourist, anyway. It had been all right as far as Puerto Rico, which of course was pretty well part of the States anyway; but the further south one went, the less the inhabitants seemed to appreciate women in halters, women in orange shorts, men in striped peaked caps, men with three cameras and a good solid waistline. So they stood in groups under the bright sun, looking round, enjoying themselves and their isolation, turning their backs on the quayside touts, telling the beggars to go to hell; until the man in charge of transportation called out: "This way, folks!" and they set off in high spirits for the historic site marked*** in the itinerary—Nelson's Dockyard at English Harbour (restored).

They were beginning to travel in their own vacuum bowl, and beginning not to give a damn about it. It was the difference between belonging to the *Alcestis*, and not belonging. Envious stares, flip remarks, inevitably went with the former, and that was all there was to it.

Louis Scapelli, a small trim figure in white slacks and a blue-striped T-shirt, had held back from the queue which was piling into the last bus.

"Gee, I don't want to go with this mob," he said to Mrs. Stewart-Bates. "Can't we fix something just for ourselves?"

"I don't see why not," said Mrs. Stewart-Bates, with that slightly flustered air which meant that she was secretly pleased. "There must be another taxi somewhere around. Is that what you mean?"

"Yes," said Louis. "That's exactly what I mean."

"If you could find one," said Mrs. Stewart-Bates, timorously, "I'd be glad to—"

Her voice trailed off; there was no need to be explicit about what she would be glad to do, and indeed, she would no longer dream of mentioning the topic. She had reached the stage when deferring to his wishes, which had formerly been a pretended submission, was now a real one. It was not that he was masterful; simply that he only remained attentive as long as he had his own way, and she needed him—desperately, tormentingly—to remain attentive. She realized, being fundamentally sensible, the degrading aspect of this companionship; at night, alone, she was ashamed of it; but in the morning, meeting once more his dark good looks, his intimate air of sharing a secret only with herself, she forgot shame and knew only joy. No-one else on board had a man like this one. He had chosen her, and stayed with his choice; if they were not lovers yet, it was only because he respected her too much. She could not see the future, but the present was ecstatic.

Louis, having secured his *carte blanche* and with it his private line of retreat—and in any case, he didn't like the *Alcestis* crowd at times like this, they were inclined to smirk and make cracks about himself and the old girl—Louis looked about him. The last passengers had climbed into the buses, and driven off; with the exodus, the quay was beginning to resume its normal air of indolence. There was a tall native, in some sort of washed-out khaki uniform, leaning against one of the buildings, smoking lazily, staring at them. He was about ten yards off. Louis gestured.

"Hey, you!"

The man did not stir a muscle; he remained where he was, gracefully, insolently private, watching Louis and Mrs. Stewart-Bates. After a moment of silence, Louis was forced to walk towards him.

"Can I get a taxi around here?" he asked, still on a note of command.

The tall native took his time about answering. He looked from Louis to Mrs. Stewart-Bates, and then back again. Then he threw away his cigarette, watching the butt curve and fall into the water. Then he said:

"I got taxi. Yes, sir!"

Even the 'Yes, sir' managed to sound mocking, a caricature of the American glad hand. But Louis pushed on through it.

"Well, you're hired."

The man repeated 'Hired' as if it it were a new word. Then he said: "Where you want to go?"

"Down to that dockyard, that harbour some place."

"English Harbour?"

"That's it."

The man gestured towards the dust of the departing buses. "You miss transportation." He said the word with a very careful, very satirical intonation, as if it were fundamentally foreign and ridiculous—which indeed it was. "Yes, sir!"

"That's O.K.," said Louis. "We want to go by ourselves."

"Pay fifteen dollars," said the man. "British West Indian currency."

"Hell, that's ten bucks—" began Louis. But Mrs. Stewart-Bates, coming up behind him, interrupted.

"Oh, what does it matter? Take it, Louis! It'll be just wonderful!"

"O.K.," said Louis, "let's go."

The man straightened up at last. He now addressed himself, with special insolence, to Mrs. Stewart-Bates.

"You pay ten American dollars to English Harbour?" he asked. The accent, carefully, was on the first word of the sentence.

"We'll pay," said Louis. "Let's go."

The man ignored Louis; his glance remained on Mrs. Stewart-Bates. She had to answer him, in spite of shamed misgivings. She said:

"Of course we'll pay. What's all the fuss? Where's your taxi?"

"Pay first," said the man. "English Harbour, ten dollars American."

"Now see here—" began Louis

"Police laws," said the man, indifferently. "Outside town limits, pay first."

"Bunk!" said Louis roughly. "That's just a racket."

"Do you have ten dollars?" Mrs. Stewart-Bates asked him hesitantly. She reached into her bag. The man was watching her, unsmiling, confirmed in his thoughts.

"Sure I have it." Louis pulled out his wallet, peeled off two five-dollar bills, and held them towards the man. "Here!" he said savagely. "Now let's get going, for God's sake!"

He was still scowling when they settled down in the taxi, an ancient mouldering De Soto with torn upholstery and cracked yellow windows.

"Please don't be angry, dear," said Mrs. Stewart-Bates. She pressed his hand; it was something they were by now accustomed to. "Let's not have it spoil our day."

He looked sideways at her. She was the same as ever, stylish, dumpy, and plain; the brilliant sunshine was not kind to her sagging skin, though it did a great deal for her sapphires. *It's going to spoil your day, he thought, just that extra little bit. . . .* With an effort he smiled, and returned the pressure.

"It'll take more than some snotty cab-driver to get me down," he told her. He spoke carelessly loud, for the driver to hear. "Now let's enjoy the view."

But the view was not encouraging. Though their taxi rattled, rocked, and ground its way round endless corners, the surroundings remained the same—mile upon mile of dusty yellow cane-fields, narrow roads untidily strewn with crushed cane-stalks, small featureless hills crowned with shabby kilns. The earth was bone dry, the air had a sickly sugary smell which never varied; there were half-naked children staring at them, and figures bowed over squeaking bicycles, and men with rounded shoulders wielding their heavy sickles as if each stroke were a lash on their own backs. Antigua was perennially short of water, they had read in the guide-books; but it seemed to be short of much else besides—short of colour, short of hope, short of life. When they bumped their way through a village, the village seemed to turn its back on them; not because of something better to do, but because it did not want to know about them, or about anything.

"What a dump," said Louis presently, when for the hundredth time the taxi groaned round the same right-angle corner at the edge of a cane-field, to show them yet another dusty stretch, another vista of bent canes lining the road.

"But it's interesting," ventured Mrs. Stewart-Bates. She was looking about her in her usual vague way, ready to be impressed by anything she saw. "We've nothing like this in America."

"Damn right we haven't!" answered Louis. "And they can keep it."

The driver turned his head slightly. "Very poor peoples," he said. There was contempt in his voice, but it was not possible to name its target with any certainty.

Louis raised his voice. "Why don't they do something about it, then?" he asked disagreeably. "Instead of just sitting around."

The driver said nothing; the poise of his head above the frayed collar-band spoke his answer for him. *We like it this way,* it seemed to proclaim; *and even if we didn't, we wouldn't change it if we had to be like you. . . .* Under the fierce sun beating down on the roof, the air inside the taxi was stifling; but it was not more stifling than the savage pride in poverty which sat, its back turned upon them, a few feet away.

Presently the road began to wind downhill; there was a view of the sea, a blue arm of a bay invading the yellow flat-lands; then they were driving at water-level on the last mile of their journey. They passed a white-washed water-catchment, its sides daubed with the names of old ships, the initials of long-dead sailors, the curving figures of old dates—"1809," said one; "H.M.S. Paragon." Then they passed through a tall gateway, and into an area of quays and roofless buildings and loading-bays overgrown with grass. The taxi ground down to a stop, its transmission shuddering.

"English Harbour," announced the driver, without looking round. "Dockyard of Lord Nelson."

"Wait for us," said Louis curtly. "Right here."

"Yes, sir!"

They got out, stepping into the sun as if into an open fireplace, and began to walk about. Except to the eye of faith, unashamedly in love with the past, it was not impressive; the efforts of reconstruction had not been able to keep pace with the decay and indifference of a hundred dying years. There were buildings, neatly labelled "Barracks" and "Store-Room" and "Capstan House" and "Sail Lockers," but they were shells of buildings, tumble-down walls, sometimes nothing save a roped-off area with a painted plaque inside it. The few yachts and motor-cruisers moored alongside were like intruders—intruders not upon the past but upon a decayed present. As newcomers, they looked too good, too workmanlike, for their surroundings.

A throng of tourists, most of them from the *Alcestis*, milled around, tracing without great enthusiasm the ancient formations of the dockyard. Young women sold souvenir postcards, and cold drinks, and cigarettes; the taxi-drivers lounged in the shade, waiting for customers, waiting for interest to fade and history to catch up. The water lapped with a sullen air against the rotting piles, the ruined facings of the dockside.

"Hell!" said Louis Scapelli. "Is this all?"

The eye of faith, unashamedly in love with the past—in the person of the Professor—was near to tears with the magic of its surroundings. The Professor had come to Nelson's Dockyard well-prepared; he had a guide-book, he had a historical brochure tracing local maritime history from the middle of the eighteenth century, and he knew a good deal about it already. But mostly he had a sense of the past, an honourable reverence for all ancestors. When he wandered, he trod softly and shakily, aware of the hallowed ground but aware more movingly still of the throng of ghosts which brushed his shoulders.

He had made his tour alone, with loving concentration. He had traced the outlines of the old Capstan House, where the ships were "heaved down" by tackles attached to their masts, so that they could be careened for repairs. He had seen the sail lockers, the pond for soaking new spars, the mouldy store-rooms for rum and salt pork and hard biscuit. He had come upon old anchors embedded in the hard earth, and flights of steps leading down to the water, and ancient ring-bolts. He had paced out the length of the rope-walk, where the huge tarry hawsers were woven and spliced.

All the time, his imagination had been at work, conjuring the past. On this very ground, Nelson himself must have wandered—1794, 1796, he could not be exact—heart-sick at his exile, wasted by malaria bred in the foetid tideless basin. His ship—the *Pegasus?* the *Boreas?*— must actually have come alongside at this very quay, not less than one-hundred-and-sixty-four years ago. But there was older history than this, a more evil past which the Professor was forced to re-live at the same time.

For here, earlier, had come the pirates, the freebooters of the Spanish Main, the slavers from the dreaded Guinea Coast, three thousand miles away to the eastwards. In the small museum attached to the dockyard, dark, musty, neglected, he had come upon evidence of this last guilty stain on mankind; a rusty slave-shackle with a great iron ball attached to it, a whip of coiled oxhide "as used by the Over-Seers," and especially a tattered poster which, across a span of two centuries, still spoke loudly of pain.

"*To Be Sold This Day on the Block at Saint John's,*" he had read; and below it, in bold face, a catalogue of wares, neatly ranged:

"1 Mulatto Cook-Boy, THOMAS, 30 years old, warranted sound.
2 Field Hands, JAMES & EZRA, from Bankrupt Plantation at the Barbadoes.
1 BOY, Martiniquan, speaks only French, aged, no warranty.
1 House Maid, SAVANNAH. A fine Clean Girl. Together with two female children (one 4 years, well-grown, one at breast.)
Also JASPER, a runaway."

Entranced, appalled, the Professor sat down on a mouldering wooden capstan, and stared seawards, his eyes moist with the easy tears of old age. Then he took out his notebook and, after a moment, began soberly to write.

"Hell, is this all?" asked Louis. They had been walking for ten minutes, peering into dark corners, reading labels which were nothing but labels. He did not like the *Alcestis* people who greeted them or pointedly ignored him, who darted here and there with cries of discovery; the whole thing was just a tourist trap, not even a good one. The sight of the Professor sitting on a hunk of wood, writing in his note-book, made him angrier still. It was time someone in this outfit went to work. . . . He kicked at a baulk of timber lying half overgrown by weeds. "Why don't they label this one?" he asked sarcastically. " 'Piece of wood.' How about that?"

"Don't you like it here?" asked Mrs. Stewart-Bates.

"There's nothing to like," answered Louis. "Have you ever seen such a crummy set-up? Jesus, even Plymouth Rock is better organized!"

"But it's historical," said Mrs. Stewart-Bates. She looked round the derelict dockyard, which the bright sun made shabbier still. "It's so English, don't you think?"

"Yeah. Maybe that's the trouble. Who was this Nelson, anyway?"

She smiled. She could always tell when he was joking. "Now, Louis! He was like our John Paul Jones. You know that perfectly well."

"I saw the picture," said Louis. "Robert Stack. Boy, that was a lemon!" He turned towards her, suddenly changing levels. "Let's get out of here, Grace."

He did not often use her Christian name; it was still a novelty, still a major happiness.

"Do you think we could?" she asked doubtfully.

"Why not? We've got the cab waiting, haven't we? There's nothing for us here."

"But we were going to that club place, the Millreef."

"Oh, screw the Millreef!" His occasional crudity was something else which he knew she enjoyed. "Look, I've got a headache. This sun is murder. Let's go back, huh?"

"Oh, you poor boy." She was readily sympathetic. "Of course we'll go back, if you're not feeling well."

"We can have dinner on board, instead. Just you and me. Wouldn't you like that?"

"You know I'd love it."

"What are we waiting for?"

They found their driver, sprawling with a dozen others in the shade of the museum. He was slow getting to his feet, slower still at opening the door of the ricketty cab. "You go back?" he asked. He spoke so that the other drivers could hear.

"Yeah," said Louis. "But take it easy. There's no rush."

"Back to St. John's?"

"Where else, for God's sake?"

"Yes, sir!"

Behind their backs, one of the other drivers repeated "Yes, sir," in a high-pitched voice, and there was a chorus of contented giggling from the rest of them.

The return journey was a replica of the out-going one; hot, dusty, and featureless. They sat back, staring out on either side, not talking to each other; when she inquired about his headache, he said: "It's O.K. Skip it!" in a voice which forbade further conversation. But presently there came a variation which woke both of them from their divided thoughts.

They were nearing St. John's, climbing one of the last hills between the lolling cane-stalks, when the driver turned his head very slightly, and spoke just above the whine of the engine.

"English Harbour to St. John's," he said, on a conversational note. "Fifteen dollars, ten dollars American."

Louis had been preoccupied, thinking and planning ahead; it was Mrs. Stewart-Bates who reacted first.

"What was that you said?" she asked. "Were you speaking to us?"

"I was speaking," said the driver. "I say, ten dollars American, back to St. John's."

"I don't understand," she said. "Louis—"

But Louis was now fully awake. "What the hell!" he said forcefully. "I paid you the fare already. You know that, damn well!"

The driver nodded twice, as if agreeing to a proposition in pure Socratic argument. "Yes, sir. You pay for journey to English Harbour. This is journey back."

"Well, God damn it!" said Louis. He was prepared to be furious. It was a perfect squeeze, almost a legitimate squeeze; he should have thought of it himself, at the beginning. "You know damn well that when you quote a price for a trip like this, that means the round trip, there and back."

"No, sir," said the driver. "Not the custom here. We make agreement, ten dollars for trip to English Harbour. You pay me."

"But surely—" began Mrs. Stewart-Bates.

"Now we go back," said the driver. He seemed to be bouncing the words to them off the windscreen, negligently skilful, sure that they would arrive, rather than addressing them directly. "This is new journey, English Harbour back to St. John's. Fifteen dollars British West Indian currency. Ten dollars American."

"We won't pay," said Louis furiously. "Not a damn cent!"

They felt the taxi slowing down. "What you say?" asked the driver.

"You heard me."

The taxi braked to a halt. A small cloud of yellow dust drifted past them on the following wind. The smell of sugar cane, mixed with burnt grass, was overpowering. As they lost way, the sun immediately gained in strength, forcing a torrid heat within the car.

"We wait here for police," said the driver.

"Christ, what a racket!" Louis exploded.

"They did warn us about it," said Mrs. Stewart-Bates. "Don't you think—"

"I'll see him in hell first!"

A silence fell, and continued; the heat began to be intolerable. Louis thought swiftly, brushing the sweat from his neck. He did not want delay; the thing was flowing his way, and must not be interrupted. A squeeze was a squeeze, but it was her money, anyway. Or rather, it was going to be her money, as soon as they got back to the *Alcestis*. He made his decision, curbing a violent impulse to pick up something—anything, a stone, a tire-lever—and smash in the back of that hated head. If this had been Central Park, on a dark night. . . .

"O.K.," he said. "But I'll report you. Don't think I won't!"

"Yes, sir," said the driver. "You pay? Lady pay?"

Louis reached for his wallet. "Cut that out," he said roughly. "I'll pay." He counted out ten dollars; it was all he had left. Then he was reminded of something which had struck him earlier, something which had not seemed worth the trouble of raising. "Wait a minute. You're too damned smart. Didn't you say fifteen dollars local money?"

The driver nodded again. "Fifteen bee-wees. That's how we say it here, for B.W.I. money. Or ten American."

"It's not ten American," said Louis angrily. "It's nine American."

The driver turned round. It was a surprise to see his face, after watching the back of that inscrutable neck for so long. It was more surprising still to see that he was now smiling, as if some extra dividend of pleasure had just been awarded him.

"*I* say, fifteen dollars, British West Indian currency," he explained, with obvious pleasure. "*You* say, ten dollars American." He produced a very fair approximation of Louis' accent. "Remember you say, 'Hell, that's ten bucks'? *You* say it, I don't say it." His voice was triumphant. "So you pay me ten bucks. You want to pay fifteen dollars now, fifteen bee-wees?"

"I haven't got it," said Louis. "You know that. And I wouldn't touch the lousy stuff, anyway."

"Then ten dollars American," said the driver.

"Nine."

The driver sighed. "We wait for police."

Mrs. Stewart-Bates laid her hand on Louis' arm. "Don't you think we'd better pay?" she suggested. "It's so hot. We could stay here for ever."

"But this is just a hold-up," said Louis angrily. "We're being clipped, twice over."

"It's only ten dollars."

"Lady right," said the driver.

After a pause, wordless, Louis passed the money across. The taxi gathered way again; presently they were at the quayside, and rewarded by the sight of the *Alcestis,* shining white among the drab fishing-boats in the harbour. There was even a launch waiting, an

Alcestis launch, something they could at last give orders to. But Louis was unappeased. It was murderously hot; he actually had a head-ache now; and he had fallen for a racket so obvious, so childish, that he could never tell anyone about it. His anger mounted as he glanced at Mrs. Stewart-Bates, sitting by his side under the ruffling canopy of the launch. It was clear that she would not look at him; she was embarrassed by their defeat. She was thinking, already, that she would have to reimburse him twenty dollars.

Close to, the *Alcestis* was enormous, a towering castle, a symbol of unscaleable power and quality. This was his true world, his own home ground. But he had been gypped by a nigger cabdriver in a frayed shirt. . . . By the time they trod the decks again, he was in a vile mood, just ripe for it.

He lay back on the comfortable bed, the pillows piled high behind his head, an eiderdown drawn half-way up his chest. She had undone his tie, and loosened his collar; she had given him two aspirins, taken his temperature, nursed him anxiously for half an hour. Now she sat down on the edge of the bed, and put her hand on his forehead. It was still cold to the touch, moist, slightly clammy. It might have been fever, though in fact it was not.

"How are you feeling?" she asked anxiously. "You're so pale."

"I'm fine." He covered her hand with his own. "Don't you worry about me. It was just the sun. I'm better already. I'm always pale. You know that."

"You need someone to look after you."

"I've got someone, haven't I?"

She had switched off all the lights except the bedside lamp; in their private world, the scene and the mood were already sensually relaxed. As soon as they had returned on board, he had pleaded a violent head-ache; it seemed that, by the time they reached her cabin, he was almost in a state of collapse. But now things were easier. A half-hour of quiet, with herself as the ministering angel, soft-footed, gentle-voiced, had worked the required miracle. They were back where they had been before—wherever that was, she could never decide, she did not want to spell it out—with all the inevitable promise that lay between two people content to spend their time with each other.

"I'm fine," he said again. When he made his move—and it must be soon—he wanted the moment to be exactly right. Shock was going to be everything; he intended her, for pleasure as well as for profit, to be so overwhelmed that her only reaction would be a fish-like gasp, followed by an abject, spread-eagled surrender. That was the way to operate. . . . He let his other hand fall gently on her thigh as she sat on the edge of the bed. He had never yet touched her there. Big deal. . . . Her come-back would be a slight confusion, a withdrawal for a breathing-space, followed by—

She got up, reacting swiftly, a pink suffusion in her cheeks. "Now, Louis. I don't believe you're sick at all!"

"Not with you around," he said. "Who could be. . . . I like that necklace of yours, Grace, It suits you."

Her hand went to her throat. "Do you really like it? It was a present. It's beautiful, isn't it?"

"That's why it suits you."

"Now Louis! What's got into you, all of a sudden?"

"You know, don't you? It's because we haven't been like this before."

"Like what?"

"Kind of close together."

But now that the moment was here, now that he had projected it into the room like a chord in music, she could not believe it. She drew back, and stood looking down at him. He noticed that her hands were trembling, and that into her eyes had come a kind of silliness, as if she were seventeen again, and face-to-face with some dream of joy. Delaying for very shyness, she asked:

"Don't you want to eat now, Louis?"

He shook his head, settling back into the pillows. "Not yet. I could use a drink, though."

"Scotch and water?"

"Just that."

She poured the drink, her back towards him; but there was something in the way she stood, the set of her head, which told him that she would never be more vulnerable, more open to astonishment. His moment had come, and with it a cruel appetite for power, as though he could feed upon her ruin. As she handed him the glass, he said:

"That cab-driver sure took us for a ride, didn't he? Twenty bucks!"

"Horrible man. . . . Oh, I must pay you back, mustn't I?"

"There's no hurry."

"While I remember."

Her bag was on the bedside table. She sat down again, and reaching for it took out a roll of bills, clipped together with an ornamental gold spring. She drew out two ten-dollar bills, and passed them to him. He took them; then he said, on a sudden note of the utmost ferocity:

"More!"

"More?" She was confused by the word, and by the tone he used. "What do you mean?"

"Give me more. Keep dealing! Give me all of it."

"But Louis—you're joking—" She was not yet shocked, just completely confused. "Why should I give you money?"

"I'm in your bed, aren't I?"

It hit her like a wave crashing upon a naked swimmer; he could have laughed aloud to see the expression of bewilderment wiped from her face, to be succeeded by a fearful shame. She was horror-stricken; the brutal tone, the brutal words, had overwhelmed her. Her hand went up to her mouth, convulsively, as if he had slapped her upon it.

"Louis!"

There was a knock on the door, and the stewardess' voice said: "Madam?"

He reached out and grasped her arm in a ferocious grip. With his other hand he ripped open his shirt, so that it looked as though he were lying in bed naked.

He had foreseen this, too. He could turn it to account. He said, in a fierce whisper: "Go ahead! Ask her in to take a look at us!"

With an enormous effort, near to sobbing, Mrs. Stewart-Bates turned her head and called out:

"What is it? I'm busy right now."

"I'll come back, madam," said the stewardess through the door. "I just wanted to turn down the bed."

Footsteps receded, silence returned; his grip on her arm remained relentless. Down the corridor, the stewardess said to Barkway, the steward:

"They're at it again."

"Good luck to 'em," said Barkway.

"Disgusting, I call it. It ought to be reported."

"Not by me," said Barkway. "They can rock the ship, for all I care."

Within the cabin, the vile scene developed swiftly.

"Now get this!" said Louis. He was sitting up, his naked brown chest gleaming in the lamplight. He suddenly seemed, to her, the very picture of masculine evil, and to himself, a god. "You'll pay me, and you'll pay good. For a start, give me the rest of that bankroll."

His grip tightened on her arm, twisting the flesh cruelly. She cried out: "You're hurting me! Stop it, Louis. You must have gone crazy! What do you want?"

"You heard me." He reached out, and snatched the money-clip from her hand. "I want this. As a starter. Call it the cover charge."

She stared at him, still disbelieving, unable to face the truth of the nightmare. "But if you need money—I don't mind—only don't talk like that."

"How else should I talk?" he asked brutally. "You want sweet talk? *You?* Don't make me laugh!" He looked down at the roll of bills. "How much is there here?"

"I don't know," she said. "I never—"

He twisted her thin arm again. Hurting her, he was at last hurting the cab-driver, hurting the world. "*How much?*"

"Oh, please! About five hundred dollars."

"You're worth more than that." He was beginning to enjoy himself, in a way which had never happened to him before. He brought his face closer to hers. "You wouldn't get everybody to agree, but *I* say you're worth more than that. Not at strip-tease, maybe, not like Miss America, but in other ways. . . . You want me to ring the bell, call that stewardess, let her see me like this?"

"No, no!" Shame and fear combined to render her powerless. "What do you want? I haven't any more money."

"Jewellery," he said. He had already appraised what she had, during the past fortnight; indeed, they had talked about it and admired it, like two old friends; he knew exactly what he would take. "The two bracelets. The clips. The sapphire earrings and the rubies. The big solitaire ring. You can keep that necklace. It's lousy!" And as a new horror dawned on her face, he said, with frightful menace: "Get them! Or by Christ I'll run out of here naked!"

"But my husband gave them to me," she said pitifully.

"I'll bet that's all he gave you. For years. Isn't that the truth?"

She covered her face with her free hand. "Oh God, how can you say things like that?" She was crying now; ridiculous tears coursed down her face, bringing ruin to the careful make-up. In a shaking voice she said: "You told me you loved me."

"Don't make me laugh!"

She had not heard him; she had retreated into a pathetic, belated world of school-girl commonsense.

"I always knew you were no good. . . . Your eyes are too close together. . . . Mother always said—"

"Mother!" He put such crude savagery into the word that she was forced to look up. "Mother! How old is mother, for Christ's sake?"

"My mother has passed on."

"By popular request." He rose swiftly from the bed, and stood over her, buttoning his shirt. The action itself had an obscene connotation; she had imagined sailors doing that, leaving a girl as soon as they had "finished," walking away with a rolling self-satisfaction. . . . "We're wasting time. Give me the jewellery. And if you ever breathe a word to anyone—"

"It's Mrs. Consolini," she said, still clinging to the rags of normality, to anything which would explain the unbelievable insult in compassionate terms. "I've seen her looking at you. . . . Don't deny it! She's been scheming to get you away from me. . . ."

He wanted to say: *You've got a point—she's next on the list,* but he resisted it. He had to keep up the pressure; he must not let her escape into any other world except the one they stood in now—the secret world of her cabin, the world she was terrified of letting anyone see.

"That's enough," he said, roughly. "I don't need any Mrs. Consolini to make me dump you. Work it out. . . . You want me to twist that arm again? You want me to shout for help? Give me the jewellery."

Her gray hair had fallen foolishly over her ravaged face, like a blurred old mask. She pushed it back, and said again: "But you told me you loved me."

"Are you nuts?" He poured into the question all the scorn he could muster; he knew it might be the last pressure he need apply. "Love you? Have you looked at yourself in the mirror lately? Do you know how old I am? Twenty-four. And you? Christ, you must be fifty!"

"I'm forty-one."

"Round the hips."

"Oh God!" she said again. Her tears were beginning to roll afresh; her sobs were like coarse hiccups, rending her whole body. "How can you say things like that? And age doesn't matter—you said so yourself."

"I said a lot of things that make me sweat to think of them. But I'm not saying them any longer. The late late movie's finished." He was ready to go now; the money was in his pocket, the jewellery case within a few feet of him. "You bought me," he said crudely, "and now you've got to pay. Christ, do you think I'd dance with you for anything except money? And a hell of a lot of it, too. Haven't you seen people laughing? Jesus, they think you're my mother—my *grand*mother! I should be in short pants! And you were aiming to go to bed with me!"

"I wasn't," she said. Her voice was shrill. "I never even thought—"

"You thought about it all the time. You're just a dirty old woman, that's all." He moved swiftly, towards the jewellery case; he plunged his hand in, and drew out what he wanted, piece by piece, while she watched him, horrified, powerless. The stones hardly had time to sparkle before they were dowsed for ever within his pocket. "I'm going now," he told her. "But if you ever breathe a word—"

He had come prepared. He drew out of his other pocket a knife, and flicked it open. Then he advanced the point towards her face, while she watched it, and the light gleaming on the blade, in absolute terror.

"Take a look at this," he said. "I can use it. I've often used it. If you say a word about this—a single word—to anyone—" he punctuated the sentences with twisting stabs, so that the knife seemed to be darting and snaking in and out of her flesh, "I'll come back and carve my name on your face. Your—ugly—old—face."

"Go away," she whispered. "Oh, go away. . . . Take anything—everything. Only go away."

"Now you're talking." The knife flicked shut, and disappeared into his pocket again. He straightened up. "But don't talk any more," he said. "Not to anyone." Then there was silence, and in the silence he was gone.

Left alone, in cruel isolation, in deadly fear still, she thought she was going to faint. She was trembling all over, and her face in the mirror was utterly distraught. Now she did look old. . . . But as her terror receded, it was not anger which was left, or the memory of peril. It was shame. It was scorned love. It was a desolate mourning for her last chance at the cherished might-have-been.

Presently she fell forward on the pillow, where his head had rested, where she could smell his young body, and, for the first time in her life, began to sob as if her heart would break.

chapter 5

THE lunch-time sessions in the Tapestry Bar were growing longer, as people shed the habits of home and developed a more casual approach to misbehaviour. The weather helped; it grew hotter, as they made their calls at Guadeloupe and Marie-Galante and Dominica; they achieved, as they drew south, a pirate thirst which could only be slaked by the long and potent drinks—rum punch, rum Collins—which seemed appropriate to this part of the world. The bar was always well-patronized by eleven o'clock; at noon, when Edgar closed the daily sweepstake and the figures for the day's run were telephoned down from the bridge, it was packed; and the pre-lunch gaiety often continued until two o'clock, at which time Edgar rang a small and discreet gong, and announced to the assembly: "Ladies and gentlemen—have a heart!"

For those few who, remaining prim, took their lunch at the normal hour, it was quite a sight to watch the entrance of these late-blooming gladiators into the dining-room. Some of the stewards ran a small sweepstake on the last one to arrive. Mrs. van Dooren was always a favourite runner.

In the bar, the talk was easy; clothes for the women, business prospects for the men; modest travellers' tales, and ship-board gossip on the same unchanging themes. They wondered how near Mr. Simms was to dying; they noted that his pretty nurse, Miss Bartlett, found time to charm the officers' table on most evenings; they reported some fresh atrocity on the part of Barry Greenfield; they confessed they didn't know how Mrs. van Dooren kept it up—or down. It was always a shame about Bernice Beddington, who really got more homely every day. It was always a disgrace about the Burrells—people said they weren't even married. It was always odd about the Tillotsons; no-one knew anything at all to say about them.

"I heard he's worth sixty million dollars," said Mr. Gerson, at one of these lunch-time sessions. Mr. Gerson was a great gossip; he enjoyed it, he could suck it out of his thumb if need be; and Diane, perched beside him on a stool at the long bar, found him useful. He was going to be useful in other ways too, as soon as he made up his mind to it. At the moment he had wife-trouble—which meant, in this area of endeavour, that Mrs. Gerson watched him like a hawk every waking hour of the day and night. It was only on occasions like this, when she was having her hair done and would miss lunch, that he managed a modest run of freedom. Diane had an idea that this time he was going to make the most of it.

"Sixty million?" repeated Diane, in awed tones. When money was mentioned, she always made her eyes go large; for sixty million dollars, she made them go very large indeed. "Gee—what does he *do* with it?"

Gerson watched her with great pleasure. He was four rum Collinses ahead, and hazily happy; he liked the shape of her, and the way her breasts touched the bar before anything else did, and the kissing mouth she made when she sucked on a straw. ("You want a piece of tail?" his friend Bancroft had asked him, very confidentially. "Go ahead and help yourself. She loves it!") He didn't believe Bancroft had had it, but he believed that he could himself, if he played it right.

"I don't know what Tillotson does," answered Gerson, "but I know what *I'd* do. Have a good time, that's what I'd do! Like they say, you can't take it with you. Isn't that the truth? Who wants to be the richest man in the grave-yard, for God's sake?"

"What's your idea of a good time?" asked Diane.

"Well, now. . . ." Their eyes locked momentarily as she turned on him a candid, inquiring glance, and he felt a stirring of the blood in his solid loins. It was true, this babe was hot. . . . Maybe Bancroft had been steering him right after all. . . . "Well, I'd live it up, that's what I'd do. Yes, sir! I'd get me a yacht—well, I've got a yacht, but I'd get a real big one, hundred feet, hundred-*fifty* feet, and I'd go around the world just having fun."

"That's for me," said Diane. "Just take me along, that's all!"

"You'd come?"

"Try and stop me!"

"It's a date." He signalled to Edgar, who came forward with a shaker to refill their glasses. "Yes, sir, that's what I'd do with sixty million dollars. Or six million, for that matter. I'd have fun!"

"You're so right," said Diane.

"They say Zucco's loaded too," said Gerson, momentarily brooding. He sipped his fresh drink. "All those guys in the film business, they make money like they printed it themselves. Course, he's a Jew, it's different. Mind you, I like Jews. Don't get me wrong. But they certainly know how to make a buck, and they certainly know how to hang on to it."

"I never could save money."

"You and me both."

Within their orbit of vision, Louis Scapelli came to the wide double-doors of the bar, glanced slowly round the room, and crossed with a smile to a small corner table at which Mrs. Consolini was already seated. By the way they fell into animated conversation, they were cordially glad to see each other.

"Isn't that your cousin?" asked Gerson, watching them.

"Yes."

"Seems to be consoling himself."

"How do you mean?" asked Diane warily.

"Well, there was a lot of talk about him giving the other old girl a whirl. You know, Mrs. Stewart-Bates. What happened to that one?"

"I don't know. *Was* he giving her a whirl?"

"You know darn well he was." But Gerson was smiling; he recognised family discretion at work, and approved of it. "He had her spinning six different ways at once. Now, bingo!—he's switched. What gives? You don't even see her around any more."

Diane decided it would be easier to play it at Gerson's level of comment.

"Lover's quarrel, maybe," she said, with a confederate grin. "You know how it is."

"I know how it is. Do you know how it is?"

"What do you think?"

"Lots of boy-friends, eh?"

"Oh, scads. That's why I'm taking a rest-cure. They just wore me out."

I'll bet, Gerson said to himself, thinking back to his friend Bancroft again. He looked down at her bosom; it was by far the easiest place to look, and it recalled once more a memorable conversation. "I tell you, she loves it!" Bancroft had said, encouraging him. "And you'll love it, too. No kidding, that babe can do more with her tits than you and I can do with a knife and fork!" "What's the angle, then?" he had asked. "No angle," Bancroft had answered. "She's like they say, an enthusiastic amateur. It's for free. *I* know." "In a pig's ear," he had scoffed, disbelieving on principle; and Bancroft, who sometimes affected a frightful travesty of an Irish accent, had answered; "That wasn't the place at all, at all!" and had choked with uproarious laughter. Then, more serious, he had added: "You gotta conscience, slip her five bucks."

It hadn't rung quite true when Bancroft told him about it—if she was all that good, why was Bancroft being such a pal, why was he spreading it around?—but now he was beginning to believe it. Sometimes they just had to have it, in triplicate; one guy couldn't keep up. . . . Anyhow, there was no harm in making a bit of time with her. She looked like the best bet in the ship, and the trip was damned dull otherwise.

He was ready to pursue the allusive topic of the boy-friends she had left behind, when there was a disturbance at one of the tables nearby, and they both turned their heads. It was, as usual, Mrs. van Dooren, insisting on her constitutional right to buy a round of drinks. Above the steady roar of conversation they caught the words: "Lunch? Don't be a radical! George! Set 'em up in the other alley!" Edgar snapped his fingers, and one of his aides hurried over.

"I don't know how she keeps it up," said Gerson. "Must have hollow legs."

"She's got pretty ones."

"You know, that's what I like about you!" he exclaimed. "Generosity! Most women, look at another woman's legs, they say 'Oof, take 'em away!' They can't stand competition. But you, you say straight out: 'She's got pretty legs.' I like that."

"Maybe I can stand competition," said Diane.

"Baby," said Gerson, "you never spoke a truer word." He leant over, slightly drunk, amorously happy. "I bet you can stand it all over. Know what I mean?"

But this was a little too raw for her. It was lunch-time; there were too many people around; at any moment his wife might duck out from under the hair-dryer, and come running. Diane looked away from him, as if preoccupied, and caught Edgar's eye; and Edgar, who had been watching and intermittently listening, and who recognized a situation when he saw one, moved across till he was opposite them.

"Can I interest you folks in tomorrow's pool?" he asked cheerfully. "We're still giving money away."

"You know it's just a racket," said Diane, smiling.

"Of course it is, madam," said Edgar. "Otherwise I wouldn't be in it, would I?"

"How much?" asked Gerson, straightening up. "As if I didn't know."

"To you, sir, one hundred dollars even."

"Put me down for two chances," said Gerson. He gestured towards Diane. "Her and me."

"No, please!" said Diane. "You mustn't do that."

"Forget it," said Gerson, suddenly a big spender. "We'll bring each other luck." He signed the chit which Edgar had passed over to him. "Whoever wins nine hundred bucks buys the other one a drink. Two drinks. O.K.?"

"It's O.K. by me. And thanks a million!"

"Forget it, baby. You deserve it." Edgar was still standing in front of them, and Gerson asked him: "Who won it today, anyway?"

"Mr. Bancroft, sir."

"Now wouldn't you know it! Jerry Bancroft! My pal! The lucky old crook!" Gerson looked behind him, at the room-full of compulsive hospitality. "Funny thing, I don't see him standing any drinks all round."

"I don't think he knows about it yet, sir."

"We'll tell him." He turned back to Diane. "Won't we? You know Jerry Bancroft, don't you?"

"Oh, sure."

"D'you like him?"

"He's O.K."

"He likes you," said Gerson, eying her. "How about another drink?"

"It's pretty near time for lunch."

"Just one more. Hey, Edgar!"

"You're getting me into bad habits."

"Give me time. . . ." He leant towards her again, gravely confidential; now he was looking down her bosom as if he were thinking of foreign policy, of life-insurance. "Are you planning to go ashore at Martinique?"

"When's Martinique? I've lost count."

"It's this evening."

Diane nodded. "Yes, I'll probably take a look round."

"How about with me?"

She considered, thinking fast, while Edgar put the two rum Collinses in front of them on their little decorative mats. This was the pass, all right, but it needed handling. She didn't want a brawl in public, and she didn't want the alternative—meeting Gerson under some street lamp in the dock area as soon as he could sneak off. Perhaps it was best to be frank, on the same sort of plane as he.

"How about your wife?"

He waved his hand airily. "Oh, she'll probably play bridge or something. She's not too sold on sight-seeing." He dropped his voice. "We could slip ashore, go to some joint, live it up a bit. How about that?"

"I think I'd like to. If you're sure it's all right."

"I'll make it all right." He raised his glass. "Be seeing you, baby. And save it for me."

The harbour-capital of Fort-de-France was all that a tourist could ask for. By day, its shabby buildings, multi-coloured in artistic shades of blue and pink and brown, had a Mediterranean tang; and by night, its sleazy air of disrepute, its cries and running feet, its smell of drains and ancient seaweed and rotting sugar-cane, all contributed to the authentic atmosphere of romance. When Jack Gerson and Diane

Loring, that unlikely pair whom fate (they freely agreed) had drawn together, set off on their tour of the city, they were able to feel that every step they took was a step into the mysterious unknown.

It was still oppressively hot, at nine o'clock in the evening; the easterly trade-winds brought no sea breezes, only the smells and the laden breath of the dark interior; the streets around the quayside, littered with refuse, policed by dogs, were not inviting. But there were still trees, and ambiguous shadows, and bougainvillaea in heavy bloom; and behind them, against the back-drop of the *Pointe des Negres*, the solid white bulk of the *Alcestis* remained constant. She was, if need be, their escape route from the hazards of foreign parts.

They were arm-in-arm; it seemed safer and, of course, nicer. There were still plenty of people about, mostly strollers doing nothing and beggars doing what they could. The talk in the streets was all French; but it was a transplanted French, guttural and opaque, the kind of French (as a Parisian would put it) spoken in a province one could never quite identify. But when they stopped at a street corner, it was to come upon an altercation which might have been transplanted direct from the Champs-Elysées.

A native taxi, rounding the corner, had misjudged the curve, and its front wheels had mounted the pavement by a foot or two. A dapper policeman, ebony black, advanced upon it, swinging his baton and then pointing it accusingly at the driver.

"*Que faites-vous sur le trottoir?*" he inquired roughly.

The taxi-driver spat, with great deliberation. "*J'attends votre soeur,*" he snarled, and drove off in triumph.

There was a roar of laughter, a concerted flash of white teeth, from everyone within earshot. The policeman retreated again to the centre of the cross-roads, with as good a face as he could muster.

"You've got to admit," said Gerson, "it's a hell of a romantic language." He squeezed Diane's arm; it seemed logical to do so. "I hadn't realized the Frogs ran this place."

"It's always been French," she answered. "Didn't you know Josephine was born here?"

He was puzzled. "What Josephine?"

"*The* Josephine. Napoleon."

"You mean, 'Not tonight, Josephine'?"

"Sure!"

"Well, what do you know!" exclaimed Gerson, marvelling. "In Martinique? I thought she was—hell, I don't know what I thought. Tell me some more."

"It was discovered by Columbus," said Diane. She was quoting from the "Tips for Travellers" column in the ship's daily newspaper, which Gerson clearly had not read that morning. "He thought it was America."

"He must have been nuts," said Gerson, looking round him.

"They had a volcano here," she went on. "Maybe they still have. It killed forty thousand people in nineteen hundred and two. In three minutes."

"Jesus! How do you know all this?"

"Oh, I know. . . ."

They had reached another cross-roads; there were lighted streets, and dark ones; the humid air stirred the trees slowly as it passed.

"Time we had a drink," said Gerson. "It's hotter than hell here. What do you say?"

"I'd like a drink."

"Let's find some lousy joint."

But joints of any kind were hard to find. They tried two hotels, but they were crowded with people from the *Alcestis*; at both of them, a sedate dance was in progress, the couples circling the room as if doomed to do so until Prince Charming cleft the forest and set them free. Then they found what they were looking for; a side-street bar with a deserted dance-floor, and a smoky atmosphere as thick as brown fog. The sign outside said: "Cafe Stork-Club"; and a printed card, on the table they were led to, announced: "Welcome, Alcestis Passengers! *Couvert*, 1000 Francs."

"Clip joint," said Gerson with a worldly air. "But they won't clip me." He hammered on the table. "Let's have a little service here!"

"But how did they know we were coming?" asked Diane.

"The boat probably calls here two-three times a year," answered

Gerson. "They just trot the signs out. Same for all the cruise boats. . . . Do you want something to eat, baby?"

"I wonder what they've got."

"Some native goo."

The head-waiter, dressed like Gerson in a white dinner-jacket and red tie, materialized at their elbow.

"Scotch and soda?" he asked. "Scotch on rocks? Scotch and Coca-Cola?"

"Rum," said Gerson. "And none of your home-made rot-gut stuff! Comprenny?"

"*Oui, monsieur,*" said the waiter.

"We're hungry," said Gerson. "How about that?"

"Hot dog," said the waiter. He was tall and well-built. "Hamburger with French fries. Ham and two eggs."

"Hell!" said Gerson. "We don't want that sort of crap! What would you like, honey?"

"I'd like something local."

Gerson looked up at the waiter. "Something local," he said. "Like —like fish *à la mode*. What have you got?"

"*Calalou,*" said the waiter.

"How's that again?"

"*Calalou,*" said the waiter. "Mixed vegetable puree with spices and special sauce."

"I guess it can't kill us," said Gerson. "Bring it on. Two double portions. And hurry up with that rum, for God's sake."

"*Oui, monsieur,*" said the waiter.

"You've got to keep up the pressure with these characters," explained Gerson when he was gone. "Otherwise they just fall down on the job." He pressed her hand. "Are you with me, honey?"

"I'm with you," said Diane.

The drinks arrived, and then the food; an enormous platter of unidentified roots and leaves and shoots, covered with a pink sauce of mysterious consistency. Gerson drank deep, talking all the while in a high-pitched, rather quarrelsome voice; he had been drinking steadily all evening, he had told a series of evasive untruths to his wife, and he was defiantly determined to enjoy his freedom. When he had taken a couple of spoons-full of the *calalou,* and masticated them thoroughly, he snapped his fingers, summoning the head-waiter again.

"What was that you called this?" he asked.

"*Calalou,*" answered the waiter.

"You can say that again. . . . D'you like it, honey?"

"Well yes, I do," answered Diane. She was hungry, and the unfamiliar dish was appetizing. "I'd hate to have to cook it, though."

"I'd hate to have to eat it," said Gerson. He looked up again. "Did you say ham and eggs?"

"Yes, sir."

"Bring 'em on. And I'll want a rain-check on half of this."

"Sir—" began the head-waiter.

"Don't argue!" barked Gerson. "It tastes like crap, and you know it. Pour it back down the can, and bring me a double-order of ham and eggs. And let's have some music. This joint is dead on its feet."

Presently an orchestra, of five young boys in tight black trousers and scarlet frilled shirts, filtered onto the stage and began to play. The music was unexpectedly moving; the two guitars, the singer, and the skin drummers presiding over an array of eight differently textured drums, combined to produce a melodious and haunting line. Under its influence, Gerson essayed a dance, though the rhythm was a tricky one, and he was inclined to stumble. The few other dancers, all coloured, made way for them with indulgent smiles. He held Diane in a rock-like grip, pushing his considerable bulk against her with exploring fervour; he hummed as best he could the intricate, off-beat tunes, and occasionally stroked her bare shoulder with a wandering hand.

"You enjoying yourself, honey?" he asked presently.

"Oh, yes," said Diane.

"Better than that old ship, eh?"

"Well, it's different."

"I told you I'd show you a good time." His grip tightened. "Come to Daddy, then. . . . Gee, honey, you feel good."

"Let's have a drink," said Diane after a couple of minutes.

"Whatsa matter—you aiming to tease me?"

Diane put her cheek against his for a moment. "I'll tease you good," she promised, alluringly, "when there aren't so many people around."

The remark put Gerson in a high good humour; when they returned to their table he ordered fresh drinks, and began to talk about the various techniques of drilling for off-shore oil. He fondled her hand throughout, and his knee kept up a steady pressure against her thigh. She might have been worried at the way the evening was going —he had really drunk an enormous amount since lunch-time, and he might turn sleepy and unambitious on the way home; but he seemed to have that occasional North American capacity for drinking endless shots of hard liquor without reacting at all. The row he was doubtless going to have over the bill should wake him up, anyway. She maintained, throughout, a reasonable return pressure on her thigh, and an unwinking expression of interest.

"Now down at Galveston, Texas," said Gerson, "they've got a rig that's a real honey." Then he broke off, and said, grinning: "What the hell—let's talk about something else." He snapped his fingers, and the head-waiter crossed the dance-floor towards him. It was past midnight, and there was now only one other couple in the room.

"Let's have a refill," said Gerson. "When's the floor-show going to start?"

"Sir," said the head-waiter, "we have no floor-show tonight unfortunately."

"It says cabaret outside."

"That is for Saturdays only."

Gerson stabbed with his thumb at the 'Welcome Alcestis Passengers!' notice on their table. "*Couvert* is cover charge, isn't it? What do we get for the cover charge? Knives and forks?"

"That is to pay for the orchestra, sir."

"*And* the floor-show. Come on, you're not dealing with peasants, you know. Give!"

"We might arrange something," conceded the head-waiter. "A

specialty. Just for you and madame. Would you enjoy limbo?"

"We just ate that," said Gerson.

"No, sir, that was *calalou*. This is the limbo dancer. She bends backwards until she passes under a bar not more than sixty centimetres from the ground."

"This I'd like to see."

"It will cost two thousand francs," said the head-waiter.

"Now what the hell—" began Gerson, and then paused. "Say, how much is that in money?"

"About four dollars, sir."

"It's a deal," said Gerson. And as the head-waiter retreated, he added: "Private cabaret, eh? Jack Gerson, the Big-Time Charlie. That's me!"

The orchestra started up again, a sinuous tune with an insistent beat and a crescendo rhythm. A long thin strip of wood, and two uprights, like a high-jump apparatus, were placed on the dance-floor, and after a moment a tall girl, almost naked, appeared and took up a position in front of it, swinging her body in time to the music. Though she was painfully thin, she was still beautiful—a ravishing *sangmêlée*, her skin the colour of cloudy white Burgundy. The music quickened in tempo; she began to bend backwards, weaving her arms, and to edge forward towards the strip of wood which was not more than eighteen inches from the ground. In time with the music, she sank lower and lower, insinuating first her knees, then her thighs, then her pelvis under the bar. There was a wavering interval when it seemed impossible that she could bend backwards far enough to allow her breasts to pass under it. But at the last moment, with the music reaching a jungle flurry of uproar, she wriggled quickly, and passed through, and then sprang high in the air with a scream of triumph. She looked exhausted, and her whole body was bathed in sweat.

"Jesus!" said Gerson. "I'd hate to tangle with that babe." But he was plainly impressed; the girl coming towards him with her thighs spread and her back impossibly arched had started an inevitable train of thought. He clapped loudly, and the girl, walking away, turned her head and gave him a brief smile.

"Must be double-jointed," said Gerson, "just where it counts most." He squeezed Diane's shoulder, and let his hand remain where it was. "Could you do that, baby?"

"I could try," she said. "But I doubt it. I just can't bend that way."

He looked at her appraisingly, his eyes roving freely. "I'll bet you could, at that. Well, what do we do now? It looks like we've closed this joint."

"Go back on board, I suppose."

"And?"

"Oh, we'll take it from there."

"You said something about teasing—remember?"

"I haven't forgotten."

"How are we going to make it?"

He was far from drunk, she decided; he was sweating freely, and his eyes looked like small boiled onions, but there was a quality of insistence about him which alcohol had not affected. So much the better. . . .

"We'll organize something," she reassured him. "You can always come and have a drink in my cabin."

"That's my girl!" With a snap of his fingers he summoned the waiter, and told him: "Let's have the bill. And keep it good and low, or I won't pay."

But he was in great spirits now, and the bill, though high, was not outrageous. He had a shot at adding it up, but this proved too difficult; it seemed to be all noughts, arranged in different columns. To the waiter he said:

"You take American Express credit cards?"

"No, sir," said the waiter, and added, surprisingly: "Only Diners' Club."

"No kidding?" Gerson looked round the tawdry twilight of the room, now completely deserted. "They must have a better list than I figured." He flipped out a travellers' check for a hundred dollars, and signed his name with a flourish. "Here—take it out of this."

The waiter went in search of change. "Never carry any cash around," said Gerson. "You never know when you'll get rolled." He looked at her. "I won't need any more money tonight, will I? Or will I?"

They had reached the stage when she could play along with that one. "For you, I'll make a special price," she answered. "Nothing."

His bellow of laughter was enough to stir the curtains. "Well, the price is right, anyway!" He dropped his hand, till it lay like a clamp made of raw steak on her thigh. "Come on, baby, let's get the show on the road."

"Well, that was nice," said Diane. And indeed, it had been; Gerson was overweight, and far from prepossessing to look at, but he had a bull-like quality of determination which was a good substitute for virility. The way that most American men made love—as if they had to prove something to the on-lookers—had in this case worked out well. In fact, it was really going to be a pity to spoil it.

They were lying side by side in the darkened cabin, smoking, staring at the ceiling; Gerson had another drink ready to hand, but he was not giving it much attention. Already he was drowsy; the mystic communion was over; only a show-off or an Italian lover-boy would make a three-act drama out of it by going on talking.

"You were terrific, kid," he said. He patted her flank fondly. "Great talent there. . . ." Then he yawned cavernously, and his eyes blinked and closed. "Remind me to give you a reference," he mumbled. "With five asterisks against it."

His voice tailed off. Presently a slight snore indicated that he was resting from his exertions.

Diane waited a long ten minutes, while Gerson gradually relaxed his position and his head fell sideways on the pillow. His snores deepened as his mouth fell open. Then she eased herself gently off the bed, threw on a robe, and crossed to the chair where he had piled his clothes.

She had noted that he kept his wallet in the inside pocket of his dinner-jacket. She pulled it out swiftly, and after a backward glance went to the dressing-table and emptied out the contents. There were a few loose bills—about sixty dollars' worth; a book of travellers' checks, a photograph of Mrs. Gerson, looking happy at a night-club table; another photograph of a blonde in a bikini, signed (or perhaps captioned) 'Prudence'; and a separate booklet with an enormous array of club cards. He seemed to have everything to which the upright citizen could attain; American Express, Hilton Carte Blanche, gasoline credit cards (Shell, Esso and Fina), Rotarians, Kiwanis, two hotels in Chicago, Hertz-Rentacar, International Air Travel card, driver's license and insurance identification certificate.

Gerson's snores continued unabated as she went back to the folder of travellers' checks. It was a thick one; it contained four checks for five hundred dollars each, eighteen for one hundred, and some smaller ones. The total was considerably more than four thousand dollars.

She weighed them in her hand. Ever since his remark in the night-club: "I never carry any cash around," she had been thinking of this particular problem, and had worked out what seemed the best way of dealing with it. Now she took the bills, and put them in her purse; then she tore off two of the five-hundred-dollar checks, and laid them on the dressing-table; and then she closed the folder, and opening a drawer stuffed it far out of sight under a thick pile of clothes. That was to be her weapon, her ace-in-the-hole; if it didn't work, it couldn't be helped. At least she was sixty bucks to the good.

After replacing the wallet, and then the coat, she looked at her watch. It was nearly two o'clock; save for the far-off hum of a generator, and the hissing of the ventilator ducts, all sounds had ceased. Ashore, when she drew aside the small curtain and looked out of the porthole, the lights of Fort-de-France were dim under the strong moonlight. There was a black, tossing crest of a hill against the pale sky, which looked like a huge breaking wave. It was beautiful—but it would still be beautiful tomorrow. She turned away, nervously strained, her heart thudding, and approached the bed. Now.

Gerson lay like a fat and ugly baby, his head turned away from the shaded lamp, his mouth bubbling gently with successive snores. She reached down and shook his arm.

"Hey," she said softly. "Wake up. Time to go."

He was only lightly asleep, and he came to the surface within a few moments. Blinking, he sat up, and put his feet down on the floor; then he grimaced as he tasted his mouth, and took a deep swallow from the glass on the bedside table.

"Hi, baby," he said. "I must have dozed off. What time is it?"

"After two."

"Jesus! My wife will give me hell if she hears me come in."

He dressed in swift plunges; when he came to draw on his coat she watched him warily, but beyond patting his wallet with an automatic gesture he made no further check. Then, when he was ready, and she was wondering what form of words to use to start the pressure, he looked down at her.

"Thanks, honey," he said. It was no more than the set form, but at least he said it. "You were sensational. . . . Look, are you short of money or anything?"

"Well," said Diane.

He gestured, dismissively. "Don't give it a thought. I know the way things are." He put his hand to his inside pocket, and drew out his wallet. Diane looked away, for delicacy's sake. She could guess, to within very narrow limits, what his next words would be.

"Well, hell!" he exclaimed, half-way between puzzlement and anger. "What's gone wrong? I had sixty bucks, and a whole raft of—"

After a long pause, she said: "Travellers' checks?"

"That's right." He had got nothing from her voice so far. "You saw them, didn't you?"

"I saw them all right," said Diane.

"They're gone!" he exclaimed, now thoroughly roused. "Some-one in that lousy clip-joint must have—" He was looking round him excitedly, and his glance happened to fall on the dressing-table. The two five-hundred-dollar checks were lying not more than two feet from him. "Well, what the hell!" he said. "Those are mine. Are you trying to be funny?"

She shook her head. "No," she answered. It was easy to harden her voice, now that the moment was here. "No, I'm not trying to do that."

He picked up the two checks and examined them, more uncomprehendingly than ever. Then he looked across at her, his eyes narrowing. "Did you tear these out?"

"Yes. I thought you'd like to have them ready."

"Ready? What the hell do you mean, ready?"

"They're for me," she said.

"A thousand bucks? You must be nuts? I was going to give you— And where are the others, the rest of the book?"

"I have them safe."

He drew in his breath, and came a step towards her. "What the hell are you talking about? Quit fooling around! What *is* this?"

"If you shout," she said, "some-one will hear you." She gestured towards herself, naked under the thin robe. "Bad public relations."

He had caught on now. He looked from her to the two checks, and back again. Then he nodded, several times.

"I get the picture. This is a straight squeeze."

As she nodded in turn, she wondered if he would lose his head, like Bancroft; or turn rough, and use force; or try to call her bluff; or walk out, and chance the whole thing. But he was tougher than Bancroft, or more resourceful, though he had only the same number of cards in his hands.

He did not waste any time; there was no nonsense about love betrayed, no surprise at the crude trickery.

"A thousand is too much," he said crisply. "I'll make it a hundred, if you're that short."

"I'm that short," she said, "and it's a thousand."

He flicked the checks with his fingers. "These are no damn good to you. You know that. They have to be signed. And how would I get the cash at this time of night, anyway?"

"Tomorrow will do," she said indifferently.

His face brightened. "You mean, I take them away?"

"Yes. And you bring the cash tomorrow morning. And I give you back the other checks."

"Oh. . . ." He considered. Then he said: "I'll see you in hell first!"

"All right." Her pose of indifference was easier now; she knew that, tougher than Bancroft, he was also quicker to size up a situation. "Then I'll go to your wife. And I'll call my uncle as well."

"Nuts! Who's going to believe you? It's your word against mine."

"I have the checks," she answered. "Three thousand dollars' worth."

"What the hell is the good of them? Be your age! You know I can send a cable tomorrow morning, and have the whole lot cancelled. I just say I lost them."

"But I have them."

"So?" His voice, however, was unsure; he was getting more and more of the picture every moment; his mind had almost caught up with hers.

"How did I get them?" asked Diane. "You want me to go to your wife and say, 'I found these in my bed after your husband had gone'? Or show them to the Captain, to prove you were here? He'd put you off the ship at the next stop!"

Gerson came a step nearer. "O.K.—where are they?" he asked roughly.

"I told you, they're safe." She looked up at him, meeting his eyes without wavering. "You try and find them, and I'll start screaming."

"There's no-one around at this time of night."

"My uncle's just across the passage."

"Is he in on this?" he asked bitterly.

"Not yet."

He swallowed; so intense was the prickling silence in the cabin that she could actually hear it. "You can't prove a thing," he told her. But it was himself he was telling, and failing to convince. "I came in here for a drink. You started throwing it at me. Don't forget, *you've* got your pants off. I haven't."

"Is your wife going to believe that?"

That was the moment when he began to swear, and equally the moment when she knew she had won. She hardly heard the torrent of obscenity which he seemed able to rip off as if he were tearing successive pages from a book; indeed, it was like background music, unheard by the inner ear, which was busy with other things. When his voice petered out, and he remained standing in furious, sweating silence, she said:

"Feeling better? Don't take it too hard, sonny. The price was a bit high, that's all."

"A thousand—dollars!"

"That's a perfect description. . . . Don't come too early in the morning. I like my sleep."

"You can sleep. I'll be thinking—but good! You won't get away with this!"

At eleven o'clock next morning, however, Gerson was in quite a different mood. It might have been a hangover, or a rueful sense of humour strong enough to survive the loss of a thousand dollars; it might even have been that she had gauged the amount accurately—she had not been too greedy, a thousand dollars was just not enough to make him drop everything and run screaming for the cops. But whatever it was, when they met out on the boat-deck there were no more reproaches. He handed her a roll of hundred-dollar bills; she produced the rest of the travellers' checks and passed them over; and that seemed to be that. When he looked at her, his glance was almost admiring.

"That was the most expensive lay I ever had," he said. "Hell, it cost more than getting married!"

"Worth it?"

"Jesus, no! Nothing's worth that kind of money."

"Too bad. I thought we might do business."

"Not at those prices." He was staring seawards, where the morning sun on the water made a clean, dancing sheen. "I've been doing some figuring. You pulled this on Jerry Bancroft, didn't you?"

There seemed no harm in telling him. "Yes."

He slapped his thigh. "I knew it! The crooked bastard! I thought there was something phoney when he was talking. How much did you take him for?"

"The same."

"A thousand bucks?"

"Yes." Even here, she would not confess to that extra thousand; it was her own triumphant secret.

"Do me a favour," he said, after a moment. "Give me back five dollars."

She stared. "Now why?"

"So that I come out better than him."

He was laughing, and after a moment she joined in. "It's a deal." He had forgotten about the sixty dollars in cash, and she wasn't going to remind him. She opened her bag again, found a five-dollar bill, and gave it him. "Your change, sir."

"That Bancroft," he said, pocketing it. "He's not so smart after all. Only cost me nine-hundred-ninety-five. Now he was *really* gypped."

chapter 6

THE evening's poker session was to be in Carl Wenstrom's suite, and there, punctually at nine o'clock, the five other players assembled. Carl welcomed them like old friends—which, indeed, they were; they were now bound by the ties implicit in the prolonged ebb-and-flow of this battlefield. Tillotson was one; the biggest winner after Carl, a tough and aggressive player with that necessary sense of humour which went with successful bluffing. Burrell was another, a Canadian, married to a French-Canadian wife whose theatrical mannerisms, curious accent, and insistence that she was a Parisienne born-and-bred, had drawn to herself a good deal of unflattering attention. He was very rich, and (among Americans) curiously sensitive, as if he went in fear of being unmasked as only a Canadian after all.

Mr. Beddington was another contestant, cautious, speechless from one hour's end to another; and Mr. Greenfield—'the father of the brat,' as Carl called him—who purged his guilt by generous over-calling, was another. The last member was a rash and cheerful man by the name of Hartmann, a New York advertising executive who, judging by some of his plays, was under-writing the whole thing on his expense account.

They were punctual, as serious poker-players always were; and they refused after-dinner brandy or liqueurs, according to the same tradition. Kathy, performing briefly as hostess before they settled down, had little to do save to pour coffee for all of them. When offered drinks, they all said, with scarcely any variation: "Not now, thanks. Got to concentrate."

"Concentrate?" repeated Carl, picking up the word as Hartmann used it. "What's this? You mean you're going to take the game seriously?"

"It's about time I did," said Hartmann, who started each session full of cheer and ended up in impenetrable mourning. "Gosh, d'you know how much I'm down on the past month?"

"How much?" asked Burrell, who was satisfied—and, indeed proud—to have broken even on the twenty-two games they had played so far.

"Eight thousand dollars, that's all," said Hartmann. He looked round him for sympathy. But at this stage, just before the game, he was never sad about his losses; he knew for certain that the balance would be redressed by the time they broke up. "If I told them back in N'York what you characters here were doing to me, they'd say to have my head examined."

"Maybe they'd be right," said Mr. Greenfield, another big loser. "And maybe I'll join you, if things go on like this."

Tillotson, who was sitting at the green baize table counting out chips, looked up momentarily.

"The trouble with you," he said to Hartmann, "is that you will come in on every hand."

"But I like playing," said Hartmann.

"Oh, I'm not complaining," said Tillotson. "It's nice to have you along. But I just thought I'd mention it."

They came to the table as soon as they had finished their coffee; before each player, when Tillotson had completed the allotment, were four stacks of red, yellow, blue, and green chips representing two thousand dollars. Carl broke open a pack of fresh cards, took out the jokers, and began to shuffle them. Cigars were lighted, chairs were drawn up; Kathy placed an ashtray beside each of them. It was the marginal moment before battle was joined, and Carl, feeling the cards slide beneath his fingers, was deeply contented. There was no moment in the world like this; the shining chips stacked, the score-card clean, the cards ready to be cut, the players hopeful and eager. Probably, apart from the game, he would not speak twenty words during the next four or five hours; Tillotson was the same sort of player as he, absolutely still, absolutely concentrated; the others would do the talking, in more or less degree, but for these two, poker was like a flag hoisted, a gage thrown down.

Kathy, standing behind Carl, asked: "Anything else I can do for you?"

"No, thank you," answered Carl. He smiled at her over his shoulder. "I think we have everything."

She gestured towards the loaded side-table. "Drinks," she indicated. "Ice—soda-water—cigarettes . . . And there's lots of coffee left. I ordered sandwiches for eleven o'clock. Barkway's off now, but there's a night-steward."

"Thank you, my dear girl."

"I'll say goodnight, then."

"How are you going to spend your evening?" asked Tillotson politely.

"Oh, I'll look at the view, and then go to bed. We're passing St. Lucia some time during the night, but I expect I'll be asleep."

She nodded to each of them in turn, and as they half-rose, she bent and kissed Carl. "Goodnight," she said. "And good luck, if I'm allowed to say that." Then she turned, and was gone.

"A beautiful girl, that," said Tillotson, on the correct note of diffidence.

"Very like her mother," said Carl. He sighed; with practise, it was not difficult to do so. "She has been a very great comfort to me."

Tillotson took the cards from Carl. and spread them fanwise on the table, with an expert flick of the back of his hand. "Draw for it," he said, his voice already changing to a curt, controlled competence. "Ace high, high deals."

It was one o'clock, and then two; while the *Alcestis* threshed on through the calm night, and the ship's interior noise receded all round them, their game continued. But as usual, with the passing hours its outlines had become blurred. The men who talked were talking more, the ones who drank had drunk too much; the heavy losers had relapsed into their customary depressed silence. Carl was a small winner again, and Tillotson a large one; Beddington, that silent, cautious man, was about even, and Burrell a little down. Hartmann, the irrepressible, had eight hundred dollars against him on the books, and Greenfield, who had held terrible cards all evening, and had drunk too much anyway, was nearly two thousand behind. It was very much like the pattern of many other games; the true players came to the top, the amateurs stayed in the ruck, and those without the gift of concentration sank inevitably into the mud.

At half-past two, Carl looked at his watch. "Gentlemen," he said, "speaking as a winner, and also as the host, I suggest we have the last rounds fairly soon."

"Suits me," said Burrell. He had had a nervous evening, with one good run and one bad one; he didn't expect to win now, he was ready to cut his small losses and call it a day.

Tillotson nodded, without saying anything. Part of the pleasure of playing with him was his unfailing good manners. As the big winner, he could not appear eager to quit; but half-past two was late, past their usual break-up time.

Greenfield was at the side-table, helping himself to another whisky-and-soda. "Might as well be drunk as be the way I am," he said slurringly. "Make it last rounds if you like. They'll have to be damn good to pull me out."

Hartmann said: "O.K. by me," and Beddington, lighting his pipe, grunted vaguely.

"All right," said Carl. "One round of dealer's choice, and one jack-pot."

When the deal came to him, he looked round the table again. "What's it to be?"

As usual, when invited, they all named their favourites.

"Straight draw poker," said Tillotson.

"Aces wild."

"Seven card stud."

"Misere."

"High-low."

Carl laughed. He was relaxed now; the game was nearly over, it had gone well enough for him, nothing much could happen at this stage.

"Thanks for the help," he said. He looked up at Greenfield, still the main casualty. "You choose," he said. "I think you've earned it."

"Jack-pot," answered Greenfield. He had won a big pot, three or four hours ago; he wanted to return to that golden age.

"But we're going to have one in a minute, anyway," objected Hartmann.

"I'd like one now," said Greenfield obstinately.

"Jack-pot," said Carl, and began to deal.

No one opened the first time, nor the second, nor the third; the pot, 'sweetened' every time with ten dollars from each of them, was worth over two hundred by the time it came to the fourth deal. But on that round, Carl found that he had given himself a pair of aces and a pair of eights—good enough to open with, by a long way. He was, however, forestalled.

"It's loose," said Hartmann, who was sitting on his left, promptly. "For half the pot—say, a hundred and twenty dollars."

There was the usual silence. After a moment, the next player, Burrell, said "Too expensive," and threw his hand in. Then Greenfield, squinting at his cards, said: "I'll come to that party," and began somewhat uncertainly to count out one hundred and twenty dollars.

It was Tillotson's turn. He would not join in unless he had something worth while, thought Carl; he might be a couple of thousand ahead, but he would never throw any of it away, neither early nor late in the game.

Tillotson said: "Double."

Two-hundred-and-forty dollars, thought Carl, to win a pool worth about the same amount. Tillotson must be good, he must be certain he was better than Hartmann the opener. Two pairs, maybe. Even threes.

Beddington, the fifth player, shook his head mournfully. "Not at those fancy prices," he said, and tossed his cards into the centre.

That left Carl himself. His two pairs, ace high, were good, probably better than Hartmann's hand. Greenfield might have anything; he was fiddling with his cards, rearranging them; it usually meant that he had a broken hand—four to a straight, four to a flush. Tillotson's call was confident. But it might be a bluff to knock out Hartmann, who, as a biggish loser, was inclined to run scared at such times.

"Two-hundred-and-forty dollars," agreed Carl, and pushed the the chips forward.

"You can't frighten the opener," said Hartmann. "Two-hundred-forty it is."

Out of the blue, almost sulkily, Greenfield said: "Double again."

Tillotson looked at him quickly, as did Carl. The call of course was nonsensical; if his hand was as good as that, Greenfield should have doubled on the first time round. But he was drunk, they all knew; he might have mistaken his hand at the first glance, and then, at a closer look, found he had something better. He was not likely to be bluffing; he never bluffed unless he was well ahead of the game. Carl placed him with two very good pairs, or else a pat hand. A straight.

Tillotson's thinking had obviously been on the same lines, but he was still confident. "Expensive," he murmured. "But not too expensive. I'm in for four-eighty."

It was Carl's turn again. It was indeed an expensive hand to join in; his two pairs, ace high, seemed to have shrunk in stature since he first sighted them. With Tillotson in, at such a big price, it meant that there would be serious competition. But two aces and two eights had a ring of gold about them. . . . He nodded. "All right. In."

Hartmann was now having serious second thoughts. He was frowning, looking from one player to another. Then he began to tap his cards on the table irritably. It was a sure sign, Carl knew, that he was going to fold.

"I'll show my openers," said Hartmann after a moment. "This is too rich for my blood."

Carl said: "Three players in, for four-hundred-and-eighty dollars." And then, to Greenfield: "Cards?"

"I'll play these," said Greenfield.

A pat hand, thought Carl again; not a bluff—he wasn't that kind of a player, and particularly not at three o'clock in the morning. A flush or a straight, which had at last swum into his uncertain ken. . . . His eyes went round in turn to Tillotson, sitting opposite him.

"Two cards," said Tillotson.

Carl said: "I believe you," and dealt him the cards. It was as he had expected; Tillotson, sitting on top of the opener, had come in with three of a kind.

It was now his own turn. He looked down at his two aces and two eights; there was of course only one thing to do—throw away the odd card, and draw one. Then he noticed something. Two of the cards which Beddington had thrown in at the first round had been flipped over, face up, when Hartman discarded his hand. They were both eights.

He looked away again, thinking very hard. The exposure was an enormous piece of luck, both good and bad. It meant that he could not improve his eights; he could only improve his aces. But equally, he now knew that if he drew one card, it gave him only one chance of improvement; if he drew three, it gave him three. Two pairs was not going to be any good against Tillotson's probable three-of-a-kind, nor Greenfield's pat hand, whatever that was. The eights, face up on on the table, were telling him to take a chance—the only chance.

He picked out his pair of aces, and discarded the three other cards. Then he said, formally: "Dealer takes three."

Tillotson raised his eyebrows at the draw. "Brave man," he said.

Carl smiled, and took the next three cards from the top of the pack. Tillotson was watching him, as usual, while he made his draw. He squeezed the cards gently, fanning them out, his face expressionless.

He found that he had dealt himself two more aces.

With no more than a moment's pause, he looked at Greenfield, and said: "It's you to speak. From four-hundred-and-eighty dollars."

But this was not Greenfield's day at all. Just as he opened his mouth to bet, he took a last look at his cards, for reassurance. His jaw dropped like a plummet, and an incredulous look came over his face.

"Jesus God!" he said. "I made a mistake."

Tillotson turned to him, courteously, not mocking his ineptitude; as usual, he was a delightful player to share a table with. "Not betting?"

Greenfield's owlish face was ludicrous in its dismay. "I thought that last card was a heart, God damn it!" he said. "It's a diamond."

"Bad luck," said Carl. With four aces, and a pot now worth nearly fifteen hundred dollars to the winner, he really did feel, benevolently, that it was bad luck. His eyes went round to Tillotson, his traditional adversary whom he respected. "You and me," he said.

Tillotson answered, without hesitation: "I will tempt you. Double."

Burrell drew in his breath. "Hell!" he exclaimed, impressed. "That's nine-hundred-and-sixty dollars."

"You have tempted me," said Carl to Tillotson, greatly at ease with the world. "I'll make it a nice round figure. Nineteen hundred dollars."

There was a silence of extraordinary intensity all round the table. This was the biggest betting they had had so far; it was clear that Carl and Tillotson, who seldom bumped into each other in any serious sense, had now met head on. At so high a figure, it was unlikely that either of them was bluffing; it meant that good cards were meeting good cards—the most expensive kind of collision in the world.

Tillotson put down his cigar, with great care. "Now that's very interesting," he said. He was being much more talkative than usual, Carl noted, even at the end of a winning evening; it meant, probably, that he was confident, that he had a tremendous hand—possibly fours also. It did not matter; his own aces were unbeatable. "You took three cards," Tillotson went on, amiably. "I took two. You must have improved. I surely hope so, for your sake. Double again!"

At the end of the normal, slow-spoken sentences, the last two words came out with enormous force, like the crack of a whip. But to Carl, they were musical; they would have been musical if they had been pistol shots. He said, keeping his voice as controlled as possible:

"And once more. Seven thousand two hundred dollars."

Tillotson's face was without expression. He did not look at his cards; he looked straight at Carl. There was silence for the space of fifteen seconds, while he weighed the probabilities concealed within this perilous maze—the trap against the bluff, the very good cards against the fractionally better. He then proved what an excellent player he was by saying, with no concession to histrionics: "No. I fold."

He threw in his hand, face down, and began to count out thirty-six hundred dollars. The others broke the silence like schoolboys. Hartmann said: "Gee! If that was a bluff . . ." and Burrell said: "That's the biggest hand we've ever had—even without the last bet." Greenfield levered himself up, and wandered to the side-table again, muttering: "Now why doesn't that happen to me?" as if he would naturally assume the role of Carl and not Tillotson. Only the two principal players remained silent, until Tillotson had pushed nearly all his chips into the centre, and Carl had raked in the total—over five thousand. Then Tillotson, as if to himself, said: "I think I was right."

Neither of them would have dreamed of asking the other what cards he had held; and no-one else in the room, drunk or sober, would have asked either. But Carl, for five thousand dollars, felt able to answer, without loss of principle:

"Very likely."

By the time they were gone, it was near dawn; the faintest possible lightening of the sky outside the porthole proclaimed the advancing day. Carl, sitting in an armchair after saying the customary slow good-nights to his guests, surveyed the abandoned room. The after-the-party wreckage was familiar, and by no means unpleasant.

Cards were strewn all over the table; clusters of coloured chips mingled with them, spangling the green cloth like Christmas-tree decorations. The ashtrays overflowed with cigar-butts, the used glasses had a raffish air of neglect. On the side-table, half empty bottles of gin and whisky and brandy stood among a phalanx of club-sodas. On the carpet below it, a frieze of bottle-tops lay like confetti. Coffee cups, stale sandwiches, crumpled napkins, told of the half-way refreshment which had kept the laggards going. There was a chair overturned—that was Greenfield, rising to stumble back to his cabin at the end of the game. Opposite Carl's place on the table was the score-card with its neatly balanced columns, and three checks totalling $5400, his triumphant share of the evening.

He would have enjoyed what he saw, whether he had lost or won; the room, with its air of Regency dissipation centered on the green baize table, conjured up agreeable pictures of noble and desperate conduct, dawn duels, ruined heirs. The drifting smoke was like the smoke over a battlefield, long in dispersal, marking great events, historic collisions.

He smiled at the thought. It was not like that at all; it was like the smoke after a party, and a wonderful party too. He stood up, and crossed stiffly to the porthole, and opened it after a struggle with the unwieldy clasps. A fresh breeze met him, and the steady hiss and roar of sea-water tumbling past a few dozen feet below him. The light was gaining now, a pale pearly glow spreading over the sea towards him. But there was a harder outline hidden within it, and presently he saw that it was land. They were coasting past an island.

He watched it take shape, emerging out of the mist and the vagueness of the dawn like a new character altogether. It must be St. Lucia, the island that Kathy had mentioned, and it was not more than a few miles off. It was only an outline, but an outline of perfect shape, rising past formidable cliffs to a tall peak in the centre. There were two lighthouses at either end, still competing with the dawn, and in between them a few straggling lights, seeming to climb the hills from the sea until their strength gave out. The water between him and this revealed paragon of landfalls was faintly ruffled by the dawn breeze, and its colour was turning to a smoky pink as he watched it.

He remained by the porthole for a long time, with a luxuriant sense of blessing; the view seemed to prove that the world was good, that God was generous this morning, after a night in which men also had done more than their fair share for him. Then he sat down again, in the only uncluttered chair, with a final whisky-and-soda and positively the last cigar of the night, and relaxed in deep contentment. After six hours of the utmost concentration, it was good to dream, to let slip the mask and reveal the liberal face.

Kathy must be long asleep by now, he thought; and of his other problem children, only Diane was possibly still awake. She had done well with Gerson, and she had shown herself very ready to pursue the same sort of effort, with other candidates. Indeed, rising from the dinner-table that same evening, she had said, carelessly confident:

"I feel good tonight. I think I'll knock off Zucco."

The dauntless vulgarity of the remark had amused him when it was made; at this later hour, he only hoped that it had come true, without complication. But he did not want to consider the topic now; he only wished to savour the peace and contentment he had won. He drew on his cigar, and looked at the checks on the table. He saw once again Tillotson's face as he had first sniffed danger, and then backed away from it, his head lowered like a wary bull. Delicious moment. . . .

Now it was after four o'clock, and his face in the dawn light was stiff and tired. Perhaps he was getting old. But what pleasures still came his way!

chapter 7

ZUCCO was a breeze, a pushover, thought Diane; he knew all about the Hollywood meat-market, but he wasn't used to it getting up and biting him in the wallet. The total operation took less than forty-eight hours, and the whole thing, as far as she was concerned, boiled down to two scenes, like in one of his lousy films.

Scene One was ashore at Barbados. Pretty colours, kind of picturesque, but a dump, old-fashioned as hell. Policemen dolled up like from Gilbert and Sullivan. A daylight session up the coast, where the attraction was billed as a Planters' Lunch. ("These are planters?" asked Walham suspiciously. "But how do we *know?*") A band knocking themselves into a coma, beating the hell out of two rows of oil drums. Then a night-club where they fried the lobster in coconut oil and even gypped you in the loo.

First, Zucco mournful, saying: "Tell you a funny story about an electric guitar. We lost a good musician that way. Bought himself a cheap guitar. Too cheap. First rehearsal, he plugged it in, gave one plonk!, and fell stone-dead into the orchestra pit. Faulty wiring. Studio couldn't figure out whether it came under the Musicians' Union or the Seal of Good Housekeeping."

Then Zucco warming up, giving the slip to his wife, saying: "Sure I'll get you a film-test, any time. I'm like *that* with Walter Warner."

Then Zucco happy in his work at last, saying: "You're stacked, kiddo. Beautiful music!"

Scene Two was Came the Dawn, or near enough to it, in Cabin A 15.

Zucco distraught, saying: "But I told you, I'll get you a film-test, I can make you a big star! I have lunch with Genghis Cohen every day!"

Zucco weakening, saying: "Hell, they don't pay those prices in Bel Air on Christmas Eve!"

Zucco in the death-throes, saying: "Christ, if I O.K.'d a script like this, they'd have me strapped to the couch!"

Zucco flouncing out, saying: "Next time I see you, remind me to tell you to drop dead!"

Cut to hands counting ten-dollar bills, and Dissolve.

Down the corridor, listening to retreating footsteps, Barkway the steward picked his teeth reflectively. Then he shook his head.

"Stamina!" he said, to the duty-stewardess. "Say what you like, you've got to admire it."

chapter 8

AT Grenada, most beautiful of islands, they viewed a volcanic lake, and Mr. Cutler the purser stocked up on fresh limes; at Tobago, the

Professor held forth on Robinson Crusoe, expanding the slim evidence which sought to establish the island as the undoubted headquarters of this ancient mariner. But in general, the main anticipation centred on Port of Spain, Trinidad, where the *Alcestis* was due to arrive in time for the Carnival. When they finally streamed ashore here, into the arms of a polyglot population perfectly equipped to deal with such invasions, they looked forward to it as one of the high spots of the whole cruise. They were not disappointed.

Port of Spain seemed to have everything, and, at Carnival time, everything was on display. Steel bands roamed the streets, exotically costumed; the rival Calypso Kings set up their tents, and embarked on the yearly warfare to advance the claims of Lord Caresser, Lord Life Expectancy, and the Edinburgh Whiz-Kid. In the streets, the range of costumes and the shades of colour were fantastic; Indian women in saris, civil servants in white duck, pure Negroes, impure Europeans, Portuguese traders, Chinese brothel touts, Spanish girls with enormous bosoms and fiery eyes. There were teak forests to be visited, and a lake of pitch solid enough to be walked upon. The mosques and temples and bazaars beckoned the eye; the competing music wove its pattern continuously; tiny humming-birds hung like bees, motionless above the red-flowering *immortelles*.

There was Creole cooking for those who wanted a change, and caustic curries for those who preferred an ordeal. For passengers who, even at this late stage, had never left New York, there was a restaurant called the *Tavern-on-the-Green*. Over it all, music and dancing and a zany pre-Lental delinquency set the tone and showed the way. It was no wonder that, allowed by the schedule to spend five days there, the Alcestians took a long look at the conventions and decided to give them a rest.

Louis and Mrs. Consolini—whose name was Belle—had at last found a place they liked. It was a night-club called the *Calcutta*, one of the few which readily stayed open as long as the customers chose to remain there. They liked it because it was dark, and unfashionable, and because very few of their fellow-passengers had discovered it.

Once there, all they did was talk, and listen to the music; Louis was handling this one with a long and leisurely spoon, and he applied no pressure of any sort. The pressure indeed finally came from her, in a form which he was to remember for a very long time.

Belle Consolini was in a curious mood. On this trip, the Captain had certainly not come up to her expectations; the impulse which had prompted her to make a third cruise in the *Alcestis* was paying many pleasant dividends, but Captain Harmer had not been one of them. Nor, up to the time of going to press, had anyone else. She had looked the field over; in plain terms, there just wasn't a field on board, save for this dubious young man who, so far, had concentrated on giving her rival Mrs. Stewart-Bates a whirl, and on nothing else. That seemed a pattern which had been discontinued, for reasons which she did not know but could approximately guess; the coming change-over, however, was going to be on her own terms. It only remained to tell him how and when.

On their second night at the *Calcutta*, the calypso singer who went the rounds of the tables paused to give them the traditional salute reserved for *Alcestis* passengers. (All the cruise-boats had their own slanted calypsos, calculated to provoke delighted squeals and two-dollar tips.) At the end, Belle Consolini unexpectedly asked the singer:

"There's one from Barbados called '*Back to Back, Belly to Belly*'. Do you know it?"

"Yes ma'am," said the calypso singer, grinning. "All the eight verses."

He sang them, in lingering detail, and departed with some solid largesse for his trouble.

"That's a pretty hot number," said Louis appreciatively. "You certainly know your way around, Belle. How did you hear about that one?"

She waved her hand; the lights caught her bracelets, and travelled up her plump sunburnt arm, and gave a dull sheen to the draped mink stole, and finished up among the gold dust sprinkled on her hair.

"We've had some of these jokers back in New York," she answered carelessly. "My husband was in the business."

It was a phrase she often used, in widely differing contexts; indeed, it was difficult to judge what Mr. Consolini's business had been, except that it had given him, and consequently her, an all-embracing knowledge of how things were organized. Once she had stopped Louis putting more money into the fruit-machines. "Those things are fixed—strictly for suckers," she told him. "My husband was in the business." Once she had asked him, when he was buying her some perfume, not to choose a certain brand. "It's the most god-awful stuff. They make it out of the trash from the stock-yards. My husband used to have the franchise." When Louis complained, like everyone else, about the band on board, she diagnosed the trouble in a single sentence. "Union rules," she said. "If you hire one player who can play, you have to take on two relatives who can't." Apparently her husband had been in that business too. On a later occasion, when they were discussing the immigration laws in America, and she had revealed an astonishing knowledge of permits, restrictions, evasions, and loop-holes, Louis had asked her what her husband's line had actually been. "He was an agent," she answered. That was all.

It had been enough on that occasion, and it was enough also to make him suspect that Belle Consolini would not be an easy target. The thought did not worry him, but it had perhaps persuaded him to take the whole thing at a very even speed.

Now, enjoying their Cuba Libres, while the calypso singer sauntered back to the bandstand and the *Calcutta* customers applauded him, they relaxed and were happy. Louis thought idly that it might be tonight that he would make his move. He could not know that Belle Consolini had come to the same conclusion, from quite a different angle, at quite a different time.

It was a chance meeting, back on board, which precipitated the next and final stage. The time was two o'clock, and though it was too late to get a drink in the bar, they agreed that they were both wide awake and still wanted one. She invited him down to her cabin; the way there led past the library, where the lights were still on. Through the open doorway, they both saw Mrs. Stewart-Bates sitting reading—or, perhaps, pretending to read; for as they passed, the book was lowered, and Mrs. Stewart-Bates stared at them over its top, like a pale ghost doomed to stand sentinel for a thousand years.

Neither of them made any comment, though Louis found the encounter slightly unnerving. But when they reached her cabin, Belle Consolini, pouring him a drink, remarked:

"Your friend's up late."

It would have been silly to say anything except: "Yes."

Mrs. Consolini brought the drink over, and set it down by his side. Then she asked, without preamble:

"How much did you take her for?" And added, inevitably, over the beginning of his energetic protest: "It's O.K. My husband was in the business."

More than two hours passed before the subject was raised again; and when it was, it developed, swiftly and subtly, on a plane which seemed to place all the initiative in her hands. She even destroyed, in advance, the shock-element in his plans—the surprise he had not yet sprung.

"Of course I knew what was going on," said Belle Consolini. She lay back on the bed, her body relaxed, her eyes alight; it placed him at a disadvantage that she seemed to take this whole situation so completely for granted. "Who didn't know? You and Grace Stewart-Bates. What on earth would you have in common? She could pass for your mother! Of course she must have hired you, and I hope it was fun."

"It was fun, all right," he answered. He tried to give his voice an edge, preparing to make his own move. "And *we* had fun too, didn't we?"

"Certainly," said Belle Consolini. "That was the basic idea."

"How about it, then?"

"How about what?"

"Paying for it."

"Oh, *that*." She nodded as if there were nothing in this conversation she had not heard a hundred times before. "How much did Grace pay for you?"

"Never mind about that. This is you and me. You'd better start talking."

She stared at him, calculating, not worrying at all about his altered manner. "You'll find a hundred-dollar bill in my bag," she said. "Help yourself."

"A *hundred!*" His voice, coming from the shadows outside the circle of the bedside lamp, was scornful. "You'd better think again. You want people to know about us?"

"Heavens, Louis, you've got some funny ideas! Of course they'll know about us, if we go on with it. What does it matter? What do you think people talk about, all day and all night?" She looked up at him, as if she were genuinely puzzled. "What's on your mind? How much *do* you want?"

"Nearer a thousand."

Now it was her turn to laugh. It had a lilt, a merry and musical sound which was infinitely disconcerting. But all she said was:

"For tonight? I think that's a little too high."

"It's not too high." This was all wrong, but try as he would, he couldn't seem to get back on the right track again. "It's what you're going to give me."

"I'll give you nothing of the sort." She might have been shopping for vegetables, with five stalls to choose from. "Look, my lad, which of us knows more about the going rates, you or me? My husband was —" she did not even need to complete the sentence. "I like you, Louis," she went on, "and I don't want to see you get into the wrong hands. I'll tell you what—I'll make it five hundred a week."

"A *week?* What the hell is this?"

"You know very well what it is. It's a deal, the kind of deal you're looking for." She lay back, entirely at her ease, as if the matter were beyond discussion or comment, except among foolish people who did not know what was good for them. "Five hundred a week, for as long as *I* choose. And you just stay in line, or the deal's off."

"What if I say no? What if I—"

"You won't say no, and you won't do anything silly, either." She looked at him, her eyes shrewd, her voice entirely firm. "I don't know what you put over on Grace, and I don't want to know, but *I—am—not—Grace*." She brought the four words out with complete authority; then she relaxed, and her tone became almost kindly. "This is just what you want, if you'd only work it out—a safe job, regular hours, let's call them fringe benefits, more money than you could earn any other way. Without throwing any compliments around, it's what we both want."

"You've got it all worked out, haven't you?" he said, between bitterness and relief.

"You bet I have!" For once, she said nothing about her husband, but it seemed improbable that the guiding principles of Mr. Consolini were far from her mind. She patted the covers, and drew them up a little round her shoulders. "Now hand me my cigarettes, there's a good boy."

"Anything else you'd like?" he asked, with an attempt at irony. It did not survive her answer.

"No," she said. "And you can get dressed now. I won't want you again tonight."

part four

"Enjoy long, thrill-packed days at sea on the way to your rendezvous at the Tavern of the Seas—Cape Town.

chapter 1

"*MAN that is born of woman hath but a short time to live,*" said the Captain, "*and is full of misery.*" He tried not to intone the words; however many times one had read it—especially during the war—it was a most moving service, dedicated always to the proposition that the man lying on the deck at one's feet, whether snug in a coffin, or sewn up in his hammock, or hidden under a flag, deserved only sincerity and sorrow. "*He cometh up, and is cut down, like a flower; he fleeth as it were a shadow, and never continueth in one stay.*"

The *Alcestis* moved slowly through the sluggish water; within a few moments, her engines would be stopped for the burial, and the run-down had to be as gradual as possible, for reasons which the Chief Engineer Officer could, if called upon, explain cogently enough. There was a slight breeze, ruffling the bare heads of all who stood in the small space below the after-deck; it came from the newly-opened void in the ship's side, the mouth of the grave. The attendance was small; four officers, a mixed dozen of the crew, and about thirty of the passengers. As far as the latter were concerned, Captain Harmer always tried to keep the occasion as unobtrusive as he decently could; a death on board, particularly during a cruise when the average age was over sixty, was deeply disturbing, and the less advertisement it received, the better. The nurse was crying, he observed with surprise; an unusual reaction for a nurse, implying—if it implied anything—that she was concerned on a non-professional basis. She had loved the dead man? She was now out of a job? She blamed herself for something not done, or inadequately done? The Doctor, always involved when people started to cry, would tell him later.

"*In the midst of life we are in death.*" said the Captain, shifting his feet as his ship rolled gently in the long South Atlantic swell. In a small way, that fact was always true for Myth Lines; on any voyage, they carried six coffins, a discreet portion of the purser's empire which lay hidden until called for. But it must have been true also—he looked down at the ever-present shape on the deck, the mound covered by the flaring colours of the Stars and Stripes—it must have been true for the dead man, George Morgan Simms, retired business executive, who had lived with death for more than ten years (so the Doctor said), on whom, indeed, death had long fed with unobtrusive appetite.

Probably he had known, when he was wheeled on board at New York, that he would never be wheeled off again; but he had chosen this sort of death, this sort of occasion, with the sun warming him for the last time and the horizon bare of buildings, of hospital walls, of relatives. Yet perhaps he could not quite have foreseen that he would leave the ship, taking the long dive seawards, in a hundred fathoms of cloudy water off the mouth of the Amazon. For an American, for anyone, the Equator was an odd place to die, and odder still for a graveyard.

"*Suffer us not,*" said the Captain, "*at our last hour, for any pains of death, to fall from thee.*" The warning words, of course, were for the spectators; if Simms could die, they could all die; let them take care to do it in piety. He glanced round, wondering what the ceremony meant to the onlookers, and why they were there. Curiosity? Religious conviction? Respect for the dead? None of them had known Simms. No-one had known Simms; not more than six people had set eyes on him during the past month and a half. Simms had been an idea within the ship, a cautionary item of lading; he was present whenever one thought of him—by accident, by overhearing his name, when sad or lonely or drunk—and absent when he passed out of mind.

Now it was time to make him absent for ever.

The Captain raised his head, and nodded unobtrusively to Tiptree-Jones, standing to one side at the back of the attendant circle. Tiptree-Jones pressed a bell twice, a prearranged signal to the bridge. Deep within the ship, they could all hear the clang of the telegraphs, and then the beat of the engines died, and way fell off the *Alcestis*.

The Captain braced his shoulders, face-to-face with the part he hated. "*For as much as it hath pleased Almighty God of his great mercy to take unto himself the soul of our dear brother here departed; we therefore commit his body to the deep.*" By the open space in the ship's side, the bearers bent and tipped the small platform bearing the coffin; it slid away from them, into the burning sunshine, and down out of sight, as if sponged away from a pale blue slate.

There was a farewell to be spoken at the same time. "*In sure and certain hope of the Resurrection to eternal life,*" said the Captain, "*through our Lord Jesus Christ, who shall change our vile body, that it may be like unto his glorious body.*"

As his voice ceased, all of them were left staring at the empty space, the astonishing void. A few faces were stony, but most betrayed a genuine bereavement. There could be no more irrevocable burial than a burial at sea. It did not need the gentle returning pulse of the engines to tell them that it was too late to do anything, that they were abandoning for ever the old man whom no-one had known.

The Captain returned to his prayer book, making his voice as strong as possible, to atone for all their guilt. "*I heard a voice from heaven saying unto me, Write; From henceforth blessed are the dead which die in the Lord; even so, saith the Spirit, for they rest from their labours.*"

As usual for the Captain, that was all; he always ended on the phrase "*they rest from their labours,*" which at such moments seemed the point of the ceremony, and perhaps the point of life. There were sentences later on which he never read out loud, which he did not believe in and could not stomach; the part where they were asked to give hearty thanks to God for delivering this our brother out of the miseries of this sinful world. Of course it was meant to cheer people up, but it was utterly false, it was a lie. Hearty thanks. . . . Life was not miserable; sometimes it was dull or ugly, but on balance it was beautiful and exciting, and it was a shame to die and a shame to be snatched away from it, and a shame to be left a mourner.

He put on his cap, while Tim Mansell, who was in charge of the burial party, set them to work dismantling the pivoted platform and securing the huge water-tight entrance-doors again. The machinery of these occasions was always a bit obtrusive. . . . Harmer nodded to the passengers, and murmured "Thank you for coming" as he passed by them. Going forward, his footfalls echoing in the long passageway, he fell into step beside Tiptree-Jones.

"Thank you, First," he said formally. "Everything went off well. See that it's logged, and I'll sign it."

"Yes, sir," said Tiptree-Jones. In this aftermath, his face and bearing were both especially noble, but for once the Captain forgave him. These things were always sad, always hopelessly final; nothing could change that, or detract from it.

"Crossing the Line," said the Captain after a moment. "When was that laid on for?"

"Tomorrow morning, eleven o'clock," answered Tiptree-Jones.

"We'd better scrub it out," said the Captain. The uninhibited, sometimes raucous ceremonies to mark the crossing of the equator might have served to cheer the ship up, but he did not feel like doing it that way. "It's not really suitable. People will understand."

"Of course they will, sir. I'll tell the purser."

"And cable head office again about Simms."

"Yes, sir."

"I won't come down to dinner."

chapter 2

EVERYONE felt like that, for a number of hours afterwards; they fell out of love with parties, they did not want to meet other people, they preferred to keep to their cabins until the blackest shadow in the world had passed. Much of this feeling stemmed outwards from the nurse, a slightly melodramatic creature whose finest hour this was.

"I shouldn't have left him alone," she declared, not once but a score of times. "He *promised* me he felt all right!" No-one blamed her, everyone patted her shoulder and told her not to feel badly about it, it might have happened any time, they knew for a fact that Simms hadn't suffered a thing. But there were private thoughts to match this gloss on reality, private pictures of an old man dying alone in terror, reaching for a bell in the darkness, not making it, gasping out his life while just above his head the band played on and the glasses clinked. As long as the memory and the pictures were fresh, no-one wanted the band to play, and they preferred to clink their glasses in private.

Diane Loring had many of these thoughts; she unloaded them onto Kathy, in a long monologue which, with death as its starting-point, moved inevitably to the only topic which seemed to promise stability in a perilous world. The topic was sex. It was one which Kathy, in her present mood, could have done without.

Diane had attended the funeral. "I'm sure I don't know why," she said. "I just hate the idea of people dying." They were in Kathy's cabin, which Diane had invaded; Kathy was lying on the bed, and Diane sitting before the triple-winged mirror, dabbing at her nails with a scarlet-edged sable brush, pausing now and them to examine herself minutely in the glass. "Fancy just tipping him into the sea like that. It doesn't seem safe. Wouldn't he float, or something?"

"They put weights in," said Kathy vaguely. She did not want to talk about this, or about anything; she had been reading when Diane came in, and she still wanted to read or to think, now that she was here. "The sailors know how to fix it."

"Well, I certainly hope so. Think of that poor old man." She moved her face within a few inches of the mirror, and turned it from side to side, scrutinizing with minute attention the skin adjacent to her nose. "Do you get blackheads?"

"No," said Kathy.

"You're lucky. Greasy skin, that's me. All brunettes have it. They say it's the natural oils. . . . That poor old man," she said again, but the thought had become intertwined with another, and she moved on to it very readily. "Did you ever sleep with an old man? I mean—well, Carl's not *old*, is he?—I mean, a real old man?"

"No," said Kathy. "No, I never did."

"Well, don't!" said Diane, with emphasis. "It's enough to turn your hair grey. They have the darnedest time getting anywhere! And then they blame you! I remember one old character down in South Carolina—" she went back to the nail-dabbing, frowning, holding her hand up to the light, "honest, it was just like a horse-race. He had to cheer himself on, the whole time. You know what he said?" She giggled. "He used to shout: 'Come on, you bastard! Come on, Silky Sullivan!' "

Kathy smiled briefly, but her thoughts were far away from the joke, if it had ever been a joke. It did not need Diane, these days, to turn her mind away from sex; for the last few weeks, she had seemed to have a blank in her mind, an area of nothingness in her body, where that was concerned. She did not want to love, she did not want to make love, she did not want to pretend, or prepare the snare, or use herself as bait, in the way they had planned. All she wanted to do was to pass the time dreamily, enjoying this wonderful voyage, soaking up the sun, *feeling* life with the whole of her prostrate body instead of a part of it. A year ago, she would have been bored with the idea, she would have thought of it as a waste of time, a routine fit only for deadbeats. But something—the sea, the sense of floating calm, the undemanding *niceness* of everyone around her—seemed to have turned her mood towards despised contentment.

Even Tim Mansell had remarked on it—juvenile Tim, simple and silly Tim, inadequate Tim who could not guess the score. He had said, out of the blue: "You may not realize it, but you're not as tough as you used to be." He had used the word 'tough' apologetically, in quotation marks; they had been talking about women, and what they could and could not do with their lives, and the hard, speculative sense necessary (he thought) to deal with each man on the exact basis he deserved. She had turned the approach aside—her hard speculative sense was certainly good enough for that one—but the thought had remained. It was true that she had softened; happily dormant, she had forgotten what she was there for. The realization should have been far more of a shock than it was; it involved complications in the future, and a sense of guilty inadequacy now; at the worst, it threatened to betray Carl, and all the interlocking confidences involved in their last six years together. But it had happened, and she did not know how to cope with it, and she did not want to know.

Diane, with no such inhibitions, was jogging along happily on her only hobby-horse. "I met a guy once, he'd got it all worked out," she said. "About seduction, I mean. He told me all about it. It was a bit late for him to tell me then, if you know what I mean, but I guess he thought it was good for a laugh. He said there's two sure-fire ways that men can always make a girl—any girl. I mean, as long as they're not out-and-out apes. First is when they dance with you, and after a bit they say: 'Honey, something wonderful's happening to me, I didn't know it was possible.' Then they say: 'This is the first time it's happened since Korea, or maybe even Okinawa. My God, I thought I was impotent!' Then they say: 'Only you could have done it for me! Are we going to let this beautiful thing go to waste?' My friend said the answer is always, No. I mean, No, we can't let it go to waste." She laughed, without malice. "Aren't men the living end? Then the other way is, they give you a long sad story about how nobody loves them, if they can't work up a relationship soon they're going to jump right out the window, and then they put the lights out and give you a great big slug of gin and get you cornered on a sofa, and then they undo a lot of buttons and start to cry. I mean, actual tears. He said that one never fails, either."

Kathy, who had scarcely been listening, woke up to the silence when Diane paused. By way of suiting the conversation, she asked: "Which way did he use with you?"

Diane frowned at her reflection. "He didn't have to use any way, darn it. He was good-looking. . . ."

Now her nails were finished; she waved them once or twice in the air and then, when they were dry, started to put away her manicure compact. "Men," she said. "Sometimes they make me sick. And what a collection we've got on board this barge! If I'd known what sort of age-group it was going to be, I'd have asked Carl to pay us over-time rates." She looked down at Kathy; she was inquisitive but not, in her present mood, challenging. "Have you got anyone going for you?"

"Not yet," said Kathy.

"We'll be in Rio next week," said Diane. "I wonder what that's like. I went with an Argentine once, he said a funny thing, he said: 'In a hundred years it will all be from test tubes. But you and I, let us make history!' What a character . . . Tell you something, that old Prof had better lay off the booze, or he'll be giving the game away. I've seen him absolutely stinko a couple of times already. It's time he did some work." She stood up, collecting her things. "Time we all did, I suppose, with Carl raking in the stuff the way he is."

"Who's next for you?"

"Walham, I guess. The mean old man from outer space. Have you got any ideas?"

"Not really." She could not possibly be friends with Diane, but she wanted to make a point, even before this tough-skinned, almost impenetrable witness. "I know I've been lazy so far," she said, with a hint of apology. "But I didn't realize it was going to be as peaceful as this."

"You like it peaceful?"

Kathy nodded. "Yes, I do."

"Well, personally it would give me the willies," said Diane. "But it's all according, I suppose." She prepared to take her leave. "See you at dinner."

"Yes."

"Think of that poor old man," said Diane, "chucked overboard, bobbing about like a cork in a kettle. There ought to be a law against it."

chapter 3

RUNNING down to Rio, the *Alcestis* regained her spirits. If Simms had been known to anyone on board, they might have mourned him longer; but he had lived and died anonymously, as far as the ship was concerned, and he passed out of mind almost as swiftly as he had quitted the after-deck on his last journey. It was not a callous reaction; the worst it contained was an element of self-delusion, designed to make those who were left behind feel happy and confident again. Of course Simms had died—or at least, passed over—but he was so shadowy a figure that his passing didn't really count. He had been a name on a list, and now the list was altered; but everyone else that one knew still figured on it, and that was the way it was going to stay.

People talked about him, avidly enough, for the space of two days; his burial—no, his leave-taking—had been original, even bizarre. Then they only remembered him accidentally, when the nurse laughed a little too loudly at the officers' table; and then he was forgotten.

The weather helped this process, and, more than the weather, their ports of call. They were coasting down from the mouth of the Amazon to Rio de Janeiro, touching at all the towns on the Brazilian seaboard where the company had any sort of tourist connections. Brazil was much written up in the ship's daily bulletins as a land of mystery, scarcely explored, hardly penetrable at all save by intrepid voyagers such as those carried in the *Alcestis*. Romantic names and words constantly recurred—Matto Grosso, alligators, gauchos, jungle-orchids, *cruzeiros,* Amer-Indians, *piranhas,* Dom Pedro II. Brazil was *terra incognita;* it was larger than the United States. . . .

As they worked their way down the coast, little of this *mystique* actually confronted them; the successive calls at such places as Belem, Fortaleza, Recife, and Salvador were like their calls anywhere else—they anchored off the coast or came alongside, they went ashore, drove up mountains, rode horses along bridle trails, looked at monasteries, wandered round museums, attended race-tracks, explored slums, took photographs, sampled the local food, spat out the local drinks, talked, quarreled, got drunk, pushed aside the beggars, and went thankfully back to civilization again, laden with souvenirs made of rare, unwrought silver.

But the places were amusing enough, the people could safely be labelled quaint, or colourful, or different; and always, present in all their minds, there was this *idea* of Brazil—part of an untamed continent, full of silences and the hiss of poisoned blow-pipes, *bigger than the United States*, and of course all matted jungle except for this tiny coastal strip. Each time they went ashore it was as if they were winning, afresh, a toe-hold on a savage hinterland. This extraordinary illusion did no-one any harm, and made very real the idea that a cruise in the *Alcestis* was a life-time adventure.

For the Professor, this was no longer quite true. Being under-employed, he was beginning to be bored; the trips ashore tired him, and he had little to do except doze in his chair on the sun-deck, and make for the Tapestry Bar as soon as it opened. His book languished, though he loved it as dearly as ever, and sometimes, if he could assemble an audience—one listener was an audience—he read selected sections of it aloud.

On such occasions his voice took on a fine sonorous timbre, and his white mane and proud old face gave him new authority. But he soon tired of this too; reading was thirsty work, he would say, after ten or fifteen minutes; he did not want to bore anyone—perhaps a little *refreshment*. . . . Refreshment marked the end of every day; he would sit in the bar, drinking at a steady rate, delivering long philosophical monologues on classical education, and public morality, and the indiscipline of the young, to whoever would listen to him; until gradually he became fuddled, and his face, paper-frail, lost its fine distinction and collapsed into dribbling foolishness, and he stumbled off to bed.

Edgar would look after him, shaking his head. "He'll be the next to go, if he don't watch out," he would say. "Stands to reason. Think of a liver that's been going full-ahead for seventy years. No resilience."

Louis, lapped in luxury, was also cushioned in servitude; his $500 a week for round-the-clock attendance was becoming harder and harder to earn.

It was not that Belle Consolini was overdoing the obvious demands; she had never done so, and she was not going to start now. She had made this clear from the beginning. "It's a matter of mood," she told Louis. "*My* mood. I'll tell you when I want it, and you'd better be on deck when I do. But we're not out to break any records. That's for kids. I'm forty-four, and I like being forty-four, and I'm going to act forty-four. I'm paying for your company, not just your—" She had a colourful way of expressing herself which Louis, a child of the gutter himself, often found shocking. "I should be very surprised if it's more than once or twice a week," she elaborated, "but I want to see more of you than that. For instance, when we get to Rio—"

Thus she made plans, disposing of his time as if she were paying him by the hour; almost she drew up a daily schedule, setting out where he was to be and what he was to be doing, from breakfast-time to midnight and beyond. If she wanted someone to talk to while she was making up for dinner, he was to be there, sitting in a chair near her dressing-table; if she wanted a handkerchief or a scarf or a magazine, he went to fetch it, and he had to come back straight away. When she felt too lazy to go ashore and buy something, he trotted off to execute the commission; when she gave a small party for some of the officers and a dozen of her fellow-passengers, he wrote out the invitations, and saw they were delivered, and subsequently helped with the drinks, passed the salted almonds, fetched the chairs, lit the cigarettes. Afterwards he had to listen to the post-mortem; and if she were 'in the mood,' he had to press that button also.

All he was excused, due to circumstances beyond her control, was the washing-up.

She had taken to calling him Scapelli; it had a finger-snapping sound which seemed to determine his status more pointedly than anything else. "Good morning, Scapelli," was certainly adequate for a head-waiter or even a secretary; but for an ardent lover it seemed less than warm, less than encouraging. He was a lazy young man, who would never have quarreled with $500 a week for performing almost any service; but when the service was of this sort—constant, humble, and emasculate—then even he, as the mileage of subservience piled up, felt a surge of impatient manhood.

Above all, there was, ever-present, Mr. Consolini, that knowing paragon who had done everything and, it seemed, everybody. She referred to him very regularly indeed, not as someone whom she mourned—they had been married for fifteen years, and for the last ten he had been spectacularly inattentive—but as a man whom nothing ever took by surprise, because nothing was new. He had travelled five times around the world, he had been in jail ("He was framed," said Mrs. Consolini, with a certain wistful admiration for some unnamed third party), he had bought and sold every single commodity from black pepper to under-age female companionship. Whenever Louis asked a question, Mr. Consolini had known the answer, and his widow, scornful or complacent, produced it now. Sometimes it was less than crystal-clear. Once he had asked her if she were fond of snails. "Good heavens, no!" she answered, almost shuddering. "My husband once told me what goes on in there."

Even his death, apparently, had been in a flamboyant tradition. He had suffered a heart attack in a motel. "The girl said he must have strained himself carrying the suitcases," said Mrs. Consolini. "*But I know better.*"

So did Louis earn his money, as the *Alcestis* curved her way past the broad pregnancy of the Brazilian coastline, and the sun, balanced overhead like a burnished shield, beat mercilessly upon the wooden decks. These, by midday, were unbearable to the touch, and the pitch in the seams bubbled and spread; while below, in the cabins and the public rooms, the forced-draught ventilation impelled upon the passengers great gusts of moist and torrid air.

It was not a climate for romance, save for a few determined characters who chanced to be awake during the small hours; and Louis Scapelli, the bonded courier of love, crept nearly every night to bed like an exhausted eunuch, a true minister without portfolio. There might, he decided, be tougher ways of earning $500 a week, but there could be none more irritating or more fatal to morale.

Diane, ideally equipped to defy the heat—or to match it, as the occasion demanded—was engaged in the weaving of a curious tapestry.

One thread of it was Mr. Walham—Walham the slow man with a dollar, the last of the very small spenders; the other was a thinner, slighter strand altogether, a customer normally to be overlooked, not least by herself—young Master Greenfield. If the first one was the meanest man she had ever met, Barry Greenfield turned out to be, within his modest resources, the most generous soul on board.

Barry Greenfield was a few months short of sixteen years old; by common agreement, by acclamation, he was the worst example of the Great American Brat that anyone on board had ever encountered. In the space of two months, he had managed to antagonize an impressive array of people, ranging from the oldest passengers (who could not stand the noise) to the youngest officers (who did not mind the noise but could not stand the back-talk.) He was legally banned from the Tapestry Room, and he now, by popular request, took his meals an hour earlier than the rest of the passengers, who had had enough of noisy scenes, ruined table-cloths, and flying bread-sticks. But that still left a number of places where he could make a thorough nuisance of himself—notably the swimming-pool, the cinema, the boat-deck during siesta-time, and on trips ashore. For these, a lively competition had developed *not* to be in the same motor-boat, bus, or taxi; there was something about the whining voice, the derisive running-commentary, the penchant for booby-traps and smeared ice-cream, which destroyed all eagerness to sample the joys of foreign travel.

His parents had long ago given up all but the rudiments of supervision. Years of varying treatment, from sudden harsh punishment to cloying and sentimental forms of bribery, had done their work; Barry now knew that he could get away with murder, and when either of them was goaded into trying to disprove this, the resulting uproar was hardly worth it. He should have been at school at this very moment, but when the cruise was at the planning stage his refusal to be left behind had been so vociferous that they had given up arguing. (He did not really want to come with them, but he wanted to go to school even less.) The authorities had been quick to agree, typically, that Barry, a delicate, highly-strung boy, would benefit from a long sea voyage. They made no secret of their view that it would not really matter how long it was. So he had found himself on board the *Alcestis;* and the *Alcestis* passengers had found themselves bedevilled by a fellow-traveller who, across an average gulf of forty-five years, epitomized all that they loathed and feared in the word 'teen-ager.'

It was this young man who presently approached Diane and asked her, in no very ambiguous terms, if he could go to bed with her.

Diane had been in her cabin when the first encounter took place. It was the middle of the afternoon, at sea between Recife and Salvador; most people were asleep after a late lunch, but she had chanced to be wakeful and was sorting some clothes to send to the cleaners. Her cabin door was open, to take advantage of the slight breeze, and the curtain half drawn. A small movement disturbed her, and she looked up, thinking it was the stewardess. But it was Barry Greenfield, his head peering round the corner of the doorway, staring at her with solemn concentration.

He said: "Hi!" in a gruff voice.

She frowned. "What do you want?"

"Nothing. I was just passing."

"Keep doing it, junior." Most people now spoke to Barry Greenfield like this; anything less was a fatal weakness, inviting insult or embarrassment.

But he remained where he was, regarding her with an unwinking stare which was, subtly, less unpleasant than usual. Presently he said:

"I thought maybe you could use some company."

She frowned at him again, irritable, not yet awake to the situation. "What the hell are you talking about? Can't you see I'm busy? Run away and play!"

He came forward a step and said: "I'd rather stay here and play." The expression on his face, as much as the words, made his meaning unmistakable.

Diane Loring was not shockable material, but on this occasion she came very near to succumbing. For five seconds she regarded him, quite unable to believe her ears; then she exploded:

"Don't talk to me like that, you snotty little bastard! Just beat it, or I'll call the steward."

"You won't do that," said Barry Greenfield.

She looked at him more closely, trying to guess what line to take, and why it had suddenly become necessary to take any line at all. As usual, he was remarkably self-possessed; his face, which had never seemed immature, was now set in a knowing, confederate grin. But there was something else, something new—and that was what it was, she suddenly realized; it was something new for him. He was doing this for the very first time; playing it by ear from a sordid fund of guesswork and hearsay; and just for once, the person he spoke to was bound to have the advantage, because he was a boy, however precocious, stepping onto adult ground.

Confidence returned to her. She was used to dealing with men; this one was a small-scale man, a miniature pressing of the brashness, lust, terror, and vanity which she knew all about. All she need use were small-scale gestures and maybe (she grinned privately) shorter legs.

She said, not relinquishing authority: "You'd better sit down. What's on your mind?"

He came forward and sat on the edge of the bed, small, self-contained, tough, and yet vulnerable in the way that all men were vulnerable, when they laid it on the line.

"You know what's on my mind." His voice, not long broken, was throaty and gruff; trying for masculinity, he achieved a rather beguiling adolescence. She recalled reading some book that said that kids of this age were at the peak of their male potency. Such language. . . . "How about it?"

"But gee, Barry, I don't even know what you're talking about."

"Knock it off, sister!" Everything he said, and every line he took, were diminished by the laws of perspective, but they were authentic none-the-less. "I've been watching you. Don't think I haven't! You and that other babe, you've fixed yourself up a nice little racket. Well, I'm a customer."

"A customer? Whatever for?"

"For one of you floating call-girls." She could see that he had all his phrases ready; he must have rehearsed this scene, afraid of making mistakes or of losing ground at a critical stage. "Just name a price, and maybe we can do a deal."

She looked at him again, more closely still. Under the brash manner, the man-of-the-world assumption, he was nervous; but it was a sexual nervousness only—he knew something, or he had guessed something, which allowed him to speak to her like this. If was difficult to know how to deal with it; a virginal squawk would have been out of place, and yet to take it seriously, to treat it as a proposition, would surely qualify her for the nut-house. It could even be illegal. . . . Finally she said: "I don't know what in hell's got into your head, but whatever it is, it's all wrong. Now just you beat it, the same way as you came in. I'm busy, like I told you."

He gave her an authentic sneer, copied from a whole saga of 'juvenile delinquency' movies and TV programmes. "I'll say you're busy! Busy with Old Man Walham. Don't waste your time, that's all I say. You want to know what's in his wallet? Mothballs! You'll never get rich that way."

"Walham? What are you talking about? You must be nuts!"

He said again, with considerable assurance: "Sister, you're wasting your time."

It was true that she was busy with Walham, and probably just as true that Walham was not going to pay her much of a dividend. He had placed the offer, from the very beginning, on a purely business footing; and the area of potential blackmail was very small indeed—he was travelling alone, he had (or so he claimed) an 'understanding' with his wife, he was not the sort of man who, faced by Carl the outraged uncle, would have crumpled up and reached for his pocket-book. It boiled down to a matter of terms, and he was, as usual, looking for a bargain.

It had started, as so often happened to Diane, with a dance at one of the ship's innumerable 'Gala Nights' involving balloons, paper caps, and moderate misbehaviour. Walham, she knew, had been gravitating in her direction fairly determinedly during the preceding five days; it became clear, when they had circled the dance-floor a couple of times, that he had now made up his mind to spend part of the allocation set out in his budget (so the Professor said) under 'Sex.' It became clear, also, that he was going to use as little of it as possible. Why he had taken it for granted that she was a suitable target, never even came up in conversation. All he said, when they presently sat down in a quiet corner of the main saloon, was:

"How much?"

After their dance, which had been explicit on both sides, it seemed silly to clutch her neckline and demand to know what he could possibly be talking about. Instead, she decided on shock tactics. She said:

"A thousand dollars."

He snorted. Clearly it gave him pleasure to do so: it must have been the preliminary to hundreds of similar discussions, in areas ranging from the selling of farm-tractors to the buying of antiques. In addition, he affected now the classic gesture of the man prepared to make a long, long fight for justice. He cupped his hand to his ear, and said drily:

"Must be getting deaf. I could have sworn you said a thousand dollars."

Diane, taking the cigarette he offered, answered: "That's exactly what I did say."

"I'm not handing out any endowment funds," said Walham.

There ensued a bargaining session, extending over several days, which was ludicrous, spirited, and distinctly pleasurable. He began by offering her fifty dollars—"and that's 'way above the market. You'll have to earn it." She indicated, disdainfully, a total lack of interest; they were on board the *Alcestis,* she argued, and he must be prepared to pay luxury rates. "By God," he swore, his voice already an angry whine, "you're talking like that damned purser!" He used every argument, including some close financial figuring which she could scarcely follow. Scribbling on the back of a menu, he calculated that, on an actuarial basis which took into account the number of available men on board, she was putting her monthly salary at more than $20,000. "Hell," he said, "the top man in General Motors doesn't rate that much!" "But he gets free cars," countered Diane. "And anyway, that's just a run-of-the-mill job." She was enjoying herself.

"But a thousand bucks!" said Walham, again and again. "I don't spend that amount in five years. I could get fifty girls for that kind of money."

"Go ahead," said Diane heartlessly. "Wear yourself out. See if I care."

"Look, I'll make you a proposition—" Walham began again.

Suddenly, talking to Barry Greenfield, Diane thought: Well, why not? Of course, he was a terrible brat, and she had never done anything like it before; but this was a pleasure cruise—they were in the tropics—anything went—in certain lights he was actually quite good-looking. . . . She said, her voice on a much more friendly note:

"All right, smarty-pants. Make me an offer."

"Well, gee. . . ." He looked away from her, fingering the edge of the pillow. "Gee, I don't know." It was most gratifying to see him, at last, embarrassed and at a loss; it must be the first time anyone on board the *Alcestis* had enjoyed such a view. "It's like this. . . ."

"How much have you got?" she asked him.

"Seventy bucks." He looked at her, trying to interpret her expression. After a moment he said: "I can get more."

"You'll need more."

"O.K., O.K."

"Where will you get it from?"

He jerked his head back. "The folks. My dad's loaded." There was a return of his flip manner as he added: "Don't you worry about the dough."

It was important that she remain in command, in all areas. "I'm not worrying," she told him crudely. "*You* worry. Seventy bucks will get you precisely nowhere. What sort of league do you think this is?"

"O.K., give it a rest," he said crestfallen. "How much?"

"Two hundred, at least. Then we'll start talking."

He rose from the bed, looking down at his feet. Consternation struggled with the need to appear sophisticated, and both of them with an important branch of virtue—thrift. "That's a lot of dough," he said.

"No, it isn't," said Diane. "It's peanuts."

"I'll see about it," said Barry. "Let you know, huh?"

"You do that."

He came closer, a step at a time, so that presently he was standing over her, and his body, when the ship rolled slightly, touched her shoulder. She suddenly realized that he was tremendously keyed up, triggered for something which, for all the tough talk and the show-off manner, he still knew nothing about. But the message was there; when the time came, it was going to be just like the book said. She put out her hand, holding him off with a very real sense of excitement.

"Down, boy," she said. "Take it easy. I'll see you when you've got the money."

"But when I have it," he insisted, "it'll be O.K.?"

"Yes. It'll be O.K. . . . How old are you, Barry?"

"Nearly nineteen."

"Good for you."

"I'll make it one-hundred-fifty," said Walham. "Not a red cent more."

"The trouble with you," said Diane, "is that you're mean."

"Of course I'm mean! That's why I'm rich." He sounded pleased.

"Well, you're not going to be mean with me. Four hundred—" (she had scaled it down progressively, just for the fun of bargaining) "—is my last and final word. Take it or leave it."

"I got an advance on my allowance," said Barry.

"How much?"

"A lousy fifty." He studied her face briefly. "Still no good, huh?"

"No."

"I'll get some more, though. Don't you change your mind, will you?"

"A bargain is a bargain," said Diane.

"But it's twice my whole allocation for the trip," said Walham, desperately.

"Well, you're going to blow it all in one."

"Three hundred dollars."

"No."

"Aw, come on. Give a little!"

"No."

"I've got a camera," said Barry. "Cost over a hundred bucks. How about that?"

"I don't want a camera," said Diane. "Cameras are for other people."

"It's a darned good one."

"You know, like the old joke. No Leica."

"O.K." He sighed, not too despairingly. "Only thirty bucks more to go. It won't be long now."

"What's that kid hanging around all the time for?" demanded Walham.

"Maybe he loves me."

"Three hundred and fifty dollars. And that's the last word."

Diane shook her head, for the thousandth time. "We're not on the same wave-band. Why don't you give up?"

"When I go after a thing, I get it."

"I believe you," said Diane. "The trouble is, I operate the same way."

"What's a Mickey Mouse watch?" Barkway asked Brotherhood, the Captain's steward.

"Ask me another," said Brotherhood. "Why?"

"That blasted kid just offered to sell me one."

"All right," said Walham finally. He was in a very bad temper. "Four hundred. But it's plain robbery, let me tell you."

"Bunk," said Diane. "You're getting a bargain."

His eyes gleamed. It was his only prospect of making a profit. "It had better be."

"Congratulations," said Diane to Barry Greenfield. They had really become great friends during the past few days. "I hope it wasn't too much trouble."

"Oh, forget it!" answered Barry. "That's a deal, then?"

"Sure thing."

"When?"

"Now, if you like."

"Thirty-one years at sea," said Barkway. "And I thought I'd seen everything!"

Suddenly, everyone started to say: "You know, I believe Barry Greenfield is actually *improving*."

chapter 4

"A VERY healthy situation," mumbled the Professor, indistinctly. It was clear that the phrase could not be applied to himself. He had a nine P.M. pallor and a very shaky enunciation; awkwardly co-ordinated, he kept dropping his pencil and strewing cigarette ash down his lapels. Carl, looking at him, thought: It was a mistake to have this meeting so late in the evening; we should have made it before lunch—before breakfast, even. But in truth, it was difficult to catch the Professor in good shape, at any hour of the day. "Very healthy indeed," went on the Professor, wiping the saliva from his lips. "Has anyone anything else to add, before I make up the figures?"

Louis, lounging back in his chair, smiled unpleasantly. "Sure you *can* make them up, Prof?"

The Professor collected himself with an effort, and glared at his questioner: "What do you mean by that?"

"You know what I mean," said Louis. "Better let me do the adding up."

"I am perfectly capable—" began the Professor.

"O.K.," interrupted Carl irritably. "Let's not make a production out of it. You heard what he said, Louis. Have you got anything else to give him?"

"Sure I've got something," answered Louis. "Steady income, that's me." But he was not particularly proud of the statement, and it showed in the way he looked round the cabin, as if daring anyone to make any sort of comment. "Another five hundred for this week. That's fifteen hundred altogether."

The Professor wrote it down laboriously in his account-book, while they all watched him, and Kathy, sitting in her armchair outside the immediate circle, took a sip of her coffee and wondered if they would get through the meeting without some sort of explosion. Once again, she herself had nothing to contribute; everyone in the room was already aware of this; it was a question as to whether Carl could head off criticism of the fact. It was a question, indeed, whether he wanted to.

The Professor, stumbling over the simple words, asked: "Who was that from?"

"Mrs. Consolini," answered Louis.

Diane raised her head. "What's this Consolini deal?"

"You know what it is," said Louis, edgily. "Five hundred a week."

"How long for?"

"For ever."

Diane raised her eyebrows. "For that, she gets exclusive rights, huh? You're certainly playing it safe!"

"Just try and do better."

"I *have* done better," said Diane. She turned abruptly. "Take it down, Professor. Walham, four hundred dollars. Greenfield, two hundred."

"*Two* hundred?" queried Louis, on the alert. "*Two?* What's the good of that? Hell, Greenfield's a rich man!"

"He's not that rich," answered Diane. She really could not correct the mistake. "Anyway, that was the best I could do with him. There've been a couple of others as well," she told the Professor. "Another three hundred altogether. Total, nine hundred." She reached into her hand-bag, and took out a roll of bills. "Here it is."

"Store prices," said Louis contemptuously. "Four different guys for nine hundred bucks. Is that what they mean by a quick turnover?"

"So what's wrong with store prices?" Diane came back at him. "Hell, I'm *working!* One of those guys—I can't even remember his name—was the quickest deal you ever saw in your life. I swear to God, I was back on the dance-floor in twenty minutes. Do you do any better than that?"

"I'm not in the taxi business," said Louis.

"You're damn right, you're not," said Diane angrily. "Five hundred a week for lighting cigarettes and running errands! Don't you try and tell me who's earning their living. We might just open a can of worms."

Carl raised his hand. He should have intervened earlier, he knew, but he was not in an intervening mood. As a team, these two were doing well enough; he could not really quarrel with any of the figures, though it might be said that Diane was cutting down on the prices—operating almost legally, in fact—and that Louis had promoted himself into a curious and not particularly appropriate role. But certainly they were showing results, they were both staying ahead of the game.

The same could not be said for the rest of the team. As far as poker was concerned, he was in the doldrums, hanging onto his substantial winnings but not adding to them. It was not that he was playing badly, or holding worse cards, but simply that, as a school, they were finding out too much about each other's play, and learning caution in all circumstances. It was now a tighter game altogether, and thus a less profitable one.

After himself came the Professor, a licenced non-earner who was squandering every cent of his allowance at the bar; and after the Professor came Kathy, who had attained no category of any sort. Carl was not angry with her on that score. He had tried, and failed, to analyze exactly what he felt. Of course it was a disappointment, of course the rest of the team were carrying her; but perhaps, if it made her happy, he could afford to let it go on. It meant, at least, that she was not wandering into danger, that he need not feel he was sharing her with anyone. The other two, however, were entitled to resent it, and it was this that made him wary of applying pressure or discipline of any sort. He could hardly tell Diane that the time had come to step up the prices, when Kathy had no prices to show at all. . . . Now, commanding their silence, he said mildly:

"Let's take it easy. You've both done well. Professor, give us the figures."

"By all means, Carl." The Professor shuffled through his papers, focusing and refocusing his rheumy eyes. "You yourself are the winner, the very big winner." He smiled vaguely and ingratiatingly at Carl; he knew that he was not distinguishing himself, and that consequently he might need a friend. "You are fifteen thousand dollars ahead—fifteen thousand, one hundred to be preshise—precise. Diane's total is now three thousand, nine hundred. That includes what she has just given me. Louis, three thousand, *eight* hundred—"

"Hey!" said Louis. "Hold on! How do you figure that?"

The Professor blinked at him. "You mean, you would like the figures broken down into their various categories?"

"I would like," said Louis, savagely copying his careful pronunciation, "to know how in hell you get that total. It's 'way out, by my reckoning."

"One moment." The Professor peered shortsightedly at his book, and at the small mound of papers lying by its side. He was not necessarily in difficulties, but it was not a good moment for close calculation. Today had been a long day, like all other days; by rights he should have been installed in the Tapestry Bar, digesting his dinner, talking at ease to a rapt audience who were enthralled by his views on literature, scholarship, the things of the mind. . . . "One moment, if you please. I certainly have the exact figures here—somewhere—" his voice tailed off as he scrabbled among his papers.

"Jesus," said Louis, "this is book-keeping?"

"Cash from Mrs. Consolini," said the Professor, at last surmounting his confusion, "fifteen hundred dollars. Cash from Mrs. Stewart-Bates, five hundred. Jewellery from Mrs. Stewart-Bates, eighteen hundred dollars. Total—"

"Eighteen hundred?" broke in Louis, angrily. "How in hell do you figure that?"

"Fifty per cent of valuation," answered the Professor, suddenly more confident because he had fastened upon a phrase written down in his note-book. "That is what we are likely to get, when the jewellery is disposed of."

"Well, of course if you're going to louse up the figures like that—"

"He's not lousing up any figures," said Diane. "He's trying to work out exactly what you're worth. It's not likely to take him all day, either."

"Total for Louis, three thousand, eight hundred," said the Professor, unheeding. "Grand total for everyone, twenty-three thousand, eight hundred dollars. A most substantial—"

Carl broke in. "I make that twenty-*two* thousand, eight hundred, Professor. Just check again."

There was silence while the old man, breathing hard, fiddled his way through the addition again. Everyone in the room knew, without any reference to the figures, that he had made a mistake. It was, sadly and brutally, that sort of occasion, and Carl, the questioner, was that sort of man.

"Well, bless my soul," said the Professor at last. "I must have transposed—" he caught Carl's eye, and checked his explanation in mid-sentence. "You are quite right," he said humbly. "The grand total is twenty-two thousand, eight hundred."

"Not bad, not bad at all," said Louis. "Even if my stuff *is* marked down like it was a fire-sale." He looked at his watch. "Carl, if it's O.K. with you, I must run, right now. I have a date."

"You run," said Diane. "Or Mommy spank."

"Now cut that out!" said Louis furiously.

"You can both cut it out," said Carl, with an edge on his voice. "I haven't finished yet." He looked round them; when his eyes turned towards Kathy, they did not change expression. "We're halfway through the trip," he went on, "and we still haven't made the price of the tickets. I—"

"Very nearly," said the Professor, almost to himself.

"What was that?"

"I beg your pardon, Carl," said the Professor, reacting to the sudden sharpness in the voice. "I must have been thinking aloud. But it's only fair to say that we have *very nearly* covered our outlay. In fact, we are only some three thousand dollars short of the target."

"So?"

The Professor looked away, deeply embarrassed. "Pray proceed."

"*As I was saying*," said Carl, with cruel emphasis, "we still haven't made the price of the tickets. Of course, it's pretty well pure profit from now on, but we've got to make sure that the profit matches the effort, that it's worth all this planning. That means that we've got to take every single chance that's offered, and see that each prospect really pays off, for every cent we can squeeze out of it."

He paused, and his glance went slowly round the table.

"Don't look at me," said Diane cheekily. "I've been doing just that."

"I wasn't looking at anyone. . . . I think, Louis, that you will probably have to break away from—from your present situation. Of course it's an agreeable arrangement, and in ordinary circumstances it would be ideal. But at the moment it does limit you. Don't you agree?"

"Hell," said Louis, sulkily, "I don't know about that. I worked hard enough to set it up. I work hard enough now, God knows. And after all, it's money coming in, every week. What's the matter with that?"

"There could be more money coming in. Perhaps with less time spent on earning it."

The suggestion echoed Louis' own thoughts very closely, but he was not yet ready to acknowledge them in public. "It needs thinking out—" he began.

"You heard what the man said," interrupted Diane. She was in a difficult mood; Louis' earlier remarks about 'store prices' still rankled; she was not missing any chances at evening-up the score. "Don't think—do! Five hundred a week for playing footsie with grandma isn't *work!* You want to get out and about, Junior. Use those rippling muscles, make with the body-urge. This isn't a soft-shoe routine."

"O.K., I'll figure something out," said Louis. The answer was addressed only to Carl; he ignored Diane as if she did not exist, as if her voice were inaudible against the continuous ship's noises. He looked at his watch again. "I guess that's it for me," he said. "I have to keep that date."

"He must have to punch a clock, or something," said Diane, looking after him as the cabin door closed. "I wonder he's strong enough."

Carl glanced round the room, suppressing a sigh. The Professor, his task done, was already dozing off; his head nodded jerkily as it settled on his chest. Kathy, he knew, would not break her long silence; she had nothing to break it with, and in that lay the seeds of conflict—the conflict he knew was coming. He could sense it in Diane's manner, in her reaction to Louis, in the stubborn self-confidence that overlaid the pretty face. She had done well; they had all had to accept it. Now she was going to make some comparisons.

He wondered how she would begin, and he did not have long to wait.

Diane was lighting a cigarette, unhurried, perfectly sure of herself. She had no worries; worries were for people who didn't measure up, who fell down on the job, who perhaps thought they were a shade too good for the situation. All she wanted was a few straight answers.

"Look," she said finally, "there are a couple of things I just don't understand."

"Such as?" asked Carl. He pitched his tone midway between indifference and a polite show of attention. He did not want to give Diane any more latitude than was strictly necessary, but in all fairness she had earned her say. "What's on your mind?"

"The whole set-up." She turned slowly in her chair, so that she was face-to-face with Kathy. "For instance, is she in on this or isn't she?"

It was Kathy who answered. "Of course I'm in on it," she said. "You know that perfectly well. I just haven't started yet. We've talked about that already."

"Sure we've talked about it," said Diane tartly. "We talked about it a fortnight ago. So what happened?"

"Nothing."

Diane waited for her to add to the answer, but no further word broke the silence. Annoyed, she said:

"Nothing? What's that mean, for God's sake? Here am I, working like a short-order cook at Coney Island, and you do *nothing!* What sort of a deal is that? Have I got to finish the trip with round heels, just because you're too lazy to pitch in?"

Carl said: "That has nothing to do with you, Diane. I make the rules, and I'm the only one who has to be satisfied."

Diane eyed him. "*Are* you satisfied?"

"Yes."

"Lucky you! Well, I'm not." Her voice suddenly changed, to a strident malevolence. "What sort of a deal is this, Carl?" she repeated. "You're working, I'm working, even Louis is working. The Prof—" she looked at the ancient nodding figure, "—well, at least he does the chores and keeps the books up-to-date. But Kathy. . . . This was meant to be a team, remember? No wonder we haven't made the price of the tickets, when all she does is sit around reading books and getting herself a tan. If that *is* all she does!"

"What's that meant to mean?" asked Kathy, in the silence that followed.

"Take it whichever way you choose," said Diane, with spiteful carelessness. "You may not be bringing in any money, but you're certainly keeping that kid officer happy!"

"I haven't even seen—" began Kathy impetuously, and then broke off. To identify was to acknowledge; to *know* that Diane was referring to Tim Mansell meant that Tim Mansell must be figuring actively on the scene. He did not do so. No-one figured on the scene. There was no scene. . . . On an impulse she got up, and stretched, and said curtly:

"I think this has gone on long enough."

"You can say that again! In fact—"

"All right, Diane," interrupted Carl. "You've spoken your piece. Now let's leave it."

"But is she going to get to work?" demanded Diane belligerently. "Because if not—"

"If not, what?" asked Carl.

"Well, hell, I'd like to take a rest myself!"

"No-one's going to take a rest."

"Well, that'll be a nice change." Rising, Diane looked across at Kathy. "I've got nothing against you personally, honey," she said, on a slightly conciliatory note. "I just want to know where we all stand."

"Well, you know now."

"O.K." The brief overture evaporated; if Kathy would not meet it, Diane could switch her mood back again just as easily. "But you can't expect me to carry the load for both of us, indefinitely. There was nothing in the contract about Carl playing favourites. Which means that you and I are doing exactly the same job. Which means that you've got nearly four thousand bucks to catch up. Let's see you do it."

The slam of the cabin door behind her woke the Professor momentarily, and he peered round him, with cautious interest. But there seemed, regrettably, to be some sort of crisis in the air; it was not a climate for tired old men who might themselves be in disgrace. He shut his eyes again; it was his only defence measure. There was a long silence, broken only by the Professor's snuffling as he dozed off once more.

Kathy looked at Carl's frowning face. "Am I making it difficult for you, Carl?"

"A little."

"Or a lot?"

"A lot, I suppose."

"I must stop, then. What do you really want me to do?"

He made up his mind, between the question and the answer. "Work," he answered briefly. "Diane's got a point, you know. How *do* you fill in your time?"

She shrugged. "Doing nothing. I'll admit it. But I am there for you."

"I think you'll have to improve on that." There was a shade of annoyance in his tone, perhaps masking something else. She might be 'there for him,' but in fact they had not made love, nor even come near to it, for a long time, and they were both aware of the fact. "Tell me, what was that crack of Diane's about the kid officer?"

"Just Diane."

"Sure?"

"Oh, come, Carl!" she said irritably. "You know me better than that."

In plays, thought Carl, that was the point where the hero put on a meaningful, middle-distance look, and answered: "I wonder if I do. . . ." But he wasn't in that sort of mood. He *did* know her well, and it was ridiculous that they should have scenes like this. He answered, instead:

"We'll be in Rio tomorrow. You'd better start working something out."

"If that's the way you really want it."

"Yes. I do."

"All right. I'll start now."

chapter 5

"I STILL maintain," said Sir Hubert Beckwith, in that clipped British accent which reminded Kathy of the film version of *Little Lord Fauntleroy*, "that as a nation we have a valuable contribution to make. In fact, quite definitely! The world," said Sir Hubert, slipping an unassuming thumb under the back of her dress as they danced, "will be in debt to the English as long as quality and integrity are held in their proper esteem. That has always been our strong point, as you know." The thumb began to explore the small of her back, conveying a discreet yet perceptible message. "We may no longer be rich," said Sir Hubert, "but we have flawless taste, and we have influence. It would be a great mistake to forget either of them."

They were circling the small twilight dance-floor of *Sacha's* on Copacabana Beach, after a day's determined sight-seeing all over Rio de Janeiro, ranging from the superb outlook of Sugar Loaf Mountain to a perfectly horrible black-bean lunch in one of the tourist-trap cafés. The rest of their party of six were sitting it out at one of the wall-tables; here and there in the room were other passengers from the *Alcestis*, eating Fish Porridge and drinking "Brahma Extra" beer in accordance with the directive in the ship's daily bulletin. Nearer the dance-floor, Kathy had observed, was a table of about a dozen of their officers, presided over by the Captain. Tim Mansell was among them, slightly flushed, audibly argumentative. She had smiled at him, but he had failed to smile back. His table included old Mr. Simms' ex-nurse, a girl from the ship's hair-dressers, and one of the two female junior pursers. To hell with him, she thought.

She and Carl were there as part of the recurrent entertainment protocol, which operated in every port they touched. This time it was the Tillotsons' party; they had invited the Beckwiths because they owed them a night out from as long ago as Port of Spain, and they had invited Carl and herself because Carl, as a fellow poker-player, seemed to be Mr. Tillotson's natural companion on board. Whether the latter had any other reason for the invitation, had not yet become apparent. She herself liked *Sacha's* very much; it had the right combination of luxury, semi-darkness, good music, and a whopping cover-charge which marked all the best night-clubs in all the best countries.

If there were things included in it which she did not relish—such as Sir Hubert Beckwith's thumb, and his unassailable self-conceit—they still did not obtrude too much. She would dispose of them, because (like it or not) she was involved in that sort of business; and she and Carl, together and separately, were strong enough (like Edgar the barman) to assimilate everyone else's problems and still do a day's work. Tonight, Carl would deal with Lady Beckwith, whose preoccupations were emeralds and status, and with Mrs. Tillotson, beset by homesickness involving her grandchildren. For herself, Beckwith boiled down to no more than a thumb massaging her spine, and Tillotson (so far) to a minute exploratory flicker of the eye.

Ranging further afield, if Tim Mansell were too sad or angry to return her smile, it only meant that he was not measuring up to his own particular problems, which involved, presumably, that stupid bitch of a nurse now toppling over into his lap.

Perhaps, thought Kathy, she was not really in a good mood at all, in spite of *Sacha's* and the other delights of Rio. Perhaps she was in a lousy one. It was a question, now, as to who was going to pay for it.

"I cannot emphasize enough," said Sir Hubert, looming over her like a rubber light-house, "that dollars are not everything. I always remember some lecturer fellow in Boston once saying that life was now a synthesis of the three D's—dollars, dynamism, and destiny." His encircling hand achieved a really remarkable subcutaneous grip. "I may have got the actual details wrong, but the sense is certainly there. And some of us—*some of us*—still prefer destiny."

"Gentlemen," said Captain Harmer, who was in an expansive mood, "with a view to encouraging thrift among my officers, the next round is on me."

At this point of the voyage, the Captain was always relaxed and content; indeed, the officers' party at *Sacha's* was traditional, and at one point or another the Captain always made his benign comment about thrift. He was looking forward with satisfaction to the run from Rio to Cape Town; it promised him over three thousand miles of sea-time with never a sight of land, with only the lonely deeps of the South Atlantic under his keel. Eighteen thousand feet, twenty thousand feet—these were real sailor's soundings, worth celebrating.

His officers needed the party for a different reason. It was all very well for the Captain to feel at his best when they were furthest from land; but the passengers tended not to like it at all, and what the passengers didn't like, the officers, in the end, paid for. Rio was their chance to relax after the varied chores of the past six weeks; but it was also their preparation for the long haul, trackless and featureless, which lay ahead. The Cape Town run had many hazards, all of them man-made.

From Rio to Cape Town, people grew bored; feuds came to a head, complaints multiplied, everyone quarreled. There was always a time, on any voyage, when any given passenger would make any given remark; this, for the present cruise, was it. *Alcestis'* only manslaughter to date—a heavy bottle through a light skull—had occurred on this section of the trip.

With no shore excursion to break the monotony, with nothing to look at save those dear familiar faces, this was where the passengers really started to wonder if they had thrown away their passage-money; and it was here, possibly, that the *Alcestis* could have done with a cruise-director—preferably a very funny one who could sing, dance, and juggle for twenty-four hours a day.

When his round of drinks was brought, the Captain raised his glass. In the murky, somewhat Latinized atmosphere of *Sacha's*, he was as trim and as English as a cold cut of beef.

"Gentlemen," he said. (They could always tell when the Captain was two or three drinks on the way; he started *all* his sentences with the word 'gentlemen.') "Here's to a successful second half of the voyage."

They all drank; the Chief Engineer, the Purser, Tiptree-Jones, Blantyre; and further down the table Beresford the apprentice, the girl from the hair-dresser's, Fleming the young engineer, Tim Mansell, Faith Bartlett who had been Mr. Simms' nurse, and the plain girl from the Purser's Office who was universally known as Good Old Joan. It was a mixed party, with expansive confidence at the top, a wary good behaviour in the middle, and unpredictable reactions at the lower levels. Mr. Cutler the Purser, for example, was in a genial story-telling mood; Tim Mansell, on the other hand, was sad, slightly tight, and resigned to a lifetime of lonely insignificance. It was he who, responding *sotto voce* to the Captain's toast, murmured:

"What was so successful about the first half?"

"Now don't be like that!" said Faith Bartlett, a wayward character who was demonstrably not like that at all. "Cheer up! Have fun! We're all going to South Africa. Remember?"

"I remember," answered Tim Mansell morosely. His eyes followed Kathy as she danced with Sir Hubert Beckwith. "What's the good of South Africa to me? I've been to South Africa. It's not going to make any difference."

"You could always get a soft shore job," said Fleming. "Cape Town agent for Myth Lines. A hundred pounds a month, and all the coloured girls you can eat."

"I think it's disgusting," declared Good Old Joan, with a shiver, "the way you men talk!" She lived, indeed, in a state of perpetual dismay; no personal hazards came her way, only second-hand accounts, filtering through the ship's grape-vine, of maidens overthrown, young men fleeing without their trousers, old men caught in the hard-won throes of carnal knowledge. "Why can't you be *normal?*"

"We are," said Beresford, an indubitably normal young man. "In fact, you're sitting at a table with the only normal characters on board." He nodded towards the Captain and his entourage; his voice dropped, theatrically. "All they do is talk about it. We *do* it!"

"I don't know what you mean," said Good Old Joan.

"Neither do I," said Faith Bartlett, with a different kind of authority. "No-one's done it to me, I can promise you." She nudged Tim Mansell. "Did you hear that, Fourth?"

"Don't call me Fourth," said Tim.

"But everyone calls you Fourth."

"Not girls."

"What do girls call you?" asked Fleming, now speaking over his shoulder. He was busy on his long-term pursuit of the hair-dressing girl, an unclassifiable blonde called Estelle. Their knees were glued together, their hands intertwined like plaits, but she wore, even now, the same totally preoccupied look with which she dealt with finger-waves and incipient dandruff. Her husband was a Brooklyn detective, long estranged; she did not even like men, only hair problems and the small, minutely-growing savings account which would one day give her independence. "What do girls call you?" asked Fleming again, dropping his free hand onto Estelle's thigh. "Just so as we know."

"Oh, cut it out!" said Tim Mansell irritably. "If you want to be funny, practise on somebody else."

"My goodness," said Good Old Joan. "You *are* in a bad way! Crossed in love? Is that it?"

"Of course he's crossed in love," said Faith Bartlett. Her roving, somewhat spiteful eyes rested for a moment on Kathy, as she swum past in the arms of Sir Hubert. "Your girl friend's doing all right for herself," she said, in a lower tone. "None of my business, and *don't* think I'm worrying. But if you really want to make good, you'd better hurry it up."

Kathy danced with Mr. Tillotson. She knew hardly anything about him, as a man, and he still gave little away. It was only a thought that she had had, buttressed by the briefest of indications, fed by tiny hints, by nudges of instinct. In the past weeks, they had sometimes mingled eyes; she had intercepted a stare, she had noticed a devious manoeuvre which placed him next to her at parties or at film shows. But even now, as he danced, he was not committing himself; the arm round her waist, though strong, was not a confessional arm, nor an intrusive one. He was either very shy, or he could not make up his mind, or he was resisting temptation for severe moral reasons, or else she had mistaken her man altogether. But she did not think so.

She liked him, as did everyone else on board. Gossip invariably tagged him as the richest man in the ship; but, save for a certain crisp command when he wanted attention, one would not have guessed it. He had the small man's compact strength without the small man's cockiness; it seemed likely that he had got where he was by merit and luck, not by swindling or manipulation.

Kathy found it impossible to guess, except at a very crude level, why, at this stage of his life, Tillotson should have become vulnerable to physical urges and needs; it could not spring from any deep division between himself and his wife. Mrs. Tillotson was, by common consent, a darling; sweet-tempered, gently-spoken, a repository for everyone else's confidences and problems. The two of them seemed ideally suited, obviously happy; no hint of a quarrel, no sign of impatience or frustration, had ever become apparent. And yet, and yet. . . . Kathy still had an absolute certainty that Tillotson wanted something from her; perhaps a brief excitement, a mere pleasurable spasm which would touch him not at all, perhaps something deeper and more fundamental—a reassurance, a flattering renewal of his youth.

There were men who, in middle age, appraised the years ahead against the years behind, and sought to prove that they could still kill a bottle, raise plenty of hell, lay any pretty girl they wanted to, just the way it used to be. . . . In men of quality, it was always a surprise. But it did happen.

Tillotson moved away from her, holding her at arm's length for a moment. His eyes below the crisp grey hair were quizzical, his firm mouth amused.

"Penny for them," he said.

Kathy smiled. "Oh, I was just thinking."

"I know that. You looked as if you were a million miles away."

"No, indeed. The exact opposite."

His eyebrows went up a fraction. "Thinking of me?"

She nodded. "Just that."

On the verge of saying something in answer, he changed his mind, and his expression grew noncommittal again. He drew her gently towards him, but it was not an approach, simply a return to normal. She realized that, even in that modest moment of invitation, she had moved too fast. He was not ready yet, and he was not going to be rushed.

She made up her mind. Tillotson would keep, perhaps for ever. Sir Hubert now stood at the head of the menu.

Entertaining the top end of the officers' table, out of ear-shot of the impressionable young women lower down, Mr. Cutler the Purser was telling a story. He was a great story-teller; he had stories for every category and every sub-division of passenger; he had stories for his superiors, he had stories for stewards. He could always suit his company, whether it were official or polite or relaxed or bawdy. But he had a taste for what might be called shaggy-girl anecdotes, and he was indulging this now.

"There was this new draft of twenty Wrens," he said, straight-faced. "They were having a full-scale medical examination on a very cold day in naval barracks. They were kept on parade for an hour, stark naked, temperature of zero, very draughty. Then the door opened, and what do you think came out?"

His audience waited.

"Forty blue-tits," said Mr. Cutler.

He got his laugh, from the Chief Engineer and the others, even from the Captain, who, a puritan soul, had a vague feeling that such stories were bad for discipline. Tiptree-Jones laughed heartily as soon as he saw the Captain doing the same. Relaxing, they looked round them, enjoying *Sacha's*, and the cool dark beer, and the beat and sway of the music. They couldn't really afford such cushioned luxury, as the passengers could, but once in a while it seemed a permissible waste of money.

Mr. Cutler, glancing down the length of the table, said:

"Young Tim looks a bit under the weather."

Captain Harmer looked in the same direction. "So he does." He raised his voice: "Fourth!"

"Sir?" said Tim Mansell, swinging round.

"Cheer up," commanded the Captain. "Aren't you enjoying yourself?"

"Yes, sir," answered Tim. "I'm enjoying myself very much."

"You don't look like it."

Blantyre, the third officer, who acted as a link between the top brass and the juniors, said: "It must be love, sir. Hopeless unrequited love."

"Oh, cut it out," said Tim under his breath.

"Who is it, Fourth?" asked Tiptree-Jones. They all knew, but they were in the mood to play along with the joke. "Maybe we could help. Is it anyone we know?"

"It isn't anyone," said Tim sulkily.

Kathy and Mr. Tillotson, circling the dance-floor, passed close by their table.

"Why don't you dance with her?" asked Blantyre, when she was out of earshot. "Give her a real treat."

"I don't know what you mean."

"Perhaps she likes older men," Beresford chipped in. "I read in a magazine once—"

"You shut up!" said Tim savagely.

"*I* like older men," announced Faith Bartlett. "And I like younger men. In fact, I like men, period."

"How can you say things like that?" demanded Good Old Joan, embarrassed. "You might as well say—well, I mean—" she broke off, floundering in shocked speculation.

Fleming squeezed the hair-dressing girl fondly, and inquired:

"Do you like men, darling?"

"I like men," said the hair-dressing girl, preoccupied as usual, "like I like enlarged pores."

"That's my girl," said Fleming.

The music ceased, with a flurry of bongo drums; Kathy put her hand lightly on Tillotson's arm as they left the dance-floor. She was looking lovely, thought Tim, watching her with hot and miserable eyes. The loveliest girl in the whole world. Hanging onto that old man's arm as if they were going to bed together. And the way she walked . . . He turned away, in absolute unhappiness, and made a desperate effort to exorcize the moment. Glass in hand, he leant towards Faith Bartlett, until he was staring directly into her eyes.

"Now, nurse," he said, "tell me about your problem."

Kathy danced with Carl Wenstrom. They danced well together, from long practise; his tall body moved gracefully, and she followed him with instinctive pleasure. They stayed near the centre of the floor, withdrawn from the other couples and from the tables close to the edge. Carl spoke softly, with no change of expression, and she answered him in the same fashion.

"Bring me up to date," he said.

"It looks like Beckwith," she answered indifferently. "Tillotson's playing it very cagey. In fact, he might never get to the point. But Beckwith will."

"How do you know that?"

She shrugged. "Oh—you know. He's pressing ahead whenever he gets the chance. Busy fingers. He's a cold-blooded fish really, and scared to death as well, but I'm getting the message. And so is he."

"I am almost jealous," said Carl.

She dared not bring her body closer to his, but she squeezed his arm slightly. "You know you needn't be. You're worth ten of these dopes. But I've got to put out some sort of a welcome-mat, haven't I?"

"Undoubtedly." He looked down at her for a moment, enjoying the warm, creamy curve of her bosom above the pale green dress. "You're looking very lovely tonight, my darling. Do I see you later?"

"I hope so." They circled once before she spoke again. "It depends how long this thing takes to develop, and what happens."

"You think it will be tonight?"

"Maybe. I haven't worked things out. It might help if you kept old Lady Snootwith busy when we get back on board. Trouble is, she has him running errands the whole time."

"So what's the answer?"

The music was coming to a close. "I haven't worked things out," she said again. Her forehead was creased with a tiny frown. "Has Beckwith ever been in your cabin? Do you think he would remember the number?"

Carl shook his head. "No. He's had a drink in the sitting-room once or twice. But he wouldn't know which of the other rooms are yours and mine. Why?"

"Just an idea. I thought it might increase the pressure if I took him into your cabin, and then told him you were likely to come back any time."

"It's a possibility."

She nodded, as the music stopped and the dancers began to move back to their tables. "Yes. I'll probably try that. You'd better stay out of the way, or use my cabin, till I give you the word."

"O.K." As they walked back, he said: "I see your *other* admirer isn't looking quite so sad now."

She glanced briefly at Tim Mansell. "Oh, him. . . . That nurse really is a menace, isn't she?"

"She makes me glad I am not ill," answered Carl. Coming towards their table, he added: "Ah, we have a visitor."

The Captain had joined them for a moment, greeting their table heartily and accepting a whisky-and-soda at Tillotson's invitation. His good-humor was infectious; their group, which had not been notable for its high spirits, soon grew cheerful and lively. But presently it was time to leave; the *Alcestis* would be sailing at first light, and they were due back on board not later than two o'clock. Tillotson, calling for their bill, frowned in mock dismay as he noted the total.

"Well, it's cheaper than playing poker," he remarked, "and that's about all you can say for it."

Captain Harmer nodded. "Ah yes, I heard you had a regular game going. Who's the big winner?"

Carl and Tillotson both answered: "He is," at the same moment, and then burst out laughing.

"You must be 'way ahead," said Tillotson.

"Perhaps a little," admitted Carl. "I haven't been keeping strict accounts. But I can feel you breathing down my neck most of the time."

"You play a heavy game?" asked Harmer.

"A moderate game," answered Carl. He smiled at the Captain; there was between them a mutual respect and liking which rose from small things, things heard and seen and reported at odd moments during the past six weeks. They faced each other as strong and competent men in their own chosen worlds. "We don't want to give the ship a bad name, do we?"

They were all preparing to move; Sir Hubert was collecting things for his wife—her stole, her cigarettes, her lighter which had fallen to the floor. But then, out of the corner of his eye, Carl noticed that Beckwith was hanging back, so that presently he was walking to the door beside Kathy. He could be heard to say, in well-bred tones whose nonchalance failed to conceal a hint of invitation:

"I must say I'm still pretty wide-awake. We might have a night-cap on board, what?"

Carl, motioning to the Captain to precede him, smiled inwardly. It sounded as though tonight would indeed be the night.

It had started, like all English love-making, as a series of merry jokes and timid ventures. How about a goodnight drink, ha! ha! My wife seems to be busy, ha! ha! More cosy in your cabin, what? Ha! Ha! Let's put the lights out and enjoy the view, ha! ha! Perhaps we'll be more comfortable on the bed, ha! ha! ha! But from then on, helped by alcohol and judicious favours, Beckwith had gained courage and a certain crude insistence; and his last throw of the dice—" Better lock the door, what?"—had been made with hard-breathing authority. She had locked both doors, and pushed the key out of sight behind a pile of magazines. Then she turned, and in the light of the bedside lamp found that the action was about to be joined.

Sir Hubert Beckwith was discarding his trousers. Even this he managed to do as if he were conferring nobility upon some female peasant. He had a monogram on his under-pants. The time had clearly come.

Kathy sat down on the bed, and said, in a very distinct voice: "What in hell are you doing?"

Sir Hubert started. Above the hum of the engines, and the creaking noises the *Alcestis* always made at sea, Kathy's words had rung out with electrifying clarity. He straightened up, a lanky and ridiculous figure in his striped under-pants, and said, in a nervous whisper:

"Sh! Not so loud, for heaven's sake! Someone will hear."

"I should damn well hope so!" said Kathy, with the same clarity and force. "What do you think this is? The locker-room at the Y?"

Irresolute, not equipped to argue from so weak a position, he said: "But I thought. . . . Good heavens, we were just talking about it! I mean, not in so many words, but. . . . I thought when you kissed me—"

"Have you gone completely nuts? I asked you down for a drink, and you suddenly start undressing! What do you think you're going to do?"

It was sufficiently clear what Sir Hubert had thought he was going to do, and equally clear that he could quickly lose his appetite for it. Already he had picked his trousers up, with a kind of sulky grandeur, and was drawing them on again. He must, thought Kathy, have felt himself excessively vulnerable, if it had taken so little to unnerve him; fear of scandal, warring briefly with desire, had overrun the position and dictated a most prompt retreat. It was worth remembering. . . . Adjusting his scarlet braces, he said, in tones of majestic reproof:

"You seem to have changed your mind. It's really quite extraordinary!"

Kathy waited. Her disgust at the situation was almost dispelled by its humour; it was all she could do not to burst out laughing in his face. Finally, when he was fully dressed again, and preparing aloofly to leave, she said:

"Not quite so fast. Do you think you can get away with this? Wait till my step-father hears about it!"

"I hope," said Sir Hubert, in perceptible alarm, "that you will not be silly enough to tell him."

"Tell him?" Kathy forced a full measure of indignation into her voice. "I won't need to tell him! He'll find out, soon enough! And so will your wife."

Sir Hubert started again, more violently, as if a painful nerve had been touched. It was the first time he had reacted naturally, without reserve or hauteur; both seemed to be melting away. "My wife has nothing whatever to do with this," he said, in a thoroughly uncertain voice.

"Not yet, she hasn't," answered Kathy. "She's up on the bridge with my step-father and some of the others, seeing the sunrise. You know that, darn well." Her voice took on a crisp inflexion. "But soon it'll be light, and then they'll all come down."

"Well?" But he knew the answer already.

"Your wife will come looking for you. And my step-father will find us here, with the door locked."

"But nothing's happened."

"Try and tell him that!"

"Why should he come here, anyway?"

"This is his cabin."

Sir Hubert, who was obviously not at his best, took a few moments to work the situation out. But when it hit him, it was a mortal wound.

"My God!" he said. "You planned this whole thing."

"Yes."

"What is it you want?"

"Money."

Sir Hubert swallowed, as if he had something very unusual to admit. Finally he admitted it. "I haven't any."

"Don't give me that," said Kathy crudely. "You can't have come on a cruise like this, and not have money. Look at those cuff-links. Look at that cigarette-case. You've got plenty! Give some to me."

"I mean, I never carry any money with me."

"Then you'd better leave me the links and the case, while you go and get some." As he advanced a step towards her, she said: "Don't try anything rough, or I'll start ringing bells and screaming the place down."

"Let me out of here," said Sir Hubert stoutly. But his front was crumbling from moment to moment; there was now a wildness in his look which was a long way from the noble suavity which had been his most detested hallmark. He turned, and tried the doorknob. "Where's the key? Give me the key."

"Give me the money," she countered, "and you'll get the key. You won't get it otherwise!"

"It's my word against yours!" His voice had sharpened a full octave of hysteria.

"Maybe. But do you really want my step-father knocking on that door? What are you going to say to him? What are you going to tell your wife? The door locked itself? You were afraid of burglars? You'd better pay up, and damn quickly!"

Sir Hubert stood looking at her for a full half minute, the sweat gleaming dull on his forehead. It was clear that he was beginning to be terrified; the idea of his wife finding him in the cabin, or even hearing about it afterwards, must have seemed in the realm of irretrievable disaster. He tried the door again, with furtive, futile energy; the fact that it was still locked seemed to push him over the edge of self-control. Turning away, he collapsed into a chair, and covered his face with his hands. From there, he mumbled indistinctly:

"I haven't any money. It's all my wife's."

They were getting on, thought Kathy; he had made the big admission, breaching the dyke of his enormous self-esteem, and soon he would make others as well. The important thing was to keep him on the run.

"Of course it's all your wife's," she answered roughly. "Who do you think you've been fooling? Everyone in the ship knows you're a full-time phoney! But you can still get some money. From her. Can't you?"

Sir Hubert would no longer look at her. By the ebbing of alcohol, by the terror of discovery, he was reduced to a small ashamed voice in a collapsing world. "She keeps me very short," he said finally. "A sort of allowance. I can't possibly ask for more. I have to account for every penny of it, as it is." After a moment he added: "You can't imagine what it's like."

Kathy stared at him. If he was acting, it was a very good act; but she knew that he was telling the truth. Only a desperate fear would have made him admit such pitiful facts. She hardened her heart, determined to make some advantage out of it.

"O.K., have it your own way. We'll just stay here till something happens. I'm not giving you the key until you pay, that's for sure."

"But I can't pay." His voice was now dull, as if many shameful blows were falling on him at the same time. "I haven't any money left. Literally none at all."

"How much does she give you?" asked Kathy curiously.

"It varies with—with how she feels. Last week it was ten dollars."

Between pity and disgust, she was almost ready to write the whole thing off, and let him go. She was using a lever against a vacuum; there was nothing to be gained from this *insect* of a man. . . . But before she could make up her mind, Beckwith was speaking again; the words suddenly began to pour out, and though his head was still bowed and he was talking to the floor, she knew that he was aiming directly at her heart, out of his terrible need.

It was as if he could not explain fast enough, nor dig deep enough for the degrading truth; it was as if he had not spoken this truth, nor even glanced secretly in its direction, for as long as he could remember. She sat down, compelled to let the torrent of words swamp her.

"You don't know what it's like, being dependent on a woman like that." His voice was a gabble, but a clear gabble none-the-less. "She doesn't let me forget it for a single second. . . . It was all right at the beginning, but that was twelve years ago. I was thirty-six. . . . She gave me everything when we were first married; clothes, cars, horses, a wonderful house, jewellery, travel. The title was new to her and she loved it, and she loved me. . . . Then it all changed, I don't know why. She saw that I'd got used to all the luxuries, all the money, and that I couldn't do without them, and she started to ration me. . . . Then she began making a fool of me in public—no, not quite making a fool of me, but using me to run endless ridiculous errands. There was one embassy party in London when I had to stand beside her with an ashtray. Oh God!" he exclaimed suddenly, as if he could stand the contemplation no longer, "give me a drink, for Christ's sake!"

She rose, without a word, and poured out some brandy, and gave it to him. The recital was disgusting, but beyond disgust was an appalled sense of pity; Beckwith was all the bad words—sponger, parasite, fake—but he was reduced now to a simpler emblem—total defeat. The haughty façade of the years, the self-deception, the armour of arrogance, all were melting away. She had a frightening suspicion that, when all was gone, there might not even be a man left.

He gulped his drink, raising his head only a fraction to do so. "You don't know what it's like," he said again. "Fetching things, finding things she's lost, buying things and bringing back the change. . . . Being sent on errands. Being *interrupted,* told to keep quiet. And making love to order. Getting ten dollars when she was pleased. . . . Once we were in Paris, and I lost a watch she'd given me, and she wouldn't believe I'd lost it, she said I'd sold it and kept the money, and she took away all my clothes and called the police. They must have thought we were both crazy. . . ." He raised his head at last; there were tears glistening in his eyes. "Let me go," he said suddenly, humbly. "I've nothing to give you. You can see that, can't you?"

She could indeed see it, and she was prepared to let him go; but remembering his manner of the past, his purse-proud, title-proud disdain, she could not control her wish to hurt. He was going to get off easily, but not as easily as that.

"Sure you can go," she said contemptuously. "Who wants you?"

"Thank you," he said, with the same humility, and stood up, his shoulders slack.

"Are you really a man?"

"I—I don't know."

Suddenly the revenge was nothing. In an absurd reversal of roles, she felt herself softening, to the point where she wanted to build up again, to restore something of manhood. Anything was better than this cringeing spaniel, in naked fear of losing his meal-ticket.

"Why not get out of it altogether?" she asked.

"How do you mean?"

"Leave her. Beat it. Find some work. Do anything. You must have been something before. Be it again."

"I was nothing before." She felt that she was now listening to an entirely natural man, stripped of all the pretense, all the shoddy gilding. "I never had any money. Just the title. There were three lots of death-duties in ten years. . . . This is all I can do."

"Why?"

"I just know it is."

It was as she had suspected and feared; the natural man was nothing, just as the fake man was nothing. She took the key from behind the magazines, and unlocked the door. Then she stood aside.

"Beat it," she said.

Awkwardly he advanced. "Thank you very much. I'm sorry about the misunderstanding."

"There wasn't any misunderstanding."

"Goodnight, then."

She did not answer, and when she was alone she stood for a long time in thought, staring at the closed door. Then she began to laugh, silently at first, and then aloud. So much for the first attempt at piracy. She thought of her accounting at the next meeting. "Sir Hubert Beckwith— Nothing." Most accurate. . . . She was still laughing when Carl came in, but the laughter was nearer to tears—tears for her own failure, tears for all the failures in the world. She was overwrought by the degrading tug-of-war; in such a contest, who was the victor, who the vanquished?

"What happened?" asked Carl, watching her with some concern. "I just came down—I was next door—I heard him go. How much did he give you?"

"Not a dollar, not a cent." And as he looked puzzled: "You know those Christmas-present ads— 'For the man who has everything'?" Her voice began to shake uncontrollably. "There should be another line of goods, for the man who has nothing. Beckwith would be a real candidate."

"Are you all right, Kathy?"

"Oh yes, I'm wonderful!" Suddenly she threw herself on the bed, and turned her face away; it seemed the most pitiable and evil moment of her life. "I'm wonderful," she repeated, her eyes now scalding. "But only by comparison."

chapter 6

EAST by south from Rio, the *Alcestis* ploughed her brave and steady furrow across the South Atlantic, traversing as quickly as possible the long haul to Cape Town. The Captain, personally, was in no hurry; he would have preferred to stay in these indulgent latitudes for ever, with only the dolphins and the flying fish for company, and two thousand fathoms of blue water to play with. But he had other responsibilities; chiefly, to see that his passengers crossed three thousand miles of ocean, and made their landfall in South Africa, without coming to blows or sending priority cables ahead for plane reservations to New York. Since, at their best speed of fifteen knots, the journey could not take less than nine days, their best speed it had to be, to minimize the chances of disaster. In the meantime, his officers put forth prodigious efforts to keep the customers amused.

Competitions multiplied, games were stepped up; there was a succession of tournaments—pingpong, deck-tennis, shuffleboard, swimming, diving, horse-racing—to take the main edge off the day; and in the evenings, fancy-dress dances, film shows, bingo sessions, and gala dinners varied the monotony of a landless passage. Above all, the passengers were encouraged, by example and by stealthy hint, to give parties themselves. The fact that the same people came to all of them could not be helped, and was, perforce, taken for granted.

The Zuccos gave a "historical characters" costume-party; there were eight Napoleons, eleven Helens of Troy, and endless bickering about the prizes. The Bancrofts gave a champagne party, and the Gersons, not to be outdone, an oyster supper. Carl gave a smaller party in his suite; it was amusing for the entirely private reason that the majority of their guests were connected by adultery. The Beddingtons gave a moonlight dance, virtually in pitch darkness, up on the boat-deck; it was in such circumstances, people said unkindly, that Bernice Beddington looked at her best. Mr. Walham, in spite of the broadest encouragement, failed to give a party; Mrs. van Dooren gave one, and didn't even show up.

But there were quarrels none-the-less; feuds sprang up, remarks were taken the wrong way, carelessly-passed drinks seemed, later, to have been spilt on purpose. There was one glorious row, which reached as far as the Captain's cabin—and stopped there—when Mrs. Kincaid told a select circle of friends, not more than ten or twelve, that the blonde girl who called herself Mrs. Burrell had better get married fast because she was undoubtedly pregnant; whereupon Mr. Burrell, a proud husband in fact and a prouder father in embryo, countered with the comment that he would sue the Kincaids for a million dollars—the exact amount, he affirmed, missing from the public treasury in the Kincaids' home-town. (Captain Harmer dealt with this affair so sternly and scathingly that the contestants, cowed, came together and swore eternal enmity—towards him.) But there was no row to match the row which developed after the ship's concert. That, as Mrs. van Dooren put it, was a real honey. She added her own obscure superlative; it had, she said, everything but pink lemonade.

The programme for the ship's concert developed somewhat bashfully at first, but during the last forty-eight hours before the performance the idea caught on, and finally everyone wanted to get into the act. The task, which fell to Tiptree-Jones, of auditioning the available talent and deciding which would qualify and which must be declined, was a formidable one; it was safe to say that by the time the curtain went up, almost the entire audience were composed of rejected performers who were not in the mood to admire anyone else's talents.

Tiptree-Jones himself led off the show with a comedy conjuring routine. It was the sort of thing he was good at; but too many of the audience, denied by this very man the chance to tap-dance or sing "Asleep in the Deep," buttoned up their smiles and sat on their hands. A flop. Nurse Bartlett sang songs from "Oklahoma" and "South Pacific"; but as a pretty girl she was unpopular with those who mainly moulded public opinion, and as a nurse she was notorious for having lost a patient, no doubt through neglect. Another flop. Two stewards then embarked on a cross-talk act; it was funny if one could appreciate English music-hall humour, and unravel a Liverpool accent as well, but not otherwise. The applause was generous rather than appreciative. It was now the turn of Mr. Zucco, who, looking like Buster Keaton and sounding like the public image of Sam Goldwyn, told a succession of funny stories. They were not at all funny; and he ended with a Jewish dialect anecdote so unmistakably crude that the audience gasped, and his wife's cheerful laugh rang out over acres of shocked silence. A flop, indeed.

That left Mr. Hartmann, one of the poker players, who juggled with pingpong balls and expendable glassware; Jack Gerson, who was far from sober and did impressions, appallingly similar, of Bing Crosby, Lionel Barrymore, and James Stewart; and two more stewards, who went through a slow-motion wrestling routine copied from an early film of Mickey Rooney. The audience, restive, began to talk out loud, complaining of favouritism and ineptitude. The husbands and wives of the performers clapped energetically, glaring round them. Tiptree-Jones, harassed beneath his easy social manner and aware of the Captain's critical eye from the front row of chairs, stepped forward and announced: "We come now to our final turn—last but not least, to coin a phrase—Mrs. Burkhart, soprano."

Mrs. Burkhart was not a soprano, but she was everything else; it was indeed unfortunate that Tiptree-Jones had used the expression "last but not least," which scored an immediate laugh as soon as she stepped onto the stage. For Mrs. Burkhart was a huge woman, on whose monumental bosom the music-sheet quivered like a newspaper caught on a mountain ledge. The piano rattled, the very floor-boards shook, as she took up a stance like a prize-fighter; then she launched forth, at full blast, her giant arms flexed, her enormous diaphragm rising and falling like some vast, ruined *soufflé*, into her song.

It was unfortunate, again, that the song she had chosen was "The Lass with the Delicate Air." Someone snickered audibly as the first words recalled the song's title; the laughter thickened and spread as the absurd phrases, appropriate only to some shy wood-nymph weighing not more than ninety-five pounds, came booming forth from this heroic amplifier. There were angry shushing noises, but not enough to overcome the laughter, which had gained a determined, cruel hold. Mrs. Burkhart only survived two verses; increasingly aware of her audience, angry with the pianist whose instrument was no match for her own, she stumbled over the girlish trill which went with the word "delicate", and came to a ragged stop. The laughter was a long time subsiding; but to match it there was in the audience another faction, grim-faced, scandalized, which now called for order and shouted "Encore!"

There could be no encore. Mrs. Burkhart swept from the stage, followed by the pianist, running to keep up with her; while from the second row of the audience a furious red-faced man—Mr. Burkhart—rose like a thunder-cloud and strode off in the direction of the Purser's office.

That was a row which was a long time dying, capping as it did an evening which had inspired plenty of bad feeling already. All over the ship argument broke out like an endemic rash; cabin doors were slammed, drinks refused, lips pursed, angry charges made. The number of people who were not on speaking terms next morning exceeded all previous figures. But the Captain, mulling it over with his First Officer afterwards, was not too perturbed. Rows were standard practise at this stage of the voyage; they rarely got by the ship's concert without some furious tribal outbreak. The *Alcestis*, however, was making good progress, under the arching sky and the benign glow of the Southern Cross; and there was a report of bad weather, about five hundred miles ahead, directly in their path. That was nicely calculated to take the mickey out of everyone.

Louis Scapelli had finally had enough of it. More than enough. It had been sufficiently annoying, though tolerable, to be at Mrs. Consolini's beck and call on a twenty-four hour basis; at least the manly incidents of the night made up for the bell-hop aspects of the day, at least he was earning part of his money honestly. But lately he had noticed a change; the fetching-and-carrying had been stepped up, while there appeared to be little or no call for any more significant activity. As a matter of fact she was bored with it, she told him coolly, when he brought the subject up, one afternoon in her cabin. It wasn't all that important; with him, it never had been. Meanwhile, she wanted to give a party, tomorrow night. About sixteen people; the list was on her desk. Would he fix it, please? Last time, there hadn't been nearly enough caviar among the canapés. He really ought to watch out for that—the ship was full of it, it was just slackness on the part of the stewards. And she had left her library book somewhere. She would like it now.

Louis finally exploded. "What do you want to go and leave your stuff around for? Do you think I've nothing better to do than—than—"

She eyed him coldly. "Than what?"

He stared back at her, bad-tempered, ready for a collision. "Than run around after you like this?"

"No."

"What do you mean, no?"

"I mean, you *haven't* anything better to do. Not as long as I'm paying the shot. You'll do what I want, and if it's my book I want, you'll go get it."

"Get it yourself," he said angrily. "I'm sick of this."

"Very big and bold." Her voice was sarcastic. Momentarily he wondered if she were staging a show-down on purpose; if so, he was more than ready for it. "But I don't pay you five hundred a week to be sick of anything. Go get that book for me, and then come back and fix up about the party. I'll want fresh flowers for it, too."

"No." He should have let the bald refusal stand by itself; but because she had always held the commanding position, had called the tune for so long, he found himself adding, lamely: "I'm tired. Just leave me alone, will you?"

But she was not going to take any excuses. It was the first time he had shown any sign of rebellion, and, one way or the other, it was going to be the last. Their relationship had now continued for nearly a month; it had been fun at the beginning, as all aspects of command were fun; but the fun ceased as soon as the command was challenged. She didn't want a contest of wills; she wanted a captive. And captives didn't argue.

"You heard what I said, Scapelli," she answered brusquely. "Do I have to tell you twice?"

He remained staring at her in silence. He had had enough, certainly, but now that the moment of crisis was at hand, he was not quite determined enough to make the break himself. Let her be the executioner, he thought, and himself the injured party. That way, he would be left with a grudge, which was the way he always preferred it.

"Scapelli—" she began again.

"Don't call me Scapelli!" he snapped. "My name's Louis. Use it."

"Scapelli," she repeated, as if he had not spoken—and instinctively he knew who would be the next character to appear. Her husband—the man always at hand to settle any arguments. "My husband always said that—"

"To hell with your husband!" he answered. "I'm sick of hearing about him. I don't believe he ever did anything worth a damn. He's dead anyway. Maybe he's better off, at that."

She looked at him levelly. "Now we're getting at the truth. It sounds as though you want out."

"I want out of this sort of thing." He swept his hand around the cabin, which in its untidy luxury seemed to reflect all the things about her he most disliked. "Doing the chores for you—I've had enough of it!"

But she did not intend to allow so quick a break; the dismissal was to be staged in her own good time. "Who's next on your list, then?"

"What do you mean?"

"You know darn well what I mean. You'll be losing five hundred dollars a week. You must have thought up another prospect, before you started acting so tough. Who's it going to be?" She smiled unpleasantly. "Maybe it's a pity Grace Stewart-Bates got away. People like her don't grow on trees."

It was not a pity, of course; it was the best thing that could have happened. Mrs. Stewart-Bates had left the ship at Rio, alleging ill-health; but before she had cut her losses, there had been, for Louis, a very uncomfortable period during which she appeared to be haunting him. He had run into her at every corner, every party, every shore excursion; there were times when the entire passenger-list seemed to have been reduced to a single pair of sad, accusing eyes, staring at himself and Belle Consolini as if the two of them were jointly responsible for all the misery in the world.

He had not felt threatened by it—he knew she would never dare confess what had happened—but it had been discomforting all the same. It was the more discomforting because the same thing did not seem to be happening to Diane, who had just as much on her conscience, if not more. She appeared to feel no embarrassment over the fact that she had to mingle with yesterday's victims; indeed, neither Bancroft nor Gerson, for example, showed any signs of resentment, and she could be seen having drinks with them, separately or together, at any hour of the day. Maybe they were coming back for more. . . . . But he was *not* coming back for more; not from Mrs. Stewart-Bates, not from this tough old bitch who treated him like dirt. Money was money, but, as Carl had pointed out, there were better ways of earning it.

"Don't you bother about that," he answered her roughly. "I'll get by, without any help from you."

But she still wanted to slow it down, to enjoy the victory on her own terms.

"What'll you bet? I'll give you any odds you'll be back here in a week, looking for a free hand-out. I know your kind. My husband always said—"

"Oh Christ, not him again!" He faced her squarely at last. "Look, let's pack this thing up. You don't want me, I don't want you. I'm sick of running errands, and it's pretty obvious you don't need me in any other way."

"You're no good in any other way," she interrupted.

"O.K., O.K." He was prepared to let it go. "Let's not tangle over who's alive and who's dead."

"Are you saying I'm dead?" She was suddenly furious; her eyes were snapping fire as she looked at him. "By God, I've picked up better men than you off Skid Row!"

"I wouldn't doubt it."

She began to swear, at that. It was no ordinary cursing; she dredged the gutter for her language, and flung it at him in great heaps of abuse, handfuls at a time. Something had caught her on the raw. Perhaps it was a sexual thing, perhaps it was the fact that the dismissal was turning out to be mutual; but whatever the trigger, the weapon spat fire. He took the tongue-lashing without reprisal, without really listening attentively; if it made her happy, it was no skin off his nose. When she paused for breath, he said: "Good for you," as if praising a child's best efforts, and turned to leave the cabin.

Opening the door, he caught her glance inadvertently, and found there the most baleful expression he had ever encountered. As he went down the corridor towards his own cabin, he suddenly realized that in the last fifteen minutes he had made an implacable enemy.

Mr. Kincaid, who had the professional politician's trick of being able to button-hole anyone in two easy moves, cornered Carl after dinner in the smoking-room. In evening dress, Kincaid looked at his most senatorial; across the ruffled cream shirt a broad black ribbon wandered, anchored to his eye-glasses which themselves set off the bushy white mane of hair. But behind the eye-glasses, his blue eyes were singularly alert, and his manner was very far from vague.

"What's the matter with the old guy?" he asked Carl, without preamble.

"Old guy?" Carl, contentedly nursing a small brandy which would last him out until he joined the poker game, an hour later, looked at Kincaid with only moderate interest. Even if he had wished to be interrupted, he would not have chosen this corrupt old weasel as a companion.

"You know—the Professor."

From the first, everyone on board had always called him the Professor; Carl was probably the only one who knew and remembered his proper name.

"What about the Professor?"

Kincaid said: "Let me top up that drink for you," snapped his fingers at the attendant steward, and said: "Two brandies, son." Then he turned back to Carl. "He was talking a hell of a lot of crap to me before dinner, that's all. Half the time I couldn't make sense out of it."

Carl smiled, not encouragingly. "Vague reminiscence is the privilege of age."

"Maybe, maybe. Only this wasn't reminiscing."

"What was it, then?"

"God knows. More like the stuff you hear on some egghead lecture-circuit. I tell you, he was 'way out! 'Course, no-one minds him being fried all the time—let's face it, everyone on board gets plastered, most days—but he certainly talks queer when he lets go."

"How do you mean, queer?"

"Oh, I don't mean *queer*." Kincaid grinned, with wolfish humor. "Guess he's too old for that sort of stuff." He signed the bar-chit which the steward offered him, and took a noisy gulp at his brandy. "He was talking in parables, he said. I'll say he was! I can't give it you word for word. You know the way he spouts it when he gets going."

"Yes," said Carl. For some reason he had become alerted. "But what was the general sense?"

"General nonsense, I'd call it." Kincaid rubbed the side of his chin with a faint, unpleasant rasping noise. "Well, I'll tell you. He said this ship was a—what the hell's that fool word—micro something."

"Microcosm?"

"That's the one. Never have occasion to use it myself. A microcosm of the world today, that's how he put it. It's financed by the Americans, but it's really owned and run by the British. He said as long as we stay on board and do as we're taught, we're safe; we're looked after and protected by the sailors—that's the British. But as soon as we get ashore by ourselves, the natives—that's the rest of the world—take us for suckers, rob us right and left. Get it?"

"Oh yes," answered Carl easily. "But I don't really think—"

Kincaid held up his hand. "Oh, I don't mind that kind of talk," he said. "You know what the British are like—always bitching about how we've edged them out of the sunshine. I've never met an Englishman yet who wasn't in mourning for the good old days before we took over world leadership. That's standard operating procedure. Take that stuffed-shirt Beckwith bastard, for example. To hear him tell it, we stole Buckingham Palace when the Queen wasn't looking!"

"Plenty of symbolism in Beckwith, too," agreed Carl. "But what about the Professor?"

Kincaid nodded. "O.K.—let's get back to him. Now, where was I?"

"The Americans are guided and protected by the British," prompted Carl.

"Yes. That was the general idea. He said the outside world was always waiting to take us for a ride. Well, we know that. But then he had a twist. He said the *real* danger was not from the outside world, but from internal corruption. While we're concentrating on people like the Russians, who are the open enemies, same as the tourist-gougers ashore, the real damage is being done by people inside."

He paused, and Carl was glad of it. He needed a space to collect his thoughts. He could just hear the Professor giving their whole position away, in a few measured sentences, and he was appalled by it. The damned old fool. . . . The only question that remained was, whether Kincaid was smart enough to have worked out the parallel.

Apparently he was not smart enough—not yet. "Thing I don't understand is, the connection with the ship. Over that last item, I mean. I can see how it's us spending the money, and the British doing the organizing, and the crooks ashore taking us for every cent we've got. But what's the danger inside the ship? Who are meant to be the bad characters here? Or does he mean all the rows that go on? Is that it?"

"Very probably," said Carl, grateful for the false lead. He tried to inject into his voice an easy confidence. "I must say I'm inclined to agree that they have an unsettling effect on our lives, aren't you?"

Kincaid rubbed his chin again. "Maybe that was it. Though it doesn't add up to danger, surely? . . . Why does he talk that way, anyway? Mind you, it doesn't worry *me*. Fifty years in politics, you get yourself a tough hide. But lots of people don't like it. They think he's needling them."

Carl shook his head. "I'm sure he's not. It's simply that he has an analytical turn of mind—"

"I call it needling," said Kincaid briskly.

It seemed to Carl that he must start mending some fences. "I can assure you, the difference is radical," he began.

Kincaid, conditioned to react to the fatal word, did so instantly. "Radical, eh? Is that the trouble? I might have guessed it! How did he get on board, for God's sake? I tell you, those bastards are everywhere."

"No, no," said Carl, stemming the flow as best he could. "You misunderstand me. What I meant was, there's a world of difference between needling—saying things to provoke or annoy—and theorizing for its own sake. I'm quite sure the Professor was simply trying to make conversation, in the realm of world politics. Probably as a compliment to you. If he got a bit mixed up in the process—" he shrugged, and smiled, as one man of the world to another. "It's understandable. We've got to remember that he's getting old."

"Old enough to know better," grumbled Kincaid. He tossed off the remainder of his brandy, and stood up; he had seen someone else he wanted to talk to. "Well, I just thought I'd mention it to you. That sort of talk's unsettling. Even when it makes sense. It might be a good idea to have a word with him."

"I certainly intend to do that," said Carl.

The Professor was asleep when Carl found him; stretched out on his bunk under a fan, wearing only a pair of patched drawers, his withered old body collapsed, his mouth open to allow the bubbling snores to escape. He must have lain down straight after dinner, and dozed off. Carl, in a quiet fury, reached over and shook him by the shoulder.

"Wake up," he commanded. "I want to talk to you."

"Eh, what's that?" The Professor, fathoms deep in unconsciousness after a day's steady drinking and a prolonged meal, struggled to come to the surface. His eyes blinked through wispy grey hair as he looked at Carl, and he sat up shakily. "Good heavens, Carl, what's the matter?"

"What have you been saying to Kincaid?" demanded Carl.

"Kincaid? That ridiculous mountebank!" The Professor, lowering his stick-like legs over the edge of the bunk, snuffled the words. "I said nothing of any consequence to him, I can assure you. It would be an utter waste of time."

"Don't give me that," said Carl sharply. He realized that he was on edge, harassed by a score of things, worried especially about Kathy, but he was unable to control his anger. "You've been talking to him —about us!"

"Us?" The Professor, collecting his wits, was beginning to comprehend. "Nothing of the sort. I was drawing a simple parallel between—"

"I know all about your simple parallels, you bloody old fool! You as good as told him that we were operating as a gang on board, that we were the real danger to him and the rest of the passengers. Didn't you?"

Deeply offended, the Professor looked down at his curling, yellowish toes. "Really, Carl! Surely you and I have been friends long enough—"

"Don't soft-soap me!" snarled Carl, suddenly beside himself with fury. "I didn't bring you along as a friend. You're hired, hired to do a job, and instead of that you're well on the way to ruining everything." He pointed an accusing finger downwards, stabbing the crass air between them. "Why did you talk like that to Kincaid? Have you gone crazy?"

"Certainly not," said the Professor, feebly trying to regain his dignity. He drew a towel round his shoulders, and thrust his feet into ancient felt slippers. "I said nothing to Kincaid which he could possibly construe—"

Carl broke in. "I'll tell you exactly what you said to Kincaid. You said—or implied—that the danger to him and to the other passengers wasn't when they got ashore, it was right here on board. Internal corruption!" He felt a fresh wave of fury exploding inside him. "God damn it, what were you trying to do? Put him on his guard? Tip him off?"

"He is much too stupid—" began the Professor, wavering.

"He's not stupid at all. He's a hard-shell politician with a nose like a blood-hound. You said more than enough to start him wondering and guessing. I know his sort. He'll worry away at it till he comes up with the right answer." He looked down at the old man. "Professor, I could just about kick you off the ship, right now. In fact, it would be a damned good idea to send you home from Cape Town."

The Professor, now cowed by an anger he had never witnessed before, much less provoked, raised humble eyes. "I'm sorry, Carl. I didn't think. . . . You know how it is when one starts speculating on an intriguing theme."

"I know how you are," answered Carl roughly. "Just a drooling old idiot. Well, I'm warning you—that's the last chance you'll get. If I hear one single word more. . . . In future, just you keep out of Kincaid's way, and don't talk like that to anyone. Anyone! You understand?"

"Yes, Carl." In spite of the hot, airless cabin, he drew his towel closer round his shoulders, shivering. "I'm sorry, Carl," he said again. "Depend upon it, I shall take especial care in the future."

"You'd better. . . . You just lay off all that sort of talk, else there'll be trouble. And lay off the booze, too. Or I'll cut you off entirely."

"I hardly think it's a matter of the amount of alcohol—"

"*And don't argue!*" shouted Carl suddenly. "Do you want to drive me nuts? You do what you're told! Don't drink. Don't talk. Don't do *anything* except be on hand whenever I want you. Is that clear?"

"Yes, Carl." The tattered patrician dignity had all but crumbled away; all that was left was the shell of an old man, half naked, stripped of much more than his clothes. "I give you my solemn promise."

"Remember it."

Making his way down the corridor again, Carl shook his shoulders, feeling a sudden load of care. If he had been rough with the Professor, it was because he smelt danger. A lot of people—their victims—knew about their operations already; for various reasons, they would not talk, but if anyone else grew suspicious, if gossip started, the entire thing might collapse. Now, at the break-even point, they could not afford that; the whole purpose of the trip was just coming over the horizon.

He turned into his cabin, bathed his face, and prepared to leave for the poker game in Tillotson's suite. How was he supposed to concentrate, when this sort of thing happened? . . . His anger cooling, he was left with a curious sense of bereavement. It was true that he and the Professor were old friends of long standing; but no friendship could survive stupidity such as this. He would just have to be watched, that was all. Like Kathy. Like all the rest of them.

The ship's doctor, Tom Hillingdon by name, was a grave young man with a sense of humour under severe and permanent control. None of the popular myths about ship's doctors—their drunkenness, their failing powers, their infamous conduct in a professional respect, their past convictions for abortion—applied to him, any more than they did to his fellow-practitioners; he was a ship's doctor because he liked the life and, more important still, because he could measure up to it. He was tall, and good-looking in a studious way; his qualifications were impeccable. He read a great deal. He had an ambition to specialize in tropical medicine—but later on, when he had seen the world and learned the ropes. Now, on the present job, he was energetic, capable and resolute. He had to be.

No seedy drunk or superannuated snuff-taker could have filled his post. On any normal voyage, Hillingdon had well over a thousand people to look after—more than to be found in the average village—and he might have to deal, at short notice, with anything from broken legs to whooping-cough, from child-birth to D.T.'s. He was always on his own; the *Alcestis* had its own clinic, operating theatre, isolation area, and labour ward, and he had to be an expert in all four of them. There were no available specialists to be called in, no *locum* to shoulder the weight or take the blame. He had to detect malingerers among the crew, and to flatter female hypochondriacs whose husbands owned 51% of any given stock. Above all, he had to be there when he was needed; and, like the Captain in another area of competence, he could be needed for almost anything.

Just at the moment, he was needed for an unusual though not unique reason, by a young woman whom he knew, by observation, to be the second prettiest girl in the ship. Tom Hillingdon, who was fond of pretty girls—it was quite mutual—was prepared to concede Diane Loring that much; though during the past month he had made certain mental reservations about her which were now proving accurate. It was just as well that he hadn't joined the queue. . . . But at least she was honest and unequivocal; faced with the same predicament, people usually said that they were inquiring for a friend.

Diane, sitting opposite him across the surgery table, went straight to the point.

"I need a bit of help, doc," she told him.

Tom Hillingdon came to the alert. She was using a phrase which he had heard, with minor variations, three times during the past two days; he had been looking for the link, which none of the complainants would give him; it seemed likely that this was it. Of course, she might simply be pregnant, or she might think she was. But in that case they usually said: "Doctor, I'm in a jam."

"Please tell me about it," he said formally, and added, with private irony: "Miss Loring."

Diane said: "It hurts."

He asked some questions, and presently made his examination and took a swab for later analysis. But he knew the answer already; it completed the puzzle which was scarcely a puzzle at all, simply a pattern of misconduct. For that reason he was not at all surprised; he had been expecting a visit from Diane Loring, or from someone like her, for the last forty-eight hours. He had thought it might be the nurse, which was a good example of a bad guess. Of course, it was not a frivolous matter; the trouble was venereal, within the meaning of the word. But it was a minor, irritant variation which posed no problems.

He told her what they had both suspected, and now knew, and added:

"I would like you to tell me who it could be."

Diane hesitated. "Well, it's like this," she began, and then stopped.

"I can assure you," he helped her, "you need not be shy with me."

"Shy? Who's shy? I'm just trying to work it out."

Now he remained silent. He had lost his capacity for surprise many years earlier. Sometimes he thought it was just as well.

"This doesn't go any further, does it?" asked Diane, on a note of caution.

"No," said Tom Hillingdon, untruthfully.

"It's probably Walham," said Diane after a moment. "I knew that old bastard would get even somehow. Or—or it just might be Bancroft."

Tom Hillingdon waited. He wanted to hear a third name, simply for the fun of it. He knew it already.

"Or it might be that dark guy who limps—what the hell's his name?—his wife plays canasta the whole time."

Hillingdon waited again. Ethically sensitive, he felt he should not prompt her.

"You know—old Log Cabin."

"Log Cabin?"

"Woodhouse," said Diane finally.

Tom Hillingdon inclined his head, content that the pattern was complete.

But the pattern was not complete. "Or it might be a couple of other people," said Diane. "Anyway, that will give you the general outline."

Hillingdon hoped so; his supply of drugs was limited. "Have you been *very* busy?" he asked.

"Hell, doc—what's busy?"

"I beg your pardon," said Tom Hillingdon formally. "It's my job to ask these things." He began to write, completing his notes and outlining the necessary treatment. "I'll give you an injection, just to be on the safe side," he told her. "And I'll make up a lotion which will take care of the local irritation. It should clear up in a day or two."

"Thanks, doc."

"There's one other thing, Miss Loring," he said, with only slight emphasis. "You should refrain from sexual intercourse for the time being."

"O.K.," said Diane cheerfully. "You're the doctor!"

He was the doctor, and for that reason he did not like the next step at all. Of all the things in medicine which he took seriously, the most serious, for him, was the integrity of his profession; and the fact that, every day he spent on board the *Alcestis*, he was under a positive obligation to violate the Hippocratic oath of secrecy, had always been troublesome. He had forced himself to come to terms with the situation, but it had never sat well on his conscience.

Briefly, he had to set out in a daily report all details of the patients under his care—their symptoms, their treatment, their prospects of recovery. Whatever it was—a broken leg, an alcoholic lapse, a bout of Asiatic flu—the Captain had to know about it, as soon as it developed. In the present case, he had to report to Captain Harmer that the ignoble link between three of his other patients was Diane Loring.

When Tom Hillingdon was younger, he used to baulk at the disclosure; once, he had even come into collision with Harmer himself, who put him straight on company policy, as opposed to medical ethics, in very short order.

"I don't care who's got what," the Captain told him forcefully, "or how disgraceful or embarrassing it may be. I've got to know about it! This ship is my sole responsibility; if something goes wrong, it's the master that takes the blame, and I am not going to take the blame for something I know nothing about."

"But surely, sir—" he had begun his protest.

"There aren't going to be any arguments," said Harmer coldly, and then, seeing the young man's crestfallen face, he added, on a more friendly note: "But I don't mind saying a bit more about my point of view. It boils down to my personal responsibility as master. Suppose you find one of your patients has signs of T.B., and for some reason you feel you want to hush it up. Because I know nothing about it, I allow that patient to land somewhere, and so I break half a dozen port health regulations, and maybe endanger a whole community. Who gets sued? The company. Who does the company take it out of? Me. . . Suppose you have a patient who develops some sort of violent delusion, and before I can have him locked up—because I haven't heard anything about it—he chops somebody up with an axe? Who takes the blame for that? The master. Because he ought to know what goes on in his ship." Harmer drew a deep breath. "I know it's a hard rule, Tom, and I know exactly why it worries you. But whatever—*whatever*—is wrong with anyone on board, I have to know about, so that I can take the necessary steps to protect the company, and incidentally myself."

"But surely there are some cases where it can't matter."

The Captain shook his head. "I'll be the judge of that," he said, with a return of his forceful manner. "As far as you're concerned, you're an employee of the company, and you'll obey the company rules. And *my* orders. When somebody is ill on board, I have to be told what's wrong with him. There aren't any exceptions, in any circumstances."

That seemed to be that. . . . Tom Hillingdon had never subsequently argued about it, and he had never held back any information in his daily reports. He did not do so now, when he saw Captain Harmer at five o'clock the same evening.

"But how serious is this?" asked Harmer, when he had digested the news.

"Not very," said Hillingdon. "It's really just a local inflammation. Over-enthusiasm, I would say. Or an infection somebody picked up in the Caribbean." He grinned. "Anyway, now it hurts, like the girl said. But it clears up in a day or two, under proper treatment."

"If she lays off?"

"If she lays off."

"You told her to do that?"

"Yes, sir."

The Captain nodded. "Very well, we'll leave it like that, for the moment." He caught Tom Hillingdon's eye. "In my young days," he said rather primly, "people had more sense of decency. Here's a girl who can't be more than twenty-four or five, apparently sleeping with everyone on board who happens to ask for it. It really is disgraceful!"

"It's the way a lot of people behave nowadays, I'm afraid."

"These girls seem to think of nothing but enjoying themselves."

"It might conceivably be profitable as well."

The Captain, brought up short, eyed him again. "Oh. . . . I hadn't thought of that. Did she say anything to indicate—" he waved his hand.

"No, sir. But some of the people she's been with aren't exactly young and handsome." He paused, rather awkwardly, and then added: "It's just an idea."

"It's a bloody good idea," said the Captain unexpectedly. "When you go down, ask the Purser to see me."

The Captain usually sent for Foxy Cutler when he wanted to talk something out; there was no man on board more likely to come up with a fresh slant on any problem. He was not to be disappointed on this occasion.

"Well, of course there's been the usual gossip," said Cutler, when the Captain brought him up-to-date on the doctor's report. "You know how it is—everyone takes it for granted that X is sleeping with Y, even if all they do is to have a drink together before lunch. But I must say, I didn't know the Loring girl had been getting around so fast."

"Well, we know now," said Captain Harmer grimly. "Do you think she's actually making a racket out of it—taking their money—call-girl stuff?"

"Could be," answered Cutler. "Perhaps with a bit of blackmail on the side."

"Blackmail?"

"Let's call it pressure. If the wife's actually on board, it wouldn't be too difficult for the girl to make the man pay up very handsomely." He mused, tapping his teeth with an empty pipe. Then he went off on another tack. "Now I remember, there was even some talk about her and the awful child."

The Captain stared at him, genuinely amazed. "Barry Greenfield? You mean that little boy?"

"The same. There was a rumour that Barkway had seen or heard something. I couldn't confirm it. He won't talk."

"I'll make him talk, if necessary. . . . But how could that possibly be true? The kid's only fifteen! He couldn't—well, think of the age difference."

"No more of an age difference than young Scapelli, and some of those old girls he's been trotting around with." Foxy Cutler's eyes narrowed. "You know, there's the germ of an idea there."

"What idea?"

"I'm just thinking as I go along. The Loring girl is sleeping around with a lot of older men—maybe for money. Scapelli is doing the same sort of thing, almost certainly for money; it could hardly be anything else. It begins to add up to a funny sort of family. And that's not all." He paused.

"What else?"

"The father, or uncle, or whatever he is. Wenstrom. He's been cleaning up, too, at poker. And I understand their stewardess is very hot on the idea that he and the *other* girl—our little Kathy—aren't father and step-daughter at all, but something much cosier."

"Any evidence of that?"

Cutler shook his head. "No. Just the way they sometimes behave to each other."

The Captain looked out of his cabin window, at the broad sweep of sunshine on the water, and the far horizon twenty miles away. He was not shocked by what the Purser had just said: years of sea-going had demonstrated, beyond any doubt, that people often told lies about their relationships, with not much harm done. Father-and-daughter, uncle-and-niece, the more traditional executive-and-secretary—these were conventional couples who often turned out to be something quite different. In this area, a hotel-clerk's easy morality was the only appropriate reaction; as long as people were discreet, it did not really matter what their closed doors hid from sight.

But Cutler had started him on another train of thought. He had raised a suspicion that the family might not be a family at all, but something like a gang, operating on the principle of plunder. That was much more serious; it came under the heading of discipline, whereas the other was merely a matter of social conformity. If it were really true—if they *were* operating like that—then something would have to be done about it. His sixth sense of the irregular was telling him that this was going to be necessary.

"Have you talked to Barkway about this?" he asked presently.

"I've given him a chance to talk to me," answered Cutler. "But there's nothing doing there, at the moment. He's been bloody-minded this whole trip, and he won't help. He just says he hasn't noticed anything."

"You'd better have another talk with him, Foxy. Or get Brotherhood to do it."

"I'll do that."

"And I'll do a bit of thinking myself." His eyes came back from the horizon. "Well, the girl's out of action for a bit, anyway. And Scapelli? What's Scapelli doing, these days?"

"Mrs. van Dooren."

Louis Scapelli had got himself cornered again, though in reversed circumstances of enslavement. It was like a bad film, or a nightmare; fleeing from the yoke of Mrs. Consolini, who only wanted him as a messenger-boy, he was now ensnared by Mrs. van Dooren, whose desires, it seemed, were exclusively animal. In her service, all he had to do was to pour the drinks, and make love to her. But her capacity for both was insatiable.

The start of the affair was auspicious—too auspicious; he should have been put on guard by her controlled handling, but he thought he could make things go his own way. He had come up to her one evening in the ballroom, when she was sitting by herself, imbibing the first of many after-dinner slugs of rye-and-water. Stopping by her table, he said:

"Good evening, Mrs. van Dooren."

"Hi, there!" she answered vaguely, and then, focussing her eyes, she said: "Oh, it's you," on a much less flattering note. When he did not immediately pass on, she asked: "What's on your mind, sonny?"

"Nothing. I thought you might like to dance."

"*Dance!*" She enunciated the word with measureless scorn. "Are you crazy? I never dance. Dancing's kid stuff. It's for people who can't go to bed together. Didn't you know that?"

"Well—" he began.

She waved her arm. "Sit down, for God's sake," she commanded. "You're giving me a crick in the neck." As he took the nearest chair she leant forward and asked, with a sort of hazy directness: "What's going on? Are you making a switch?"

He smiled, and said: "Yes," and took it from there; it seemed silly to respond in any other way. By ten o'clock they were in cheerful accord, and by eleven they were in bed.

Even at that stage, he should have taken warning. For some reason—something he had heard, something he had read—he had formed a conviction that women who drank too much were likely to be frigid; this extraordinary notion led him to adopt some odd manoeuvres, picked up in God-knows-what sexual gutter, in order to satisfy her. It was another mistake. Presently he found that she was staring at him, in critical appraisal, and then she asked, in a voice both cold and sober:

"Are you actually enjoying that?"

He decided that he was not going to accept the rebuke; he had had enough of female superiority from Mrs. Consolini. Equally forthright, he answered:

"No. I was doing it for you."

"Well, don't bother. Where do you think I was brought up? In a circus?"

"I don't know where you were brought up."

"On Easy Street."

After that, they got on much better.

Indeed, they got on too well. She had a compulsive appetite for making love. The alcohol had been a substitute; now she rationed the one in favour of the other. At first he enjoyed it; he was re-establishing his manhood after an unhappy holiday, while she flowered into a fierce and flattering sensuality which put a positive glow upon her whole body. They would spend hours in her cabin; sipping slow drinks, taking baths, falling into bed again. She was never really satisfied. At each final goodnight, still brisk as a spring lamb, she would say: "Bye now! But don't forget—come back real soon!"

They had no financial arrangement. After forty-eight hours she gave him a thousand dollars. When he went through the motions of protesting that it was too much, she said "O.K., lover-boy, earn it!"

He was the first to tire; it was inevitable; a prolonged effort, particularly in this area, had never been his strong point. On the third evening he said: "I guess I'll take an early night tonight. I'm feeling kinda bushed."

Lying on the bed, taking off her earrings, she shook her head. "Don't be chicken. What's the matter with you? We've only just started."

Something in her voice stirred his misgivings; it was an echo of an earlier servitude. "But I'm tired."

"Snap out of it, then. Take a drink. Do some setting-up exercises." After a moment she added, with seeming irrelevance: "I heard about you from Mrs. Consolini."

"What do you mean?"

"She said you were an awkward bastard."

"What else did she say?"

"That she paid you five hundred a week, and you didn't deliver. So you were fired."

"That's a lot of bunk!"

"I'm not so sure. . . . What do you want *me* to say about you?"

He frowned, disliking—even fearing—the way the conversation

was going. "I don't want you to say anything about me. Jesus, don't you want this to be a secret?"

She shrugged. "I don't mind. I'm not shy. . . ." Then suddenly she was staring at him, and her eyes were dead level, not at all vague. "Look, Romeo, let's get this straight. I drink all the time, and I'm not ashamed of it. If I make love all the time, I'm not ashamed of that, either. I do exactly what I like, and I just don't give a damn. You can't scare me like you scared that poor old dame. And you can't hold out on me, like you held out on Belle Consolini."

His sulky expression was a mask for much uncertainty. "You seem to know it all."

"You bet I know it all! Do you want me to start *telling* it all?"

"No. Of course not."

"Well, behave yourself, then."

He decided to play it safe. "Hell, I was only fooling. I'm not tired." He approached her bed, and relapsed into their personal jargon. "Baby wants it?"

"Baby wants it eight times. . . ."

He did not leave baby till four o'clock in the morning; at noon, a note enclosing a hundred-dollar bill summoned him again. He did not dare to disobey; he was sure that she *would* talk, and talk loudly and shamelessly, if she did not get her way. She knew or guessed too much, and she was tough enough to use all of it.

So it went on, seemingly for ever; he had fashioned himself a nympho neck-tie which he could not discard. When he hung back, she laughed at him, or threatened; when he did what she wished, all she said was: "More."

Nearing Cape Town, utterly exhausted and unnerved, he knew that he must somehow escape.

chapter 7

ABOUT two hundred miles west of the African coast-line, on the last day's run, the *Alcestis* began to move uneasily, as they edged towards the bad weather system which for a week had been lying in wait for them.

The Captain knew all the symptoms, as a doctor knows a difficult patient, or a man his quarrelsome wife. The glass had been dropping swiftly, and the wind, veering, now blew stiffly from the south-east; as the long South Atlantic swell developed a cutting edge, the *Alcestis* began her traditional misbehaviour. With the wind ahead, she had never been a good sea-boat; there was some flaw in the sheer of her bows, or the length of her keel, which started her butting and pitching while other ships could still shoulder their way smoothly ahead. Now, with the wind getting up, and the sea beginning to run against her in good earnest, the *Alcestis* showed what she could do when, like a girl unwillingly talked into a picnic, she took a dislike to the weather.

The Captain had been called to the bridge at midnight; on his way up—he had been watching a film-show, three decks below—he listened to the sounds of his ship, and knew what was in store for her. She was working and creaking loudly, as all old ships did; down the long corridors, a dozen groaning sounds came to meet him as he made his way towards the main companion-ladder. She was already pitching heavily, rolling more than a little—the wind must be on the starboard bow, as the forecast had warned them. Even as he mounted the bottom step of the ladder, he heard and felt the first solid crunch as her bows slid down an enormous switch-back to land squarely in the trough of a wave.

Now, wedged in a corner of the bridge, accustoming his eyes to the darkness, he weighed their prospects. It was likely to be a south-easterly gale—the traditional Cape weather—and it was likely also to last a couple of days. Faced with this, he could either alter course slightly to the northwards, and press on towards the shelter of the coast-line ahead; or he could hold his course, and make the best progress he could into the eye of the wind. Even as he considered their choice, the *Alcestis* came down heavily again, with a huge solid crash, and he heard from far below the tinkle of broken glass. That must have caught the bar off balance. . . . But it meant that he would now have to ease off, whatever course they were steering; the *Alcestis* was too old, and too much loved, to be punished like this. He turned abruptly, and called to the officer of the watch.

"Second!"

"Sir?" came a voice out of the darkness, somewhere beside the quartermaster.

"Reduce by twenty revolutions."

It was bad luck, but it couldn't be helped.

The wind got up with astonishing swiftness; at one o'clock he gauged it to be Force 6, and at two it was nearer 9 or 10—over fifty miles an hour. He stayed where he was on the bridge, duffle-coated against the vile weather, because that was his job; it was how he earned his pay, not by handing round drinks or preserving a social armistice among the idle rich. He could not have got to sleep any-way, the way that they were moving. . . . Under the sullen sky, there was moon enough to see the white walls of water rushing to-wards them, and to watch them explode into foam under their bows; moving into the teeth of the gale, the *Alcestis* laboured and rolled as if she were tired and defeated already, while from outside the bridge-house there was a mounting uproar as the wind screamed and tore at every surface it could reach.

He had to ease their speed every half hour; by the time dawn came up, they were virtually hove-to, making three or four knots at the most, in a grey waste of furious water which every few minutes broke as high as the boat-deck. Pinned down by the storm, the *Alcestis* suffered and took the staggering blows, with a heavy, hang-dog per-sistence. Every now and again, like a steeple-chaser misjudging a fence, she came down with an almighty, rivet-starting crash which shook the whole hull; while tons of water swept over the fore-deck and cascaded down into the well.

He had no choice now; they would have to stay where they were till the storm blew itself out. It meant that they would be a day late at Cape Town—maybe two. He smiled wrily, rubbing his stiff bristly face. At least it would take the edge off all their quarrels, and keep the children quiet.

Kathy had risen early, at about six o'clock; she had found it hopeless, trying to sleep while the whole ship and everything on board was being thrown about so unmercifully, and in the close air below she was feeling seasick. She dressed in slacks, and the thickest sweater she could find, and made her way slowly to the boat-deck; it was a matter of clinging to handrails, walking a few steps, pausing often to get her breath back. As she mounted, the full noise of the storm began to reach her; at the boat-deck level, even inside the armoured glass walls of the sun-room, it greeted her in a frightening crescendo.

The sun-room gave her a view of the whole upper deck, dripping wet, swept by scuds of spray which every few moments were whipped into a hundred small whirlpools by the driving wind. A notice on the door said: "In the interests of safety, access to this deck is temporarily forbidden." Surveying the wild and universal turmoil, she could not quarrel with that. The fresh air revived her; she wedged herself into a deck-chair, and sat down to a grand-stand view of the storm.

She had never before experienced a storm at sea; its strength and fury were unimaginable. Everything within her view was drenched with spray—the funnels, the line of canvas-topped boats, the railings; and the noise seemed to her tremendous, a whole orchestration of tortured notes, from the howl of the wind round the main deckhouse to the vicious twanging and plucking of ropes and wires. When a sea hit them, it was like a blow from a murderous fist. From where she sat, she was looking aft, down the whole length of the *Alcestis*; whenever the ship rolled, and the horizon lurched into view, the entire surface of the sea seemed to be fleeing away from her, torn to ribbons by the wind and flung into a boiling twilight far astern.

She found it awesome—and then, after the accustoming of time, magnificent. The sea was clearly their enemy, but the *Alcestis* was a match for it; she was riding the storm as if, for all the punishment it meted out, she knew she could outlast it in the end. As Kathy sat there, time was forgotten; only the nearness of danger, the sense of triumph, was real. She would rather have been where she was, alone, than anywhere in the world.

Presently—after an hour, two hours, when it was full daylight, and the outlines of their ordeal grew even clearer—she became aware of a new noise added to the tumult. It was a thudding, a crashing, a rhythmical shock which she could feel through the thin soles of her shoes. She sat forward, uneasy, and presently identified it. Quite close to her, the second boat in the long line of eight swung out of sight, towards the sea, and then came crashing back inboard, with a monstrous shock. It had broken loose from its lashings. She knew enough to realize that if the plunging and swinging continued, the boat would soon be smashed to matchwood. She knew also that its ponderous weight, and the great lift of the sea urging it to and fro, could maim and destroy anyone who tried to secure it.

Even as she watched, appalled by the prospect of destruction, the men came running—four of them, unwieldy in dripping yellow oilskins, led (she had known this would happen) by Tim Mansell. He, and they, looked tiny as they collected in a group underneath the enormous lifeboat, which first swung free and then crashed against the davits. She almost cried out: "Run away—don't touch it!" as they stood within the shadow of that hideous pendulum, and took stock of what they had to do.

But presently it was a pride and a joy to watch him. He was not a boy any longer, he was a man, he knew what he was doing, even when life could be at stake, when an arm could be torn off, a chest crushed to bloody ruin. He—no, it was they, a brave team of men marshalled by a young lion—worked gradually, perilously, but surely. It took four tries to throw a heavy line over the boat, in the teeth of the wind, and as many more to bring the line inboard again. Tim Mansell himself did that, darting forward within inches of the hurtling keel and hauling in the line as if possessed. When he shouted, his men jumped forward, lending their weight, taking a turn round a stanchion; when the line snapped on the reverse roll, they were all flung off their feet, in a comical, heart-rending overthrow.

Catlike on the heaving deck, they tried again, with a thicker line; this time it held, while the four of them, straining, sweating, dashing the spray from their faces, made it fast and inched it in. The boat came sullenly under control, and was edged back into its chocks. Gradually the danger passed, while the wind, robbed of its sport, screamed with haphazard fury. It had taken more than an hour to turn crisis into nothing, to shrink a series of desperate chances down to a single log-entry.

Kathy found that for a long time she had been standing up, her body pressed against the glass of the sun-room; she had become so bound up in the struggle that she was exhausted by the end of it. When finally Tim Mansell, surrounded by his men, stood back, hands on hips, to look at their completed handiwork, she felt a deep admiring pride. This was what it was like, to be a man, a sailor. . . . The sea-voyage had never been real until this moment; nor had Tim Mansell ever seemed part of the grown-up world, until in this brief contest, under her very eyes, he had suddenly overtaken and surpassed all that she knew of men.

The four sailors struggled forward again, leaning their squat bodies against the wind, brushing the streaming spray from faces pinched with cold. Last of them all, with a backward glance at the tamed boat, was Tim Mansell—but as he passed the windows of the sun-room he glanced inside, and found her there watching him. She smiled brilliantly as she met his eyes, and then, on an impulse, she clapped her hands together, offering him silent applause for what he had been through, for what he had done. As he saw it, his expression changed again, from competent sternness to a familiar boyish immaturity. But she would never believe the latter again; she had seen the fabric of the man within, and now she was shaken by its power to move her.

He waved in answer, but dismissively, as if to say: "Sorry—busy." She sat on alone, watching the scudding spindrift, hearing the wind, feeling the *Alcestis* lift ponderously to the enormous waves. For a hundred reasons, she was nearly in tears; but beneath a marvelling emotion she was deeply content. She could not analyze it; indeed, it did not seem to matter what anything meant. The whole ship, and all sorts of other things, seemed suddenly to have been cleansed by the wind and the sea, and by heroic men who were not daunted by either.

Table Mountain came up over the horizon like a noble blessing; after two days of foul weather, they were gliding into Table Bay as if across a carpet, quartering the calm sea towards peace and the long-hoped-for landfall. The mountain itself was cloud-topped, wreathed in misty white; it stood poised above the town, which straggled up its slopes until first the houses, and then the tree-line, surrendered to rock and scree. Sunshine seemed to fill every part of the horizon, reflected on pink and yellow buildings, on bronzed green roofs, on exotic trees; the gateway of Africa opened to them in hot splendour. They edged into the harbour, past a bright-painted Union Castle ship which was just getting up steam. People waved a welcome; black faces looked up at them; flower-sellers offered tiny pin-points of red and orange and blue; the quays sprang to life as they nudged a way gently into their berth. On the deck of the *Alcestis*, all storm and stress forgotten, the passengers counted their blessings and basked in the sunshine. Cameras clicked and whirred. Over all, the mountain stared down on them in hazy blue detachment.

The Professor, gazing round, threw out an arm and declaimed:

"Cook's son, duke's son, son of a belted earl,
Forty thousand horse and foot going to Table Bay!"

"What was that?" demanded Kincaid from nearby. He often followed the Professor round nowadays, standing within earshot, hoping for ammunition. "Who said it?"

"A poet of Empire," answered the Professor courteously, "singing of our past glories."

"This is the twentieth century, you know," said Kincaid, with unpleasant emphasis.

"Oh, yes," said the Professor. He sighed. Though it was early in the forenoon, he was tired already. "Let us try to make the most of it."

part five

"Listen to the heart-beat of savage, untamed, mysterious Africa."

chapter 1

"YOU'VE all seen what the choice is," said Carl. "There's a trip by air up to Johannesburg, and then on to the Game Reserve. Or there's a bus-tour along what they call the Garden Route, between here and Durban, with various stop-overs. The ship itself stays here about four days, before moving on to Durban. That's where we all get together again." He looked round them, trying to curb the nervous irritation which had lately been plaguing him. "Personally, I'm going to stay with the ship, and I think you might as well do the same. There'll be plenty of people left on board."

It was after lunch, on the first day of their stay in Cape Town; the delay in arrival had meant some last-minute changes in the routine, and only now had the choice of arrangements been made clear. They were all with him in the day-cabin, except for the Professor, who had retired to bed with a headache; Diane and Louis sat silent on the big sofa, while Kathy had her usual station at these meetings, standing close by the open porthole as if she belonged to two worlds, and could not make up her mind between them. There would be no shore excursions until the morrow, when Tiptree-Jones set out with the Johannesburg contingent, and the Purser headed the cavalcade by road to Durban.

Diane was the first to speak, and she prefaced it with a yawn and a stretch.

"It suits me O.K. to stay on board," she said, in an off-hand voice. "I don't want to go chasing after any wild animals. I'm tired!"

"How about a little work?" said Louis snappishly.

"I'll work when I'm good and ready."

Kathy turned from the porthole momentarily. "Do you happen to know who's staying on board?" she asked Carl.

He shook his head. "No. Everyone's been thrown out—they're still making up their minds."

Diane asked: "Who do you *want* to stay on board?"

"No-one special," answered Kathy. Her voice positively forbade any further discussion.

"What's the Prof going to do?" asked Louis.

"He'll stay too," answered Carl. "I want to work a few things out with him, maybe mail some of the stuff home." He looked at Louis. "That leaves you."

Louis also yawned, not so convincingly as Diane; where she had looked tired, he seemed almost theatrically indifferent. Finally he said:

"I was thinking of taking in the Johannesburg trip."

There was silence after he had spoken; his words had been normal, his choice hardly worthy of note; it was only his manner which drew attention to both of them, so that those who heard him were left wondering what it was all about. Carl spoke for all of them when he asked:

"What do you want to go all the way up there for?"

"Just for the hell of it," answered Louis off-handedly. "It's all part of the cruise, isn't it?"

"I'm not so sure of that," answered Carl. He hardly knew why he was arguing, except that Louis' manner had put him on his guard. "We're not here to enjoy ourselves."

"Hell, chief!" said Louis. "I've been cooped up in the ship since God knows when. I want to get away."

There was another silence. Once again, the phrase 'I want to get away' was entirely normal, like the line of thought behind it; it was the way Louis said it, as if he had rehearsed it earlier, and was now coming in on cue, which nudged the attention. This time it was Diane who challenged him.

"We all want to *get away*," she said aggrievedly. "But it means you'll be gone for nearly a week, just loafing around. How about that?"

"I won't be loafing."

"What, then?"

"Gee, I don't know!" said Louis, with somewhat overdone irritation. "There'll be a big party going up. Maybe sixty people. I'll find someone to work on."

"Mrs. van Dooren?" inquired Carl.

"Could be."

"And could be not," said Diane. "I heard she was taking the other trip."

"So what's the difference? I'm nearly two thousand bucks ahead, there. I've just about run through her."

Diane said: "It's the other way round, by the look of you."

Louis did not answer. He was indeed looking wan and pale; a nervous twitch at the side of his mouth spoke of tension and tiredness. At the beginning, he had given them all a ribald account of Mrs. van Dooren's tastes and demands, but latterly he had not been at all communicative, on this or any other point. Yet Carl, looking at him, decided that he would let the thing go. Louis had earned a rest, if it was a rest he was really looking for. There could be no possible harm in giving him a run ashore.

"O.K.," he said briefly. "Let's leave it like that. We all stay on board, except Louis who does the Johannesburg trip. I may do a bit of shopping here, but that's about all." He glanced across at Kathy, still stationary by the porthole. "I suppose we should really buy some souvenirs, while we're in this part of the world." There was almost a coaxing quality in his voice; she had been very remote lately, he could not get near her at all. He supposed it to be due to her embarrassment that, even now, she had not contributed a single cent towards their earnings. "Would you like that, Kathy?"

"If you would," she answered, without feeling.

Diane sniffed. "Try me," she suggested caustically. "I'd like some nice souvenir bars of gold."

"They've got diamonds here too," said Carl jokingly, to ease the moment. "Up at Kimberley. They just dig them up out of the ground." He recalled a guide-book phrase. "They say it's the biggest man-made hole in the world."

"Now take it easy, Carl!" said Diane, in pretended alarm. "You'll get Romeo all worked up again."

Snugly berthed in the inner harbour, sheltered by the enormous mountain at its back, the *Alcestis* fell silent. More than two-thirds of her passengers had taken one or other of the shore trips; and this was the time when the Captain, aware that most of his crew needed a break, granted leave-periods of two and three days at a time, to anyone who could be spared. Cape Town was not the ideal place for this; not for nothing had it been nick-named, for over three hundred years, the Tavern of the Seas; almost always, someone landed in trouble, and had to be rescued, or bailed out, or, in extreme cases, left behind to languish in jail. Apart from the formidable domestic brandy, it was not that opportunities for sin were anything out of the ordinary. It was just that the local rules were perceptibly stricter. All he could do was to see that knowledge of this filtered down to the lower deck. The most important could be summed up in a succinct phrase: "Coloured girls are illegal."

"But is that really true?" asked Beresford, the apprentice, when he was told of the ban. He had not touched at a South African port before. "You mean, you can actually go to prison for sleeping with one?"

Blantyre, his informant, nodded. "Immorality Act, they call it. If they catch you, you both go to jail."

"But what are they afraid of?"

"They're afraid you might get to like it too much," said Fleming.

"Well, *I* wouldn't," declared Beresford stoutly. He came from a strict North of England home. "I think the whole idea's absolutely horrible. Good heavens, who wants to go to bed with one of those black birds?"

Fleming, a more worldly character, grinned cynically. "You'd be surprised. . . ." His face assumed the smooth, slightly crafty air which meant that he was initiating a leg-pull. "South Africa's a great country for birds," he said. "I mean, real birds. Vultures, flamingos, great crested eagles. . . . There's one that I know you'd like. You see it everywhere."

"What's that?"

"The Rosy-Breasted Pushover."

"I never heard—" began Beresford, and then stopped, discomforted by the laughter. He was even blushing. "I knew you were fooling," he said lamely.

"This isn't fooling," said Fleming. "It's *real*."

There was not much for them to do except talk, on this or any other topic; the *Alcestis*, relieved of the necessity of being ready to sail for five or six days, was allowed to relax and run down. Pressure fell off the boilers; the bridge-house was locked and deserted; the radio operators took a holiday, for the first time in nearly two months. At meal times, the stewards looked out over a waste of unoccupied tables; at night, the empty cabins gave the long passageways a lonely, even desolate air. The only people who had not taken off for Johannesburg or the Garden Route were the lazy, who never went ashore anywhere; the bridge-players, who never even looked out of the portholes; and those with ulcers and dietetic problems, who preferred to be miserable in familiar surroundings. When every meal, three times a day, was limited to the softer parts, boiled, of certain bland fish, there was not much point in going ashore to eat it.

Of them all, the Captain had the most leisure. He knew no-one in Cape Town and, being a predominantly solitary character, he did not want to know anyone. He spent his time reading—the books were mostly heavy historical novels borrowed from the doctor's library—and in thinking about what he now called, in his private mind, the Gang.

He was aware that all of them, except Louis Scapelli, had remained on board; there was nothing surprising in this, except that it was a further hint, a small pointer towards their solidarity. All he could do, of course, was to wait; but he waited in confidence. If something important or critical were to happen, this was a good moment for it; when the ship was in harbour, people could be disciplined, people could even be sent home. . . . In the meantime, he reviewed the evidence.

He had a little more to go on, since he had last talked to Foxy Cutler. Diane Loring had sent another casualty to the doctor, a secretive man called Hathaway who was resolute in his insistence that his complaint was a form of sweat-rash. Talking to Hartmann, one of the poker-players, and cross-checking with Burrell, another, the Captain had confirmed that Carl Wenstrom's poker winnings were indeed enormous, by any standards—something like twenty thousand dollars. No-one was complaining about that, but it certainly had a professional touch to it. And there was ample evidence that for the past week, Scapelli and Mrs. van Dooren, that unlikely pair, had been breaking a number of records. It seemed possible that some of them were financial.

The Captain had gone so far as to interview Barkway, on this and some related topics. Barkway, still sulky and unhelpful, made it clear from the outset that he was not going to talk; but his manner made it equally clear that he could have talked plenty if he had chosen to.

"I do my job, sir," he had said at one point, with the air of a man appalled at the injustice of it all. "There's no call for me to go spying on the passengers."

"I'm not asking you to go spying," said the Captain hardly, "so you can cut out the injured innocence. I'm asking you if you've noticed anything out of the ordinary."

"No, sir."

"You haven't heard any talk?"

"No, sir."

"What about the Greenfield boy?"

"Sir?" said Barkway, elaborately mystified.

The Captain sighed. He was getting nowhere; it was just bad luck that, out of all the stewards, Barkway, the key one, was labouring under a sense of injustice and would never co-operate in the slightest degree. At a venture, seeking another avenue of approach, Harmer said, in a different tone:

"It's about time you forgot that pay I docked you, back in New York."

Barkway's wooden face became positively teak-like. "I don't understand you, sir."

At that, the Captain let him go, with a bad-tempered, rather unfair command to take that silly expression off his face. It had been a waste of time, as he had feared; he was no further along, in any direction. But presently, that very evening, he was given something else to work on.

It was the second purser, Wexford, in charge when Foxy Cutler was ashore, who brought him the story. As sometimes happened when the *Alcestis* was berthed alongside in a foreign port, there had been a minor outbreak of pilfering; it was difficult to keep track of the various messengers, dockside workers, porters, and delivery men who had to have access to the ship at all times, and the result was the disappearance of easily-pocketed articles such as cameras, flasks, and loose change. Short of a complicated search system on all the gangways, twenty-four hours a day, there was nothing to be done about it. But now, apparently, there was a chance that the latest rash of thefts was not an outside job at all.

"It's a funny story, sir," said Wexford, "and I'm not sure if I've got the rights of it." He was a young and simple character, not yet branded by a purser's ingrained cynicism; he still had some way to go before he automatically thought the worst of everybody. "But you know we've been having various things missing from the cabins on B deck. A lot of them are empty. Well, this evening, Mrs. Youngdahl —she's in B 44—went down to her cabin at dinner time, about ten minutes after the gong had gone. She wanted a scarf, or something. But when she got there, she found someone inside her cabin, and she swears that he was opening one of the drawers in her dressing-table."

"Who was it?" asked Harmer.

"The old man—the one they call the Professor."

The Captain came instantly to the alert. This might be an important part of the puzzle. He was certainly not going to neglect any aspect of it.

"What happened?"

"Nothing much, sir. He apologized immediately, and said he must have gone to the wrong cabin by mistake." Wexford smiled hesitantly. "You know, he *is* a bit vague, even at the best of times. His cabin is actually B 64, down the next alleyway. Apparently it was all quite friendly, and they joked about it, and then went in to dinner. But afterwards—this was about an hour ago—he came up to her, and said he was awfully sorry, he must have picked something up by mistake, and he gave it back to her."

"What was *it?*"

"A gold wrist-watch."

The Captain felt a prickling sensation at the tips of his fingers; it had always happened, as long as he could remember, when there was a need for caution or a hint of danger. But all he said was:

"What did Mrs. Youngdahl do?"

"Well, of course, she was very surprised, and probably a bit flustered. She thanked him—rather coldly, I imagine—and he went off again. By that time I gather he was more than a little tight. Then she thought about it for a bit, and then she came and told me."

"Does she think he was stealing it?"

"Frankly, yes."

"Has she ever lost anything before?"

"No, sir. But there was that wallet that disappeared from B 42, next door. She mentioned that."

"Has she told anyone else?"

"I don't think so, sir. I asked her not to, and she promised she wouldn't."

The Captain, silently commending this piece of discretion, sat back in his chair, and gave himself to thought. It all fitted in, but it was not going to be easy to pin any of it down. The old man, even when he was not drunk, was a well-known eccentric; it was perfectly possible that he had wandered into the wrong cabin, and conceivable that he had picked up the watch in mistake for his own. But at that point, coincidence began to wear a strained expression. Women's wrist-watches were nothing like men's wrist-watches, and the difference was immediately apparent, even to a drunk man. When a wrist-watch was picked up, it didn't go into a pocket, it went onto a wrist—there to be discovered, instantly, to be the wrong shape or size or feel. It was as impossible to make a mistake in this respect, as it was with someone else's hat.

He made his decision. "See Mrs. Youngdahl again," he ordered. "Explain that I have been told about this, and that I'm making the most rigorous inquiries. Ask her, again, not to say anything about it to anyone else, for the moment. Make that as a personal favour to me."

"Yes, sir," said Wexford.

"And ask the Professor to come and see me, now."

The Professor was really magnificent; his performance could not be faulted, whether he was guilty or innocent, whether he was covering up a crime or retrieving a social embarrassment. He was drunk, of course—so much the Captain recognized; but he was drunk in the way that true *habitués* were drunk, solemnly and owlishly proud of the fact that the rest of the world had not quite caught up with him. He was as good a man drunk, he seemed to declare, as a hundred lesser men sober. . . . As regards the incident, he made no effort to argue the facts, or to minimize them. It had simply been a deplorable mistake.

"I'll forget my own name next!" he exclaimed, with infectious, positively bouncing good humour. "I cannot imagine what came over me. I must indeed be getting old! . . . I thought things looked a little odd in the cabin—you know, clothes and things—and then poor Mrs. Youngdahl came in and found me there. She must have had the most terrible shock. I do hope she is not too disturbed."

"She *is* disturbed," said the Captain. He looked at the old man, seated in a corner of the cabin, and his eyes were unwinkingly direct. "So, in a way, am I. There's the matter of the wrist-watch."

"God bless my soul, yes!" agreed the Professor heartily. "That *is* an extraordinary affair, isn't it? I was picking up a few of my things—at least, I thought they were my things—small change and so on, and I must have dropped it into my pocket." He sighed. "Habits, habits. . . . We are creatures of them, I'm afraid. If I had only stopped to think, instead of allowing my attention to wander—"

"Professor," said the Captain suddenly.

The Professor's rheumy eyes came round to him. "Yes, sir?" he answered politely.

"What sort of watch have you?"

The Professor shook his head, as if he could scarcely credit what he was about to say. "Now that, if I may so express it, is the most ridiculous part of a ridiculous affair. Believe it or not, I don't even possess a wrist-watch! Affected sort of things—I never could abide them!" With a wavering hand he dug into the pocket of his braided evening waistcoat, and drew out a ponderous pocket-watch on the end of a heavy gold chain. "This, sir, is my watch, and it was my father's before me. Designed and made by the Swiss firm of Wechsler, in 1885. It doesn't lose five seconds in an entire year! I can assure you, they don't make watches like this nowadays."

"Quite so," said the Captain, with incisive irony. "There could be no similarity." He waited, but as the Professor, brushing tobacco-ash from his lapel, did not appear to have heard him, he added: "You see the difficulty, don't you?"

"Difficulty, sir?" The manner was fractionally stiffer. "I don't quite take your point."

"You were in the wrong cabin—a natural mistake." The Captain put into his voice a disciplinary emphasis. "You picked up certain things from the dressing-table—a natural mistake. Then you picked up a wrist-watch—a natural mistake. Then what did you do?"

The Professor's air of bonhomie evaporated sharply. "Upon my soul," he said, with dignity, "I don't understand."

"Upon my soul," said the Captain, "nor do I. You could not conceivably have mistaken that watch for your own. It must have been less than half the size. You could not have put it on your wrist, because you don't wear a wrist-watch. You slipped it into your pocket. Why?"

After a moment's heavy silence: "I take the very strongest objection," said the Professor struggling to rise to his feet, "to the expression 'slipped it into my pocket.' It savours of—" he waved his hand, "—you are perfectly well aware what it savours of. I made a mistake, and I am sorry. I *put* the watch in my pocket, among my loose change, and I am sorry. But I utterly repudiate the suggestion, the charge that—"

"Professor," interrupted the Captain curtly. "I am not making any charges. All I want is *your* explanation of how you came to mistake a wrist-watch for anything else, and why you put it into your pocket."

There was another silence, much longer. The Professor was looking down at his patent-leather shoes, which were old, cracked, yet highly polished; if he were playing for time, it was done with a wonderfully natural air. Finally his head came up, and he looked at the Captain with simple humility.

"Captain," he said, "I have a confession to make. It is intended for your ears alone, and I would be grateful if you would honour that confidence. The truth is, I—er—have been under the weather lately. As a consequence, I was somewhat in liquor this evening—there, I won't try to dissemble any further! I must have thought I was in my own cabin, dressing for dinner, and I naturally took everything off the dressing-table and put it in my pocket. Without thinking." The eyes went down again; it could have been shame just as well as shiftiness; the Captain could not make up his mind. "I beg you to understand," said the Professor, "that I am deeply sorry for this lapse of behaviour, and it certainly will not occur again."

It was thin, thought the Captain, in the silence that followed; thin as a liar's web, thin as a poor man's soup; but it *might* be true. . . . He was aware that he could not take the thing much further, at this stage; short of a direct charge of theft, which would be difficult to substantiate, all he could do was to exhibit a wary, qualified acceptance. He realized also that if this had been a single story, told by a single man, he might have passed it without question; it was only because he had the 'gang' idea ever-present in his mind that he was suspicious.

But he was again brought very sharply face to face with this, and the ground was altered, when the Professor, preparing to leave, said out of the blue:

"I would be extremely grateful also if you would not mention this—ah—matter to Mr. Wenstrom."

This was, in the circumstances, such an extraordinary request that later, when the Professor had gone, it was the thing the Captain remembered most vividly, of the whole interview. Reduced to its essentials, in the light of what he knew and suspected, it could only mean that what the Professor regretted above all was to have been involved in failure.

Sitting alone in his cabin, debating what to do next, the Captain's suspicions returned in full flood. His hunch had been right. The Professor *had* been stealing; he *was* part of a gang; and they were all involved, all five of them. What they would do next was a matter of guesswork; but whatever it was, he had to be ready for it.

chapter 2

KATHY was not at all sure how she came to be leaning over the rail of the boat-deck, side by side with Tillotson, towards midnight forty-eight hours later. It was simply that he was that sort of man; when he wanted to, he made things happen, he fashioned events to his own will. He was like Carl. . . . In his case, it had seemed a most natural sort of progress; they had met while ashore, had a drink at the Mount Nelson Hotel, made a vague date for later on, and kept it. Clearly he had planned it that way; but the planning had not shown at any point, the manoeuvres had not been perceptible. The two of them were there, according to schedule—his schedule. That was all.

It was a wonderful night. Their berth in the inner harbour gave them a view, across pitch-black water, of the glowing aura of the city; and beyond it, straggling up the hillside, the yellow pinpoints which were street lamps, and lonely houses, and then the vast inky looming of Table Mountain. Their side of the ship, away from the quay, was completely silent; voices came to them, but they were far away, like echoes off the mortal stage; only the night, and the pale quarter-moon, and the hot smell of Africa, were real.

Real also was the man beside her; she could feel his presence, the force of his personality, the coiled spring of will and determination which set him apart from many other men. He drew evenly on his cigar; its recurrent red glow was like a signal flare, marking the nearness of an unusual hazard. He was silent, he was thinking—but what was he thinking? This was an extraordinary, even fantastic situation for a man of his quality. Was he thinking of that? Or had he passed that self-regarding stage?—was he merely wondering how to begin?

She straightened up, and turned away from the water, and then leant back against the rail again, pencil-slim, the line of her body candidly displayed. It was an advance she had to make; this much was due from her. It came as no surprise when he moved suddenly, and took her in his arms, and kissed her fiercely.

He smelt of cigars, and expensive after-shave lotion, and his body, pressed against hers, was as she had imagined—small and tough and thrusting. It meant nothing to her—she had expected that also; he could not communicate sensuality, because there was not an atom of sensuality in him—not for her. But he communicated other things, in disconcerting abundance. Strength, determination, and a burning hunger were among them.

She said: "Oh!" on a neutral note of acceptance, as she always did, and waited.

He had turned back to the rail and was staring down at the water again, as if he had completed one part of a pattern and was taking his time over the next section. Presently he said, quite calmly:

"I knew you would feel like that. . . . But you should have sounded more surprised."

"I wasn't surprised," said Kathy.

"Oh, I know *that*. . . . But isn't it part of the act?"

If there had been the slightest edge to his voice, the words would have been deeply offensive. But there was none; he might have been making casual conversation; he might have been saying: 'Isn't it warm tonight?' Nonplussed, she waited for more; and more came, in a controlled confessional flow like nothing she had ever experienced before.

"I'm not a fool," he said quietly. "You must have realized that, by now." The cigar glowed brightly as he drew on it. "I know what you're doing, I know what your step-father is doing, I know all about the others, too. I know you've been available, ever since you came on board." He paused; a slow drift of smoke crossed between them, like a gauzy curtain falling and lifting again. "Available isn't exactly the right word, is it? It sounds cheap, and in spite of this *racket* you're running—" on the word 'racket' his voice was briefly contemptuous, "—you are not cheap. I really meant ready, ready for selected customers. Each of you may have fooled a lot of people, but you haven't fooled me. I'm not that sort of material."

It was important to answer this just right. "But now you want to be fooled?"

She saw him nodding, his grey head clear against the darkness on the other side of the rail. "I guess that's about it."

"Why?"

"I have to have it," he answered immediately. "I felt that, when I touched you, *before* I touched you. You must have felt it in me. I know it's wrong, I know it's silly, I know it's expensive, and maybe dangerous. But there it is. I've had a—what's the common term?—an itch for you, ever since I first saw you. I have to have you. If it's free, wonderful. If it's not free, it's wonderful just the same."

"But why?" she asked again. She was astonished. "You're not like that at all."

"You know nothing."

She shrugged. "O.K."

"Nothing about this. . . . I am fifty-eight," he went on, in the same tone of detached narrative, "and you are young and very beautiful. Do you know what it's like to be fifty-eight? No—how could you? Let me tell you that it can be hell, in lots of ways. But it can be the worst hell as regards women. When at last it catches up with you. I've been happily married for years, for thirty years. I have three grandchildren. I haven't thought about women, except casually, for five years at least. Then I saw you."

He paused. Kathy could not speak; she did not want to. In a way, this was how she had thought it might go, and in another way it was fantastic. He had been a long time coming to the point, but only because there were huge obstacles, of habit, will, and propriety, barring his path. She had guessed some of them, but the essence of the man she had not guessed.

"When I saw you," he went on, in his unchanging, level voice, "I knew straight away I wasn't dead, after all. Sexually dead. Then I got to wondering about how many more women I'd sleep with, before I died, and the answer was none. *None*—if I didn't do something about it. None—and I just couldn't stand the idea. I used to do a lot of it; why should it be over, for ever? Suddenly, I want to go to bed with many women, before it's too late. But you first."

Before she could really consider what she was saying, she produced a standard reaction. "That's not very flattering."

"Don't be childish," he said, curtly. "You are not childish. . . . You've triggered something—how and why, it doesn't matter. You've started a train of thought that tells me that I *cannot* be fifty-nine, and then sixty and sixty-five and seventy, and never make love to another girl." His voice changed, taking on a more urgent note; he was speaking from his deep need, but he knew about it—he did not mind, he was not ashamed. With a flash of insight, she understood why he had the capacity to command men, why he had gained his pinnacle of success. It was because he knew himself, completely, from the pinnacle down to the most odious of his desires. "I have to have you," he said again, "because I can't bear the thought that I'll never sleep with someone like you again. Does that make sense?"

"It makes sense to *you*," she said carefully.

"Ah. . . ." He got the point immediately. He was very quick, astonishingly sensitive. "So it won't be free?"

"No."

He said: "All right. . . . I'm a rich man. . . . But I guess you know that already."

"I'll need to think about it, anyway."

He said, again: "All right."

She stood up straight; the small of her back was sore where she had pressed it against the rail. Around them the night was warm and still; far away, at the edge of the dock, there was the clang of a bell—an ambulance, a police-car—to recall them to the world. As they stepped apart, and the link between them dissolved, she was struck by an enormous self-disgust. This was so utterly sordid. . . . He was such a good man, basically; in spite of what he had said, the wild lust for youth and softness would vanish; the moment it was slaked, he would be a grandfather again. . . . All he wanted was the transient use of her body, and she was going to sell it to him, though she wanted nothing of his—it would have been the same if he had been made of wood, of rubber hose. . . . Twisting the suicidal knife, because she loathed what she was preparing to do, she said: "How much?"

His cigar-butt described a wide arc, up and away, and fell thirty feet below into the invisible water.

"You can have anything you want," he said.

They began to walk away from the rail, towards the lighted sunroom. There was someone inside, a woman, sitting in the same chair as Kathy had used, when she watched Tim Mansell being young and brave. . . . Tillotson pushed open the door, and stood aside to let Kathy pass though. The woman within rose, as if a signal had been given, and took a step towards them. It was his wife.

It might have been an electric moment, but it was not; the principals involved were too well-disciplined, and perhaps too adroit. Tillotson closed the door behind him, and advanced into the light.

"Hallo, dear," he said, without hesitation. "I was wondering where you were."

Mrs. Tillotson, though she had risen with alacrity, was also entirely calm; her plain and pleasant face showed no important emotion; only a certain watchfulness as she glanced from one to the other told Kathy that there were reservations and tensions beneath the surface. How much she had seen, or had guessed, was problematical; the two of them had been standing within a corner made by the third and fourth lifeboats; the deck was virtually unlighted; they might well have been out of sight. But they had, indubitably, been together, in circumstances which aided the imagination, particularly the imagination of a wife.

"I was reading," said Mrs. Tillotson, on a quietly social note. "Then I thought I'd like some fresh air. But it seemed a bit chilly outside. . . . You'll catch cold!" She looked at Kathy's exiguous off-the-shoulder dress. "Both of you."

"Oh, it's warm enough," said Kathy. Try as she would, she could not look quite directly at Mrs. Tillotson; her eyes were focused a little to the side, in a neutral area which promised safety. "We were enjoying the view."

"One way of getting warm," said Tillotson, "and that's a drink. How about it?"

"Can we get one?" asked Mrs. Tillotson. She glanced at her watch. "It's after twelve, you know."

"I'll fix it. . . . Whisky-and-soda?"

"Just a small one, then."

"Kathy?"

"I'd love one," said Kathy. She knew what was going to happen now, but there was no way of avoiding it. Perhaps she did not deserve to avoid it.

"I'll bring it up," said Tillotson, and turned, and was gone.

It was all right for him. . . . As she smiled and sat down, she wondered why he had left so promptly; a drink was a welcome idea, but a drink did not need fetching, on board the *Alcestis*—there were bells for drinks, all the way round the clock. It was not due to cowardice, because he was not that sort of man. Perhaps it was something more directly connected with his wife and his background—a belated social sense, even, which told him that he had spent quite enough time with a young unmarried woman, and must absent himself for a space. . . . Whatever it was, it left herself in an awkward position. If the thing became emotional, or competitive, or unpleasant, she would scarcely know how to deal with it. In her present mood of confusion, she did not even know whether she wanted to win or to lose.

She need not have bothered. Mrs. Tillotson was far too kind a woman, too genuine a person, to vulgarize or to out-face. She had some points to make—so much was quickly clear; but she was going to make them in her own fashion, and her own fashion was subdued, oblique, and above all civilized. Nothing she said over-stepped the limits of social exchange; it was the foot-notes, known to both of them, which supplied the key to their communication.

"Bill is so energetic," said Mrs. Tillotson, looking after her husband as the swing door closed behind him. "I can hardly keep up with him, these days. This cruise has really made him feel young again."

Kathy, busy with her cigarette, remarked that it seemed to have had the same effect on a lot of their fellow-passengers. The sea-air—could that be it?

"And the people themselves, I think." Mrs. Tillotson seemed to be considering the point judiciously; her eyes were turned towards the boat-deck. "You know how one makes new friends. . . . And then, I suppose, as soon as one gets home, everything goes back to normal again."

"That's rather a sad idea," said Kathy. She was content to supply the linking, not the material; her eyes, following Mrs. Tillotson's, had noted that from this vantage-point the boat-deck was dark and shadowy; if they had been seen at all, it could only have been as two people emerging out of the twilight between the two boats, after a lengthy absence. Perhaps, in the circumstances, that was enough.

Mrs. Tillotson shook her head. "Oh, I don't think so. It's like waking up suddenly, in the middle of the night, and then falling asleep again. It's almost a shock; the sleep is so much more natural." She laughed softly, as if this were a domestic joke they could easily share. "Don't let me give the impression that Bill is asleep all the time! Far from it. But after all, he *is* nearly sixty."

"He doesn't seem that," said Kathy.

Mrs. Tillotson's head came round, inquiringly. "Not to you? I'm surprised—considering that you're so very much younger. Bill and I must seem like antiques. Set in our ways . . ." She rummaged in a brocade bag at the side of her chair, and produced her knitting; it accented what she had just said, more delicately than any further words could have done. "Socks for the grandchildren," she murmured; "Bill just adores them . . . Perhaps he gives people a different impression—on a holiday trip like this, I mean—but he's very much a family man. He won't be really happy till he gets back home. Nor will I. Ridiculous, isn't it?—to come all this way, and see all these new things, and then settle back again as if nothing had happened."

Kathy kept her silence.

"Of course, it's different for you," Mrs. Tillotson went on. "Being young, I mean. . . . When *you* meet someone new, it might change your whole life. A young man, I mean. . . . You might even meet the man you're going to marry. . . . " She sighed, as if the thought made her happy and contented, for Kathy's sake. "Of course, there's no-one really suitable on the boat, is there? Except those nice officers."

Kathy said, lightly, that for all sorts of reasons she couldn't imagine marrying a sailor.

"Perhaps not," agreed Mrs. Tillotson. "I only meant, of all the men on board, they're the only ones really *available*."

Kathy wondered how much more she would want to say; the targets had all been hit, the information passed on. . . . She could never have argued with Mrs. Tillotson, or tried to put another point of view; there could be no battle, when most of her own thoughts and feelings were so confused and, where they were clear, so self-disparaging. She wanted to shut her eyes, and fall asleep, and have the whole of the last hour vanish without trace. This warm-hearted, quietly determined woman at her side would certainly help her to do that. Perhaps Tillotson himself would, when he came to think it over, when he saw the knitting and re-entered the even flow of their shared life. Perhaps he would not really want to wake up from that sleep, even for a brief dazzlement.

Mrs. Tillotson seemed to think so.

"Yes, we've certainly enjoyed this cruise," she said, as if Kathy had asked a question and she were answering it. "Do you know, I had a terrible time getting him to take it. He likes to work, and he likes to sit at home, and that's really all. It sounds dull, doesn't it?—dull but safe. . . . I don't think anything will ever really change that, but if it did, he'd probably regret it very much. Almost immediately." There was a step on the stairs behind her, and she turned. "And here he is, bless him, looking after me as usual. My dear—" her hand rested briefly on Kathy's arm, "—don't tell him I said so, but I just hope that when the time comes, you get as good a husband as mine."

Tillotson approached, balancing a loaded tray. "Sorry to be so long, dear," he said. "They tried to tell me the bar-supplies were locked up. Imagine!" Handing them their drinks, he looked from one to the other; his eyes dwelt on Kathy with a curiously varied expression, half confederate, half withdrawn. "Well, have you settled the affairs of the world?"

"Some of the affairs," said Mrs. Tillotson. She raised her glass, almost gaily. "I guess the rest will keep."

Tense yet listless, shaken by doubts, fatally aware of misgiving, Kathy knew she would not sleep. She sat on in the darkened sunroom after the Tillotsons left her—they went off arm-in-arm, without a backward glance—and watched the moon go down and the lights of Cape Town grow pale and spectral, and was conscious of nothing but a wretched isolation. She had to do a job for Carl, and she had started on it at last, well enough; and then she had suddenly hated it, felt shame instead of satisfaction—she doubted now, if she *could* make love with Tillotson, unless it was pitch-dark and they were both drunk. . . . It left her nowhere, nowhere in anyone's world. She was no good to Carl, and less than no good to herself.

Her thoughts went round, in a dreary endless circle; it was after two o'clock when she rose, stiffly, and began to make her way three decks below to her cabin. Turning a corner of the stairway, at the A-deck level, she saw a shadow move and heard footsteps, light and brisk, coming up towards her. She stopped, uncertainly, hoping it was no-one she knew, hoping above all it was not Tillotson returning to clinch the deal; she was dead tired, and absolutely spiritless. The shadow broadened and lengthened, and then the owner was standing three steps below her, as startled as she. It was Tim Mansell.

She looked at him, without saying anything. He was out of uniform, wearing a sports jacket and grey flannels; in unfamiliar colours, he still seemed broad and young and tough, and infinitely confident. She went down the three steps, and stood before him; a head shorter than he, her slim body drooping, her face pale.

His expression, which had been cheerful, as if he were *en route* to a party or a special rendezvous, grew grave as he stared at her.

"You look sad," he said unexpectedly.

"I am sad."

He did not ask why. He said: "You should really be in bed, shouldn't you?"

She smiled wanly. "So should you."

"But I've just got up!" Cheerfulness broke through again, as if he had suddenly remembered where he was going, and how much he was looking forward to it. "This is my day off, so I thought I'd start early. I've got a whole twenty-four hours, and I've only wasted two of them in sleep."

"Where are you going?"

"For a drive, a long drive. I've hired a car—it's down on the quay. I'm going up to the Karroo."

She repeated the unfamiliar word. "Karroo?"

"It's a kind of desert, but it's beautiful." Suddenly and, she guessed, bravely, he took a step forward. "Why not come with me?"

She smiled at that—it was so like him, shy and impetuous and quite unconnected with graver matters. "Now how could I do that?"

"Easily!" And he looked as if it would indeed be easy, the easiest thing in the world, presenting no problems at all to people like themselves. "It's only three hundred miles or so. Six hours, probably less—the South African roads are wonderful. I was going to spend the day there, picnicking, and be back by midnight tonight. In fact, I have to be back. Sailing tomorrow—remember?" He was young and not-so-young at the same time, full of careless ways of spending his energy, but equipped to trim them down to a disciplinary size. He would be back in time, and sleep like a puppy after it. . . . He said again, on a note which held something of compassion for her: "Come with me."

Suddenly it was the only thing to do.

"All right," she said, on the impulse. "I'll go and change. Ten minutes?"

He nodded; his face now had an extraordinary lightness and happiness in it. "Ten minutes. . . . Bring a coat; it's cold now. And a bathing-suit."

"You bring the pretzels, I'll bring the beer."

"Beer?" he repeated, puzzled.

"It's a song," she said.

Presently it was.

chapter 3

"KEEP warm, curl up, and go to sleep," he commanded, as soon as they were settled in the car; and she was glad to obey so reasonable an order. She had a fleeting impression of long gloomy lines of dock-sheds, the squeak of opening gates at the customs check-point, and a large blond policeman peering in at her as if she were some luscious form of contraband; then they were moving up the broad main thoroughfare which she knew as Adderley Street, and thereafter she dozed off and fell into grateful sleep. He was obviously a careful driver; she trusted him.

It was his hand which awakened her, touching her shoulder gently, without intrusion, until she opened her eyes. She looked round her, puzzled, and then remembered where she was and how she had got there. She became aware that it was light outside—a paleness in the gloom which had already overcome the beam of their headlights. Then he slowed down the car, and stopped it at the side of the road, by a low wall.

"This is the first good view," he said.

Opening the door, and stretching her stiff limbs, she asked:

"How long have I been asleep?"

He smiled. "Two whole hours. It's just getting light. This is the top of the first pass—Du Toit's Kloof. I wouldn't have woken you up, but it's worth waking for."

She had only to look briefly about her before exclaiming: "Oh yes!" And then, without thinking, charmed by new-minted magic: "Always wake me."

They were indeed at the top of a pass; over the rough stone wall beside the car, the slope fell away in a sheer drop of hundreds of feet, crossed and recrossed by the winding road they had climbed, which now snaked its way down to the misty Cape Flats. The dawn was already creeping across the enormous spread of the valley beneath them, but the plains were still shrouded by the night mist; nearer to their vantage point, delicate drifts of spider's web matched the luminous white carpet below. They were still within sight of the coast; away to seaward, a light-house was feebly blinking at the dawn; there were lone yellow farms, noble mountains, birds wheeling and calling, rock-rabbits peeping timidly at the new day. The two of them seemed to stand at the very top of the world, flanked by purple hills, gazing down on a broad private kingdom. They were ahead of the day, ahead of everyone. . . . And as if showing them how to keep ahead, behind them the road cut through a slim passageway between two outcrops of rock, and disappeared downwards into the next valley.

Enchanted by everything within view, from the pink-frilled clouds in the eastern sky to the sombre buttress of Paarl Rock, two thousand feet below, Kathy sighed her pleasure.

"But it's wonderful! Why do we live in towns?"

"I don't," answered Tim, with a touch of pride.

"All right, sailor. . . ." She gestured through the magnificent arc which lay below their platform. "Is it all going to be as good as this?"

"Every bit. Right up till midnight." He suddenly added: "Cinderella."

She looked at him, and inclined her head. There were things between them already, new things, things apart from the ship and the crowds they lived in. She did not care; if it were going to be that sort of day—the first for many years—then she did not want to change it. She said: "Right now, Cinderella is cold," and he took her arm and led her back to the car. The tone was being set, thus early, thus happily; it might falter into discord when midnight struck, but that mattered not at all at 6 A.M.

He drove on, down a winding round which followed a deep-cut river bed, while she warmed to the day, and watched him driving, and listened to him talking, and enjoyed it all. Away from the ship, away from other people, he was a different person; he had her in his charge now, for the first time, and he seemed to have grown up suddenly, as if only a man could deserve this honour. He talked of everything—about his job, his hopes, the people on board, the way a ship was run at sea, the way a sailor was treated ashore; and she listened, and grew interested, and presently found herself joining in. She had not talked like this for years; it was innocent and intriguing at the same time, a tremendous contrast with every aspect of the past. Of course, he was her contemporary. Perhaps she had been searching for a contemporary, even longing for one.

The plunging mountain road gave way to a broad plain, and long vistas of fruit trees, and a straggling town called Worcester. Kathy proclaimed that she was hungry, and indeed she was; they stopped at a small hotel where, although it was barely half-past seven, everyone was already astir, and the rocking-chairs on the *stoep* had a dozen slow-talking customers. Apparently South Africans rose early, to greet their beautiful dry sunshine. In the hotel lobby, furnished in musty yellow-wood, smelling already of coffee and something savoury which presently turned out to be the breakfast steaks, she said:

"This is going to be fun. Order me a big breakfast. Have you any money?"

"I have twelve pounds," he said, with satisfaction.

"Heavens! Lend me a penny."

They both burst out laughing, the sort of laughter from which everything good can stem, a guarantee that nothing could go wrong. Later, in the dining-room, they continued this mood of shared nonsense, so that even the old waiter, and the grumpy 'regulars' who stamped in, wordless, and bull-dozed their way through mealie-porridge, and steaks crowned with fried eggs, topped off with mugs of beer, grew brighter as they listened to the laughter and eavesdropped on the foolish jokes. At one point, Kathy, catching sight of herself in the blotched, fly-specked mirror, said: "We've no right to be so cheerful, after two hours' sleep." But she was wrong, and she knew it. Today, for some reason which they would learn as they went along, they had a cast-iron option on happiness.

"Now we've really got to drive, instead of dawdling," announced Tim, when they were outside again in the morning sunshine, and surveying the main street of Worcester with disbelieving eyes, as if they had newly landed on the moon. "It's at least another hundred miles before we come to the best part of the Karroo, the part I want you to see."

"What does Karroo mean, exactly?" she asked, as she got into the car.

"It's a Hottentot word—no water, waterless," he answered—and those were the last words he spoke for many miles. The road was excellent, and he drove fast and with great concentration, up the rising pass of the Hex River Valley, past sleepy, sun-baked towns with outlandish Afrikaans names—De Doorns, Touws Rivier, Matjesfontein—and then across a huge level plain where the road stretched like a straight black ribbon ahead, and the landscape on either side was a lonely wilderness. They covered a hundred miles in under two hours, and slipped downhill through Laingsburg, and out into the deserted table-land again. There, driving past a big outcrop of rock, its top weathered to the baldness of a thousand years, he let their speed fall away, and relaxed, and said:

"This is the beginning of it."

It was arid, austere, featureless, and very beautiful. They could see, in any direction, for fifty and sixty miles—miles of brown-baked earth and stony wastes which, close to, were discovered to be living after all, carpeted with millions of tiny flowers, green-brown cactus, pink and yellow protea, succulents seeming to grow out of the bare rock, thorny stunted bush which thrived miraculously on nothing. Tim commented: "They say this is the oldest part of Africa—perhaps the oldest part of the world," and though she did not really see how one part of Africa could be older than another, she accepted the fact. It had to be. . . . The desert which was no desert stretched as far as the eye could reach; here and there, close to the road or on the far horizon, were conical ridges and hill-tops, their outlines layered by a million years of the relentless erosion of wind and sun and rain, starkly sculptured against the pale sky.

The light was wonderful—clear as blue water, transparently bright; and though it was very hot, the heat was dry, and the shimmering air like thin wine. They seemed to be transfixed in brilliant isolation, the only people left in a world which had been dead since history began.

"But it's wonderful!" she said, for the second time that day. "Do stop, Tim—I want to get the feel of it."

The feel of it was very strange. With the engine switched off there was utter silence all around them; when they got out of the car and walked to the roadside, they found there a dried-up watercourse, bleached by the endless sun, and beside it the horned skull of an animal, cruelly whitened, the eye-sockets staring blindly at the sky. There was nothing else in sight—no house, no human being, no living creature. Away on the far horizon, there was a clump of trees, and a windmill turning, its blades catching the sun. That was all.

"It's absolutely incredible," said Kathy. She was staring about her as if in a dream. "Doesn't anybody live here?"

"Well, farmers."

"*Here?*"

"Oh yes. They raise some of the best sheep in the world—the Karroo mutton tastes absolutely perfect—I don't know how they turn out so well, but they do. They must eat rocks. . . . Of course, the farms are enormous, thousands of acres. In the old days, when they were giving the land away free, you were allowed to mark out as a boundary the distance you could ride between sunrise and sunset. That could be fifty miles—perhaps more. So you could get yourself a farm fifty miles square."

She was still looking about her, entranced by the burning sun, the vast stretches of brown earth, and the raw-boned hill nearby, shaped like a crouching lion. At its base, across miles of shimmering heat, she caught a movement, a patch of colour which had shifted imperceptibly. She pointed excitedly. "There's something there!"

He had brought his glasses from the car; now he searched, and presently found the quarry.

"It's a buck, a *springbok*," he reported. "Beautiful. . . . Take a look."

It was indeed beautiful—a sleek brown shape, dappled with orange and white, its horns curving proudly back; alone and heraldic, it seemed to rule the desert landscape. But even as she looked, the buck moved again, melting away behind a rock as if not choosing to be thus surveyed. They were alone once more.

Presently she said: "Have you noticed how the whole earth seems to be moving, after so long on the ship? You can actually feel it roll."

"It always does that."

"O.K., professional! But it's new to me."

He grinned. "I can't help being a sailor."

"I suppose now you're going to tell me you've wrung more seawater out of your socks than I've ever sailed on."

"Now where on earth," he asked, startled, "did you hear a thing like that?"

"I heard one of the deck sailors say it."

He shook his head, mock-serious. "You really mustn't listen to what the deck sailors say. Particularly when they don't know you're there."

"Oh, I'm tough."

He looked at her, gravely, searching her face for clues, for answers. "No, you're not."

"Not today, anyway." Now she in turn was looking at him; their eyes were held fast, exchanging signals, forming alliances. She thought: He wants to kiss me. Perhaps he would try to, perhaps she would let him. Nothing would have been more natural, alone in the sunshine. But it was not quite the moment for kissing. Not yet.

She turned away, staring at something, anything, and said: "What now? How much further?"

"Fifty miles or so." His voice was constrained, but he was bringing it under control. "Then we'll picnic, and bathe, if we're lucky."

"Bathe?"

"There's a dam, off the road. Or there was, last year. It shouldn't be dried up now."

"Let's go, then."

It was only when he had already started the engine, and put the car in gear, that he said: "I love you."

They drove in silence for five miles or more. She did not know what to say; one thing was following another, but though she could guess the outlines of the pattern, she could not really see it clearly. It was a day for love, and a place for it also. But somehow it was too early. She wanted more things to happen, more things to be said and felt, before his arms were round her. If that was where they were going to be.

It was Tim who broke the silence. "Don't tell me," he said—and there was blessed laughter in his voice—"that you didn't hear."

"Oh, I heard, all right." She put her hand on top of his, and it rested there comfortably. "Girls always hear *that*."

"What do girls answer?"

She affected to treat the question seriously. "Some girls say: 'Who —little me?' Some girls say: 'Cut it out.' Some girls say: 'Uh huh!' Some girls say: 'So do I.' "

"I like the last girl best."

She shook her head. "Much too forward. In and out of juvenile court, all the time."

After a silence, he spoke in a different voice; the appeal in it was very strong. "Kathy?"

"Yes?"

"What does this girl say?"

She took her hand away from his, but gently, not making it a matter of denial. "I don't know at all. . . . Let's not talk about it now. I want that bathe, and that picnic."

"I want them too. I want everything."

"I know."

She liked, very much, the way he could straightway break the tension, to suit her mood exactly, and answer: "We will now do things in the proper order."

He was making, he said, for a turn-off marked '*Mooikraal,*' though the 'beautiful village' was now no more than a deserted ring of ancient mud huts. Presently they reached their cross-roads, and branched off onto a bumpy track leading up hill towards a clump of trees. A couple of miles away, they could see a pink-and-white farm-house, with four windmills turning lazily in the faint breeze; the clump of trees, when they reached it, marked the edge of a small dam. The brown earth surrounding it was cracked and dry, and as the car stopped a drift of their yellow dust moved past them and away, losing itself in the parched ground. But miraculously there was water in the dam, quite a lot of water; it shimmered in the heat, and sparkled where it caught the sun; it might have been trapped there for their delight.

"It's our lucky day," said Tim, and edged the car into the shade. When they were at rest, he turned towards her, but he made no other movement; he really was doing things in the right order. "Bathe now? It looks just what we want."

She nodded. "Try and keep me out of that water."

"Change in the car," he said. "I'll try the trees."

Within minutes she was wading into the dam. The water was warm, almost hot, and muddy where her feet stirred it; but the soft feel of it was a blessing. When Tim joined her, she was already swimming round and round in lazy circles.

"Slow," she called out.

"I like to give a lady a fair start."

He had a beautiful body, as she had already observed on more formal occasions at the ship's pool; lithe, muscular, the hips narrow, the chest deep and firm. He had developed also a handsome tan, as she had herself; when presently they waded out again, and sat on the edge of the dam to dry out, there could be no denying his strong physical appeal. It was clear that he felt the same about her, and she was glad of it; he must have seen, many times on board, the brief green swim-suit she wore, and the contours of her body candidly displayed by it, but now he admired them frankly, and let her see him doing so. She felt that this was entirely right; if they were young animals in the sun, let them give this pleasure to each other, without furtiveness, without peeping. . . . She lay back, crossing her slim legs, and when he had enjoyed this, and the lift of her breasts under the clinging material, he said, as she had hoped he would:

"You're the most beautiful girl I've ever seen."

She smiled back at him, without guile. "When you look at me like that, I feel it."

"Do you mind?"

"No."

"We're doing all right today, aren't we?"

"Extremely well."

"I was afraid we wouldn't."

"Why not?" But she knew exactly what he meant. "You mean, the ship and everything might still be here?"

"Yes. But it's not, is it?"

"Nothing's here."

Tim smiled, in pure joy, and leant across and touched her shoulder. His hand was strong, but the grip was as tender as a girl's. He said: "Are you hungry yet?"

"Absolutely ravenous. What is there?"

"Iron rations," he answered. "But well up to *Alcestis* standards. I know the Chief Steward."

He pulled her to her feet, without making a production of it, and they walked back to the shade of the trees, hand in hand. On the way, she asked:

"How old are you, Tim?"

"Just the right age."

She thought: This is hardly fair. . . .

But just as he was manhandling two very large wicker baskets, and a carrier-bag which clinked agreeably, from the back seat of the car, there came a most odd interruption, one they could have done without. It was other people.

They were walking in procession along the edge of the dam towards them; an old man with a white beard, an old Negro, and an old dog, all moving very gently at a pace suited to age and authority. Close to, the old man was a tremendous sight. He was very tall, even with his stoop; he wore a wide-brimmed sun-hat, and under it his lined face was like a hawk's, proud and watchful. He had wrinkled yellow trousers, and a bush shirt of faded khaki, and dusty *veldschoen*, and he carried a long staff as bent and gnarled as himself.

He stopped when he came opposite to them, and surveyed them unwinkingly. His eyes were blue, with a faraway fierceness. The old Negro also stopped, a pace behind him, and scratched the grey-white wool of his head. The dog, a ridge-back hound with enormous sinewy shoulders, growled once, and lay down stiffly in the middle of the pathway.

It was time for someone to speak. "Good morning!" Tim called out, with more confidence than he felt. "I hope we're not trespassing."

The old man said nothing; he continued to stare at them, as did the gaunt black man and the dog. Standing outlined against the sky, he had an infinitely patriarchal air; when his eyes shifted from Tim to Kathy, and took in—though without impertinence—her slim body and tiny swim-suit, it would not have surprised her if, then and there, he had called down a Mosaic curse on such a fleshly display.

Tim said, in a low tone: "Probably he only speaks Afrikaans," and then, raising his voice again, he called out: "*Gooie môre, meneer.*"

Surprisingly, charmingly, the huge old man swept off his hat, with a tremendous courtesy, bowed to Kathy, and returned the greeting: "*Gooie môre.*" His voice was a deep rumbling bass, and his mane of white hair gleamed like a halo before he put his hat on again.

"That's all I know, damn it," said Tim, aside to Kathy. He came forward, smiling as broadly as he could, and gestured round the clump of trees; as his arm moved, the dog growled, and half rose on its haunches. Tim tried to convey with his gesture and in his expression a triple idea—that they knew they were on the old man's land, that they thought it was very beautiful, and that they would like to stay there, if they could have his permission. The synthesis would have taxed the most highly competent actor; but it was possible that he did succeed in communicating some of it, for after a long moment, during which the old man let his steady gaze wander from the car to the picnic baskets, from Tim to Kathy, and from the baking sunshine to the cool shade of the trees, he took off his hat again, bowed, and prepared to move on. The old Negro, whose face was shrunken to a tiny birdlike mask, raised a skinny arm in salute, said something that sounded like "Ow!" and followed him; and the dog, heaving itself up stiffly, drew back a lolling tongue and padded after them.

"Whew!" said Tim, in relief, as soon as the cavalcade was out of earshot. "That's better! I thought they'd come down to throw us out."

"You mean, this is his land? He didn't look as if he had a cent to his name!"

"He probably owns every mile you can see from here."

"But what a terrific old man!" Kathy looked after their late visitor as he made his way slowly up the hillside towards the distant farmhouse. "He must have been at least eighty. Didn't he bow *beautifully?*"

"They have wonderful manners, the old Afrikaners," agreed Tim.

"Wonderful hospitality, too. Some of the younger South Africans are terrible thugs—we've had some on board, they talk like I imagine Hitler used to—but the old folks, the old Boers, are real charmers."

"Talking of hospitality," prompted Kathy.

"Coming, madam," said Tim, with a fair-to-middling caricature of the Chief Steward, and started to break out the picnic baskets. But he took his time about it; returning solitude seemed once more to have eased them of all cares; they were sure of their day, they could enjoy it lazily, happily, at a pace incomprehensible to the outside world.

The *Alcestis* kitchens had done them well; there was a chicken, half a ham, Russian salad, plovers' eggs, fruit, cheese, some coffee in a hot thermos and some Vichyssoise in a cold one. "So this is where the profits go," commented Kathy, as she surveyed the feast spread out on one of the dining-room's spotless tablecloths. "No wonder your fares are so high."

Tim was about to reply when his eye was caught by a faraway movement, up the slope near the farm-house. But it was not the old man and his small procession; they had already disappeared; it seemed to be a younger man, more agile, running towards them with long loping strides.

"We might as well be in Piccadilly Circus," Tim grumbled. But he was intrigued none-the-less.

As the runner drew nearer he could be seen to be a boy, clad in ragged shorts and a torn brown jersey. He was carrying something with great care—a box or a basket, held out in front of him like a votive offering. When he reached the edge of the dam he broke stride, and walked the last few yards. He was pale-skinned—a Cape Coloured, probably—with curious reddish hair and a brilliant grin. As soon as he reached them he bobbed and bowed, jumping from one foot to the other, and then set down his burden on the ground. Then he laughed, very merrily, and turned and ran away, with never a backward glance.

"This must be one of those days," said Tim dubiously, and pulled the box towards him. It was cardboard; it had once held soap-flakes

But packed inside there were now two fruits, like melons, only glowing golden and orange, and a dripping bottle without a label on it.

"What are they?"

"Paw-paws," answered Tim. "They have a funny taste—a cross between a melon and a soapy kind of marrow, only much nicer than that sounds. And this—" he drew the cork from the bottle, which was cold to his hand, and sniffed at the contents. Then he poured some out, and sipped it. It was white wine, cool and tart, like thin cider.

"Well," he said, astonished, "this really is our day. Instead of being thrown out, we're given wine to drink and paw-paws for dessert."

"What lovely presents," said Kathy. "And what a sweet thought. Aren't people nice to us? He must have liked us after all."

"It's probably his own wine, too," said Tim. He poured out two tumblers of it, and they drank inquiringly. "Tastes rather like Rhine wine, only thinner."

Kathy sipped hers. "It's just about the nicest thing that ever happened, anyway," she said, happily. "Do you think it's strong?"

"Oh, I hope so."

It was like Christmas, with the presents, and New Year's Day, with the promise of the future close at hand; and all in the middle of a South African desert within sight of a dam, which in the noonday sun shone like a burnished mirror. The sun filtered down through the leaves overhead, dappling their bodies with just-moving shadows; they ate and drank, and talked lazily, and looked at each other, and felt happy on the edge of love. Kathy found herself sinking slowly back into a slothful, sensual peace; there could be only one thing to happen now, one way of taking their delight after the wine and the meal; she was ready for it, she did not quarrel with it, she wanted it. But she knew more of the man already; she knew that he would not, even now, make love to her except by direct invitation. Of course he wanted her, under the trees, in the shade; his eyes were saying it, there was even a message from his body, across the few feet between them. But he would not take her, he would only be received and welcomed. . . . She put down her empty glass, and said:

"Oh dear! What a huge lunch. I'm going to sleep, I think. Perhaps we should both do that."

"Yes."

She looked behind her at the trees. "If we went further in, we'd have more shade."

"Yes." There was a tremor in his voice; he had his invitation now; the enormous joy was beginning to possess him.

"Let's move before we get too lazy."

He stood up.

"Do we need a rug?"

She looked up at him. He was smiling gravely, but his lower lip was trembling a little. She smiled back, with an equal joy, and said: "Obviously."

Walking before him into the deeper shadows, her knees already a little weak, she suddenly wondered, like a young girl on the very threshold, how sailors made love.

Sailors made love, she found, with shattering eloquence; a blend of sensuality, competence, and tender adoration which brought its own tempestuous end. Now that they were agreed, she was in his hands, and presently she was overjoyed to be so. He asked, before they lay down, "Am I the first?" and when she shook her head (with an absurd sense of disappointment) and answered: "No—the second," he nodded to himself, and then to her, as if this were the answer he had expected, a natural part of the day's progress. After that, he said: "You know I love you," and after that they were lost. But through it all she was conscious of direction, of control; even when he was on the edge of delight, he took care that she was there too. She had not been wrong; it was what she had guessed when she watched him securing the life-boat, during the storm near Cape Town. Sailors were men, not boys, and this sailor was a true man among them.

After their love-making he thanked her, with glowing eyes which might have held tears a moment before, and they dozed off and slept deeply, while the sun drew round to the westward, and the shadows of their arbour began to slant away from them. When they awoke they swam again, rejoicing in freshness, shedding their languor; and then they made love once more, their bodies still cool and only half-dry—but this time it was a kind of happy frolic, light-hearted, laughing—they made each other smile, even as they made each other wild—they knew enough to be confident now, they could drop the guard and take loving chances. And then, too soon, the sun began to go down, and it grew cool, and they would have to go—indeed, they would have to drive like the wind if they were to be back in time.

So he drove like the wind, but his arm was often about her, and she would lean across and kiss him when he asked her to. Her thoughts were chaotic, and yet secure; none of this made sense, part of it was unworthy, part almost wicked, but she could not wish to change any of it. When he said: "I adore you—I wish I could stop the car," she felt swamped by a tender longing, as real as his body had been real.

On that return journey, they drove for nearly an hour towards a fantastic Karroo sunset, streaked with orange and red and green and purple; she had never seen anything like it before. "It's the dust in the air," he said; "it filters the light or something." She believed him; she would have believed him if he had said that it was controlled by the F.B.I. There was a moment when she had a fierce urge to tell him everything—all about Carl, all about the gang; it might free her, partially, from the deadly sense she had had lately, of being trapped in evil, so that she would end her days as the kind of woman one saw in old gangster movies, dyed, dilapidated, crying into her beer as the leader slapped her down or deserted her for younger, fresher meat. . . . But the moment passed; confession did not seem necessary; when they were in this mood of sensual release, when they had made love so well and so wonderfully, she could not be trapped by anything except an extreme of gratitude.

They had had their day; it had been heaven; he had taken her by the hand, and she had re-entered with him a young world of innocence and ardour, a world she had lost, a world she had never known. That was today, and it had been set apart. Things were still to be done in the right order. If there were tears in their future, they could not dry them now.

Going down the long hill into Cape Town, he suddenly said:

"I'll be able to sit for my mate's ticket, in about three years' time."

It seemed to her, at that moment, the happiest, the most comforting prospect in the whole world.

Carl Wenstrom was coming out of the smoking-room when she and Tim stepped over the top of the gangway onto the 'square' of A-deck, blinking at the lights overhead. One look told her he was absolutely furious, with her and perhaps with a lot more besides. He stared at her, and then from her to Tim, and asked very curtly: "Where have you been all day, Kathy? Do you realize it's nearly midnight?"

"Don't we know it!" She laughed, careless of his mood, and turned to Tim. "You left that sprint a little late, Ben Hur."

"I told you we'd make it." Tim stretched, luxuriantly stiff; then he intercepted a speculative glance from the gangway quartermaster, and straightened up. "It's a good road, isn't it?" he ended, on a much more formal note.

"Where have you been?" Carl asked again.

"We went for a drive. A picnic." She waved her hand vaguely; she was overwhelmingly tired, and it was the most wonderful tiredness she had ever felt. A day which had started with Tillotson had somehow escaped its shoddy origins, and ended in Paradise. " 'Way up there."

"You should have told me," said Carl. "You should have left a message."

Tim broke in. "I'm afraid—" he began.

Carl, insultingly, took Kathy's arm and drew her to one side, without looking at Tim. He knows, she thought; he knows already, or he guesses, and I do not care, either way. . . . Over his shoulder, Carl said: "Goodnight, Mansell," and almost propelled her down the corridor towards their room, leaving Tim, red-faced, to swallow his hurt as best he could.

When the door was shut behind them: "That was terribly rude, Carl," said Kathy. "He's been so sweet to me, and we've had an absolutely wonderful—"

"Shut up!" said Carl, suddenly snarling. He *was* angry, fantastically so, she realized; his face was pale, and the veins at his temples fluttered uncontrollably. "We'll take up what you've been doing, later on. I hope you'll be proud of it, when we do. . . . Right now, you'd better realize that I've had enough for one day. I've had one hell of a session with the Captain. He seems to know everything! About Diane. About the poker game. About the Professor making an idiot of himself all over the ship. And that's not all." He stared down at her, his eyes smouldering. He knows, she thought again; but at the moment it was, for Carl, only a little thing, compared with something else he knew. She could not guess what that something else might be, until he said, with extreme loathing in his voice:

"I think Louis has taken off."

chapter 4

CARL had good reason to be angry; it had been a most ominous day, one which had seemed to threaten their whole undertaking. They were under suspicion—so much had been made clear, in an interview with the Captain which had left him nervous and irritated at the same time; and the suspicion involved the future as well as the past. If, as the Captain obviously suspected, they had been "operating," it was, from the disciplinary point of view, so much water over the dam; as of that moment, it was in the past, there had been no specific complaints, it was just a black mark in a ledger which did not greatly matter. But if they now tried to continue on the same lines, they would do so under an official microscope which would make profitable operation very difficult indeed.

He could not but admire, even in his annoyance, the swiftness and competence with which the Captain had drawn the lines of battle to his own exact taste. It had been mid-morning when the Captain, summoning Carl to his cabin, had greeted him immediately with the words:

"Mr. Wenstrom, I've been hearing some funny things about you and your family."

Carl had not displayed any reaction, either of guilt or fear; he was not that sort of man. "Well now," he had answered, with the easy condescension of the big man towards the small, "I don't think we need to—"

The Captain, noting and disliking the manner, had not hesitated to kill it stone dead. He had held up his hand, with undeniable authority. "Just a minute!" he said, sharply. "At this stage, I'll do the talking."

"He was damn right, he did the talking!" Carl now recalled to Kathy. He was walking up and down the day-cabin, in unusual, indeed unprecedented agitation; it was mostly a build-up of anger, Kathy judged, but on top of it was an uneasy sense of vulnerability, as if he had been brought face to face with the astonishing idea that he might have met his match. "He hasn't much to go on, and he was guessing quite a lot, but he certainly did a good job of presenting the evidence."

"What sort of evidence?" asked Kathy. She was still half-way between two worlds, and she was very tired; it was an effort to take this seriously, to feel herself involved in things which for the space of a whole day had retreated out of sight. Did she have to come back to this ridiculous circus? . . . She knew that she was being fundamentally disloyal to Carl; but many things were now in flux, things which for six years she had treated as part of an immutable universe. Love was changing—had already changed—to independent appraisal and activity; she was tied to Carl by a hundred strands, of gratitude, appreciation, and memory, but physical love was no longer part of this weaving, and she could not now pretend, even to herself, that it still figured as an entry in their joint account.

"What sort of evidence?" she repeated, as he did not answer. "What does he know?"

"He knows too much." Carl had been marshalling his thoughts; the sum was not a pretty one, and his voice showed it. "To begin with, he's found out that Diane has been sleeping around. You know how? A lot of her chums had to go to the doctor. . . ." Meeting Kathy's shocked expression, his own face hardened cruelly. "Wonderful, isn't it? He *doesn't* know she's been making money out of it, but he suspects it, and he hinted as much. Hinted!" He jerked his head back with intense irritation. "What he actually said was: 'The age of the men involved indicates that love didn't have much to do with it.' That's a kind of damned English way of putting it!"

Kathy, interested in spite of herself, said: "There's still nothing illegal in that. If one or two men choose to give her presents—"

"The word 'illegal' was not used. The word used was 'unbecoming'." He mimicked Captain Harmer's pronunciation with savage precision. "The word 'unbecoming' was also used about the Professor. I knew he'd been getting conspicuously drunk during the past few weeks, but I didn't know that he'd been wandering into other people's cabins. Did you?" And as Kathy shook her head: "The damned old fool—Mrs. Youngdahl came down one night and found him in her room, drunk as an owl! The story got to the Captain, of course, and he had him on the carpet. And I'm the last one to hear about it!"

"What did he do about the Professor?"

"Gave him a blast—threatened to cut the tap off if he didn't behave himself in the future." Carl frowned grimly. "I've dealt with the Professor myself. But the harm's done. Between him and Diane—"

"But it's still not so terrible, is it?" interrupted Kathy. "What can the Captain do about it?"

"He can watch us. Everybody can watch us. Don't you see—" Carl's voice suddenly cracked out. "*—we've attracted attention!* In future, whatever we do, however innocent, we'll probably have half a dozen people trailing us. The Captain even said something about the poker games!"

"But there's nothing wrong there."

"There's been a hell of a lot of money coming my way, and it all ties in with the rest. . . . Then we had a long bit about Louis, and his 'unusual choice of companions'—" the angry mimicry came into play once more. "In the Captain's mind, it all fitted into a pattern. And the pattern's something like the truth. He made that clear." Carl passed a weary hand over his face, and crossed to the side-table for a drink. From there he spoke, his back to the room: "I could have done with your help today, Kathy. Where were you?"

"I went for a drive. I told you."

"All day? With that little sailor boy?"

"Yes."

"How was it?"

Carl's tone carried considerable innuendo, but she passed it by. "We had a lot of fun."

"I wouldn't doubt it. But I don't suppose you picked up much loose change, did you?"

After a moment, Kathy said: "Carl, I'm terribly tired. Let's not have this. . . . You haven't told me the important part yet. About Louis leaving, or something. What was that?"

Carl turned round to face her. "You prefer to change the subject? Very well. . . . Louis called me up this afternoon. He was high—high as a kite. He was also in some place called Bloemfontein, instead of being in Johannesburg or the Game Reserve, where he's meant to be. And he wasn't there by himself, either. He's picked off a real beauty this time."

"Who?"

"Bernice Beddington."

"Oh *no!*" Kathy reacted in astonishment, and then, in spite of her tiredness, burst out laughing. "*Bernice?* He must be out of his head."

"He's out of his head, all right," answered Carl roughly, "but for a different reason. Of course she's ugly and stupid, but that's not the point. She's young, and her father and mother are here on board. If he's started something with her, he's going to land us all in a load of trouble."

"*Has* he started something?"

"Yes. He says so, anyway." Carl heard again, in his inner ear, the crackling hum of the long-distance wires, and Louis' voice, cocky and blurred at the same time, saying with foolish affectation: 'We drove down here to get away from it all!' And a little later, after Carl had begun to sort out the picture: 'Sure I've laid her! And she's not going to come unlaid, no matter how much people squawk!'

"He was drunk as a goat, the God-damned little bastard!" Carl so rarely swore that it was a shock to hear the words. "Or he wouldn't have called me up in the first place. I don't know whether he *will* come back, or when. I told him to break it up, to go right back to Johannesburg, and then meet the ship at Durban, like we planned. Or there'd be hell to pay. But I don't know whether it took. He sounded—he sounded 'way out!"

"But what can he do, that he hasn't done before?"

"He can tie us all up in knots, maybe get involved with the police. That's what he can do! Oh, I know the girl's over-age, but there's such a thing as abduction, undue influence, all that kind of trouble. And it'll start the Captain up again, in high gear. The only good thing is, no-one knows anything about this yet. Louis told them up there he was going to take a drive, instead of following the normal schedule. We've got to cover this up somehow, if I have to go up and fetch him back myself! We just can't afford—"

There was a loud knock at the door, which sprang open immediately. It was a woman—Mrs. Beddington—in such an obvious state of excitement that Carl's heart sank at the sight. She was a small woman, of most ordinary appearance, but at this moment she radiated personality on a very large scale. She had a piece of paper in her hand, and, as she advanced into the cabin, she waved it with furious energy.

"What's this mean?" she cried, explosively. "Just tell me that! What's it mean?"

The piece of paper became a telegram, and, guessing with some confidence what it meant, Carl searched for a non-committal answer. He was still searching when Steward Barkway appeared in the open doorway, and said, with unmistakable relish:

"Captain's compliments, sir, and would you please see him immediately."

chapter 5

IT would never have happened, Louis realized, if they had not been sitting side by side in the plane going up to Johannesburg. The last thing that Louis wanted to tangle with was another woman, however pliable; as a fugitive from Mrs. van Dooren, he was a fugitive from the entire sex, and he was really taking in the Johannesburg tour to give himself an essential breathing-space. But chance put him beside Bernice Beddington, that forlorn young female who was safe wherever she went, for the space of three-and-a-half hours; and the rest—as he himself phrased it, in a night-club flight of fancy, three days later—the rest was history.

Their plane took off early in the morning; at such a demanding hour, he had been quite happy to plunk himself down beside Bernice Beddington, who was making the trip alone (her father had a troublesome sinus infection), say "Hallo, there!" on the customary note of insincerity, buckle-on his seat-belt, and doze off to sleep. This was one who wouldn't cause him any grief. . . . He slept through the breakfast service, and for an hour afterwards; when he woke up, they were flying over flat, featureless country as dull as the girl who sat beside him, staring at a fashion magazine as if it were a Sanskrit papyrus. More out of habit than anything else, he turned slightly towards her, and said:

"Boy, I sure needed that sleep!"

She started as if he had stuck a pin into her. So few people in her entire world ever volunteered a conversational opening that she had no machinery to deal with it. Blushing vividly, she said the first thing that came into her head:

"Did you know you were snoring?"

He grinned and stretched. "Was I? I was deep down. . . . Hope it didn't worry you."

She found this even more embarrassing. "Oh, I didn't mind a bit. . . . You must be terribly tired, I know. . . ." She ventured a timid side-glance, as if to be sure that he were real. "You go to so many parties, don't you?"

"Doesn't everyone?"

Searching for an answer, she again produced the one that arrived first. "But I hate them!" she exclaimed.

Louis turned and looked at her more closely. She really was remarkably unattractive. Everything about her was wrong; the great moon face, broad flat nose, awkward figure, and enormous feet added up, not just to the girl least likely to succeed, but the girl least likely to be judged a girl at all. Of course (he had noted the point already) she must spend a fortune on her clothes, even though they looked as if they were hanging out to dry after a rough night in the barn; and the bag from which she now took a cigarette-case was crocodile, and the case itself was platinum, with her initials ('B.B.,' for God's sake!) in emeralds. . . . He felt rested after his sleep, and he had left Mrs. van Dooren safely committed to a different tour, and it was good to be running his own life for a change. Vaguely he found himself thinking: What the hell? Why not?

"You mustn't feel that way about it," he said, as convincingly as he could, and began to talk—as if they were both plagued by the same kind of problem—of the various methods of picking people up at parties.

Louis could be very amusing when he wanted to; and he wanted to now, for no very clear reason except that the girl must have plenty of spending money and was thus rendered desirable (Confucius say: Parents loaded, girl stacked), that she would never do anything to or for him except run errands, and that this was the way he wanted it now. (She had actually given him a cigarette, and lighted it for him. That was a good switch. . . .) Presently he ordered drinks for them both; it was only ten o'clock, but South African Airways always opened up the bar, any time of the day or night, anywhere in excess of two thousand feet, and their hospitality was tempting. One hour and four Martinis later, Bernice Beddington began to come to life.

No-one had ever talked to her for so long at one time; the fact that the talker was Louis Scapelli, who everyone said was so wicked, whom Daddy himself had been overheard to call a woman-chasing wop, was just about the most exciting thing that had ever happened. Indeed, the only thing. . . . Flowering in this fantastic radiance, she had given him her views on teen-age crime, the true and terrible story of her coming-out dance, and her entire life-history to date, by the time their plane began its slow descent towards the mine-dumps of the Johannesburg Reef.

Tiptree-Jones, the man in charge of the party, walked down the middle gangway, and paused by their seat. Having had Bernice Beddington, dumb as an ox, at his table for more than two months, he was astonished to see that she was now carrying on an animated conversation, glass in hand, cigarette puffing away merrily. . . . The fact that she was talking to Louis Scapelli caused him a minor pang of uneasiness, but he found it preferable to rise above it. If there was anything wrong, he didn't want to know.

"Are you enjoying yourselves?" he asked heartily.

Bernice Beddington, instead of letting her mouth drop open with embarrassment, actually answered: "Of course!"

"We might have a party or something, when we get to Johannesburg," said Louis, as Tiptree-Jones passed on. "I hear it's quite a town."

"Could we be—you know—by ourselves?" Bernice ventured.

"I don't see why not." Louis turned to smile at her. "Sure you don't want to take Tiptree-Jones along?"

She giggled. "But he's so dull . . ." Then she put her hand to her mouth. "Oh, I shouldn't say that, should I?"

"Say anything you like," said Louis handsomely.

"I want to go horse-racing, too. And to a native dance. And down a gold-mine." It was the Martinis speaking, but the ideas were none the worse for that. Nor was the next one. "Daddy always gives me lots of money to spend," Bernice confided. "This time, I'm not going to save any of it!"

Louis thought again, much less vaguely: Why not?

They had three days in Johannesburg, and they spent all of them together, by-passing the regular tours and excursions; while Tiptree-Jones, worried yet relieved, decided that this was much the best way of solving the Bernice Beddington problem. Scapelli might be the most terrible type, but no-one else had come anywhere near solving it, so far. . . . To begin with, the two of them had hired a car, in most auspicious circumstances.

"Wouldn't it be nicer to have our own car?" asked Bernice, on the first afternoon, when they had taken a very long and expensive taxi-drive out to the local country club. "I can drive, if you can't."

"I can drive," said Louis, not too enthusiastically.

Intensely vulnerable still, reacting to the smallest hint of anything that might threaten her capture, Bernice went on pleadingly: "I know it's extravagant. But taxis are extravagant, aren't they? And it's silly not to spend all this money."

"All what money?" asked Louis.

Bernice opened her handbag, and, in one of those enormously awkward gestures which had long been her mother's despair, positively shovelled a wad of bills and travellers' checks towards him. "All this," she answered. "Let's spend it! It's just wasted, otherwise."

Louis held the money very easily, very openly in his hand. At a rough guess, aided by a discreet touch of the thumb, it was not less than five thousand dollars.

"Gee, honey," he said—it seemed an appropriate moment for an endearment—"do you really carry all this around with you?"

"Not normally." She was, as usual, meeting criticism with humble argument. "But on a trip like this—it just seems to mount up. I haven't had anything to spend it on, so far." She looked at him, almost begging for her chance to give him something, to do something for him. "Please fix up a car, Louis. Then we can go anywhere we want."

"All right." He held out the money. "Here, you'd better have this back."

"No," she said. "I've got lots more in my room, anyway. Daddy likes me to be independent. . . . You be the banker, and pay for things."

"But I can't just spend your money."

"We can take it in turns, then," she suggested, timid once more. "We'll spend some of mine first, and then some of yours. Wouldn't that be all right?"

"I guess so," he agreed, with reluctance. "But don't forget now—fair shares!"

"I won't forget *anything* about this," she said fervently.

In her delight and excitement, she became, if anything, more ugly than ever; now, at any time of the day, wisps of matted hair lay dankly on her forehead, and her pudgy face shone with a moist rapture which no powder could cope with. She had never had a man-friend before; she had no idea what to do; she had nothing to charm him with—and yet, incredibly, he was there! Life became, for her, a series of ecstatic 'firsts,' blazing a private pathway of joy. There were times, often, when she would cheerfully and humbly have died for him.

There was the first occasion when he said, meeting her at breakfast-time: "Hi, beautiful!"

There was the time when he held her hand, walking back from a night-club, and he said: "You have very sensitive fingers—did you know that?"

There was a time, in the bar of the Carlton Hotel, when she felt that other people from the *Alcestis* were staring at the two of them, and probably laughing, and she ventured to say something about it, and he answered: "Forget it, baby—they're just jealous of us."

There was a time when he kissed her (only her spectacles rather got in the way,) and another time when he stood at the door of her hotel bedroom and said, most movingly: "I mustn't, honey—I respect you too much."

There was the time when he said: "You know, you and I have got to do something about this."

What he did about it was to suggest: "We don't want to go to any old Game Reserve, do we?"; they then cashed the remainder of her travellers' checks, and drove down to a small hotel in Bloemfontein, where he disposed of her virginity with as much enthusiasm as he could muster. It was under the influence of the alcohol necessary to confront that broad moon-like face, those myopic, cow-like eyes, and that spread-eagled acreage of body, that he had telephoned to Carl. (Years later, he was to recall: "Boy, I sure had to get into the sauce, that night!") But from then on, drifting on golden tides, they organized her entire future in half a dozen sentences.

"I don't want to go back to the ship," Bernice declared. She was already fathoms deep in astonished rapture. "You know how I hate it!"

"Then we'll stay here in Africa. Easy!"

"And—and get married, like you said?"

"Jesus, honey!" answered Louis, "you don't think I'd let you get away *now?*"

"I know what," said Bernice happily. "We'll send them a telegram."

"Sir, I can't imagine where they've gone," reported Tiptree-Jones on the long-distance telephone from Johannesburg. Beneath the smooth manner there was some agitation; he felt that he was going to be blamed, whatever happened. "The position here is that we move on to the Game Reserve, early tomorrow morning, and neither Scapelli nor the girl have been seen by anyone, for at least twenty-four hours. They didn't sleep at the hotel last night, either."

"It's your job to keep an eye on them," growled the Captain. But he was not yet worried; passengers did strange things, but he could not imagine anyone doing a strange thing to Bernice Beddington. "I suppose, if the truth was known, you were damned glad to have her taken off your hands."

"Well," said Tiptree-Jones, detecting benevolence in an unexpected quarter, "there *was* that, sir."

Captain Harmer glanced down at his watch. It was nine o'clock in the evening; he himself had to take the *Alcestis* out, at first light, for

Durban. "There's not much you can do except wait," he decided finally. "Ring me up again at midnight. If they haven't shown up by then, we might have to tell the police. Of course, it's probably nothing at all. I don't trust Scapelli in any area known to God, but I think I *would* trust him with Bernice. I dare say their car broke down somewhere."

"I'll ring again at twelve, sir," said Tiptree-Jones. He sounded relieved—on one point, at least. "And, sir—"

"What is it?"

"Do you think you could switch this call to the doctor? I'd like to speak to him."

"The doctor?" said Harmer, irritated. "What do you want the doctor for?"

From a long way away, rather faint, Tiptree-Jones answered: "Well, it's a personal matter, sir."

The Captain allowed himself a single short laugh, for the frailties of human nature which could be thus betrayed in odd areas; then he switched the call, and hung up. He was still not worried; it was just a question as to whether, at this stage, the girl's parents should be told. If it were anyone but Scapelli. . . . After the second call at midnight, with no further news, he was still debating the next step when Mr. Beddington himself stormed into the cabin, and almost shouted:

"I want an explanation of this, Captain!"

"I beg your pardon," said Harmer coldly.

"We've been having dinner ashore—only just got back." Small like his wife, Mr. Beddington supplemented his stature with a towering indignation. "There was this telegram waiting for us! My wife has it!"

"Telegram?"

"Our little girl's gone off with that wop!"

chapter 6

"IT'S disgraceful!" said Mrs. Beddington, for the twentieth time; but already she was calmer, and there was less conviction in her voice. Carl, faced with the most crucial moment of the voyage, and aware all the time of the Captain's deep resentment, was doing a masterly job of spreading a thick layer of soft soap over the entire area. To restore any kind of normality to the situation, he had to make two points: firstly, that Louis was actually a highly desirable character, and, secondly, that Bernice Beddington had brought off something like a *coup*, something for which her parents had been praying for years.

The first requirement was in the realm of the impossible, and the second was difficult to press home without seeming offensive. But in his singular display of skill, with the Captain prepared to jump in, any time he faltered, Carl had never shown better form on any track in the world.

To begin with, anger and alarm had predominated; the Beddingtons, ready to blame anyone remotely concerned with the outrage, were all for action—action in any direction. They sat side by side on the Captain's long sofa, a small tough team armoured by a just cause, and belaboured anything they could reach.

"You must have him tracked down, and arrested!" declared Mrs. Beddington. Her main target was Carl, sitting opposite her on a hard upright chair. "It's your responsibility! He's your nephew, isn't he? You're liable for whatever he does wrong! It's the law!"

"Technically, that is not so," answered Carl, with judicious calm. "I was his legal guardian when he was under age, but that of course is no longer true. He is now an adult, with an adult's freedom of action."

"Freedom!" exclaimed Mrs. Beddington. "Don't you dare talk to me about freedom! If he's your nephew, you should control him! Everyone knows he's got a terrible reputation, everyone knows he's been chasing after every woman in the ship! Most of them old enough to be his mother, too!"

"But obviously," said Carl, "he has now decided to settle down."

"Of course he's decided to settle down," it was Mr. Beddington's turn to explode, "with a girl who owns half a million dollars of my company's stock in her own right!" He swung round to the Captain, sitting watchfully at his desk. "What I want to know is, how a thing like this can happen. A young single girl goes away on a trip like this, surely there's someone in charge? A chaperone, or something? Is this your idea of proper supervision? Let me tell you, if this was a business deal, you could be sued for gross incompetence!"

The Captain kept his temper; it had been a very long time since anyone had spoken to him in these terms, but he realized the genuine distress behind the outburst. His own anger was reserved for Carl, and for this whole shoddy gang who could make a farm-yard out of a decent ship. . . .

"Naturally we exercise supervision," he said, as firmly as he felt necessary. "But you must realize that we are not dealing with children. Most passengers resent any kind of control; they feel quite capable of organizing their own lives. And after all, your daughter *is* of age, and presumably you must trust her, or you wouldn't have allowed her to make this Johannesburg trip alone. I would have thought she was the very last person to get into any sort of trouble."

"What do you mean, the very last person?" inquired Mrs. Beddington, with an edge to her voice.

"I mean," said Harmer, "she's a most sensible girl, well able to take care of herself."

"And now she's been seduced!" said Mr. Beddington bitterly. "And by one of your own passengers—the biggest bastard in the ship!" He looked round at Carl. "I agree with my wife—I think you've got a hell of a lot to answer for, as well."

Carl assumed a highly shocked expression. "Did you use the word 'seduced'?" he inquired, as if he had overheard some rude version of a hymn. "I must say I am very surprised. Your daughter's telegram said nothing of any such—ah—development. All she said was—" he glanced down, and read from the fatal piece of paper, "—'*Staying here till I can marry Louis Scapelli very happy don't worry best love*

Bernice.' " In the silence that followed, Carl went on: "That seems to me, if I may say so, a telegram that any mother and father would be glad and proud to receive."

"Glad and proud?" said Mr. Beddington, stopped in his tracks. "What the hell do you mean, glad and proud? She's run away, and she's going to get married—maybe. The man involved is a woman-chasing bastard, probably without a cent to his name. What is there to be glad and proud about?"

"Young love," answered Carl, on a most sober note. "The most precious thing in the world."

"Where does young love come in, for God's sake?"

Carl tapped the telegram with his forefinger. "In every word of this message. She is happy, she is excited, she is going to get married, and she sends her love to you, her parents. She wants to share her love, she wants you to be as happy as I am sure Louis is making her, at this moment."

"But he's not meant to make her happy at one o'clock in the morning!" said Mrs. Beddington, obviously appalled by the idea. "It's disgusting! How do we know what he's doing to her? What will people say?"

"They will say," intoned Carl, with sudden dramatic piety, "that love makes its own rules. . . . Of course she and Louis have been foolish," he continued, on a more man-of-the-world note, "but what does that prove?—simply that they are deeply in love and want to marry as soon as they can." He felt the Captain's frosty eye upon him, and he rallied himself for a decisive effort. "Of course it is a surprise, of course they have been naughty—in keeping it a secret—but when were lovers *not* secretive? It is part of their joy, part of the excitement. . . ." He addressed himself especially to Mrs. Beddington. "It is a great shock to you, I know—but there could be worse shocks, couldn't there?—and worse disappointments. *At last*—" he lent a very delicate emphasis to the words, "—your little girl has found the happiness she deserves. She is going to be married! There may be grandchildren! Surely you must be glad about that?"

"Well," said Mrs. Beddington, and paused to look at her husband, while Carl watched both their faces. He was aware, as if he were dictating it himself, of the train of thought which he had been able to start. Their little girl—married at last. . . . Their little girl—so huge in reality, so long unmarketable. . . . And grandchildren already over the horizon. . . . "All the same," said Mrs. Beddington, after a long silence, "it *is* disgraceful."

It was then that Mr. Beddington asked: "What sort of a young man *is* Scapelli? What's his background?"

"It's an old Boston family," said Carl readily. (The Beddingtons were from the far west of Arizona.) "His father—who married my favourite sister—incidentally in the same kind of runaway match—his father made a great deal of money in real estate, and lost his life in extraordinary circumstances in a typhoon in the West Indies." *Steady now,* thought Carl to himself, aware of a baleful glance from the Captain: *keep it vague, keep it general* . . . "Louis, I believe, has shown great promise in the business world. I would say he had an exceptional future."

"But what does he do?" inquired Mr. Beddington.

"He has been looking for an opening, and taking his own time about it."

"He has money, then?"

Carl shook his head. "Not a great deal," he answered. "I happen to know there was some unfortunate litigation—as only too often happens, with these very old families. But of course," Carl went on, largely, "he has a few thousands, and naturally I will do the best I can for him myself, on this—" he caught Mrs. Beddington's eye, and smiled suddenly and disarmingly, "—you know, I *must* call it, this happy occasion. I have long wanted to see him settled. Bernice is a dear girl," he continued, stretching a point, "and Louis has undoubted qualities which will bring him to the top in his chosen sphere." He stood up suddenly, taking subtle control of all their problems, all their worries. "Why don't we," he said, with the most insidious charm he had ever displayed, "begin to be happy about this whole thing?"

When, much later, the Beddingtons had gone—reluctantly prepared to be brave about what had happened, ready, with misgivings, to be resigned to it—Captain Harmer surveyed Carl across the width of his desk. It was well past one o'clock, and he would be lucky to get three hours' sleep that night; but there was no limit to his dislike of the man opposite him, and this gave him the energy for what he had to do next. Obvously, they were nearing the end of the line, and he intended to dispose of this whole thing in unmistakable terms.

"Well done!" he said sarcastically, as soon as they were alone; and then, on a much harder note: "This is the second time we've met today, Mr. Wenstrom. As far as I am concerned, there will only be one more of these meetings."

Carl, who had been enjoying the quiet satisfaction of having disposed of the Beddingtons with rare skill, was brought up short by the remark. Of course, the Captain was of tougher calibre, as compared with the bemused parents, and he could not be expected to come out in favour of sentimental surrender quite so readily; but it did not seem to Carl that he had left any loose ends which the Captain could jump on. Hell, they were getting married, it was practically legal. . . . He was about to express his surprise when the Captain continued:

"What I mean by that, is that I'm not putting up with any more of these incidents, from any member of your family. If we have any further examples of *young love*, as practised by Mr. Scapelli or Miss Loring, I shall be taking immediate action. And this is the only warning you will get."

"I'm not sure I understand you," said Carl, coldly. "I certainly used the term 'young love' in connection with Louis and Bernice, and I see no reason to object to it. It's obvious to me that—"

The Captain held up his hand, in sudden brusque denial. "Mr. Wenstrom—cut it out! You are not dealing with the Beddingtons now, you are answering to me. . . . We both know enough about the respective characters of Scapelli and Miss Beddington—and their respective appearances, if I can make the point—to be quite certain that this is the culmination of a racket, on his part. He has been auctioning his favours for the past two months. I am absolutely sure that he has now picked out the most impressionable girl on board, made certain that she has money, and trapped her into marrying him. Whether you yourself planned this—"

"I knew nothing about it."

"Well, you know now." The Captain stood up, and after a moment Carl felt obliged to follow suit. "Let me make myself quite clear. I *know* that Scapelli has got away with murder, and I can't do anything about it. But I can take care of the future." He stared at Carl with very direct, very level eyes; he seemed suddenly a much bigger man, undeniably powerful, ready for action against anyone or anything. "If I hear of one single more instance of anything that *I* consider irregular—and I shall be the sole judge of that—I will put the whole lot of you ashore at the first port we touch."

Carl met his glance with an equal firmness. He had been taken seriously aback, but he was not going to show it. After a moment he answered, with careless calm:

"I doubt if you can do that."

The Captain raised his eyebrows; then he laughed, very shortly, just enough to demonstrate that Carl had blundered into an area of which he knew nothing. "I understand that you're a betting man, Mr. Wenstrom," he remarked ironically. "Would you care to have a bet on that? With me? Let me assure you that I can have you, and your family, and all your luggage, carried down the gangway and out onto the dock, *within the next five minutes,* and you would have no conceivable redress, either now or later. My company would back me up, one hundred per cent, in any court in any country in the world. . . . And now, goodnight!"

He sat down at his desk, and Carl, indubitably dismissed, turned to go. As he reached the door he heard the Captain's voice behind him, relaxed, almost mocking:

"And while I remember it, Mr. Wenstrom—they don't have typhoons in the West Indies. They have hurricanes."

chapter 7

CARL awoke suddenly at five A.M., when the familiar trembling deep within the *Alcestis*, the polite shudder which fifteen thousand horse-power was bound to give when moving into action, made itself felt throughout the ship. He awoke in irritation, which presently turned to rage; this was the damned Captain again, interfering with everything, showing off his strength. . . . It was a rage which, in a greater or less degree, was never to leave him.

Presently he got up, and looked out of his porthole. They were taking a lovely farewell of Cape Town; Table Mountain especially, square-cut like an immense grey monolith, tipped with gold at its peaks, had a matchless splendour which seemed to grow more noble as it receded. Carl stayed where he was at the open porthole for a long time, while the *Alcestis* steamed southwards at mounting speed, and rounded the Cape of Good Hope, and dipped her bows for the first time into the warm Indian Ocean. Then he dressed, and set out on the prowl.

Even in his anger, he had sense enough to realize that he was looking for victims, as the Captain had made him a victim, a few hours earlier. He felt that he had never been angrier, with any man or any situation; a few weeks ago the whole thing had been under control, they had been swimming along to victory, they would land at New York with a wonderful tan and a hundred thousand dollars; now, if the Captain could be believed—and he was a man to be believed, in this area—they would be lucky if they landed at New York at all.

It was not that the Captain was a match for him—Carl would never admit that. But it was true that Harmer could manipulate the rules to suit himself, and no-one else; at sea, in command of his ship, he had the same power and the same limitless discretion as ship's captains had held for five hundred years; history might blame or exonerate them, but in the meantime, "Go!" meant go and "Stop!" meant stop.

It was something which Carl Wenstrom had never met before. It stood in his way. It must be someone else's fault.

Kathy was asleep—or at least, her cabin door was locked, and she did not answer when he knocked. He would deal with Kathy—strange Kathy, unpredictable Kathy, perhaps retreating Kathy—later on, in his own good time. . . . The next door he knocked on was Diane's, and Diane was in.

Indeed, she was in bed, enjoying a light breakfast of fresh sliced peaches, devilled kidneys, and fingers of anchovy toast, when Carl made his entrance. He waited while her stewardess added a touch of cream to her coffee, patted the pillows behind her head, and withdrew, before he asked:

"Sure you're doing all right?"

Diane, who had her own instinct for moments of drama and violence, looked at him warily and said:

"What's the matter, Carl?"

"You know damn well what's the matter!" He was finding it easy —fatally so—to switch on anger as soon as an appropriate target showed itself. "While you're lying around like the Queen of Sheba, I'm doing all the work and carrying all the weight! Did you know that Louis has taken off into the woods somewhere? Did you know that the Professor practically gets his name printed in the ship's newspaper, among our more prominent drunks? Did you know that the Captain is going to put us all ashore at the next stop, unless we behave ourselves?"

"Gee, Carl," said Diane, alarmed. "I didn't know any of that."

"Well, you know now!" (Now who had said that before? The same damned man. . . .) "A lot of it is your fault, you stupid little bitch!" The words came easier as his early morning anger found its chance targets, the things he was prowling for; the words were not even the words he would normally have used, they were more like Diane herself losing her temper, like Louis doing some cheap show-off act. . . . "In fact, a *hell* of a lot of it is your fault. *You* started the Captain making all these inquiries, adding it all up. Good Christ, if I'd known you were going to send half the ship to the doctor's office, do you think I would have brought you along? I could get more mileage out of a plastic doll!"

"Now, see here, Carl!" Diane sat up with a jerk, spilling a good deal of expensive food in the process. She had never heard Carl talk like this before, and it emboldened her to answer back, in the same crude idiom. "If you're talking about mileage, you haven't done so badly out of me! What have you had from Kathy, I'd like to know? Precisely nothing! You want to work off a hangover, go and do it on her. I was doing all right until one of those cheap bastards—oh, for God's sake!" she finished suddenly. "Give it a rest, will you?"

"Leave Kathy out of this!" Carl said, menacingly.

"Why not?" she shrugged. "Everyone else does. Except maybe that sailor."

"What do you mean by that?"

"Write your own novel," said Diane, with a sneer. "What do you think they were doing all day in the woods?—twiddling their thumbs?"

"What the hell does a cheap tramp like you know about it?"

If he was thus harsh and crude with Diane—and there was more of it, much more, before he had finished—he was positively murderous with the Professor. He found him, as usual, lying down in his cabin, half stripped to his meagre skin against the Indian Ocean heat; even as he went into action he despised himself for hammering away at this poor old ruin of a man. But it did not stop him. Today, nothing was going to stop him.

"Get up!" he commanded immediately as he stepped into the cabin. "What the hell do you think you're doing, lying around half naked! If you've got nothing better to do, put on some of those early Victorian rags and take a walk around the deck. You might just sweat out some of the alcohol!"

"What—what's this?" said the Professor, struggling to sit up. This was the second time in as many days that Carl had stormed in and abused him; his nerves were already ragged, and his exhausted body shaking at the very first contact. "I've just woken up!" Sitting up, clutching his ridiculous flannel pyjamas across his chest, he said waveringly: "Carl, I meant to ask you. . . . I did exactly as you said,

I had nothing to drink yesterday. . . . But a man of my age needs the occasional stimulus—"

"The occasional skin-full, you mean," answered Carl derisively. He leant back against the door, a strong tough man scornful of all the old and the trembling. "I have news for you, Professor. Those days are over. Let me tell you, you're not going to have another ounce of Scotch till we get to New York. And damned little then, by God!"

"But Carl, I need it," wailed the Professor. And indeed, he did need it, at that very moment; the hand that brushed across his flaky lips was visibly shaking. "A man of my age. . . . It's not my fault if I went into the wrong cabin. It could happen to anyone! And I honestly thought that the watch was mine. I thought—"

"Watch?" asked Carl sharply. He glared down at the Professor. "What watch? What are you drivelling about?"

"The watch I picked up," said the Professor, suddenly in fear. "It was very like mine, and—"

"*You bloody old fool!*" Carl's voice, low-pitched, had an extreme menace in it. "What's this about a watch? Did you take a watch? Did they catch you *stealing?*"

"But I thought you knew." The Professor was almost hiding his face in his hands. "You said yesterday——the Captain told you—"

"The Captain told me you were found wandering about in the wrong cabin," said Carl. With a huge effort, he stopped himself walking forward to chop the old man into the ground. "He said nothing at all about a watch. *Did* you take a watch? Was it you who started this whole thing?"

"But I was taking it for you, Carl." Caught in abject guilt, he might have been a dog offering a retrieved stick. "Not for myself! They were saying I never earned any money. . . . So I. . . . But it was for you! I swear it! Oh God, Carl—" he whispered, as Carl came forward with his fist raised, "it *was* for you."

"I hit him," said Carl to Kathy, half an hour later. "I hit him hard. I had to. Christ, do you realize this is all his fault? He was caught trying to steal a watch! That must have been when it all started."

Kathy, drinking her morning coffee, shook her head. The picture was ugly enough, but it seemed faked also, based on lies or half-truths, invented for the purpose of making brutality seem to be justice. "I doubt that, Carl. There are lots of other things. And you won't cure any of them by hitting the Professor, will you? Is he all right?"

"I don't care if he's dead and buried," answered Carl, and at that moment of continued fury it was the plain truth. Sulky and vicious, he looked down at her as she sat in her armchair, cool and elegant in slacks and a pink-checked shirt. She was always beautiful in the mornings. Beautiful and suspect. "So what have you been doing, Kathy?"

She looked up, surprised at the extraordinary borrowed falsity of his tone. "My dear Carl, what do you mean, *so* what have I been doing? You sound like Louis practising the dialogue for *Guys and Dolls!*"

He stared back at her in cold fury, and said: "That doesn't really answer my question, does it?"

She had been in the mood for gentleness, for friendship; but something about his tone—unpleasant, basically hateful—provoked her to the same response, the same careless cruelty.

"You would really like to know?" She dropped another lump of sugar into her coffee cup, and stirred it deliberately. "I have to decide between two proposals, Carl. You must really help me to make up my mind. . . . One is for marriage—or it could be, very easily. The other is to go to bed with someone. Just once. For five thousand dollars. Or ten. Or any number . . ." Now she was looking at him, and for the first time for many years she felt that whatever he said, in whatever tone of voice, he could not affect her decision, by the breadth of one hair; her next words were thus merely formal. "If you were in my place," she said, levelly, even sarcastically, "would you lie down for love, or for ten thousand dollars? Or would you not lie down at all, for any man on earth?"

"I can't," she said to Tillotson, later that day. It was twilight, twilight off the coast of Africa; the *Alcestis* was ploughing steadily through the fantastic phosphorescence of an Indian Ocean night, with the Southern Cross beginning to beckon them over the last horizon in the world; it was an excellent moment for decisions, however crazy, however harmful. "I thought I could—I wasn't just fooling—but now I can't."

"What is *now?*" asked Tillotson, picking out the weasel word. As always, he was calm and competent; all he had done was to walk near her as she sat in a chair by the deserted pool, smile, and say: "Referring to our recent communication. . . ." At some other time, in some other life, she had thought, he would have been quite a man. . . . But these present times were out of joint, by many a crooked mile; and Tillotson seemed, most subtly, to realize this when he said: "What's happened in the last forty-eight hours, to change it? Did I leave it too long? Surely we were agreed."

"Oh yes."

"Then?"

"A man," said Kathy.

"Ah, that's different." As usual, he was smoking a cigar, and the ash flicked over the side of the ship in a broad curving arc. "That's a development I can understand. I thought maybe it was something I could deal with."

She smiled; this was the most civilized person she had talked with today. "What can you deal with?"

"Most things involving organization. Things that come up. . . ." He looked sideways at her. "Something could have scared you, for instance. I've heard a few rumours flying around. . . . You can be quite sure that you and I wouldn't be getting our names on any Captain's list of undesirables."

She could not guess how much he knew; it seemed best to assume that naturally he knew everything. "It's not that," she answered, shaking her head. "I've nothing to be afraid of, so far as I know."

"Except that you belong to this rather unusual family."

"Are we unusual?"

She could hear a smile in his voice as he answered: "I think it's a very fair word to use." And then, more soberly:"Ah well, these are speculations—you said it was a man, anyway. That must mean a young man."

"Yes."

"I am jealous." But he said it, once more, very calmly; he might have been saying: *I am Tillotson.* He was in a curious mood, a mood which coupled exploration with acceptance; perhaps that was part of his strength, that he could gauge quickly and, if need be, abdicate gracefully. "When did this happen?"

"It didn't really *happen.*" She did not want to talk about it at all, but she felt that she owed him more than a few sentences of banal rejection. "It's more of an idea, really."

After a long silence, he said: "The idea being that you should reform."

Astonished, both at him and at herself, she answered: "Yes. That's it exactly."

"Now we know." He leant across and laid his hand on her arm; its only message was one of encouragement. "I am in the best position to tell you," he said ruefully, "that such a reformation is perfectly possible. . . . Did my wife make you feel ashamed?"

"A little."

"She is a very clever woman."

"Darling, I can't," she told Tim Mansell, about midnight that same night. They were in his cabin, a slim box of a room with a single berth, a curtained wash-basin, and a desk covered with papers; it looked out, bleakly, onto the derricks and hatchcovers of the foredeck.

"But I only wanted to kiss you," said Tim. It was almost true; though he continued to hold her slim body encircled, his own was not yet urgent. "This is the only chance we've had. Why don't you want to?"

"It's no good in the ship. It doesn't feel right. It feels kind of mean, and sneaky."

"It feels wonderful to me."

But she was not at all in that sort of mood; she was ready to be irritated. On board, in his fresh-pressed white uniform, he was so damned young again. . . . "I must go," she said briefly, turning away.

"What's the matter, Kathy?"

"Nothing."

"But it was so wonderful last time. Wasn't it?"

"Of course it was." She felt she had to destroy this; she did not want it, after all—not yet, anyway, or not on these terms. It was as bad as the idea of Tillotson, the idea of Carl. "That was what we made the trip for, wasn't it?"

"Kathy!"

She had not wanted to shock him, and the sight of his face hurt her. But something was making her continue, a compulsion to put him back in his place.

"Oh Tim, don't be such a baby! That's what people do on picnics. Didn't you know that? They eat, and then they make love. Don't tell me you didn't have that in your mind, from the very beginning!"

"But it was different," he answered helplessly. "Of course I hoped that we might. . . . But you didn't have to—I wasn't going to make you—"

"It's not a question of making anyone do anything. I was in the mood, that's all. And so were you." Kathy did not know why she was doing this to him, except that too many things had been closing in on her today; she wanted to clear a space around her, she wanted to push Tim away, just as she had pushed Tillotson, and breathe some free air. "Of course we made love. What do you think we were there for?"

"Kathy, why are you spoiling it all?"

"Spoiling it all. . . ." It annoyed her more than ever that he had found the precise word. She *was* spoiling it; making herself forget or disparage his tenderness, his ardour, his flat stomach; the sunlight through the leaves dappling their naked bodies; the world that moved. "I think you've got the wrong idea, young man," she went on, in a voice which disgusted her even as she used it. "That wasn't deathless love, you know, it was a good run-of-the-mill open-air lay." The phrase was Diane's, and she searched for another one in the same explicit terms, without success. She should have listened to Diane with more attention . . . "What had you got in mind, anyway?—" she tried another tack, "—that we should settle down in some slum in Liverpool until you passed some kid's examination for—"

Tim suddenly reached over and gave her a very precise, very firm, not too harsh slap on the side of her face. The slight sting was just enough to astonish her, to stop her in mid-sentence. She blinked, and when she could listen again, it was Tim who was doing the talking.

"That's the first of many," he told her cheerfully, "if you talk to me like that." Swiftly he had grown up again, to a person, to a man; it was the yearning of love which had diminished him, and now he was not going to be diminished any longer. "Now just you listen to me, and stop being so hopelessly disorganized. . . . Of course I want to make love to you—" he pointed, "—in that very bunk, which is just big enough for what I have in mind. We loved it last time, and we'll love it again. I'm not ashamed of that. Nor are you." He took her by the shoulders; he was as strong, at least, as Carl. . . . "I don't know why you're talking like this, Kathy, and I don't want to know—I've forgotten it already. You can't scare me. . . . But just you remember a couple of things. *One*—" he shook her, "I don't mind what you've done in the past. It hasn't changed you or spoiled you—we found that out by the dam. You have a future, and I am in it. *Two* —" another shake, "—I am not going to stop being a sailor, just because you don't like it. *You're* going to make the change. It's not so terrible, anyway. And *three*—" but here his voice altered subtly, not towards weakness but towards cherishing, "—will you please be careful? You and the others, I mean. I don't want to lose you at Durban. I want to talk to you, and kiss you, and maybe go to bed with you, all the way back to New York. But if you want to save going to bed with me until we're married, that's perfectly all right with me."

She looked up at him. Out of all the surprises, she chose the biggest one of all.

"You knew, then."

"Yes."

"Who else knows?"

"We all do, pretty well." He smiled, and then he kissed her without any possibility of a denial. "I told you that the past doesn't matter. . . . And now," he ended, "the time being twelve-thirty, I'm taking you half-way back to your cabin, and I hope you sleep as well as I do. I'd like to be doing it with you, Kathy, but confidentially, that bunk is hell."

chapter 8

THOUGH it was mid-morning, and the upper decks of the *Alcestis* were crowded with people taking long-distance photographs of the hundred-mile range of blue mountains far away on the port beam, Carl was still in bed, staring fixedly at the ceiling, when Kathy came to see him. She stood at the doorway, surprised, and then, moving forward, said: "I'm sorry, Carl. I thought you would be up."

He was smoking. He watched a spiral of smoke drift upwards towards the fans before he answered:

"You don't have to apologize for coming into my room. At least, you used not to apologize, two months ago."

Warned by his tone, which indicated a difficult mood, she said lightly: "Well, it *is* your room. . . . We're just coming up to Port Elizabeth. It really is lovely. You ought to get up and take a look at it."

After the same sort of loaded pause, he asked: "What's Port Elizabeth, for God's sake?"

"Just a place, I suppose." She had taken a cigarette from the box on the side-table, and was lighting it. When she had finished she said: "It's half-way to Durban."

He raised himself on his elbow, and looked across at her. He was frowning. She had been wrong about his mood, she decided instantly; it was not a difficult mood, it was a hideous one. But she was still not prepared for the extreme sarcasm with which he said:

"Thank you for coming to tell me that we are now half-way to Durban."

For some reason, Kathy felt brave this morning. Perhaps it was a chance feeling, perhaps it was the first of many brave mornings. But whatever its origin, she felt that it was good enough to take care of Carl, or of anyone else who wanted to impress his personality on the wretched female race. She looked back at him with equal directness, and answered: "I came to tell you some other things, too. . . . The Tillotson deal is off. I didn't go through with it."

He raised his eyebrows. "Why not?"

"There's no special reason. . . . I didn't want to, I suppose. Anyway, I've told him it's no good."

After a moment, Carl said: "You are lucky to be able to pick and choose."

But she was not going to take that; not on this morning, perhaps not on any morning. "Carl, do tell the truth," she said, rather sharply. "Did you actually want me to sleep with him? For five thousand dollars, or whatever he would have paid?"

"I would always want you to make five thousand dollars," said Carl, without expression.

"Carl!"

"Yes?"

"Don't talk like that! Answer what I asked!"

His eyes were positively murderous as he said: "You will not give me orders! That *was* my answer."

It was a mood she could not deal with; all she could do was to remained unaffected by it. She shrugged her shoulders. "All right. . . . If you don't want to be honest. . . . Tim Mansell says that all the officers know about us."

Carl, in a brief change of humour, laughed sardonically. He had imagined that the Captain would probably put out some sort of general alarm; but it amused him that the news should come from this innocent source.

"That should take care of your other problem."

Warily she asked: "What does that mean?"

"You are suddenly very obtuse," he snapped. His manner changed again, becoming charged with the spite she had been aware of earlier. "I would presume that your young sailor friend thought of you as a combination of Venus, Madame Curie, and one of the more dependable Vestal virgins. If he 'knows about you,' as you put it, what does that do to this ideal dream of love?" Carl expelled some smoke towards the ceiling. "I can visualize a slight but perceptible cloud coming between him and the sacred vision."

Kathy said, almost without thinking: "Perhaps there's less to know about me than about the others."

"You have obviously taken good care of that."

She came back to hard reality. "Oh Carl, you're impossible when you're in this mood!"

"Jesus God!" he burst out suddenly. "What sort of a mood do you expect?" He turned again and looked at her, with venomous concentration. "All right—you *haven't* slept with Tillotson, and you *haven't* slept—today—with that stupid child in the white uniform! What do you expect me to do? Burst into tears? Call for champagne? Here we have one of the smoothest operations of its kind ever planned—it was working like a dream—and then suddenly it falls to bits, and instead of cleaning up we'll be lucky if we break even—in fact we'll be lucky if we keep out of jail. . . . What do you expect me to do?" he repeated. In the warm air, his tense body was sweating. "You come here and tell me, we're half-way to Durban! Do you think I don't know it?"

Even as he spoke, she knew that she must help him. There had been many changes during the past two months; some people had grown, others had diminished, others yet had changed their area of vision, so that they could hardly remember the past and had a new hope of the future. She herself could claim to be in this category, and, try as she would, she could not be ashamed of it. But when she was with Carl, the strands of the past were bound to pull her back. She was with him now. It was when he said the word 'Durban,' on that note of foreboding, as if it were in truth the end of the road for him, that she felt most guilty and most responsible.

On an impulse, she crossed the cabin, and sat down on the side of his bed. There, putting her hand lightly on his arm, she said:

"Carl, why *don't* we leave the ship, anyway? Why don't we get off at Durban?"

He answered her instantly. "That is without exception the most stupid remark I have heard in the last twenty-four hours. And I've heard plenty. . . . You might as well ask why we don't all become priests and nuns." But it became clear that he must, at least, have considered the point she had raised, when he added, "For one simple reason—that wasn't the way we planned it, when we started out."

"I know that, Carl." She pressed his arm. "But what does that matter? We've had a wonderful trip, we've made a little money. Why don't you write it off as a free holiday?"

"Because I'm a professional."

Kathy smiled. It was a remark she had heard on countless occasions to justify anything from poker-marathons to the necessity of flirting with old ladies on the Italian Riviera. "You used to say that at San Sebastian," she recalled, "when I tried to persuade you that the Chief of Police wasn't fooling about that tourist visa. . . . I still don't believe it."

But he was not to be charmed, either by memory or by manner. "I didn't think you would believe it, in your present mood. The fact remains that we are committed to a certain programme, and I have invested a great deal of money in it. I am not going to change all my plans, and take a loss on the deal, just because a few uniformed nonentities get in my way. That isn't how I operate. You know that by now."

"But even you and I can't operate for ever."

Though she had made the remark naturally, it came from a deep inner compulsion; it did not surprise her when Carl seized upon it as if she had suddenly produced, between them, some naked emblem of the truth.

"Now that," he said, slowly, rather theatrically, "is a very interesting observation. Explain it."

"I only meant that sooner or later—"

"*Explain it!*"

"All right." It was a fine and sunny morning; why should she be afraid? "I've had six years of this kind of life, Carl, and you've had—well, lots more. But how long is it going on for? How will I finish up? How will you? We've had some wonderful times together—" her pressure on his arm was strong and sincere, "—but they *must* come to an end, some day. This could be the end."

He went straight to the heart of her dilemma when he asked: "What do you want to do instead?"

"I don't know at all. But I know what I *don't* want to do—and that's to finish up as a sort of gangster's moll, like in the late-night movies, getting older and older and crabbier and crabbier. I want a different sort of life, a different sort of future. In fact, I *must* have it."

He turned away, and stared at the ceiling, and said, with complete finality: "You will be nothing without me."

A few months earlier, she would have agreed; now she could argue the point, with passionate conviction.

"Carl, I am nothing *with* you! Don't you see that?"

"But you have been."

"Less and less. Every year less, every *day* less. You made me into something, and then—and then—" she felt ready for the tears of frustration, but she thrust them back, "—somehow I was out of date, or *you* were out of date, and it didn't make sense any more. . . . Carl, *please* let's leave the ship at Durban, and do something else!"

There was a silence; the *Alcestis* rocked slightly, disturbing the benevolent sunbeams; a harmonious gong sounded from down the corridor—the first call for lunch. Carl waited until the tinkling echoes had faded, and then he said:

"This is the only thing I can do."

"That can't be true."

"I've made it true!" His voice was strong, even proud; he was not excusing anything, he had nothing to mourn. "Good God, do you think all this happened by *accident*? I like being a crook! It's the only thing to be!" He suddenly snatched his arm away, and brought it down with a sharp smack on the coverlets. "I'm going to tell you something, Kathy, and after that we won't have any more discussion about the moral aspects of being a criminal in a criminal world. In fact, we won't have any more discussion about *anything*. . . . When I was your age—and that's a long time ago, as we both know—my younger brother was shot in New York. You didn't even know that I had a younger brother, did you? I do not blame you—he does not figure in my normal conversation—he has been a paralyzed idiot, lying flat on his back in hospital, for more than thirty years. . . . You know who shot him? A cop—an honest cop, one of New York's finest. You know why? My brother was *lent* a car by a friend, and it was a stolen car, and he didn't stop quickly enough when a zealous policeman held up his hand at a road-block. A warning shot, the zealous man said—he doubtless got a reprimand for it—only the warning shot missed the wind-shield or the tire or whatever it was meant to warn, and just *scraped* a little nerve at the back of my brother's head." Horrified, Kathy watched as Carl's hand moved up to touch the back of his own head, fingering a spot which he must have fingered a thousand times in the past, which she herself must often have caressed.

"He was sixteen-and-a-half," said Carl, "and he never spoke again, he never moved again, except by the law of gravity. He just became an expensive lump of meat—in the interests of reducing the number of cars driven away without the owner's consent in the city of New York in 1930. . . . I used to go and see him in hospital—with the priest, with the policeman, by myself—and then pretty soon I didn't go any more. What can you say to a lump of meat that has to have a nurse to shut its mouth when the mouth falls open? Do you say you're sorry, like the policeman? Do you cry, like the priest? . . . I used to cry, when I saw my brother—he once played the Spirit of Self-Indulgence, in our school play at Christmas—but by God I didn't cry for long! I went home, and I swore a very simple oath. I swore that if they could make an idiot out of my brother, I would make an idiot out of them."

He lay back, staring hard into the loathed past; she could not have interrupted him, even if she had had the words to do it with.

"I have made a very large-scale success out of that oath," said Carl. Where before there had been hatred in his voice, now there crept back a sullen and unmistakable threat. "I will continue to do so until I die, and so will anyone connected with me. We have had some set-backs on the present trip, but there aren't going to be any more. . . . " There was now an absolutely hypnotic quality in his voice; she had no choice in the world except to listen to it. "Louis has left us," he went on, silkily. "Diane is out of action. The Professor has proved useless. But that is as far as this particular roll of honour goes. There aren't going to be any more deserters, there aren't going to be any more flops or failures." He turned towards her, and grasped her hand with terrifying intensity. "I hope I have succeeded in convincing you, Kathy, because that is positively my last word on the subject. . . . I am staying, and you are staying. . . . Now, if you will please press the bell," he broke off, obscenely polite, "I think we have earned our lunch-time Martinis, don't you?"

chapter 9

DIANE was bored, for the best of all reasons. She sat on a bar stool in the Tapestry Room, late after dinner, and, between occasional small-talk with Edgar the head barman, mused on the dullness of life. The ship was passing East London, so Edgar had informed her; for all the gaiety involved, it might have been East Lynne. There were other obvious drawbacks to this part of the world. The Indian Ocean climate was intolerable, even at sea; wafts of steamy air circled and re-circled through the ventilation-system; at meal times, the butter melted at the table, and ran to yellow ooze; people lay about in attitudes of sweating boredom, too lazy even to look at the sharks which followed the ship in large-scale, faithful attendance. There was nothing to do, especially for Diane. . . . All that was open to her was to sit at bars, and, while waiting for her clearance-papers, to day-dream on the traditional preoccupations of a small but dirty mind.

No sex, no fun, she thought, sipping her brandy and staring at her reflection in the mirror behind Edgar. When she'd started out on this trip, she had thought it would be just another chore; but it had turned out to be a lot better than that. . . . Must be the boat rocking, or something. . . . But now she'd been off it for a whole fortnight; even do-it-yourself didn't work any more. . . What was that story the guy told her in New York? 'What happened to Eartha Kitt?' 'I guess it's all these do-it-yourself Kitts.' What a character. . . . When she was a kid, it had driven her nearly mad. Sometimes, in school, she had to hold up her hand, and go out and do it in the toilet, she couldn't even wait for recess. . . . But later on, it had been much more fun. Like this trip. Even the old old guys had come across. Must be the boat, again. Take old man Walham, for instance. He was so mad to get his money's worth, he really took some trouble. . . . And Tiptree-Jones—like the girl said, he's a pill, but a big pill. And young Barry Greenfield, he started out real wild, two seconds' fireworks and goodbye, a real flash-in-the-pants—but in the end he improved, too. He had to. . . . And Zucco—like all the Jews, it was practically religious, you could almost feel him praying—though what the hell he was praying for—maybe the second coming—

"Would you like another one, Miss Loring?" asked Edgar.

Now *there* was a question, she thought, as Edgar tipped the bottle of Courvoisier and added another half-inch of brandy to her glass. . . . Of course she'd like another one, she'd like another one right now. And she could be having it, if the doctor hadn't been such a square. 'Please continue to refrain from sexual intercourse,' he had said, as though it didn't matter if it was for ever. He was good-looking too, he must be a fairy. . . . She felt perfectly all right, perfectly normal. Maybe the time had come. . . . Carl had been so tough lately, so damned rude, he ought to be pleased if she came across with a few hundred bucks. Why not? she thought, looking along the length of the bar. She felt perfectly all right, it didn't even tickle . . . Carl was always bitching about her not doing enough work—and ha! ha! to that, with Kathy doing sweet nothing at all—it would be fun to come up with a surprise, to show him that he'd got at least one good trier on the team.

The prospects at the bar were not encouraging, but that didn't matter. In the past, some of the funny ones had turned out to be the best bets. . . . After a few moments, she called out to the only man within reasonable range:

"Mr. Kincaid, I know it's not like a lady, but can I buy you a drink?"

When they were gone, Edgar took a bar-chit, and wrote on it: '*No. 4 and Mr. Kincaid. Edgar.*' Then he snapped his fingers, to one of his junior aides who was collecting ashtrays in the near-empty bar, and called: "Fred!"

"Yes, Mr. Edgar."

"Take this up to the Captain, right away." He passed the piece of paper across, and then looked at Fred with the coldest possible glance. In the Tapestry Bar, there was never any doubt about who was boss. "You'll very likely read it on the way," said Edgar, sternly. "But if you *talk* about it, God help you! I'll see that you're back to kitchen-boy tomorrow!"

"Yes, sir!" said Fred earnestly, and hurried on his way.

"Mr. Kincaid," said the Captain, after listening in silence for two minutes, "I've been expecting you. Please sit down."

"How come?" asked Kincaid suspiciously. "You know this thing has been going on? If that's so, all I can say is—"

"We have suspected it," said Captain Harmer, "and we have therefore been watching it. The Loring girl was one of the people we thought were involved. It was reported to me that she took you to her cabin. The rest was easy."

"Now hold on a minute," said Kincaid. "I'm not sure I like the sound of that 'She took you to her cabin' stuff." He touched his crest of white hair almost primly; if there could have been a cross between an Old Testament prophet and the woman taken in adultery, this was it. "She says to me, let's finish our drinks down there in comfort, and I say, O.K., and then suddenly she threatens to scream rape and murder unless I give her five hundred dollars. But that's not the same thing as—"

"Mr. Kincaid."

"Yes, Captain?"

"You are not giving evidence on oath. You are telling me something, in confidence, which might possibly lead to formal charges against a third party. You will have ample time to consider the final form of your evidence."

After a moment Kincaid grinned, and said: "I get it, Captain."

"You went to her cabin?"

"Just that. One thing led to another, and I thought it was all fixed. Gee whiz, I mean—we're not children, for God's sake—everyone says she's on the menu—"

"Quite so," said the Captain.

"Then suddenly she ups and says, that'll be five hundred bucks."

"Was that before, or after?"

Kincaid, astute as a fox, trained and battered in a thousand political brawls, looked at the Captain for a long time before he said: "It was after."

Harmer nodded. "What next?"

Kincaid expelled his breath, as if a difficult corner had been passed. "Well, I said to her, what the hell, I don't mind twenty or even fifty dollars, I know the score, a working girl has to work, but five hundred, what happened, did we do it in caviar or something?—and then she says, it's five hundred or I'll call my uncle. Then I got the message." He nodded, as if congratulating himself; perhaps he was. "Yes, sir! But it wasn't the message she thought. Suddenly it all connects—Jesus, the Professor!"

"The Professor?" inquired the Captain.

"That's it—the old guy with the Old English line. Long time ago, when he was really corned, he said some damn fool thing to me about internal corruption, like there's a gang here on board taking us for everything we've got. I've been thinking of that for a long time—I used to belong to an organization that paid me a lot of money never to forget things—and suddenly I came up with the answer. This is it! This is the gang at work! The old Professor wasn't fooling after all. They're working the bruised-thigh routine! So I said: 'Go ahead and scream.' "

The Captain waited, happy and alert at the same time. He would never have thought that such a deplorable recital could sound like music to him, but it was so. "The bruised-thigh routine?" he prompted.

"We used to have names for all these plays. Remind me to tell you about the Mann Act squeeze, some time. . . . Now don't get me wrong. I'm not a hero, there's my wife on board, I have my own problems. But I knew for sure this girl wouldn't be doing any screaming. I've met plenty of this before—" he gestured, "What the hell, I've been in politics a long time—and they never, but *never*, scream. Well, almost never. In the end they say: 'You must know the mayor, or something', and then they fold. This girl folded. . . . Oh, I gave her twenty," he went on, as if reassuringly. "Don't think I robbed the girl. And then—I got to thinking about the Professor—and I've heard a few rumours, you can bet there are rumours flying around, it's like a really good convention—and so I came to you."

The Captain sat back, deeply satisfied. Whatever the theme, this *was* music.

"You did right, Mr. Kincaid," he said cordially. "You did right, and I respect you for it." He coughed. "Of course, this whole situation is entirely disreputable, and I do not for a moment condone—"

Mr. Kincaid was watching him closely. For the very first time in his adult life, the Captain felt his voice tail away under the impact of someone else's gaze. In the silence, they stared at each other for at least fifteen seconds before they both smiled broadly, and then the smile became laughter, and the Captain rose. "What will you drink, Mr. Kincaid?"

"Scotch and water, Captain."

"I think I will join you."

Toasting his host, a minute later, Kincaid said, out of the blue: "I can see now why you're captain, Captain."

"Well, thank you!" answered Harmer, surprised. "Your good health!"

"The same. . . . You said you've had your eye on this outfit?"

"That is so."

"Maybe this is the evidence you want?"

"It's a most valuable link," agreed Harmer. "I think we can take it that the girl and her family will be leaving the ship at Durban. In the circumstances, I'm sure you would not wish to press charges."

"Well now," said Kincaid, enjoying the moment, "of course I've been held up to ridicule and private embarrassment—"

"But in the interests of discretion—"

"I won't be pressing charges," said Kincaid.

"I think you are wise," said the Captain. "In return, I feel qualified to offer you some advice." He paused. "Some medical advice, in fact. I recommend a precautionary visit to the doctor."

It was delightful, within this entirely squalid framework, to watch Kincaid's face fall, from cheerfulness to a kind of mournful disillusion, and then to professional gloom.

"Now, Captain, that's a different matter," he said aggrievedly. "To begin with, it's a misdemeanour, where I come from. Legally, that girl could be—"

"It is probable that I am wrong," said the Captain, ignoring all this nonsense. "But the sooner you take certain elementary precautions, the better. You will find that the doctor is waiting for you."

"Gee, Captain!" said Kincaid after a moment, admiringly. "You've certainly got things under control in this ship."

"Thank you, Mr. Kincaid. I believe that I have."

"I won't ask you to sit down," said the Captain, "because you won't be here long enough." He looked up at Carl with almost cheerful unconcern. For once, he did not mind being a small man. This was a good night for small men. "Mr. Wenstrom, I told you yesterday that we would only have one more of these meetings. This is it."

"I don't understand you," said Carl, completely taken aback. "What's happened? What are you talking about?"

"You and your party are to leave the ship at Durban."

Carl, who had heard nothing until summoned from his poker game a few moments earlier, felt a sudden appalled sense of disaster. Something crucial had happened; he would hear what it was in a moment; but he did not need any details to recognize the executioner's note in the Captain's voice. This was it. . . . But, astonishment or not, he was in the mood to fight back; soon, anger would come to aid him, as had happened almost continuously since their last meeting; there was no merit in polite submission, when neither politeness nor submission could improve their chances during the next twenty-four hours. . . . Staring back, he said, as coldly as he could:

"You certainly owe me an explanation for that last remark."

"I will *give* you an explanation," said the Captain, equally coldly. "I don't owe you anything. . . . You will find, if you don't know it already, that your niece, Miss Loring, is confined to her cabin, until we reach Durban. There is a watchman posted at her door. She is not to come out, and no-one is to go in except the two designated stewards who will bring her meals."

"But this is an outrage!" said Carl, and he meant it. "It's tantamount to imprisonment without trial. What can she possibly have done—"

The Captain, who was now in great form, interrupted him. "Allow me to tell you. . . . I have the clearest possible evidence that your niece has been guilty of attempted extortion. In simpler terms, Mr. Wenstrom, she tried to blackmail a man who had made love to her, and he called her bluff. I told you— I *promised* you—that if there was one more incident like this, you would all leave my ship. This is the one more incident. Therefore you will all leave. The complainant has agreed not to press charges—"

"Who is the complainant?"

"That is no direct concern of yours. But in fact, it is Mr. Kincaid."

"For God's sake!" said Carl. "That cheap political hack!"

"I know very little of Mr. Kincaid's background," replied the Captain, "but I accept his word in this matter. He has offered this evidence at some personal embarrassment." He could not resist elaborating. "I think you must agree that he has played a decisive role in your defeat."

Carl, furious, seized on the word. "Defeat? What defeat? If you think we're going to walk quietly off the ship, you'd better guess again! We've paid our passage-money back to New York—your company signed a definite contract—"

"Mr. Wenstrom," said the Captain, "we have a department that takes care of contracts. Suitable arrangements will be made to fly you home from Durban, probably at the company's expense. There will no doubt be a refund of the unfulfilled portion of your ticket, from Durban to New York. But that again is a matter for the accountants." Harmer knew that he must be sounding high-handed, even crudely arrogant; it gave him a great deal of pleasure to achieve this impression. "And now, if you have no further questions—"

Carl finally lost his temper. "What in hell do you mean, no further questions?" he asked furiously. "You seem to think you're dealing with a lot of stupid sailors who are paid to jump when you crack the whip. You'll find out that you're making the biggest mistake of your life! If you even *attempt* to put us off the ship at Durban, you'll be faced with the toughest law-suit you ever heard of. Not only will it cost you your job, but your company will have to pay damages for breach of contract, for the inconvenience caused to me and my family, for slanderous attacks on our reputation—"

"Plus entertainment tax," said Captain Harmer, with rare schoolboy spite. Then he grew serious again; with luck, it would be for the last time. "Mr. Wenstrom," he said, "I didn't intend this to be a long interview. It is only you who is making it so." Now he was very much the master of his ship, and Carl knew it, and could do nothing about it. "You still seem to have some sort of delusion about the extent of my authority. Whatever law-book you consult, you will find that my authority is absolute. At sea, I can do anything—anything in the interests of the safety of my ship, anything to preserve decency and good order. If I do wrong, legally, I answer for it, like any other ordinary citizen. But in the meantime, I can take whatever steps I choose. The steps I choose now are to put you and the three other members of your party ashore at Durban, and to forbid you to board the ship again before she sails."

"Damned stupid rigmarole!" Carl snapped. He was nearly beside himself with anger; he had discovered something he could not even fight, much less conquer. "We'll just see how it stands up in a court of law."

"It has stood up for many hundreds of years," answered Harmer. "You can try to knock it down, if you wish. Of course, you will have all the petty thieves and shysters in the world on your side. There is an American consul at Durban who will be glad to listen to you. At least, he will listen to you. He is paid to. . . . " The Captain rose to his feet at last. It had gone on long enough; he had indeed indulged himself by playing out the scene to this agreeable length. "You've tried to make a pig-sty out of a fine ship," he said grimly. "It takes time to catch up with that sort of thing, but believe me, we *do* catch up with it. . . . He glanced down at his watch. "It's twenty hours' steaming time to Durban," he continued, "and therefore I have only twenty more hours of your company. That, Mr. Wenstrom, is one of the happiest thoughts of the whole cruise."

chapter 10

IT was midnight. Diane he could not reach. Kathy he could not find. There remained only the Professor. But the Professor, perhaps, was his real target.

Carl had expected to find the old man asleep; it would have been a pleasure to shake him awake, to shake him until his stupid skull rattled. . . . But he was awake already; indeed, he seemed to be working, sitting crouched over his desk by a shaded light, going through some papers. But he was not working for Carl, it seemed. He was working for himself. He was reading his manuscript of the history of piracy.

Carl, who had entered softly, in frightening contrast to his mood, stood by the door watching him. *God-damned syphilitic old idiot,* he thought. . . . As the Professor worked, or read, or whatever it was he was doing, he fingered gently the great bruised weal on the side of his face which was the legacy of Carl's last visit. Carl, on that occasion, had not meant to hit him so hard; now, fresh from a defeat to which he knew the Professor must have contributed, he wished he had taken his whole head off. . . . The Professor snuffled as he read, and touched his discoloured cheek, and presently refreshed himself from a glass, discreetly drawn from behind a pile of library paper-backs on the desk. He sniffed, and sipped, and suddenly exclaimed: "Brilliant!", and pushed the glass, of amber-coloured liquid, back into its hiding-place. *Disgusting old soak,* thought Carl; *he's back on the bottle again.* . . . Carl came forward a step or two, until he was inside the cabin and the circle of light, and said, on a false note of friendship:

"Good evening, Professor. Getting ahead with the good work?"

The old man jumped, and then stood up, trembling and shaking as if he were at the height of a fever. *Jesus,* thought Carl, *he's far gone.* . . . Carl came further forward, and very deliberately, very cruelly, reached behind the pile of books and drew out the glass of whisky. He raised it, and sniffed. Then he said: "You actually *like* tomato-juice?"

The Professor trembled again; his hand went up to the hideous bruise on his cheek, as if it were the only thing he was sure about. He looked at Carl fearfully, at a loss for words. There had been so many punishment-sessions recently; at this late and horrible stage, Carl coming into his cabin could only mean Carl angry, Carl violent and shouting, Carl swinging his fist at him as if he were cutting wood, pounding meat, killing lice. . . . He said, in terror and anguish:

"Forgive me, Carl. . . . It's the first today—the first for two days. . . . I swear it. . . . But when you get to my age. . . . A little whisky, I happened to find it in my flask, I must have forgotten it was there. . . . " He laughed, on a frightful note of nervous despair; he might have been some old, old comedian, coaxing the last laugh from leaden bellies, from stony Northern faces, before he retired to teach comedy-routines to the young. . . . "I hope you'll understand a slight lapse. . . . "

"Oh, I understand you all right, Professor." There was still no hint in Carl's voice of the volcano of fury within; only the genial manner, as false as porcelain teeth, would have given warning to a younger man, a man more alive to danger. "I understand you better than anyone in the world, I would say. . . . What exactly are you working on now?"

The Professor, doubtful, glanced down at his manuscript. "You really want to know, Carl?"

"Certainly I want to know."

"Well—" the Professor drew courage, foolishly, from the calm perfidious air, "—I wasn't so much working, as reading through something I wrote last week. . . . I try to add a little each day, as you know. . . . But perhaps you don't know, Carl—" again the laugh, the invitation to murder, "—that on the next section of our voyage we will come to a part of Africa which used to be called the Slave Coast, the Bight of Benin. West Africa, that is—they call it something different now, and I hope to heaven they are more fortunate than in the past—but in those days, in those days. . . ." He had sat down again at his desk; his hand reached shakily for the whisky glass, and then, remembering, he withdrew it, and touched his raw cheek again. "The Slave Coast," he muttered. "Infamous. . . . Brutal. . . . It was a kind of piracy, Carl," he said looking up, a scholar ready to justify his area of research, "otherwise it would have no place in my book. There was one terrible story—one of many terrible stories—which I believe is new. It will reach the world for the first time in this volume." With thin-veined hands he stroked his manuscript, dog-eared, tattered, as if it were some ancient altar cloth, an offering for the Lord. "At the time of the suppression of the slave trade in 1807, on the very coast towards which we will soon be sailing, it became imperative for one of the slave ships to conceal the fact that she was carrying slaves. She was about to be searched on the high seas—there was a British man-of-war within a few miles, coming up to board her—" his old eyes glittered, one could not tell which side he was on, "—and the captain of the slave ship, a most wicked man, had two hundred of these poor wretches, in iron fetters, battened down below. You know what he did, Carl?—you know what he did?" The Professor's voice rose to a scholarly extreme of indignation. "He brought them all out on deck, and he shackled them onto the anchor-chain, one man to every five links, and then he lowered the chain down into the water—slowly, slowly—and then he let it go. Two hundred wretched human beings, Carl! Two hundred black souls, dropped fathoms deep into—"

"Professor," said Carl.

There was so much idle menace in his voice, such loaded disinterest, that even the Professor, enthralled with his terrible story, was brought up short. He turned in his chair, shakily, reluctantly, and cupped his livid cheek as if it would help him to hear. "Yes, Carl?"

"Do you remember my giving you a message for Diane?"

"A message, Carl? Now let me see. . . ." The Professor, in an absurd caricature of efficiency, actually looked at his desk calendar, completely bare of any writing, before he said: "I don't seem to recall the exact particulars, Carl. . . . Was it about the costume ball?"

"No, it wasn't about the costume ball. That was more than a month ago." Try as he would, under the extreme pressure of his anger, Carl could not prevent some of the tension creeping into his voice. "This was the night before last. I asked you to tell her something. Remember?"

The Professor was aware of danger now. The hand touching his ruined cheek became protective, actively frightened. "Not exactly, Carl. . . . I have so very many things on my mind, these days. . . . If you could just say—"

"So you didn't give her the message?"

"Well, Carl—it's quite possible—"

"I told you," said Carl, with crystal-clear enunciation, "to tell Diane to do nothing—*nothing*—unless she cleared it with me first. I told you to tell her the heat was on, and she was to drop everything and keep absolutely quiet. I gave you that message, right here in this room." He came forward a step or two, as if the air round him had suddenly grown too hot. "Did you, in fact, tell her?"

"Well, God bless my soul!" exclaimed the Professor. The wavering laugh bespoke the edge of terror. "It must have slipped my mind completely. But I'll tell you what, Carl. Would you like me to go along now—"

"*You imbecile!*" The burst of fury, when it came, was like a thunder-clap. "You stupid, rotten, drunken son of a whore!" His hands came up, and the Professor, shielding the bruised side of his face, was knocked nearly senseless by a back-handed blow on his other cheek. "Do you know what you've done?" asked Carl. He was nearly screaming. "You've ruined this whole deal! You *didn't* give my message to Daine, and she *didn't* lay off, and now she's been locked up, and we've all got to leave the ship at Durban! And when I come down here, you're sucking down the Scotch and writing a book!"

He raised his hand again, and the Professor, half-conscious, cowered away. But it was no good, simple violence was not enough. Carl's eyes turned to the manuscript, the ridiculous bundle of old pages lying on the desk. He seized it; it was bound in stiff card-board covers, and these he stripped away with swift motions, with tearing hands. He was left with the bare pages themselves; the top ones were yellowing, the whole dog-eared collection was ripe for the trash-can.

A few feet away from him was the open porthole—an invitation to any furious man. He moved swiftly till he stood by the gaping space. Then he tore off the top few sheets, and threw them out into the darkness.

The Professor, waking from a blow which might have killed him, suddenly realized what was happening. He started forward, as if he would have attacked this much bigger man. Then he stopped, a few feet away.

"Don't, Carl!" he begged. "Stop! Please stop!"

Carl was working methodically. More pages went whirling away into the black opening, from which the sea noises, the steady hiss of their passage, now sounded loud and engulfing. Already half the manuscript—it must be the oldest part, thought Carl savagely, joyfully—had disappeared into limbo.

The Professor could only think of one thing, one hope; to achieve this, he even fell on his knees.

"Carl! *Please.* . . . It's twenty-five years' work. . . . It's all I have. . . . If I don't publish it, I will never be free. . . . *Carl!*" He was beginning to sob now, as he saw the precious pages disappearing into the darkness, and more pages, newer pages, the toil of only three and four years ago, being laid bare for the slaughter. "Carl! *I haven't even got a copy!*"

Carl stopped, for the pure pleasure of doing so. The hissing sea outside the porthole seemed to retreat. He held in his hand the last few pages—perhaps twenty of them, almost fresh, almost new; possibly the work of the last two years, laced with much alcohol, much rheumatism, much despair, age, pain, and hope. He looked at the old man, grovelling at his feet. Then he kicked the old man, in the breast-bone, under his heart, so that he fell sideways, murmuring a word which sounded like 'peace' or 'please.' Then he tore the last pages across and across, and tossed them through the open porthole, as if he were offering the cheapest possible sacrifice to the most alien of all gods.

The torn pages fluttered in a shaft of light, they even rose for a moment on a current of warm, errant air, before disappearing astern, for ever and for ever.

chapter 11

IT was one o'clock, and the ship was quietly settled for the night, when Kathy knocked at the door of Carl's cabin, and went in. She had known that he would not be asleep; the clue was the Professor, a shocked and wandering ghost, whose ironfisted jailer must still be alert and awake. When she came in, fresh from happier topics, she asked immediately:

"Carl, what's happened to the Professor? Did you do something to him?"

Carl was sitting on his bed, half-undressed, irresolute, afraid. The spasm of hatred and brutality which had taken possession of him, half an hour earlier, was now entirely spent; having punished with such wicked cruelty the old man, he was now left to face a shrinking world in which the only target was himself. Emptied of fury, he had nothing to put in its place. Nothing, he thought, looking up at Kathy, except love. That must be the answer.

But he could not ask for it out of the blue. He had to go through the accepted forms of intercourse, the territory which lay between recent anger and promised desire. He said, abruptly, looking down at the floor again:

"What about the Professor?"

"He was wandering down the passage. Carl, he was in the most terrible state—I doubt if he even saw me! He was holding his side, and his mouth was bleeding. When he passed me he said: 'A slave ship. A slave ship.' What's happened to him? Did you hurt him again?"

"He let me down."

"Oh, Carl!"

"Oh, Carl!" he mimicked. "What does that mean?"

"When things go wrong, you shouldn't take it out on a poor old man like the Professor. It's like hitting a child. . . . What did he do, anyway?"

"He let me down," repeated Carl. Then he looked at Kathy, more closely, searching for the welcome signs of tenderness, the hated evidence of other men, other embraces. She was unruffled, beautiful, flawlessly groomed; if she had been making love, it had scarcely moved her at all; if the light in her face were happiness, it could still be shared with himself. "Have *you* let me down, Kathy?"

"Of course not."

"What have you been doing, so late?"

"Talking."

"I missed you."

With rare spite, she said: "If I had come back with five thousand dollars, would that have made up for it?"

"Oh Kathy, don't be like that!"

"But when I asked you before, you wouldn't even say if you wanted me to earn the five thousand. You pretended that only the money would exist, not what I had done to get it. You wouldn't involve yourself, only me."

He rose to his feet, and crossed the few feet of space between them. Then he put his hands on her shoulders, and said: "I can tell you now—I would have hated it. Kathy—help me!"

She stiffened, involuntarily. In this context, 'Help me' could only mean 'Make love with me'; there was absolutely no doubt of that, and the swaying pressure of his body presently confirmed it. The idea appalled her. Everything was wrong. She did not want to. He had been cruel; perhaps a few moments ago he had been hitting the old man. It was hot. She had spent the last two hours talking to Tim—silly, cheerful nonsense which meant more than it said. Between herself and Carl, she could now feel nothing but the chasm of the twenty-eight years that divided them. It had been so for many fatal weeks. She did not want to. Not now, and not again.

She put her hand up to his chest; the powerful muscles pushed back against her palms. The message was there, and it came near to revolting her. "Carl—it's so late. I really must go to bed."

"With me, my darling."

Panic-stricken, for a whole world of reasons, she said: "You don't really want me. . . . It's so hot, it wouldn't be any good. . . . And you have all these things worrying you. . . . Let's just go to sleep."

"With you," he said. His arms were round her waist now; he was pulling her towards the bed. "I must have you, Kathy. It's been so long. Please!"

She did not want to. She hated the idea, and feared it; her whole body was coiled tight against it, her very womb was dry; she was afraid that it would make her ill, that she would vomit on the pillow

But for pity of the past, she found that she could not refuse.

As she lay down, she said, to herself and to him: *Forgive me.*

Even as he took her in his arms, he should have been warned. She felt utterly different; her actual skin seemed armoured, unsensual, inimical to love. It was terribly hot. In the close cabin, visited only by moist mechanical air, the pulse of the engines faded to nothing, the ship's motion seemed to disappear. He had no allies, no help, no thudding oar-beat or gypsy music. Just himself.

He lay face downwards, his face buried deep in the pillow, refusing to meet the world's eye, or hers. His whole body, ridiculously and fatally slack, was bathed in sweat. He could have shouted aloud his rebellious rage, his conviction that this could not be true, that all they need do was to wait. But shouting was reserved for potent men.

He muttered: "I'm so ashamed, Kathy."

She had never heard the words from him before. They were terrible, and wonderful; they were like sign-posts, like blessings. Presently she would found a whole future on them.

"It doesn't *matter*, Carl." She had said this when he was writhing, in furious and futile effort; she could say it now, when he had given in. "It's only because it's so hot. . . . And you've got so much on your mind. . . . It doesn't matter."

"I must be getting old."

"No, you're not."

Lying there in the darkness, unbroached, faithful still, she could have sung for joy. It was her release—she could work none of it out yet, there must be many hills still to climb, limitless penances to be made—but it *was* her release, the only one he could have given her. She was free!

She had not seen how that could happen, and she had been in terror of her endless captivity, even as he had lain on her body, desperately willing himself to be a man. But it had happened, at that very moment, when nothing else had happened. She was free!

Turning aside, withdrawing for ever from the past, she said:

"It's so hot. . . . I think I'll go back to my room."

part six

"The ULTIMATE in cruise adventure."

chapter 1

THE Professor should have been seen by half a dozen people in the course of his wanderings, and led back to his cabin or to the sick bay; but he was not seen. The Master-at-Arms, making his rounds, missed him twice; the shoe-cleaner was dozing, the night-stewards enjoying their mid-watch brew of cocoa; and when he was once glimpsed briefly, from the bridge, it was too far away to notice anything amiss, and the single figure was presumed to be a wakeful passenger, searching for cooler air in the torrid night. He finished his wretched journey at the boat-deck level, on a deck-chair in the lee of a funnel, musing—at first miserably, and then vengefully—on the pitiful pass to which the corroding years had brought him.

He had known Carl for a very long time; originally they had worked together on certain London share promotions which required, as a front, a middle-aged man who looked like a retired clegyman; and in later years, when the Professor grew truly old, Carl had been kind, and generous with commissions and odd jobs. It was hard to recognize, in this long-term friend, the cruel man who had grown so gross and remorseless in his bullying, and who had finally destroyed a life-time of work in a few terrible moments.

The Professor pressed and stroked his chest, where he had been kicked. It hurt excruciatingly whenever he made a careless movement, and his head and battered face stabbed with pain unceasingly. Without the precious manuscript which was now lost, he was nothing; he had no hope in the future at all. He must play out his life, tied to a friend who was no friend, who had become a hated enemy. He was trapped, he was powerless. Of course, he had the money, and the jewellery. . . . But he had Carl as well. Thus bound, he would never make any harbour. Life was a cruise from which one did not return.

Just as in a slave ship. . . . It seemed to him suddenly that he was like a galley-slave, chained to his oar, doomed to row for ever, to starve and suffer for ever. He would grow old and blind, and finally be shackled to an anchor-cable and dropped overboard into engulfing waters.

Unless he revolted against this vile bondage in time.

Spartacus!

The revolt of the Roman slaves at Capua in 73 B.C., against a wicked tyranny which promised to make brute beasts out of men, was led by a man who. . . . Now *there* was something he should have written! But if he could not write it—he would never write again now, it was too late—perhaps he might presume to lead it. A blow for liberty! He had the money and the jewellery, after all. He had, also, this terrible pain.

But he must not think of the money. It was not a matter of money, it was not that sort of thing at all. It was a moral crusade, a public cleansing. In the Greek city-states, in ancient times, certain humble citizens, scandalized by the vice and corruption which infected the whole republic, took counsel together, and swore an oath to the immortal gods. . . .

There was a duty to be done. Carl had cursed him, and torn up his life-time of work, and shackled him to an oar in the slave-galley, until he bent double in agony, and died upon his chains.

So, for a long time, surrounded by darkness, this demented man, in a torment of pain and despair, pondered on the ancient Stoic virtues, the rule that all tyrants must be overthrown.

Carl could not sleep, for rage, for shame. It had never happened before. It was the beginning of getting old, of saying goodbye to Kathy. He had felt that message of goodbye in her body, in her skin;

by the time he had turned to embrace her, she had left him already. It was one of the reasons why he could not make love to her. To want, one had to be wanted. He had not been wanted, and so he had failed, like a boy, like an old man. . . .

Sleepless, his nerves on edge, he dressed and climbed slowly up to the boat-deck. It was the beginning of the dawn; a wonderful pale light was creeping towards them over the calm Indian Ocean, pushing back the night. As he stood at the rail, in a small space between two lifeboats, he watched first the sky, and then the grey-black water far below.

The water was still phosphorescent, and it was possible to see the school of sharks which had been following them tirelessly, day and night, for the past forty-eight hours. Baleful darting shapes, they almost nuzzled the ship as they swam along with it. The crew sometimes threw them lumps of offal, to enjoy the swirling, snapping, often bloody battle which ensued. Now, in the half-darkness, their sleek black bodies and pale bellies left greenish trails as they wove a criss-cross pattern of attendant murder.

There was one huge one, a monster, just below where he was standing. Carl climbed up one step of the rail, for a better view, and leaned far out-board. Out of the corner of his eye, he thought he saw a shadow dart forward behind him. But when he turned, it was too late.

The Professor screamed: "Tyrant! Slave-master! Wicked man!" and pushed with all his might. The lunatic strength was too much for any resistance, the surprise too great. Carl, toppling over, clawed at nothing, embraced the free air, and went plummeting down to the ferocious jaws below.

The Professor, momentarily astonished, surveyed the space which his skill and resource had rendered empty. Then he beamed happily, and started to giggle and to caper. He was still cackling and pointing, like some poor crazy showman, when the Master-at-Arms found him, an hour later, and said:

"Now then, sir. It's bed-time for you!"

chapter 2

It was three days later, and the *Alcestis*, delayed by official inquiries, was still at Durban. The police had been and gone; they might or might not return—they were large blond men, armed, preoccupied, who had bigger things to worry about than the chance death of a passenger aboard a visiting liner. Diane was on her way home, discreetly wafted ashore in time to catch an early flight; the Professor, not ceasing to babble, had begun what must be a very long sojourn in hospital ashore.

Over Kathy, the Captain had held his hand. "Sir, I swear she's not like that—she's a good girl!" Tim Mansell had told him, with such intense fervour that Harmer's imagination had been caught. Privately, and cynically, he wondered if any girl who promoted such strong feeling could truly be classified as 'good'; but he relented none-theless. Of all the gang, she was the only one remaining on board; he felt now—as he had always felt—that the *Alcestis* was strong enough to take care of one small enigma, one female question-mark. Kathy would be allowed to remain on board for the return journey.

"But no funny business!" he warned sternly.

"Sir, we're going to be engaged," protested Tim Mansell.

"That's exactly what I meant," said Harmer. "If you have any spare energy, use it to work up on your navigation. It's still bloody awful."

Now they stood in the sunshine, looking down on the odd, straggling, almost unclassifiable city of Durban. The cruise-brochure described it as colourful, and that was as good a word as any. It was impressively hot, as well. The bright sun shone down on the yellow façades of great buildings, on the lines of surf which marked the bathing beaches, and on the grotesque rank of ricksha-boys—feathered, beaded, sea-shelled, crowned with buffalo-horn head-dresses—who (in an intriguing reverse play) made every tourist pay a minimum fee of two shillings for the privilege of taking their photographs.

Kathy was still deeply shocked. She could be handled gently, or not at all. The disappearance of Carl had had its own natural, inevitable prelude; he had been gone already, by the time he had crucified the Professor, by the time he could not make love to her. But there were six years of the past still to be counted, six years which could not disappear. They were a part of her, they were the reason why she dressed so well, talked so persuasively, looked so beautiful and aware. They were the formative years, changing her from a half-awake child to a woman. They could not be forgotten, nor disparaged.

She was not happy, but she was ready to be so, when the time came. Instead (she realized) she was lucky. She could shed the bad part of the past, and she could remain the heiress, for ever, of the good. There were all sorts of troubles ahead, but she had a man to help her. A man who she had thought was a boy, but who was not.

It was remarkable, she thought, looking at Tim, pressing his arm, how one such man could sum up the virtues of discipline and order, the merit of good behaviour.

He could make love beautifully, too.

"Darling," she said.

"Yes?" Standing guardian for her, with love allied to watchfulness, his voice had the correct, cherishing blend of both.

"What's a mate's ticket?"

New York—Ottawa—London—Barbados.
April, 1959—March, 1960.